"What's it like," I say, after a silence, "living on the road?"

"Ah, it's grand," Travis says. "You can't beat it." And he starts talking then, about how tramping in the summer's a lovely thing; a white country road on a summer evening with a faint sickle moon just above it. But on a winter's night, when the wind cuts notches in your spine and you're drenched through with rain, that's when many a tramp gives up and heads for the nearest workhouse. But not Travis. He doesn't like any kind of house, but especially not the workhouse. If anything, he loves the winters more. The stars hang so low over the moor, you can almost touch them, and the moon's as bright as the sun. He even loves the hail and the driving sleet, because that's when you find something out about yourself.

"What?" I say in spite of myself. "What do you find out?"

"You find out whether you want to live or die," he says. "And in the end that's the only thing you need to know."

OTHER BOOKS YOU MAY ENJOY

THE
WHISPERING
ROAD

Livi Michael

PUFFIN BOOKS

To Robert Williams,
a great reader, who wanted more books to read

ACKNOWLEDGMENTS

The author would like to thank H. Gustav Klaus Janson for permission to draw on the fascinating material in *Tramps, Workmates and Revolutionaries* (1933), Journeyman Press; Tony Taylor for many consultations over coffee; Mike Kane for unstinting technical support; and Ian Pople.

PUFFIN BOOKS
Published by the Penguin Group
Penguin Young Readers Group, 345 Hudson Street, New York, New York 10014, U.S.A.
Penguin Group (Canada), 90 Eglinton Avenue East, Suite 700, Toronto, Ontario, Canada M4P 2Y3
(a division of Pearson Penguin Canada Inc.)
Penguin Books Ltd, 80 Strand, London WC2R 0RL, England
Penguin Ireland, 25 St Stephen's Green, Dublin 2, Ireland (a division of Penguin Books Ltd)
Penguin Group (Australia), 250 Camberwell Road, Camberwell, Victoria 3124, Australia
(a division of Pearson Australia Group Pty Ltd)
Penguin Books India Pvt Ltd, 11 Community Centre, Panchsheel Park, New Delhi - 110 017, India
Penguin Group (NZ), Cnr Airborne and Rosedale Roads, Albany, Auckland 1310, New Zealand
(a division of Pearson New Zealand Ltd)
Penguin Books (South Africa) (Pty) Ltd, 24 Sturdee Avenue, Rosebank, Johannesburg 2196, South Africa

Registered Offices: Penguin Books Ltd, 80 Strand, London WC2R 0RL, England

First published in the United States of America by G. P. Putnam's Sons,
a division of Penguin Young Readers Group, 2005
Published by Puffin Books, a division of Penguin Young Readers Group, 2006

1 3 5 7 9 10 8 6 4 2

THE LIBRARY OF CONGRESS HAS CATALOGED THE G. P. PUTNAM'S SONS EDITION AS FOLLOWS:
Michael, Livi, 1960–.
The whispering road / Livi Michael.—1st American ed.
p. cm.
Summary: In Victorian England, poverty-stricken, orphaned siblings Joe and Annie escape from the
abusive farmer they work for and try to survive in Manchester, with help from a friendly tramp,
a mysterious dog-woman, and a renegade printer who supports the rights of the poor.
ISBN: 0-399-24357-7 (hc)
[1. Orphans—Fiction. 2. Brothers and sisters—Fiction. 3. Poverty—Fiction. 4. Child labor—Fiction.
5. City and town life—Fiction. 6. Supernatural—Fiction. 7. Manchester (England)—History—
19th century—Fiction. 8. Great Britain—History—Victoria, 1837–1901—Fiction.] I. Title.
PZ7.M5798Th 2005
[Fic]—dc22   2004015627

Puffin Books ISBN 0-14-240724-0

Printed in the United States of America
Design by Gunta Alexander
Text set in Janson

CONTENTS

PART III ♦ *Journey's End*

PART I
Road

1

Shovel

I had to get her out, that was the main thing. Annie, that is—my sister. When I saw her lying on the kitchen floor, Mistress towering over her and Annie all white and still, something cold went through me, like a shadow.

"What have you done to her?" I say, and Old Bert gives me a ringing clout round the ear.

"Don't talk to your mistress like that," he says.

I fall to my knees beside Annie. I can see blood on the stone slabs of the floor where her head is. "Annie," I whisper.

"Get 'em out," says Mistress—with a face like a slab of stone herself—and Old Bert, arms like trees, swings Annie up easy, over his shoulder like a lamb or a new pig, and with his other arm hauls me off the floor by the scruff of the neck. Off we go, my feet bumping and scraping, into the freezing night.

Old Bert kicks open the door of the chicken shed and slings first me then Annie inside. All the hens squawk at once. Annie lands on a sack with a soft thud and her head lolls to one side. I land on my knees and my hand hits something sharp, and hard. The edge of a shovel.

"Barn's full," says Old Bert. "You'll have to stay here the night. And mind . . ." He leans closer with his big, meaty face, and breathes all over us with his sewer breath. "Don't stir the hens. I hear them hens in the night and come morning I'll feed you to pigs."

That were his favorite threat. I wish I could say I didn't believe him, but I've seen him feeding the pigs before. Buckets of swill with lumps of things that look as though they might once have been a nose, or an eye.

Old Bert looms over us a few moments more, his breath rattling in his chest. I expect him to kick me and all my skin tightens up, but nothing happens. Then he says, "Milking's at four. I'll be back. Don't—stir—th'hens."

Then he's gone, all the hens rising in a great flurry as he shoves the door open and kicks it to. I hear the big wooden plank pulled across the outside as a bolt.

Have you ever tried not disturbing hens? I move my hand and the shovel scrapes and they flap up, clucking. There's only six of them but they make enough row. I shuffle over to Annie and they start again, softer this time. "Annie?" I say, and they all start squawking. I hold my breath. I try again, softer, "Annie," and take her hand. It's frozen, like mine. I push my face close to her chest and I can make out her breathing—just. I've seen her knocked out before, but not like this, never this white and still.

"Don't die on me, Annie," I mutter, and a soft clucking ripples round the shed. "Don't you die on me."

High up there's a hole where a bit of the roof's fallen in and a pile of snow after it. A shaft of moonlight turns everything gray; gray scraggy hens watching, and Annie's gray face. If she dies I'll be all alone—with them. Old Bert, Young Bert, the master and mistress. I've never been on my own before. There's always been Annie.

The shed stinks. It's full of chicken dung. Plus it's freezing. Hardest winter in twenty years, Old Bert said. Every morning we have to break the ice round the cows' faces where their breath has frozen over them. I can't feel my fingers and I'm starving. I only had bread at breakfast, bread hard like a stone but crumblier. I catch myself looking round at all the gray, scraggy hens and wondering if I could eat one raw and if Old Bert'd notice. Hunger must be making me mad. He'd kill me of course, but then maybe I'll die anyway, frozen over and starved in the dark. Maybe I'd rather die chewing on a hen.

The nearest hen looks at me like it knows what I'm thinking, with its round, hard eyes, gray as pebbles in the moon. I look at that hen and it looks right back at me. I'm thinking about the last time I helped out in the kitchen and Mistress made a meat pudding from one of the sheep that had wandered from the flock and froze. She mashed stale bread with boiling water and boiled up the meat in a pudding cloth till the juices ran, and all the time I'm clemmed—my stomach's stuck to my spine. The smell of mutton fat wafts in through my nostrils till I can feel my head fizzing like a pint of ale gone bad. Me and Annie are supposed to be clearing up but we can't stop watching Master sink his toothless gums into that pudding and all the juices running down his chin. Then he starts up with a snarl and a curse and drives us off without even the usual piece of stale bread to gnaw on through the night.

That's what I'm thinking when I look at that bird.

I know if I touch the hens I'm done for; but maybe I don't care. I know they haven't been laying in this weather, or I'd look for eggs. But they'd raise the roof anyway if I took their eggs. Maybe I'd rather be hung for a chicken than an egg. Slowly, without taking my eyes off that bird, I begin to move.

And at that moment, Annie moans. I yelp in fright and all the birds cluck and yammer. Annie takes no notice. She rolls over with her little roly-poly body that never seems quite shrunk to skin and bone, and tries to get onto her knees. She can't do it. She sinks down again, hitting the floor, and makes a noise like she's going to be sick. Only she hasn't eaten either. I grab hold of her under her arms and haul her up.

"Annie," I breathe. "Are you all right?"

Daft question. She only moans again and her head lolls sideways. I'm so glad she's coming to that I hang on to her tightly, then prop her up against the wall. She doesn't open her eyes. But after a minute she speaks.

"Cold," she says. I rub her arms, but my hands are so cold, I can't feel either them or her. She turns her head into my shoulder. "Drink," she says. I look at the pile of snow. Propping her up again so that she doesn't fall over, I crawl on my hands and knees and scoop up some of it. The hens seem to be getting used to us now—they don't flap and cluck, just stare at me bead-ily. I hold the snow to her bluish lips and after a moment she makes little sucking movements. I feed it to her patiently like you have to feed the calves that come early and can't suck, and gradually the snow disappears.

Maybe the cold of it in her throat wakes her up, because slowly her eyes open, pale and glassy in the moonlight. She doesn't seem to be looking at anything, just staring. I pass my hand in front of her face and she doesn't blink. Then she says, "They're looking," and turns her face into my shoul-der again.

I don't know what she means. The hens?

"Annie, it's all right," I say. "It's me, Joe. You've had a knock on your head, but you're all right now. You'll be fine." But she only turns her head even farther into my shirt.

"Stop it," she whimpers. "Make them go."

"It's all right, Annie," I say, wishing I believed it. "There's no one here but the hens." Annie only moans and shakes her head. Her whole body is shaking.

I don't know what to do, so I stroke her hair that clings in little damp rats' tails to her shoulders and neck.

"Sssh, Annie," I say. "Try to sleep." She doesn't stop shaking, but slowly her grip on my shirt loosens and she shuts her eyes.

"Hungry," she says.

Well, there's not much I can do about that. I stare around the shed, won-dering if there's any food for the hens, but I can't see anything. There's a scurrying noise and a rat runs across the far side of the wall and disappears. That lifts my spirits a bit. In the workhouse I got quite good at catching rats, but I've never had to eat one raw. I stay with Annie until her breathing changes and I can tell she's fallen asleep. I cover her up with the sack she was lying on. Then I start to look around the shed.

Nothing. Some crates and an empty barrel. Another barrel full of frozen water. No sign of the rat even. All the time the hens watch me nervously, but they don't start squawking. I find a big wooden pole that might once have been a broom, and a bucket. No food there either.

"Looks like you get fed about as much as we do," I say to the speckled hen, and she cocks her head at me as though listening. I rattle the door, just in case, but as I thought, it's barricaded on the other side. I wonder how long it'll be before Old Bert comes back, then turn the bucket upside down and stand on it. I climb from there to the wooden crates stacked up near the door, trying to see through the gap in the roof. All I can see is a slice of moon and a star. It's not snowing, though.

Somewhere out there, only about a mile away, there's the workhouse where we were a few weeks back. And we thought we were badly off then. I think about the other kids there, cracking the ice and picking oakum, and wonder if they're all asleep now, and if any of them are warm. I press my fingers into the rough stone and try to haul myself up, but my fingers are like wood and I can't do it. With a sigh I clamber back down from the crates and go back to Annie. I press up close to her, under the sack.

I'm cold. I thought it was just my fingers and feet, but now I can feel the cold inside, as though even my stomach has started to freeze. Somewhere inside me there's a small round pebble of ice, like a hen's eye, only bigger. And it's growing. I can't get warm.

To cheer myself up I think about the workhouse. Now that's something I never thought I'd say. I think about a teacher we had. Not for long—they brought her in from somewhere to teach us to write our names. She read to us from the Bible and made us copy stuff out. Well, she tried. None of us really managed. Sometimes she'd just give up and read us stories. That were all right. I remember the one about David killing Goliath. And other stories too, about trolls, and boys called Jack killing giants. When she left I used to tell them to the other kids, and make more up myself. About Jinny Green-teeth who lurks in ponds with her long, mossy teeth, and giants throwing boulders at one another across the valleys—which is how the hills got so stony. And hags in graveyards and trolls who suck the bones of babies.

Sometimes I could keep a whole roomful of us awake right through the night. I was cock of the poorhouse. But I don't feel like cock of this henhouse. I look balefully at the speckled gray hen and she looks back at me. Somewhere in her empty eye I see a flicker of something. Like she understands that both of us are stuck here without a chance, and her fate'll be the same as mine. I look a bit longer and think, *Not if I can help it.*

And then suddenly I know. I know, sure as I'm looking at that chicken's eye, that we have to get out of there. I know we're stuck in a shed, in a farm like a prison up a hill in the middle of nowhere, but I don't care. I think about the miles of deep snow between us and anywhere, but it doesn't matter. Suddenly I'm thinking like the heroes in one of them stories. Old Bert may look like a troll, or a giant, but I'm Jack. Jack the Giant-killer . . .

Jack the Giant-killer killed loads of giants, though he was only a kid—like me. In them days there was giants everywhere. But Jack was brave and fearless, and he decided to sort them out. So he set off with a pickax and shovel, a lantern and a horn. He dug a pit for one, then whacked him over the head with a pickax—*thunnk!* Then he met one with two heads, so he tricked that one into gutting himself and stole his sword. Then he met one with three heads, so he knocked them all together with a plank. Next giant only had one, but he was so huge, Jack could only reach his legs, so he cut them off with the sword and then hacked his head off too—*whuk! Urrgh!* Then the next one he called out of his castle with the horn, jumped up behind him and whacked him over the head with his shovel—*bamm!* And knocked him into the moat. Then he ran him through with the sword.

Well, I haven't got a sword. Or a pickax or a horn. But I have got a shovel.

Jack the Giant-killer climbs up on the bucket, then the crates. Swings the shovel down hard so that it whistles through the air, once, twice—*pheeeew, clunnk!*

All he has to do is to get the giant through that door.

Then he has to get away with his sister, and at least one hen . . .

First things first. I go back over to Annie and shake her. I've remembered now that it's dangerous to sleep when it's too cold. Old Bert once saw a shepherd froze to death with his flock.

"He'll have fallen asleep," he says to Mistress. "Cold sends you to sleep, then you never wake up."

So I remember now, before it's too late, to wake Annie.

She grumbles and moans as I haul her to her feet. "Sleep," she says.

"No, walk," say I, and pull her across the floor. She pulls back, complaining, and tries to sit down.

The hens start clucking and there isn't much time. "Walk, Annie, walk," I say, pulling her along. "We're not staying here. We're leaving. You've got to walk or I'm leaving you here."

Annie's eyes open again but she's not looking at me. Seems like she's looking at thin air. Then she lifts a finger, pointing at thin air. "Are they coming?" she whispers.

If I could've felt colder, I did then. "Don't start that again," I tell her, then go on pulling and shoving her across the floor, back and forward, forward and back, till finally she's walking on her own.

"Why?" she says.

"Because we're going," I say.

"Where?"

I haven't got as far as that. The workhouse'd be the obvious place, but somehow I don't think they'd take kindly to us running away. It was the master of the workhouse himself who farmed us out.

"I've found a good place for you," he said. "And you can both go together. That's what you wanted, isn't it?"

I'd *good place* him if I saw him again.

"Don't know," I say, and she opens her mouth and points inside, meaning, *What'll we eat?*

Typical Annie—says nowt and still manages to argue. But I can't think about that now. I've got to think about getting us both through the snow. I pick up the sack. "Here, give us a hand," I say. The top of it's frayed and the seam's coming loose. With a bit of a struggle we manage to rip strips off it to bind round our hands and feet. Not much, but better than nothing. We need the rest of it for the hen.

I step quite close to the hen without looking its way and act as if I'm thinking of nothing in particular. Then I lunge round at it. Of course I miss and it shoots into the air, squawking, which sets off all the others. I don't mind the commotion—Old Bert'll come running, but that's part of the plan—and I'm damned if I'm leaving without a hen.

Have you ever tried catching a hen? They're flapping up and squawking fit to burst, and I'm diving here, there and everywhere, falling over the bucket, scrambling over the crates and swearing. Annie's got her mouth open, screaming without making a sound. There's feathers flying and enough noise to wake up Adam in the Garden of Eden. Finally, when I snatch at my last hen and miss so that it goes screeching forward, Annie seizes the shovel, lifts it and belts the hen for all she's worth. It flies into the wall like a football, then hits the floor, kicking and twitching. I grab it and wrench its neck. In my hurry I pull too hard and its head comes right off. And the thing's still flapping there under my arm and suddenly I'm gagging, doubled over, just as if I had something to throw up. Then Annie freezes.

"Door," she says as it rattles.

No time to think. I drop the hen and grab the shovel. I clamber up on the crates, hearing Old Bert cursing outside. Through my mind flashes the image of Jack the Giant-killer and I lift the shovel up, but suddenly I'm scared to death. We hear the plank across the door being dragged off and thrown away. Annie's face is dirty white like the snow. I shut my eyes and see the giant's head bowling across the floor—*whack! Whack!*

Of course it doesn't work like that. Old Bert flings the door open so hard, it nearly comes off its hinges, and I bring the shovel down as hard as I can, and next thing I know Old Bert's turning round, roaring like a bull. I slam the shovel at him, right between the eyes, and he staggers back. But he must have a head like an anvil because he just keeps on roaring and lunging.

He grabs the shovel. I go flying off the crates and Annie screams. Somewhere outside all the dogs start barking at once. I see him lift the shovel high above his head. I shut my eyes. The next moment there's a terrific crash, then silence. I open my eyes. Old Bert's sprawled crossways over me. He's hit his head on the stone wall and lying still.

Annie rolls out from beneath his feet. She must have rolled in front of him, lickety-split, when he went for me. But now she's up and tugging at my arm.

"Shovel," she says, then, "hen."

I struggle out from under Old Bert. All I can hear are the dogs, then Young Bert and Master are outside, calling and cursing. The door's wide open. I can see a lantern flare. Annie drops the shovel and the hen into the sack, then we're off, running like tinkers over the slippery cobbles, round the back of the shed, into the snow-filled night.

2

Chicken

Oi!" roars Young Bert, and sets off across the yard with his bandy legs. His lantern bobs and flickers as he reaches the shed and takes in the scene.

"Da!" he cries. "Da!"

Young Bert's even bigger and uglier than his da. If he gets to us first there's no hope, none at all, we'll be libbed to death and he'll suck on our bones like a troll, but I keep on running because what else is there to do? Past the stables where the horses set off whinnying, round the back of the barn. I'm thinking about the back wall, and how there's no way over it that I know of.

Master loosens the dogs' chains, snarling, "Fetch!" and all the dogs bound forward, howling murder. There are four of them—mean yellow hounds kept half starved and savage. Me and Annie just keep running and slithering. Blood's pounding in my ears and all I can think is, *No chance, no chance*, in time to the banging of my heart. Past the tool shed we go and suddenly we're up against the wall, six foot high with a bolted gate. I'm about to start climbing when Annie tugs me to one side, and there's a miracle.

A small hole at the bottom where the wall's collapsing and neither Old nor Young Bert have ever done owt about it. We plunge into it and are soon sorry—there's a thick thorny hedge beyond. We've no choice but to push through the thorns as best we can because the dogs are on us now in a snarling rush. They're at the wall, baying for blood and slavering. All my shirt's tangled in thorns but I rip myself free and suddenly I'm falling, tumbling over and over, too fast to even notice how much it hurts. From the corner of my eye I see Annie flashing past and I wonder if we'll both be dead by the time we hit the bottom. Then I realize that even if we're not we soon will be, because at the bottom of this drop's the river, groaning and gushing past in flood, full of drifts of ice and boulders.

I hit a rock and bounce, and one hound tumbles past, yelping, then I fly past a branch that's jutting out and grip hold hard. The world swings round then steadies itself. I see three hounds prowling at the top but they won't come down, even though Young Bert and Master are driving them on with sticks. Then one more falls, tumbling over and over. Another puts back his head and howls, a heart-stopping, lonely sound that nearly makes me lose hold of the branch. The other joins in, and the sound echoes around the hills. I look down at slow black circles in the foam, searching for Annie.

I can't see anything at first, though I crane desperately to left and right. Hoping the branch'll hold, I scramble to one side under a little ridge so that no one can see me from the top. I try not to feel sick when I look down.

Nothing.

Annie must be floating downriver with that dog.

I'm not crying, I never cry, but the snow's stinging my eyes.

"What're you waiting for?" I hear Master say to Young Bert. "Get down there after them!"

"Me?" says Young Bert. "Not me, Master—I'm feared!"

"Get on with you!" says Master.

"I'll not go where dogs won't!" says Young Bert, then I hear *Thwack! Thwack!* as Master starts beating him with his stick, and Young Bert cries loudly, "Da! Da!"

"I'll give you Da!" shouts Master, more enraged than ever, but Young Bert, only three teeth in his head and even less sense, hasn't got the sense to stop crying. And the dogs start baying again, so there's a right racket, and suddenly it happens. A huge ridge of snow comes crashing down.

Down and down and all around me before there's time to shout. The branch breaks and I'm spinning forward and there's snow in my mouth and ears. I land with a thud in a mound of snow and a great weight of it falls on top. I'm buried, and for a minute I think I might be dead. Then I try to move.

I can't move my arms but I manage to kick a bit, and wriggle and struggle backward till I've tugged myself clear. I'm cold and battered and wringing wet. My ears are full of roaring, which I realize slowly is the noise from the river. My chest hurts and my heart seems to be banging in my head, but at least that proves I'm alive. On the stony riverbank, with the river surging and boiling and gushing out of its bed.

Usually there's a big wide bed to this river, full of stones. I remember when the teacher, Miss Julie her name was, managed to talk the master of the workhouse into letting her take us all out one day. "It's such a beautiful day," she said to him.

And Master grumbled and gurned, but he was a bit sweet on Miss Julie, like we all were, so that was how we all came to go out, walking along the riverbed, looking at flowers and fish, under the big blue sky with the sun burning down. And we weren't meant to get our workhouse clothes wet or soiled, but soon we were splashing through the river and throwing stones and laughing.

"Don't worry, children," Miss Julie said, "your clothes'll dry on the way home."

So that's what I'm thinking about now—sun and flowers and fish—because it stops me thinking about Annie, and the fact that I'm all alone and there's no chicken and I don't know what to do next. I scramble along just above the level of the river because it's so swollen now, there's no bed left. From time to time spray catches me and it's like knives on my frozen skin, and I slip and slither on wet rock and there's no sign of Annie or the chicken. And I'm getting tired, so tired I'm not even hungry anymore, just numb, and it would be easy to let myself just slide into the river and be carried along, let the darkness close over me. I'm not even thinking anymore. I go round a bend in the river and think, *Just one more bend, one more rock and I'll be there*, but I don't know where *there* is. And then I'm too tired, and instead of climbing over the next rock I just lie across it.

The river churns on black and brown where the foam's rising. It's been frozen all winter but now it's free and roaring like a hungry animal, roaring and tossing stones and branches. There are voices in it too, hundreds of voices. Old Bert's voice is in there, and Master's, and Miss Julie's, and if I listen hard enough I can hear, faint and far away, the voice of my mother. So I lie there, just listening to what the river has to say and almost, not quite, making out the words, when suddenly it says, "All right, laddie, up you come," and there's hands beneath my arms, pulling me up.

I kick feebly and turn my face away, but I'm pressed against some rough material that reeks of mildew and smoke, and I'm carried along roughly, jolting and jigging, and the river's turned into someone big and brown that's carrying me away, but I don't care anymore and anyway, it all feels like a dream.

Then whoever it is bends forward and pushes his way through a branch that catches at my legs into a kind of opening in the hill. And then I know I'm dreaming, because there's a fire and some kind of skins on the floor, and on the other side of the fire is Annie, wrapped in a skin, calmly plucking the chicken and looking up at me with her light eyes.

"You're late," she says.

Whoever it is that's got me puts me down then, on the other side of the fire. I'm near the flames but I can't feel a thing. I could be scorching. Then he starts rubbing at my hands and feet with snow. I can see black wispy hair on his bent head, and reddish scalp showing through. Then slowly I can feel pain in my hands and feet, tingling and burning so that I can't stand it and I start to struggle up, swearing. But he holds me down calmly and starts stripping the rags off my back. Well, I'm not being stripped by no man, even if he has just saved my life, and I dart backward, kicking in earnest now, and he looks up at me with huge, pea-soup eyes, thick-lashed.

"You'd better get them wet things off, lad," he says, and I glare at him. He shrugs. "I'll go and get some sticks to dry them on," he says, and crawls back out through the opening of the cave.

I look toward Annie, half expecting to find that she's disappeared but, no, she's still there, covered in fur and feathers. And the chicken looks gray and puckered now and nothing like a bird.

"Who's he?" I demand, and she shrugs. There's about a thousand things I could say, but the pain in my hands is killing me and I tuck them under my armpits. "Where did you find him?" I ask.

"Fell on him," she says. Then she looks at me and tugs my clothes.

"Off," she says, and goes on plucking the chicken as if nothing out of the ordinary's happened.

Nothing makes sense, so I start to peel off my clothes. And it's agony, just touching anything. My fingers feel huge and raw and it hurts so much that I groan and swear and spit. And my feet are killing me; I can't put them down. But I manage to peel the clothes off and wrap myself in a big shaggy skin of something that might have been a wolf, before he crawls back in.

He drives two big sticks into the earth and holds his hand out for my rags. None of us say anything but he whistles as he starts to spread out my clothes.

Then I say, "Who are you?" and he looks at me with those green eyes.

"Who are *you*?" he says, and we stare at one another for a minute, not giving an inch, and the words of a song go through my head . . .

> *Here come I, Beelzebub,*
> *And over my shoulder I carry a club,*
> *And in my hand a dripping pan,*
> *And I think myself a jolly man.*

"Food first," says the man, and he picks up the chicken and rips it apart with his big hands, dropping some pieces into a pan and skewering the rest on a stick, holding them over the fire. And I huddle closer to the fire. I can feel it now, scorching the flesh of my face. And the wet rags start to smolder and steam, and fat runs off the chicken, spitting in the flames, so all I can think about is meat. He puts the hot pieces down on a stone to cool, warning us not to touch them too soon, but I'm famished and I fall on it, burning my mouth. I tear at the flesh with my teeth and feel the juice run down my chin, and chew and chew, and have a nightmare feeling like I won't be able to swallow, like I've forgotten how. But I chew some more and gag and stuff it down. When I look, Annie's doing the same, only more slowly, and the man's looking at both of us with a peculiar smile on his face.

He has a broad, flat face and he looks at us sideways, then quickly away. He picks up the smaller pieces of chicken and eats them slowly, leaving most of it for us. As though he's not really hungry at all.

I don't know what to think about him. He starts talking while we eat, in a soft, singsong voice that sounds funny. Not like from around here. He says, "It's a fine night with plenty of moon. I walked from Huddersfield yesterday and fetched up here, tired as a dog. Drifts of snow high as my shoulder along the tops. I was looking for somewhere to spend the night and found this place. I made the fire and thought now all I need is some food, but all the way over I hadn't seen so much as a bird, or a hare. So I walked out, looking for what the good Lord might provide. When suddenly I was struck on the head by a chicken.

"Well that's not the usual way that the good Lord provides, so I couldn't help looking up, wondering if he might throw down some taters or peas to go with it. But the next thing that lands on me's the little maid. Don't worry," he says with his sideways smile, "I'll not try to cook you."

I've stopped cramming the chicken down, though I'm still eating. I say to him, "Are you a tinker?" Because we used to get tinkers stopping off at the workhouse, selling stuff, or looking for a night's shelter in bad weather. Some of them stank to high heaven and were bad-tempered with it. But some of them were all right and told us stories.

He stops eating and wipes his mouth. Then he rakes the fire up a bit.

"I've been a tinker," he says, "and a soldier and a sailor. I've been a poor man, a beggarman and a thief. But I've never been a rich man. I think the good Lord must've overlooked that one." He laughs to himself silently.

"What are you now?" I say, though Annie nudges me. She doesn't want him to start asking questions about us.

"What am I now?" he says, looking upward. "I don't know that I can rightly answer that one. . . . I sell skins," he says, waving at the pile of furs, "to rich men that deal in fur. Sometimes I sew them together, into capes or wraps, and sell them myself on the markets. You could say that makes me a tailor." He laughs his silent laugh, then looks at us, very keen. "What about you?" he says. "What are you?"

I look at Annie and Annie looks at me, her face all shut up like a box.

"We're lost," I begin, not knowing how to go on. "We were with our mam and dad, in a big town, then we lost them. We've been looking for them ever since."

It's not a good story, not one of my best, but it's the best I can do without thinking. He nods. "You'll be looking for the workhouse then," he says.

"No," we say together, and he laughs again.

"Me neither," he says. "But how'll you find your mam and dad? They must be looking for you."

Annie looks at me but I can't think. My head's filling up with the heat from the fire. But I don't want him taking us to the workhouse. If we go back there we'll be beaten and sent back to the farm. Or to a worse place, if there is one. So I say nothing and he says nothing either. Then after a minute I say, "What's your name?"

"Well, now," he says. "That's an awfully personal question to ask a fellow. I don't know when I last gave out that piece of information. What are your names?"

Annie says nothing and I'm too tired to think. My head's nodding. Annie's light eyes stare at the man, who stares back.

"What'll we call you?" she says, and he laughs.

"That's better," he says. "It doesn't do, to go giving your names out to every Tom, Dick or Harry who asks." He straightens, and stretches his legs.

I can see that he's not a tall man, but broad. "You can call me Travis," he says, and looks at us expectantly. "Well?"

"Tom," I say, very low, and he laughs again.

"And is this Dick or Harry?"

Annie says nothing. I say the first name that comes to me. "Julie."

"Tom, and Julie," he says, as if trying the names out. He looks at us consideringly and nods. "Tom and Julie. That's good."

Now I can't stay awake any longer. My eyes close and my head drops forward. I can hear Travis moving around, and through my closed lids I can still see the flickering flames. I droop forward, sighing.

"Mind the fire," Travis says, and he hauls both me and Annie backward onto soft fur. And I forget to be afraid, I forget everything but the sleep welling up like deep, deep water into my head. I feel Annie curling into my side, then nothing else.

3

Travis

We must have slept for a long time. I wake up feeling cold again. Gray light's in the cave and the sound of the river. There are skins on top of us, so only my face is cold, and Annie's still curled into me, so I tuck my face back under the skins. Travis isn't here, but I don't want to think, I just want to stay where I am and the next thing I know there's a voice saying, "Tom, Tom?"

I've forgotten I'm called Tom, so I say nothing, but try to get back into my dream. It's one I've had before, the one where the master calls me into his office and says, "There's someone come for you, Joe, you're free to go," and I look up and there she is, my mother, only I can't see her face, and that's what bothers me most, and I keep trying. So I don't want to wake up, and only when Travis says, "Tom?" a third time do I remember and turn onto my side. Annie's already rolling onto her knees, pulling the covers with her, and there's Travis, lighting the fire again and placing fish on a stone in the middle of it. I sit up, yawning hugely, and remember to cover myself up.

"It's late," Travis says. "I've been out all morning."

The sound of water's louder now, and where light comes into the cave I can see rain bouncing down. Travis is wet through. Steam rises off him as the fire gets going. He holds chunks of fish out to us on sticks.

"Breakfast," he says. "Though it's more like lunch."

I'm starving again and for a while none of us says anything as we bite into the fish. The soft flesh comes away from the bones. I choke on a small bone and Travis passes me a pan full of water. He's brewing something like tea for himself, boiling water over bits of leaves, and he offers us some. Annie pulls a face when she tries it, and I try a taste but it's bitter, so we stick with the water. Just like last night he lets us eat most of the food, and as we finish it off, he starts talking.

"I've had an interesting morning," he says. "Found some things." He lifts up something and I recognize the shovel. "Met some interesting people." He looks at us and the firelight glows in his eyes. "Two of them in fact—a farmer and his hired hand—out hunting with dogs."

I stop chewing at this and glance at Annie, but she doesn't look up.

"They shout down to me, 'Hey, you,' they say, which is not the most civil way to greet a fellow, so I go on my way. But they just keep on shouting and waving. So eventually I look up and . . . you'll never guess what they ask me."

Suddenly the fish in my mouth seems like a huge sticky lump I can't swallow.

"They ask if I've seen two children, a boy and a girl."

I look at Annie again and Annie looks at me, but her face gives nothing away. I have to say something, so I say, "What did you tell them?"

"I told them I had, of course," Travis says, and my stomach lurches so badly, I feel like I'm going to be sick. "I told them I'd seen the bodies of two children, swept down the river in the flood."

Relief flows through me, upward and into my face.

"Seemed like disagreeable types to me," Travis goes on, toasting another fish. "I wouldn't be in a hurry to tell them my business."

I look at Annie and she's smiling her hidden smile. I look back at Travis. "Thanks," I start to say, but he lifts his hand, then starts clearing stuff away.

"It's nothing to do with me," he says. "And I'll not ask. You make your own story and stick to it. If you're going to live on the road, that's the first thing you learn."

"What's it like," I say, after a silence, "living on the road?"

"Ah, it's grand," he says. "You can't beat it." And he starts talking then, about how tramping in the summer's a lovely thing; a white country road on a summer evening with a faint sickle moon just above it. But on a winter's night, when the wind cuts notches in your spine and you're drenched through with rain, that's when many a tramp gives up and heads for the nearest workhouse, or lies down in the snow to die. But not Travis. He doesn't like any kind of house, but especially not the workhouse; that he calls the poor man's Bastille. If anything, he loves the winters more. The stars hang so low over the moor, you can almost touch them, and the moon's as bright as the sun. He even loves the hail and the driving sleet, because that's when you find something out about yourself.

"What?" I say in spite of myself. "What do you find out?"

"You find out whether you want to live or die," he says. "And in the end that's the only thing you need to know."

I remember the chicken shed and the hen.

"Listen to me," he says, his face half lit up, half in shadow. "I was born into bad times. My mother and father were farm laborers, starving to death when the crops failed and rich folk took what little land they had. They were owned by other people, and worked to death for other folk's profit, but that wasn't for me. I took to the road. I said to myself that it was a foolish game trying to do anything in this world but sleep and eat and enjoy the sun and the sea and the rain. I've not worked for other folk for twenty years and I've never done a fellow man an injury. That's my religion and I live by it—live like the birds, free."

"But you said you'd been a soldier," I remember, "and a sailor."

Travis waves a hand impatiently.

"Long gone, laddie," he says. "I wasn't much older than you when I took off, and men'll try and own you, buy and sell you like so much wheat and chaff. But I soon learned. When I had a day's work I'd give it up again, before I got too attached to the money. It's a thing with me to spend all my money at once, before I leave a place, and to set out on the road with empty pockets. For you'll never own money before it owns you. And food's easy to come by."

I've never found that. So I ask him. "How?"

"Anyhow," he says, looking stern. "I sell skins if I've got them; if not, I can sing for my supper and tell a tale like anyone else. And if you do go hungry it's no big thing. Work for other people and they'll keep you hungry all right."

"You mean you can get food just by telling a story?" I say, thinking, *Any fool can do that.*

"Of course you can," says Travis.

"What kind of stories?"

"All kinds," Travis says.

"Go on then," I say. I don't know whether I believe him or not.

He sits back on his haunches and looks at us consideringly and nods to himself. Then he begins.

"Did you ever hear the one about the angel of the Lord coming to earth on the night the baby Jesus was born?" he says, and we both nod. I'm a bit disappointed, though. We had enough Bible stories at the workhouse.

"Well, what they don't tell you is that some of the angels who came down that night took a good look around and liked the place. So instead of clearing off with the rest of the holy host, they decided to stay. Well, the angel of the Lord didn't think much of that. He said, 'You have to come back with me; there's no place for you here.' He had a deep shining voice, like a bell. But still the others hung back, and already they were losing that glow around them that angels have, and becoming more like men and women. Because when you look at an angel," Travis says, "you can't tell one from the other."

We are listening now, hard. We can see a hill in winter, same as these hills, with a big group of shining angels hovering above it, and the blinded shepherds lying on the earth, and a few darker figures, still glowing, standing on the hillside.

" 'You must come back,' said the angel of the Lord. 'You have never been mortal, you have never known free will.' But one of the figures was already becoming a woman, tall and craggy with wild white hair, and she could feel the earth through her feet. 'We have chosen,' she said, and the angel of the

Lord didn't know what to say to that, because choosing was not something he knew. Just by choosing, these creatures—whatever they were—were no longer angels. So he beat his wings fast and hard and lifted his finger and spoke with many voices.

" 'Your choice is on you, and choice will take you where it will. But you have no place here, so all you can do is follow that star. Men will despise you and turn you away, and only the star and the memory of that star will drive you on, each in his or her own way, until your story ends.' And with that, he and his company of angels rose into the night, and the beating of their wings was like a fiery storm. But the others stayed on that hillside, feeling their feet grow solid and strong, like the earth, and they looked at one another without words, then turned and went their separate ways. And they became the wanderers—gypsies in some countries, tramps in others—spurned and outcast. Yet to this day, when one true wanderer meets another, they recognize each other by a light in the eyes that comes from that original star."

Travis pauses there, but we're still listening.

"I suppose that makes you an angel then?" I say, a bit scornfully, but Annie says, "What did they do?"

"They told their stories," says Travis. "True angels have no stories because they can't choose. But if you travel any road long enough it'll tell you its stories, and they soon learned how to tell them. Every road's got stories of its own. And that's why," he says, "it's good fortune to feed a traveler."

He stands up then.

"I tell that story at inns sometimes," he says, "and it'll generally get me a pint of ale and some bread."

"Tell us another," I say, but Travis only laughs and says there's work to do.

"I can't stay here all day telling tales," he says. "Rain's easing off and it's time you got dressed."

I haven't even noticed that the downpour has eased to a mizzle. I'm all fired up and ready to run off along the nearest road, but Travis says mildly, "You'd better put your clothes on first."

I'd forgotten our clothes, pegged out on sticks, dry and stiff now like boards. Travis stands at the entrance for a while with his back to us while we put them on, then he goes out. My shirt's all torn, with patches of blood, and Annie's skirt is ragged and muddy. But they were already in bad nick when Mistress gave them to us. I never thought I'd miss our workhouse clothes. My shirtsleeves are hanging off and there's a gaping hole in my trousers. I pull them on somehow though my feet hurt so much, I can hardly stand on them, then I go out to find Travis. He's a little way downstream, bent over something on the riverbank. I hobble over, but stop when I see what he's doing.

It's a dog. One of the old yellow hounds that fell over the cliff, hunting us. Travis is slitting its belly.

Now I never liked that dog, of course, but I don't want to watch it being skinned. Still, I do watch, fearfully, Travis's long knife glinting and turning red, until he looks over his shoulder and says, "Go back awhile. I'll be with you in a minute."

A long shiver runs through me but I do as I'm told. When I get back, Annie's still sitting where I left her, staring at the wall of the cave. She turns to me and her eyes are fearful and strange.

"They're following," she says.

Somehow I know she's not talking about the farmer and Young Bert.

"Give over," I say roughly, then, "shift. Travis is coming."

She scuttles sideways, then clutches my arm. "Listen!" she says.

Now I grab her arm, hard. "Shut it," I say.

Annie looks at me with her pale eyes full of fear, but after a moment looks at the floor. We sit in silence, waiting. Too many things are running through my head. The thought of Travis, kind and telling us stories, and then cutting the dog open with his long knife. The thought of us being on the road, and me telling all the stories I know.

After a long time Travis reappears, carrying a big, grayish-yellow skin with stains round the edges. I try not to look at it, but I can't help thinking there's a lot of it for one lean old hound. I glance at all the other skins and suddenly the cave seems full of death.

Travis spreads the skin out on the sticks he used to dry our clothes. He doesn't say anything, but after a while he looks at us and says, "Those clothes aren't fit to stand up in." When we don't say anything he says, "Have you got no shoes?"

We haven't had shoes since the workhouse.

Travis bends over and starts inspecting our feet, lifting them up, pulling us closer to the light, muttering to himself. Cuts and blisters, chilblains and bruises. His mouth twists. "You've got to take care of your feet," he says, "or you'll never last on the road. It's your feet that tell you where to go. Your feet and the road, see, they get to know one another. And that's when the stories come. Most folk think you get stories in your head, but that's not it. You get them through your feet, from the feel of the road. The road whispers to you, through the soles of your feet. You look after your feet and they'll tell you all you need to know."

He sits back on his haunches, considering us.

"Wait there," he says, and disappears. Me and Annie look at one another and wait. We hear him scrabbling around outside, then the noise of him fades. But after a few moments he returns, carrying long mottled leaves. He rubs these on the soles of our feet, gently, until a kind of juice is released.

"Comfrey's better," he says, "but you'll not get comfrey yet."

He carries on rubbing till my feet tingle. "There's one thing you can always do for your feet," he says. "When you pass water, make sure it gets to the soles of them. It'll harden them up like leather." He looks at me and I pull a face then close my eyes, feeling only the rub of his thumbs.

There's a burning, stinging sensation, but it's somehow soothing. With my eyes shut I can see his face the way it was when he told his story, half lit, half in shade. Something tells me that the shaded half won't want to be followed. Even so, I can see the three of us together, on the road.

Outside the rain's increasing again, in a steady spatter of drops that run into one another like the running river.

"My own feet are like hobnail boots," Travis is saying. "They've had to be. Good feet'll take you anywhere, lad."

I open my eyes. Travis's feet are wrapped in skins like the rest of him, bound on by strips of leather. They seem almost as broad as long.

"Let's see now," he says, and he takes one of the smaller skins and begins cutting it into ragged squares. Then he takes out a strip of leather and cuts narrower strips from it. Me and Annie say nothing; we just watch. It's a good knife he's got and he works fast. Then he kneels in front of Annie, lifting her foot in his hand and wrapping the skin round it, then two long strips of leather round the skin. He ties the strips of leather above her ankle, then does the same thing with the other foot.

"Is that all right for you, little maid?" he asks. Annie doesn't say anything but her eyes are smiling. Now it's my turn. He wraps my feet up like two swaddling babes and adjusts the straps once, twice.

"Too tight?" he says, then, "Tight enough?" and finally, "Go on—try them out."

We stand up and take a few steps round the cave. It feels funny, with the rough skins slipping a bit, but warm. Soon I'm stomping round and Annie's clapping.

But Travis hasn't finished yet. He's putting some smaller skins together and wrapping them round Annie. "Try these for size," he says, and offers me some more.

"Eh—thanks," I say, a bit awkward.

"Well, you'll not last the night in those rags," he says, and grins as I stamp round in my new clothes feeling like a hunter. Like Travis. But they keep slipping off.

"A few stitches'll hold 'em," he says, producing a long needle from his skin bag and some thick thread. He takes the skins back from us, sits cross-legged and starts to sew.

At the workhouse it was only the girls who sewed, but there's nothing girly about Travis as he drives the big needle through the tough skins with his huge hands. Seems like there's nothing he can't do.

"With any luck you'll be taken for two bears when you go through the forest," Travis says, and I stop stamping and stare at him.

"The forest?" I say. I've never heard anything good about the forest. It spreads for miles through the valleys, and at the workhouse they said that it was full of wolves and bears and murdering thieves, not to mention strange fey creatures that lead you astray so that you lose all sense of time and come back to a world where everything you once knew had gone. The matron used to say that folk wandered into the forest but they rarely wandered back out again, and even if they did they were changed forever. Most folk took the road, though it was much longer, curving all round the outside of the forest.

All I can say is, "Forest isn't safe."

Travis shoots me a sharp look. "It's the safest place there is, if someone's looking for you."

"But you told 'em you'd found our bodies—"

"I know what I told 'em, lad," Travis says, "but how long do you think it'd be before news of two children traveling the road together got back to the farm? You'd have to pass houses, villages, other travelers. News spreads fast on the road."

"But what about wolves?" I say. I can't bring myself to say "and murderers and demons and feys," but that's what I'm thinking.

Travis finishes sewing our skins together and tugs them hard.

"There are not so many wolves around today," he begins. "You might have to look out for the Dog-woman, though."

We sit down. "The Dog-woman?" I ask.

Travis hands us the skins. They're sewn together unevenly from differ-

ent kinds of fur, but they wrap round us snug enough. We look at one another and laugh. We look like two animals, like we should be living in the
forest ourselves. Travis smiles, his face thoughtful. Then he tells us this
tale. . . .

Dog-woman was left alone on the cold hillside. The angels had left and
the sky was empty. One by one the company of them that had been angels
had disappeared down the hillside, each going his separate way. Dog-woman
felt lonely. She put back her head and howled. It was unexpected. She'd
never done that before. She looked down at her arms that had been white
and shining and saw that they were covered in shaggy hair. She could smell
the smell of the sheep, sharp and rank in her nostrils, and the smell that the
shepherds had left before hurrying away after the star. When she looked at
the sheep they huddled away from her nervously. She felt an urge to fall on
all fours but resisted it. She had been an angel.

"Dog-woman didn't know why she, of all the company, had been singled
out to become not human but animal, and there was no one left to tell her.
She looked around and the world looked different through her new eyes;
black and white in the snow, but lit by a peculiar glow. It seemed like her
nose, rather than her eyes, was telling her where to go, so she set off following it down the steep hill. Soon the path was so rough that she was
forced to go on all fours to get her balance. And soon she realized that what
she was following was a trail of blood.

"It didn't take her long to find a wounded hare. It looked at her with its
dying eyes and she sank her teeth into its neck and killed it quickly—that
was the mercy she gave. And quickly, without thinking about it, she ate its
flesh and heart. Then, when she had finished, she wiped the blood from her
jaws. She wanted to cry, but the only form her crying would take was a long,
eerie howl. And this time there was an answering howl, then another.

"Dog-woman set off, running faster and faster down the hill. The
thought that was driving her now was the thought of the pack, and she ran

on all fours to be with others of her own kind. She ran easily, with long lop-ing strides toward the edge of a thick forest, and before she reached it she could see dark shapes appearing silently. Their smell was strong in her nos-trils and they smelled like kin. Thick and fast they came, then thicker and faster, all running with her into the forest as though with one body. And for the first time a fierce joy came to Dog-woman as she felt the strength in her muscles and veins. She leaped, sure-footed, over branches and thickets, and did not slip.

"In those days the forest was endless, and they ran on until finally they came to a clearing. There Dog-woman stood up, towering over the other hounds, and surveyed her pack. They were a motley, savage bunch, half starved and scraggy. Dogs as well as wolves were among them. They cow-ered a little before her as if they knew she was their leader and had been waiting for her all their lives.

" 'You are my people,' she said to them, or rather, howled, and they howled back at her, understanding perfectly.

"From that time on Dog-woman lived with her pack. They hunted and slept together and shared out their spoils. She learned to avoid humans, who drove them away with stones and left out poisoned meat. She mated with different members of the pack and had young. She mourned, howling, when one of the pack died, as though she had lost her own life—and she mourned often, for she outlived them all. The young of the pack grew elderly and died, and still Dog-woman survived, hunting and breeding.

"One time when she had been left alone to give birth to another litter, and the father of the litter had gone to find food for her, Dog-woman real-ized she was not alone. She looked up, and there was the angel of the Lord, leaning against a tree.

" 'You again,' she said, or rather, snarled. 'What do you want?'

"Now an angel'll never answer a direct question, and this one just went on looking at her. She remembered what she had always intended to ask.

" 'Why am I like this?' she asked, nudging her young who were suckling. 'Why am I not human, like all the others?'

"The angel of the Lord was silent for a long moment, then he said, 'Many centuries have passed. What have you learned?'

"Dog-woman had lost all track of time. She thought a bit, then said, 'I've learned that there's nothing sweeter than the scent of the chase, and the moment when another animal gives up its life—that's the sweetest feeling of all, like peace. I've learned what it is to give life, and I've learned grief at the death of my kin. I have learned to tell fresh water from foul, good meat from bad, and that there is no place for me in all the world except for running with my pack. . . . What have you learned?' She asked him this sourly, giving him a look.

" 'You were the first who wanted to stay,' said the angel, 'because of your strong love of the earth. Men and women are lonely, but you have your pack. Your life is vivid to you. You have lived many lifetimes and still the earth is the most powerful thing in your eyes and ears and nose. What would you change?'

"Dog-woman thought of her grief, inconsolable when one of her young had died, or her last mate. She thought of hunger, and the long, bitter winters. But she had chosen the earth.

" 'Nothing,' she said eventually, looking at the angel. He shimmered before her and no longer seemed quite clear. 'I wouldn't change a thing.'

"The angel smiled. 'Then that's all you need to know,' he said, and lifting his finger he spoke again with several voices.

" 'Live as long as you desire to live,' he said. 'And when you are tired, become one with the earth.'

" 'And then what?' Dog-woman asked, but the angel had already gone. And that was the last she saw of him, or any angel. She went on living with her pack, roaming the forests, and she lives with them still. . . .

"People know her hereabouts," Travis says. "You get tales of people seeing a shaggy woman surrounded by hounds. Of food disappearing when a door's left open, or sheep and chickens killed. They say if you see her in the distance it's in her human form with her wild white hair, but if she enters a house it's always as a dog. They say the bite of her will either kill or cure."

There's a long pause after he finishes the story, then I say, "You mean she lives around here now?"

"In the forest," Travis says. "If you run into her be sure you have some meat for her dogs. If you're kind to her dogs she'll be fine with you."

"Have you met her then?" I say. I can't help asking even though, of course, I don't believe his story.

"Many times," says Travis. He gets up and goes to the entrance of the cave. "Rain's easing off again," he says.

"If I see her," I say, "I'll throw her some meat and say, 'Here, girl, heel.'" I grin at Annie and she shoots me a look. "Maybe I'll teach her to sit up and beg," I say. "And she'll show us the way through the forest."

"Or maybe she'll gut you and eat you," Travis says. "But we've got work to do for supper."

We go out with him then, slipping around a bit in our skins, and all that afternoon he shows us how to spear fish on a sharp stick. I try and try but I'm not as fast as Travis. We slip on the wet stones trying not to get our skins soaked, and laugh. He shows us how to throw a stone so it skims the surface, but I can't do it.

Snow still clings to the hills in spite of all the rain, but close to the earth is soft and soaked with a wet, strong smell. By the time we've finished Travis has speared four or five fish, and I've got one, small and spiny, that thrashes around on the end of my stick and I'm shouting with excitement.

"Hold your noise," Travis says, splashing over, but he says it kindly enough, pleased with my catch. Annie's given up and is sitting on a rock, drumming her heels.

Then he takes us to a small copse of trees and shows us how to find dry sticks of birch, even in the rain, by scrabbling through the undergrowth. If he's surprised that we don't know birch from any other tree, he doesn't show it—just goes on pointing out birch that burns and willow that bends and how well they go together. I get fed up after a bit and just start banging the trees and grasses with my sticks, but Annie's good at it and soon has a bundle tied round with strips of willow and tucked under her skins.

By this time the light's fading and it's time to get back to the cave. I'm starving again and I can't wait to light a fire and cook the fish. I'm thinking all the time about what it'll be like to live on the road, and about hunting for real meat, not just fish.

The cave's starting to feel like home. I can imagine the three of us living there, but as he's cooking the fish Travis says, "In the morning we'll set off, first thing."

I suppose we can't stay too long, so close to Bent Edge Farm. And anyway, I'm happy, so long as we're with Travis. I've forgotten I ever distrusted him.

It's raining again and darkness falls like a wet, wet blanket. We strip off our skins and peg them out to dry like we've been doing it all our lives, and we sit with our faces to the flames and Travis tells us about traveling: when the spring comes that's not far off now, and the moors whisper and rustle, yellow with gorse and broom, and you can hear the call of the larks and the moorhens, and the soft, lonely cry of the curlew, and up over the hillside comes the great orange sun turning the whole world to flame then quickly, quick as blinking, back to green again.

We listen to Travis and eat the soft fish flesh with our fingers and feel the heat of the fire, and drift into sleep. And it seems to me then, as it always has done, ever since, that this must be what it's like in heaven, to be warm and fed and without fear. To have found everything that you thought you'd lost.

4

Rabbit

Seems like I've hardly been asleep when I wake up and find Travis clearing stuff away in the cold gray light.

"Always cover your tracks, Tom," he says. "Never leave anything for anyone to find."

I get up stiffly and give Annie a kick, then pull on my skins. Everything seems different in the morning light.

"Here," Travis says, handing me the shovel. "Never forget your tools."

I take the shovel and stand there, stupid-like. Annie stirs and groans.

"Right," says Travis. "Pick up your things."

We wrap ourselves in the skins Travis made for us and hand him the ones we'd been lying on. He's cleared everything else and the cave's empty and dark, as if no one had ever been there. It's a lonely feeling.

Travis hitches the bundle on his back. "Nothing like setting off early," he says.

It's freezing. Travis sets off at a great pace and we hurry after. My feet are numb, slipping and slithering in the skins, which aren't tied on tight enough. When I stop to tie them on again, Annie waits but Travis doesn't, and we have to run to catch up.

The sky's pale with a few stars. Everything's dim and gray. There's a kind of mist coming off the river, swirling into strange shapes. Travis takes a track that leads steeply away from the river. Soon there are copses of trees, dark and silent. So much silence everywhere that I want to talk.

"We could have stayed in bed a bit," I say, my breath coming out like smoke, but Travis makes no comment. "Where are we going?" I ask, but he still says nothing. Annie says nothing either, her breath coming in smoky gasps. I can feel a stitch in my side from hurrying uphill, and I begin to wonder about breakfast.

We pass through a field that's wet with rain and dew, the long grass brushing our legs. Then we climb through a stile into another field and Travis stops, bending over.

"What?" I say. "What are you looking for?"

Travis's fingers close round a stone and he stands up. He unslings his bundle and takes out a strip of leather, folding it into a loop. "See there," he says, nodding toward the far side of the field. I look but I can't see anything.

"Look again," says Travis, and I peer through the gloom until I think I can see dim shapes, bobbing and weaving. Travis fits the stone into the strip of leather and swings it round his head. It whistles through the air and there's a soft *ptth!* as it falls. I still can't see anything but Travis seems pleased. We hurry across the field after him and there, sure enough, is a rabbit—eyes wide open, legs still twitching, and a dark smudge near the ear where the stone's hit. Travis picks it up by the legs and slings it into his bundle.

"Eh, that's amazing!" I say. "Can I have a go?"

Travis makes no comment but I'm getting used to this now. We walk on to the next field and he hands me the leather sling. "Here," he says. "Aim for that hare."

I try to fit a stone into the sling and it falls out immediately until Travis helps. Then I swing it round my head and it falls behind me. The hare doesn't seem worried. It goes on munching the grass, one long ear flopping over its eye. I try again and the stone falls just a couple of feet away. The hare bounds off.

"You can keep the sling," Travis says. "You'll need the practice."

The next field we come to, he takes out another sling and fells another rabbit before I've even seen it. My stone falls uselessly at my feet.

Travis picks it up. "Like this," he says, walking to a fence. He balances two large pinecones and a chunk of rock on the fence, steps back and sends a stone whizzing at them. It hits the first cone and that topples, then the second, and then the rock—*clunk!* One after another, like that!

"How do you do that?" I ask him, running after, but he only says, "Practice," over his shoulder, and climbs the fence. We follow, Annie gathering her skirts up, me pushing her from behind, a bit harder than I need to.

We can hear the first birds now, gathering and calling to one another overhead, and soon Travis stops again. "Look," he says.

Everything's gray and still. The sky's gray, the grass is gray with dew, and the wind holds its breath.

Then there's a sharp streak of green to the east and, suddenly, the sky turns a faint pink and goes pinker until it blazes like fire. Over the gray hillside comes the first sliver of sun, a thin curve of pure, white fire, already blinding. We all stand and watch as a big ball of light grows, pulsing and throbbing, fit to burst.

I look at Annie and she's smiling, tucking a strand of hair behind her ear. There can't be anything better than this—to be on the road forever with Travis. Except breakfast.

Travis still says nothing but he swings on again at a great pace, whistling. We run after, laughing now, until Travis tells us to be quiet. "Listen," he says.

I can't hear anything apart from birds. I walk on, listening to the tramp and swish of our feet through grass, then suddenly I can hear it. Silence.

Over and above the cries of birds there's a big, big silence in the sky and, beneath our feet, a big, deep silence from the earth. We tramp along, just listening to it. Seems to me that I can tell how big the world is, just from the silence.

Travis stops one more time to kill a hare. I see it at the same time, but he's felled it before I get the stone in my sling and, once again, my stone falls at my feet.

Hopeless. I'm starting to think I'll never be good enough to travel the road. But Travis is heading toward some trees.

"Breakfast," he says, and I forget to be cross.

We run into the copse, scrabbling through the undergrowth for the driest sticks, and soon Travis has a small fire blazing. He lets us help skin the rabbit. It's harder than it looks and I'm a bit clumsy, but Annie's small fingers strip the fur back nimbly and Travis cuts it open to let the blood drain. I watch as he slides the knife in toward the back legs and tail, taking the legs out just by twisting, then cutting through the spine to release the tail. Then he cuts off the head and puts it in his bundle.

"Stew," he says. He goes on cutting through the spine and splitting the ribs, pulling out the innards and cutting out chunks of muscle from the back, spearing them and holding them over the flames.

If you've never ate rabbit at dawn sitting under a tree and looking out across an open moor, you've never lived. That's what Travis says, and I believe him, licking the juice from my fingers.

"This is the best," I say. Travis is already clearing away.

"It's the best thing, this," I say again, to make him answer.

"It's one of them," he says without looking up. "Not the best."

"Well, what is then?"

"The best thing," he says, "is to live your life without leaving a single trace."

Seems daft to me, but I don't argue. Right now, with the sun in my face and rabbit warm in my belly, I'd believe anything at all. We help him clear away, to leave no traces.

"Where to now, Travis?" I ask. For answer he walks over to the edge of the hill.

There below us spreads the forest. A few trees gather into a copse at the bottom of the hill, then that copse runs into another and another until the forest spreads like a thick green darkness for miles. Up here you can just about see the end of it, faint wreaths of smoke from cottages where the sky meets the earth.

Travis sets off down the hill, walking in great zigzags, and we follow. It's hard going because the tufts of grass are slippy and there's mud between and little pools of icy water. I have to slide down most of it on my bum.

Farther down I can see that a road branches away from the forest—the road that farmers take to market. But now that I'm closer to it I can see that a thin track goes from it through the forest, twisting and winding. The dangerous path that no one takes. But as long as we're with Travis, I don't mind.

Down the long hill we bump and slither, reaching the first clump of trees, then a place where the hill begins to level out, until finally we stand on the road, breathing hard. The dark edge of the forest looms up before us. The sun doesn't seem to have risen at all in there. The track runs into it a little way and disappears, swallowed up by the darkness made by great branches. We peer into the gloom, then look back up at Travis.

"This is where I leave you," he says, and my stomach gives a lurch and goes on falling. Travis doesn't look at me. "The track goes right through the forest," he says. "When you come out on the other side, you'll see the first houses, and then the town begins."

"But . . . aren't you coming?" I say with a little laugh. I can't believe he expects us to go in there alone.

Travis doesn't answer. He squints at the sun, which has turned white, and says, "No one'll find you in there because no one'll come looking."

I stare at him. There's a white-yellow light on his face from the sun; everything's lit up in a cold glare and still he won't look at me.

"It's a good day's walk," he says, "which is why we set off early. You'd not want to be traveling through the forest at night. But with any luck you'll have reached the town by nightfall. You'll be all right," he says, "if you stick to the track."

I feel a hard, bitter knot in my stomach. "You're leaving us then," I say. I want to shout and kick. Annie says nothing, but her eyes are open wide.

He looks at us then for the first time and spreads his arms. "I'm not looking for company," he says.

I hate him then, for ruining my dream. I might have known it was too good to be true. I kick a tree stump savagely, and hurt my foot. The pain makes my eyes sting, but I'm not crying, because I never do.

"Tom, Tom," says Travis.

"That's not my name," I spit at him. "You don't know my name!"

"And don't you go telling me," Travis says, very stern, then he sighs and squats down so that his face is a little lower than my own. "How old are you?" he says.

Now you might think that's an easy question, but the fact is I don't know. We used to get visitors at the workhouse, looking for apprentices, and whenever they asked the master of the workhouse how old I was, he changed the story to suit them.

"He might look small but he's nearly fourteen," he'd say. "Old enough to work on a building site. And feel those muscles." Or, "Oh, no, ma'am, he's no more than eight, very biddable, easily trained."

So it's anyone's guess how old I am; somewhere between eight and fourteen, and Annie a couple of years younger. So now when Travis asks me I just glare at him.

"Ten, eleven maybe?" he says. I shrug. "Old enough," he says, nodding as if to himself and I want to ask, "For what?" but I won't give him the satisfaction. "All over England there are boys and girls just like yourselves, tramping the country. Better to be on the road than inside—you can't trust people in houses. They'll buy and sell you and you'll learn to be slaves, not free. You've got a chance now, to earn your freedom."

He stands up then as though he's had enough, and dusts the mud off his breeches.

"Where are you going?" I ask, still bitter, but he doesn't answer. I want to beg him to tell us more, about when he first took to the road as a child; I want to run by his side, begging for stories—but Travis isn't like that. I can't beg or plead with him any more than with a tree. Already his eyes are focused on the far distance, unraveling the road like a spool of thread. I feel a sour pain at leaving him but it seems to me he doesn't feel anything at all. There's nothing left to say, though, so I resort to muttering, "I suppose that's one way of getting rid of us—bringing us here."

Travis unslings his bundle. "Take this," he says, holding out his tinder-box, "and this." He takes out the rabbit that he killed.

Now, I know this is a big thing—a traveler won't give up his tinder. But I won't take anything from him, so he lays them gently on an old tree stump and it's Annie who steps forward and slips her hand in his. "Thank you," she whispers, and I see Travis's face change, quick as shade. But he just nods and slings his bundle back across his shoulders.

"Don't trust houses," he says to us. "Or people in them." He tightens a knot in the rope round his pans. "Look after your tools," he says, and looks for a moment as though he might say more, but then changes his mind. He nods his head once more at Annie and turns his back.

I watch him for a minute, then take one or two running steps after him. "Where are you going?" I call after him, and, "Eh, Travis—where are you going?" When he doesn't answer I stamp my feet and shout, "What's to stop us following you, eh?"

But I know the answer to that one. For starters he walks too fast, his great stride lengthening into the road, arms swinging. For another thing we have to keep ourselves hid, like he said, in the forest. Still, I can't take my eyes off him as he walks right out of our lives, a solitary broad figure, shaggy in his skins, the brown of his clothes and hair already starting to blend with the brown of the moor and the road.

I try to go on feeling angry but I just feel hollow inside, like there's a Travis-shaped space inside me. I watch him till my eyes blur, but I'm not crying. I rub them and watch some more. You don't need to know some people for long to know that you'll never forget them. Travis was like that.

5

Forest

A few steps into the forest all the light disappears, like it's been snuffed out or swallowed.

I hold Annie's hand and she holds mine. Twigs crackle under our feet and great trailing branches brush us and make a whispering sound as if no one has ever passed there before.

We go farther and the trees crouch nearer.

Everything looks like something else.

The stump of a hollow tree looks like a bear . . . holes in the tree trunks make ugly mouths at us as we pass . . . the pattern of moss on the trees looks like faces . . .

Annie trips. She stumbles over a branch, but gets up without a word. I pull her along, trying not to listen to the stories my feet are telling me. It's all right having your feet tell you stories, but not if they're ones you don't want to hear.

It's stuffy, with a dim, musty smell—of things growing without light or air. We trudge on and our breathing is loud in the silence. I wish we made less noise, that I couldn't see faces wherever I look. Or rather, wherever I *don't* look.

Then a pattering begins, like falling leaves only sharper, over our shoulders. First one way, then another. It takes a few moments to realize that it's only rain, falling without ever reaching the forest floor, but it sounds like nothing so much as the patter of tiny, fast feet, in front, behind and to all sides. Annie's face whitens and I suck in my breath and hurry on.

The path gets more tangled, so we can hardly follow it. First Annie trips over something, then me. Something darts out ahead of us, close to or far away I can't tell.

I understand now, about the forest, how you could wander in and not find your way out again, lose your sense of time and place. Already I don't know how long we've been here or how far we've come. The forest has swallowed us up.

The pattering increases till it sounds like hail on the dry leaf carpet spread all around us. It sounds like running, like the whole wood's running hard, chasing, closing in on us. We begin to run too, losing the track as we weave away from fallen branches and sudden holes.

The third time Annie falls she lies still. I don't want to talk, because I feel like things are listening, so I try to pull her up but she won't budge.

"Get up," I hiss, and the trailing branches quiver and shake. Annie says nothing, crouched over, breathing hard. I kick at her and tug, but she's gone heavy like the bole of a tree. "Move!" I hiss.

She shakes her head. Her whole body's quivering. "Rest," she says.

That's the last thing I want to do. I squat down by her side.

"Come on," I whisper. "We've got to keep going." Don't know why I'm whispering, except for the feeling that something's listening. I shake her shoulder. "Annie," I say.

"Rest."

I'm tired too, and hungry, but I don't want to stop here. I think of Travis's tinderbox, and the rabbit, but I can't think of lighting a fire in here.

"Come on," I say again, but she turns her face away.

"What is it?" I say, getting annoyed.

"*Them,*" she says, or rather, whimpers, and she raises a finger and points behind.

Now that makes me wild. As if we don't have enough problems in this haunted hole. I pull her hair and she scratches me, so I dig my fingers into her shoulder. "Shut it!" I hiss, and, "Get up now, or I'm leaving you here!"

I can feel Annie's bones, and the muscles between them, clenched and quivering, but I pull her head up by the hair, then seize her wrist. She stumbles back to her feet, and I haul her along.

It's not likely that I'd leave her and plow on through the forest on my own, and she must realize that because she's not helping. It's like tugging a dead weight but I plow on anyway, no idea where, through all the whispering and pattering of the forest.

One thing I know I don't want is for Annie to tell me what she's talking about. But even so, I need her to cooperate, so I remember the story that always makes her listen.

It's about our mother, and the night she left us at the workhouse. I can't have been more than four years old, Annie still toddling. The woman without a face knocked at the big door until the master opened it. I can remember *his* face, worse luck. And I can remember our mother crying, and Annie clinging like a burr.

I'll have to leave thee now, but I'll come back for thee, she told us. *However far I go, however long it takes, I'll be back for thee. Dost hear me?* And she took off a trinket from round her neck and put it round Annie's, who was crying loudly. *Look after your sister, Joe,* she said. Them were the last words she spoke before the door slammed shut on her.

I've told that story over and over, till I don't know how much of it's real. But Annie's still got the necklace. It's just a piece of string with a few wooden beads and half a coin on it—if it'd been worth something they'd have taken it off us, but Annie screamed and spat when anyone tried.

"Do you remember, Annie?" I say, and she nods like she always does, following me quietly now, listening. "What?" I say. "What do you remember?"

And she answers as she always does, "Warm smell—like milk."

Well, at least she's got that much to remember our mother by—some wooden beads and the smell of milk. More than I've got. Because she never did come back for us, of course. In the end I gave up waiting, but Annie never did. So now all I've got is a memory without a face. And Annie.

I'm pulling her along, telling her all this, and what I can remember about the long walk up to the workhouse. It was snowing, my mother carried Annie all the way, she fell over twice and I thought she wouldn't get up again; and I get the feeling that the trees are listening, bending forward because I'm speaking so quiet. I try not to look at them, but in the end my voice dies away to a mumble.

Annie tugs my arm. "Go on."

"No."

She tugs again. "Go on."

"Not now."

I've got this empty feeling, like an ache, like I always get when I tell this story, but Annie can never have enough of hearing about the time before the workhouse.

"More," she says. I clench my jaws together and shake my head. She shakes my arm. "Why?"

"Because," I say. But I know she won't give up without a reason, so although I don't like saying it I nod toward the trees. "I feel like they're listening."

Annie stands stock-still so suddenly, I nearly fall over. "Yes," she says. "Listening."

She doesn't mean the trees. . . .

That's it. I've had enough. I turn round to face her square on. Her face is all white and staring.

"Go on then," I say, hands on hips. "Get it over with." And when she doesn't say anything I say, *"Tell us,"* and my voice cracks out like a shot through all the pattering.

Annie bends forward, mumbling so that I can hardly hear. "Two," she whispers. "Boy and girl."

"Who are they?" I say, still loud, though all the hair's prickling at the back of my neck.

Annie nods fearfully over her shoulder. "Behind," she says very low.

I look but I can't see anything, just the twisted fingers of trees.

"There's no one there," I say scornfully, though my heart's thudding a bit. "You're talking through your arse as usual."

And I'm about to pull her on again but she says, "Light hair, like straw, the boy has. Blue fingers. And a pattern like bilberries—here." She traces an outline across her own cheek and over the eye, though she's still not looking. Her eyes are fixed and staring a long way inside.

There's no one like Annie for putting the scunners on you. People used to shout at me for scaring all the other kids with my stories, but Annie—she'd put the fear of God in a stone. I remember once when there was a big plague at the workhouse and all us kids were shut in together, sick and well alike, sweating and puking. Annie got sick and I thought she'd die but instead she kept having these fits, crying and trembling, and when she called out a name everyone knew that kid'd be dead by morning.

There's nowt like a bit of prophecy for making you popular—she were nearly lynched twice. Old Meg who'd been in the workhouse nearly thirty years'd cry and scream if Annie went near.

"Keep her from me," she'd screech. "Owd Nick's halfwit spawn!"

One way or another it weren't much fun, trying to look after Annie. But the thing that shut most people up was that she was right, most of the time. I remember once, an apothecary bloke—Kaberry or Kewberry his name was—came up to the workhouse with some potion or other and Annie looked at him with her huge eyes and pointed and said, "Bitter."

"You what?" he says.

"Your mother," says Annie.

"What're you talking about, lass?"

And then Annie's throat worked and her voice changed and she said, "It was a bitter medicine that you give me, son." And you should've seen his face. He ran off looking as sick as a dog. Then another time we had a rough-looking fellow come to stay and Annie wouldn't go near him; she hid her face when he walked by. He had a girl's arms clinging round his neck, she said, and sure enough, after he'd gone, constabulary came looking for him. He was wanted for strangling his niece.

Oh, I could tell you lots of stories of Annie scaring everyone to death. She hasn't done it for a long time, though, and I can only think that the blow on her head's set her off again. But right now, in the thick of an evil forest that seems half alive, it's all we need.

"A boy and a girl," I say. "Well, what do they want with us then?"

She doesn't answer, so I say it louder. "What do you want, eh?"

Nothing.

Annie says, "They won't tell you."

"Why not?" I say. "Can't they talk? They've followed us all this way but they won't talk?"

Annie shakes her head.

"Very friendly, I'm sure," I say, kicking a large twig out of the way. "If they're going to keep us company you'd think they'd talk to us at least."

"They're whispering," says Annie.

"Well, speak up, can't you?" I say loudly, then suddenly I'm shouting, "SPEAK UP!"

Then we hear the howling.

Annie clutches me and I nearly fall over with fright. One howl, then another, closer. Coming our way.

I freeze solid all the way through.

One howl joins another and soon they're coming at us from all sides.

I find my breath. "Run!" I gasp, and set off pulling Annie, who doesn't need to be pulled anymore. Both of us are running for all we're worth.

We don't know where to run, because the howling's everywhere. But we run anyway, stumbling over tree roots, branches whipping our faces. Running through a black forest, with howling ghosts behind us.

We don't get very far before a monstrous form appears. Huge and shaggy with yellow eyes and teeth. Wolf, not ghost. Snarling.

I fling the shovel at it and we run the other way. So much for looking after my tools. Then another one appears, then a dog. Lips curled back, growling. Then another dog. We stop dead in our tracks. Fresh meat for starving hounds. I stare at the biggest one and he stares right back at me.

"Rabbit!" I say to Annie, then, "Annie—give them the bloody rabbit."

For a minute I think she might be too scared to hear. Then slowly, too slowly, she pulls the rabbit out from under her skins and throws it to the nearest hound.

We don't stop to watch him eat it—we're off. Running in the one direction that's clear of wolf, and they're bounding after us, and any moment I think I'll feel their hot breath on my neck and their teeth ripping out my throat. But still I'm running blind.

The good thing about panic is you can't keep it up for too long. It'll either kill you or wear off. Soon, even with the blood pounding in my head, I realize that these hounds could've had us by now—we're not that fast. They're running *with* us. I can't tell how many. Six maybe, or eight. As soon as we try to run in one direction they close us off, snarling; when we run in another they let us pass.

Taking us somewhere, I think, and I'm not sure if that thought scares me more or less.

They're not all wolves. Two of them are maybe, but the others are huge dogs, shaggy and lean. One of them presses up close whenever we falter, and another, the first one we saw is still holding the rabbit in his jaws. That much strikes me as strange, that he hasn't eaten it, but I've no time to think, for my breath's bursting in my sides and I can hardly see. Just behind me Annie's staggering and whimpering and I'm willing her not to fall over.

Then, just as I'm beginning to think I can run no farther and I'll fall over dead, save them the trouble of killing me, there's a parting in the trees. We stop before it and the big gray hound nudges us on. Into a clearing, and in the middle of the clearing there's something squatting, like a weed-covered boulder. But as we stumble in, it moves, rising up, taller and taller, into a shaggy, gray figure with wild white hair. Somewhere between woman and hound, walleyed, with long yellow teeth that she bares in a kind of smile as the hounds nudge us toward her. Her voice rasps out like it's unused to speech.

"You've come," she says.

6

Dog-woman

I've lost my shovel, or I'd fling it at her. But she doesn't attack—just looks at us with her head cocked to one side.

"Sit," she says. Annie's already collapsed against a fallen branch and I can't think what else to do, so I sit down the same.

The woman-beast, whatever she is, is squatting again, and the hounds are all over her, licking her face, and I swear she's licking theirs. They're making husky, whimpering, greeting noises at one another and I can't do anything but stare, thinking I've gone mad. I've been running so far, I've run clear out of my own mind and straight into one of Travis's stories.

Dog-woman is shaggy and wild, just like Travis said. She's got some kind of ragged weeds on her, but mainly she's dressed in her own hairy skin. At the end of her long bony feet there are curving yellow nails, like dog's claws, and her movements aren't human. She picks up the rabbit that the gray hound has dropped for her and sniffs along its length before starting to tear it apart and eat it, just as it is. Then she stops with her mouth full and looks over to us.

"Hungry?" she growls.

Not now I'm not. I look at Annie, but Annie only huddles closer to me. Helpful-like.

Dog-woman bounds over and I can't help but stiffen. Then she checks herself and stands up, so that she looks more human.

How tall is she? Taller than Travis. Taller, maybe, even than Old Bert. She tears a chunk off the rabbit with her yellow hands and drops it at our feet.

"Eat," she says.

I look at Annie again, and Annie looks at me. I'm wondering how to refuse. Then I remember the tinderbox.

"Can we light a fire?" I say suddenly.

Dog-woman listens with her head on one side. "Fire?" she says, as if trying to remember.

"You know," I say, eagerly now, "to cook the meat."

Dog-woman's listening hard. I swear I see her ears prick up. Then she laughs, surprising us; a low, rasping laugh.

"Good," she says. "Cook meat—good," and laughs again.

I can't see what's so funny, but I'm glad she thinks it's a good idea. I get up awkwardly and fumble for the box. I've tucked it into my trousers for safekeeping. Dog-woman seizes it at once and sniffs suspiciously. I start to look for dry wood and all the dogs gather round, growling.

"I make fire," says Dog-woman. "You sit."

Suits me. I'm worn-out anyway.

She squats over a bundle of twigs, cups her long fingers and sparks the flint, grinning to herself. Her face lights up. It's the strangest face I've ever seen, before or since—craggy and wezilled, but covered in fine, downy hair. Her long yellow teeth are sharp as a hound's and I can see the reflection of the flame in her crooked eyes. It's enough to scunner a stone. I look away but Annie looks up.

"Angel," she says, and I nearly laugh. *Yes, very likely*, I'm thinking.

One of the dogs keeps sniffing me suspiciously, glaring at me with baleful eyes. I glare back. I'd kick it if I felt any braver. *How did we end up here?* I'm thinking. And, *What kind of a mess are we in now?* And, *I hope she's not going to use all that tinder*.

Soon there's a small fire blazing. Dogs don't like it at first, but she croons to them and they gather round, lying down in the heat. I can see their long tongues and the movement of their ribs, panting.

Dog-woman drops chunks of rabbit into the fire. Overhead some branches have been pulled into a rough shelter, and one branch is strung across at the back with bits of dead animal hanging from it. She pulls strips of meat down and feeds the dogs, then pokes at the fire with a stick and the smell of burnt rabbit fills my nostrils. Seems like the dogs get to eat first. But then she cocks her head at us. "Come," she says.

I'm wary but Annie gets up right away, goes over to Dog-woman and sits by her side, so of course I have to follow. Never seen her do that before. One of the dogs growls but Dog-woman shushes it. I squat down on the earth, next to Annie.

Dog-woman rakes bits of burnt rabbit out of the flames and onto a stone to cool. There are lots of things I'd like to say, a lot of questions in my mind, but all I can think about is the meat. Dog-woman picks up a chunk of meat and offers it to Annie, holding it in front of her mouth. Annie holds back, then bites it, right from her fingers. Dog-woman bares her teeth, pleased, and holds out another chunk, and Annie takes it. Then she holds one out to me.

"I'll get my own, thanks," I say, and I reach over to the stone, grab a couple of pieces and retreat, stuffing them in my mouth.

It's not up to Travis's standards. Burnt on the outside and raw on the inside, but I'm starving, so I chew it anyway. Dog-woman lifts up her head and drops a chunk inside and chews hard, her mouth snapping open and shut, the juices running down her chin. Then she feeds Annie again.

"Good," she says, watching me. "Good?"

For answer I grab more meat. Soon there's no rabbit left and Dog-woman turns to the strips of meat hung up.

God only knows what they are, but I don't feel like refusing, so I chew a bit when she hands it to me. Leathery, and a stronger taste than the rabbit. Soon I've had enough and I'm thinking, *What happens next?*

"Sleep now," says Dog-woman. "Eat, sleep."

Not likely, I think, eyeing the nearest hound. I want to know what Dog-woman's planning but I can't think how to ask. Some of the hounds are circling now, or going a little way into the trees to squat down, and the air fills with the smell of what they're doing. At least they don't do it here. I scrunch my nose up and look around.

"Do you live here?" I ask.

Dog-woman grunts. Pig-woman. But I'm thinking about Travis's story.

"Have you always lived here?"

She turns her strange, walleyed gaze on me. There was a cross-eyed woman in the workhouse and everyone said she was a witch. I feel like making the sign of the evil eye.

"Long time," she says. "Long time live in forest."

I get the feeling that when she says *long* she means it—like thousands of years. "Well . . ." I say, thinking hard, "where did you live before you came here? Where do you come from?"

Dog-woman doesn't answer but she looks as if she's thinking.

"Do you come from around here?"

Dog-woman thinks harder. You can practically hear the wheels going round. Somewhere in those ash-colored eyes there's a little flame of memory, if you could just poke it hard enough.

"You must've lived with people sometime," I say.

Still no answer but the frown lines on her bony forehead deepen.

Then Annie says, "With angels," like that explains everything and Dog-woman sighs noisily, staring off through the trees.

"Yes," she says.

Of course she would say that. Who wouldn't rather be an angel instead of living like a dog in a pile of muck? I wanted her to tell us herself.

Dog-woman pokes the fire moodily, till it flares up a bit, then goes on talking. "Long time live in forest," she says. "Long, long time. Meet many people."

"You do?" I say, surprised.

"Many people get lost in forest," she says, turning that ashy gaze on me again. "Wander in—can't find their way. I find them. They stay with me."

That's nice for them, I think, but I say nowt. Annie strokes Dog-woman's stringy arm and they look at one another as though they're talking without words.

I've had enough of this. Seems to me they're both daft.

"Can you tell us how to get out of here?" I say.

"Out?" says Dog-woman, as if she's never heard of such a thing.

"Of the forest," I explain patiently. "You know—to the outside world."

Dog-woman looks blank. She's good at that. For a moment I think she won't answer, but then she says, "Where?"

Good question. Just as I'm thinking of the answer Annie says, "We're lost."

I nudge her sharply, but Dog-woman says, "Many wander into the forest, and few leave."

Because you feed them to your dogs, I'm thinking, so I say, very firmly, "We're not lost. We're looking for the town—we've got to get there before nightfall. So if you'd just show us the way, we'll be grateful."

Dog-woman says nothing to this.

"We're not lost," I repeat. "At least," I add darkly, "we weren't until your hounds chased us. So maybe you can show us the way again."

Dog-woman turns her ashy eyes on me. One eye, that is. The other one's staring at her nose. "Dogs bring you here," she says flatly, as if that settles it.

I'm not happy about this. "Yeah, they brought us here, and now we'd like to go again," I say, thrusting my chin forward.

Dog-woman looks cunning. "Road takes you to town," she says. "Big road, people come and go all the time. Not go into forest. People come into forest to hide."

She squints at me and I squint back. Perhaps she's not one egg short of a basket after all.

"We are hiding," Annie says, and if it wouldn't look too obvious I'd kick her, but Dog-woman doesn't seem to hear.

"To hide—or to find something," she says to herself, poking at the fire. Then she looks at me again. "What looking for?"

Now there are lots of answers I could give to this. "Work," I could say, or even "Travis," but somehow they all stick in my throat and I can't think of a thing to say, so I say nothing. Feels like Dog-woman's good eye is boring straight into me, but Annie says, "Mother."

There it is—she's said it. The daft idea I knew she'd had all along. It hangs in the air between us and all I can do is look sullen. But Dog-woman nods.

"People come to forest," she says, still talking to herself. "Men and women, children too—look for shelter, look for food. For safe place," she says, staring into the fire. "Long, long ago a woman came. Broken heart. Needed mending. She left her children in a bad place, over the hill." She nods outward and suddenly I'm listening hard, even my skin is listening, because I know she means the workhouse. I don't want to listen but I can't help it.

"Two children," Dog-woman says. "Boy and girl. Girl only a baby. It was winter like this—snow thick, soft. She had nowhere to go."

Annie is clutching her beads and Dog-woman's arm, craning forward to see her face. "What did she look like?" she whispers.

Dog-woman touches Annie's face with a bony finger. "Like you," she says.

I leap up suddenly, scattering the twigs from the fire. "I don't believe you!" I shout, and several dogs spring up, barking and growling, but I don't care. "Don't tell your lies to us!"

Dog-woman hardly moves. She's still touching Annie's face, Annie's staring into hers.

"El-len," Dog-woman says, without looking up. "El-len."

I can feel my blood running thick and cold, my tongue stuck up in my mouth. Because that was our mother's name—that much I know. I remember her telling the master of the workhouse, and him writing it down in his book. *Joseph and Ann Sowerby, children of Ellen Sowerby, widow.*

"I don't believe you," I mutter again. It's all I can manage to say. But Annie's face is shining. She's staring speechlessly up at Dog-woman, and this makes me mad all over again.

"Well, so what?" I say loudly, setting the dogs off barking. I lower my voice. "So what if you did see her? That was years ago. How's that going to help us now? She left us years ago and she never came back for us—never!"

"She not want to leave you," Dog-woman says, and I feel a pain in my heart that makes me even angrier. If she didn't have the dogs with her I swear I'd lay into her there and then.

As it is, all I can manage to say is, "But she did," and glare at Dog-woman's ugly face.

Dog-woman looks back at me for a long moment, then turns back to Annie. "Your mother go to town, look for work."

Manchester, I think. *The big town. I've always wanted to go there.*

"She say she go back for you when she can."

I snort loudly. "Well, she's taking her time."

"She come back if she could."

Dog-woman says this very definitely and I glare at her. What would she know? And I feel like saying something bad, the worst thought that's in me, so I say, "She's probably dead then."

"No," says Annie, very definitely.

Well, that's that then. I expel my breath noisily and kick the nearest tree, wishing it were Annie, or her houndlike friend.

"All right then," I say. "Now what? You've told us this—now what are we supposed to do?"

"What do you want?" Dog-woman says, and both she and Annie are staring at me with their eyes all lit up by the fire, and it's like all my words are jammed in my throat.

Dog-woman stands and her hounds get up as well. "You rest now. Sleep," she says.

I find my voice at last. "But we're supposed to be in town by tonight."

"Night now," Dog-woman says.

I look up at the overhanging branches. How can she tell?

"Sleep now," she says.

I don't like the thought of sleeping here, with some half-human woman and her stinking hounds, but it doesn't look like there's a choice. I rub my fingers across my forehead. "But how will we get out of the forest?"

"Sleep now," Dog-woman says, and more and more of her hounds gather round. "In the morning I take. I take your mother, I take you."

All the dogs are surrounding her now, panting up at her with their long tongues. I look at her suspiciously. "Where are you off to?"

"I hunt," she says. "You sleep."

Just like that, I'm thinking. Yet the thought that she won't be here makes me feel better. She's leaving us alone. We could run off. But we don't know the way, and it's night, and we're dog-tired, so to speak. Besides, there's nowhere to run to that she couldn't find us.

No choice then. No choice about being left at the workhouse, or sent to the farm. No choice about having to trust Travis, or to believe this creature, who's sniffing the air, making strange doglike noises in her throat, shaking herself like a dog. And the dogs bark back at her, wagging their shaggy tails so hard that even the branches are shaking with them. Then she crouches, tense as a bow, and you can feel the dogs tighten into a pack, so solid, they might be one beast. Then with a single bound she's off, and they're all off after her, leaping through the forest that's thicker than night.

I look at Annie and she looks at me. But when she sees the expression on my face the light in her eyes dies down. She settles herself near the fire and turns away from me, lying on a heap of leaves facing the flames. It's the best spot.

"Move over, can't you?" I say.

Nothing.

"Come on—shift," I say, kicking her.

"No."

"Move your arse."

"You!"

"No, you."

"You."

We glare at one another. It's not like Annie to talk back. Her chin's stuck up and her face all shut up like a box, and I can see she's not going to back down. About moving, about Dog-woman, about anything. She turns over on the leaves with a sigh that means she's not going to talk.

"You'll talk to Dog-face," I say. "You'll chat away to her all right—'Oh, you must remember when you were an angel. . . . Where do you keep your wings? . . . I didn't know they had such beautiful angels in heaven.' No wonder the shepherds near died of fright. You'll talk to *her* all right but now you clam up. Eh?"

Annie says nothing to this so I say nothing either, though I'm thinking plenty. I lie down on the other side of the fire from Annie, not looking at her because I'm still mad, and I watch the firelight dancing over the leaves and the forest yawning beyond, thoughts of what's happened and what's been said chasing themselves round and round in my brain, but no answers coming, no ideas. I just lie there, thinking hard, doing nothing.

No choice.

7

Pack

I'm woken up by a hound licking at my face, breathing all over me with its stinking dog breath.

Disgusting.

I scramble up, sharpish, rubbing my eyes.

Dog-breath shifts position and starts licking my hands, then my ears.

"Clear off!" I tell it. "I'm not your breakfast."

My head's aching and I feel stiff and bruised. But I can smell food. Dog-woman's lit the fire again and is sitting a little way off, chewing something that's still got fur. There's blood on her chin and bits of meat and gristle caught in the hairs on her face.

Lovely.

Most of the dogs are lying around, worrying at chunks of meat between their paws. My friend with the bad breath's still gazing at me hopefully. And Annie . . .

"Where's Annie?" I say very sharp, and when Dog-woman doesn't reply I say, "Eh, you, where's Annie?"

Dog-woman looks at me. Her eyes are yellowish in the green light. "Fetch water," she says.

I'm not happy. "But where is she?" I say, getting up stiffly.

"Here," says Annie, coming through the trees with her stumpy walk. She's carrying a misshapen wooden bowl with water sloshing over the sides. She brings it over to me and I slurp at it noisily, like a hound. Then she takes it to Dog-woman, who nearly tips it over, sloshing it all down her front, and then Dog-woman puts what's left down for the hounds, who all gather round it at once, nudging one another out of the way.

Then Dog-woman brings us the carcass of whatever it is she's been chewing. "Eat," she says.

I can't even tell what it once was. I point at the fire. "Cook," I say. I sound like Dog-woman. Soon I'll start to look like her.

She gives me a look, as though I've amused her, but starts tearing off chunks and flinging them onto the fire, where they crackle and curl. She hands me a stick with a pointed end, and me and Annie take turns at spearing the chunks of meat, then eating them hot.

I start to feel better. New day, new hope, as they say. There's a ray of white light coming through the trees and a breeze lifting the branches. My head starts to clear. Dog-woman means us no harm or she'd have done it by now. Chances are she'll show us out of the forest, then we'll be on our own again, heading for the town. We'll find work, and a place to stay, and Annie might forget the daft idea of chasing our mother.

Course, pigs might fly.

I start on the last chunk of meat, wipe my chin and look up to see the dog that licked me awake staring at me and wagging his tail.

"Here, boy," I say, holding it out to him, and he eats it out of my hands, his teeth just tickling my fingers. I laugh.

"What's his name?" I ask.

Dog-woman's tearing off chunks for the others from some other animal.

"No name," she says, without looking up.

"What—none of them?" I say, looking round. "What do you call them?"

"Names for people, not dogs," she says, twisting the meat. The movement of her hands reminds me of Travis. I look at her curiously.

"What about your name?" I say.

Dog-woman doesn't answer at first, then she says, "No name," under her breath.

I look at Annie, but Annie's poking the fire and her hair's hanging over her face.

"You must have had a name once," I say, but Dog-woman doesn't answer.

Hard to imagine having no name. What kind of life has she lived, with no one giving her a name? Still, I'll say this for her—she seems at home here in the forest, like Travis did on the road. Like we're not.

I get up, wiping my hands on my skins. "Will you show us out of the forest now?" I say.

So that's how we come to be running with the pack.

At first I don't like it. Dog-woman sets off at a cracking pace and it's hard to keep up with all the dogs milling around. Hard enough not to fall over tree stumps without falling over dogs as well. I'm desperate not to be left behind, though, and I jog on until my lungs are near bursting point. I want to tell her to stop, but she's too far ahead.

Then something happens. Suddenly I'm not staggering and stumbling along anymore. I get into a kind of rhythm and my feet go faster and faster. I look across at Annie and she's keeping up too, all her teeth bared in a wild grin. It's like Travis said; my feet are telling me where to go.

We're running with the pack, their dog smell filling my nose along with all the smells of the forest—and the strangest thing happens. I start to feel like I'm one of them, one with all the pounding muscle and shaggy fur. Faster and faster we go and I don't want to stop at all. I want to put back my head and howl.

Time vanishes and I don't know how long I've been running, but I do know I don't want to stop. I could go on forever, bent nearly double, my feet skimming the earth, and when the trees get thinner and the light grows I'm almost disappointed.

Dog-woman slows down and the slowing down seems to go on forever. I can feel my feet again and I start to straighten. We come to a stop, all of us, in a shaggy, panting mass, and I want to find my voice, to say "That were great," but I've no voice left. We stand in a kind of clearing, and the light's really bright now, I can hardly see. Dog-woman sniffs the air, then she raises her finger and points.

"That way," she says.

We look down a long slope and there are the first roofs of houses. Just one or two at first, the smoke curling up from them, then more and more, until in the distance they all huddle together round a big steeple. The town.

I look at it and feel afraid, somehow, of the mass of houses. How long is it since I've been in a house, other than the workhouse?

Dog-woman sniffs the air again. "Snow coming," she says. "You go now. Hurry."

I look around. It's a bright day, very bright; broad bands of sunlight across the fields. But there is a whitish tinge to it, though, not like summer. She could be right.

"Best get going then," I say, turning back to Dog-woman. But Annie's already there, holding up her hand to touch Dog-woman's withered, shaggy face. And Dog-woman bends down and down so that Annie can reach, and the next thing I know is she's planted a great lick on Annie's forehead.

Disgusting.

But all Annie says is, "Angel," looking up into Dog-woman's bent eyes. And I could say something but this time I don't feel like laughing. I don't feel fear or pity, not after that run through the woods. I swear when I look in her eyes that I can see something in them, like the memory of a star. Though if heaven's full of angels who look like that, I think I'd rather go to hell.

Anyway, I cough to break up the touching scene and say again, "We'd best be going then," and, "Er—thanks, and that."

Dog-woman straightens and says, "Dog-woman not go where people are. You go now. Do not trust people in houses. Not safe. Stay nowhere long."

Just like Travis, I'm thinking.

She nods at us again, gazing earnestly at our faces, then turns, her dogs gathering about her quick and smooth in a gray flow, and without looking back she disappears into the forest behind. Just like that. One moment we're looking at her and the next she's gone.

Whooff!

8

Snow

Annie's dragging her steps behind me. Seems like she's cut up about leaving Dog-woman, like I was about Travis—though that seems a long time back now. Well, that's life for you, I suppose. People coming and going. Thistlefluff in the wind.

Talking of which, sure enough, hardly have we set off than the first flakes of snow come down. Tiny feathers they are at first, drifting this way and that, like they haven't quite made up their minds and what's the hurry anyway? And as soon as they touch something, grass or branch, or my arm, they disappear—*pouf!* Like that.

Then more of them come down but I'm not worried. They look so pretty, dancing around in the yellowish light, that I'm too busy looking at them to think of where we're going. We start whirling round with them, catching them on our tongues. Annie's dancing and clapping, trying to catch a snowflake in her palms.

Soon it stops being fun. The light vanishes and more and more snow comes down. When I look up, the sky's dead white, and big flakes of snow look dark against it, hurtling down.

Back into the forest is my first thought. *Shelter.*

Annie seems to have other ideas, though, and she starts pulling me along a different track, through a field.

"Eh," I say. "Where are you off to?"

Annie doesn't answer but keeps tugging us on, through a hedge, then a ditch, then by the side of another hedge that's tall, for shelter. I don't argue. I don't want to go back through the forest, or spend any more time with

Dog-woman, even if she has just saved our skins. I'm surprised that Annie doesn't, though.

All the time I'm worrying about the snow because I know the kind of storms that can fly up, burying travelers or freezing them to death. We've had snow up to the windows of the workhouse before now, but this storm starts clearing almost as soon as it blows up. *Thank you*, I'm saying silently, because I can see again through the flakes. We have to find some shelter, though.

We're trudging alongside the road now, but a field away. The snow dies down to a few flakes but it's hard work on this path, since it's already started piling up. Sometimes we sink in it up over our feet, but in parts it's hard and icy and we slither along easily enough. Annie's pace never slackens and she grips my wrist as though she knows exactly where she's going.

Naturally, she hasn't thought of telling me.

"Annie," I say. "Where are we headed?"

No answer. But I'm out of breath now, with a stitch in my side the size of a poker. "Hold up," I say, slowing down. "Where are we going?"

For answer Annie just tugs my wrist hard. Then she pants out, "Got to—keep—up," between her teeth.

At first I think she means that I've got to keep up, but then I see that she's staring ahead, with that same fixed stare she had in the cave. Enough to send the willies through you. I dig in my heels hard and pull her round.

"Annie," I say very stern. "What's going on?"

She tries to twist back but now I'm holding her wrist, and her eyes roll right back in her head.

"Hurry," she moans.

I've had enough of this. Seems like all my life Annie's been trying to spook me out. I brace myself and hold on tight.

"*Hurry!*" Annie says again, in that funny voice not like her own.

I tug her arm. "I'm not hurrying anywhere," I say, "until you tell me what's going on."

Annie struggles and strains but I'm doing my bump-on-a-log bit by now, same as she did in the forest, and in the end she gives up, shivering.

"Lost them," she says in a small voice that's definitely hers.

"Lost who?" I say, and when she doesn't answer I shake her again.

"It's them, innit?" I say suddenly. "That boy and girl."

Annie still doesn't answer, but I know I'm right. "We're following *them*?" I say, shaking her again for good measure. "Why are we following them, Annie? Do you know where they're taking us? Eh? Have you asked?"

Annie stares at the snow, breathing hard.

"I mean," I carry on, "how do you know they're not leading us straight to hell? Are you trying to take us with you?" I say loudly into the silent air. "Because we're not coming! We're not going to hell today, if it's all the same to you."

Annie finally looks up, her eyes full of light from the snow. "Not hell," she says, and her voice is raspy again. "Manchester."

This time I grab her shoulder and shake her in earnest. "Are they talking to you?" I say, furious now. "What are they saying?"

"Hurry," Annie says, and points. "Mother."

She's pointing upward, into a copse of trees. And there, though it might just be the snow, for one second I think I see two flickering lights that quickly fade.

Fear catches in my throat. "If you think I'm following two boggarts through the snow," I say, "you're wrong."

Annie twists round to look at me. "Hurry," she says.

And just because I can't think what else to do I let her tug me along.

"Hurry," she says.

And that's how we come to one of them man-made waterways I've never seen before. A canal.

It's amazing—the water all still and flat like a mirror. Hills, sky and trees all upside down in the surface. I bend over and something leaps back at me, making me jump backward. I bend forward and there it is again. Horrible. Then I realize it's my head with the hair all stuck up like a nest.

"Annie, Annie! Look at my head!" I shout, and I run along the path, looking at it, for I've never seen it before—only I can't make out my face, it's too dark.

Someone came up with this—turning a river into a road! All that flat, still water going on for miles. And a pathway either side so that horses can pull the boats.

I'd be more amazed if I wasn't so cold. Seems like I've been cold for so long that in spite of Travis's skins, I can't remember warm.

My thoughts run on like this, getting jumbled. Tall trees on the banks drop their reflections on the water, making it darker yet, and the reflections are all broken up with patterns of ice. Like my thoughts are all broken up with not knowing exactly where we're going, or what to do when we get there. So I just keep going, with Annie in front, and soon the canal opens up into a wide pool. And there are some barges tethered up to great iron rings in the pathway, and covered over. Something else I've not seen before, but I've heard about them. Some of the tramps in the workhouse used to work the barges, legging them through tunnels.

Everything's so still that it doesn't seem natural—water that doesn't run, boats that don't move. But then as we get up to the wide part, we can hear voices, singing and laughter. And there, in a clearing, is the gable end of an inn.

Traveler's Rest, it's called. Sounds good to me.

A couple of horses and carts are tethered up outside. I'm not feeling brave enough to try the front door, so we slink round the back. Kitchen door's open and there's the juicy smell of ale and meat. We cross the yard with its stacked-up barrels and stand in front of the open door. Dogs start barking inside. Soon a man appears, face like a shovel.

"What do you want?" he says, but not as if he wants to know. "No beggars here—be off!"

"Water, please," I say, but he scowls till his eyes disappear.

"Did you hear me?" he bellows. "Beggar off, before I set dogs on you!"

A dog thrusts its nose through the doorway and we scuttle backward across the yard. He goes in again, dragging the dog back and cursing. Slams the door. So much for begging.

When the barking dies down and I think he's gone, we try again. This time I send Annie. I've seen a fat maid, throwing out slops.

"Go up to her," I whisper, "and bob down a bit, like a curtsy. Say, 'Excuse me, ma'am, could I trouble you for a little food and water for myself and my brother who's sick . . . no—dying.' Say you need a glass of water for your dying brother."

I've heard them begging at the workhouse.

Annie looks up at me like she might refuse, but when the maid comes out again I bundle her in.

This doesn't work either. Just as the maid's leaving the kitchen Annie bobs out at her from behind the barrels, glowering like a boggart. The maid drops the water; Annie forgets to curtsy. "Food," she says, and the maid shrieks like a steam engine.

"Save us!" she cries, running back indoors, and all the dogs start barking again. I hear her screaming, "Help, help," and I grab Annie by the neck and we run off.

We hide in a clump of bushes while I think what to do. Because this close to food, I don't want to give up. I stare hungrily at the shut gate. What was it Travis said? *Food's easy to come by.* And I said, *You mean you can get food just by telling a story?* And I thought, though I didn't say, *Any fool can tell stories.*

So this is it, I'm thinking. *Story time.*

We make our way round to the front of the inn. Someone else is hitching a wagon up and another bloke arrives with a bundle on his back.

I've always told stories. Kept the kids in the workhouse up all night. Somehow, that's different to walking into a full pub and trying to get strangers to listen.

You've got to walk in looking brave.

I take two steps forward then stop, looking about. There's an outhouse with a door on a rusty hinge. "You'd best wait here," I say to Annie, and she grabs my arm but I shake her off.

"No use begging," I say, as much for my benefit as hers. "Folk just drive you off. I'm going to try my luck with a story."

She doesn't say "No, don't" or "It in't safe" or owt like that, just looks at me with her milky face. I feel sick to my stomach. Still, what can they do? They can only chase us off again.

I shove Annie into the outhouse. "I'll be right back," I say, though I'm hoping I won't be. Not without food.

I take one step toward that door, then another.

I'm Jack the Giant-killer, I'm thinking. *I've killed the giant with one head,* thinking of Old Bert, *I've killed the giant with two heads,* thinking of Young Bert and Master, *and now all I've got to do is to walk in through a gaping doorway and tackle one with hundreds of heads.*

That's what it feels like.

No one's seen me yet. I could still run away.

Nowhere to go but forward, that's what the matron used to say at the workhouse when I didn't want to go before the board.

I clear my throat and square my shoulders and walk in through the door of that pub.

It's dark inside, gaslights burning. Walls and ceiling are painted black to hide the damage done by flaring lights, and the windows are tiny. More than dark, though, it's smoky—there's a dull smoky fire and everyone's smoking long clay pipes. It's hard to see anything else and I'm glad of it, for I can walk right past the bar and no one notices. Men are crowded round tables.

I don't know where to start or who to pick. My eyes are stinging in all this smoke. It gets up your nose into your throat—and suddenly I'm coughing. I try to choke it back so no one notices but it gets bigger, and next thing I'm bowking for all I'm worth—just like the tramps on a winter night.

Someone turns to me from one of the tables. "Now then, what's all this?" he says, then, "Eh, Seth, your customers are getting younger!"

There's an apron coming toward me through the mist, all greasy with food. Suddenly I'm caught. "Why, it's the beggar boy—I thought I'd seen you off."

It's Shovel-face—the man who chased us off before. He's got me by the scruff of the neck, which isn't helping me speak. I can't even deny I'm begging.

"Hold on a minute," the man at the table says. "Give the lad a drink." And from nowhere a jug of ale is thrust under my nose.

There's cries of "Give over" and "Leave off," but I grab the jug and slug the ale down before the landlord wrenches it away. Tastes bitter.

"You'll not waste good ale on the likes of him," he thunders, shaking me as though he wants me to throw it all back. "He's only come here begging!"

"I've not!" I squeak, trying to free my neck. "I . . . I've got a story to tell!"

The smoke clears a bit and the face of the man at the table looms through it—a long, weather-beaten face, big faded eyes and a nose that looks like it's been hammered out of shape.

"A story, eh?" he says. "I like a good tale. Put him down, Seth—you don't know where he's been."

Landlord shakes me even harder. "I'll not have beggars in my pub," he growls.

"He's just told you," says Bent-nose, "he's not begging. The lad's got a story to tell. Put him down."

The landlord hardly looks minded to do as he's told, but there's general cries of "A story, a story" and "Give the lad a chance" and "Put him down," so with a final shake he drops me back onto the floor. I slip on something and Bent-nose holds me up.

"Now then, young'un, what do they call you?"

And suddenly I'm aware of about a hundred faces, all bent toward me.

And I haven't got a clue what I'm going to say. I can only gawp at them like a loon.

"I hope this tale's a good'un," one of them says. "He's taking long enough to tell it."

And all around me I can feel interest draining away, like ale from a jug. Any minute now, they'll let Shovel-face haul me off. Bent-nose lets go of my arm and turns away.

Suddenly I know I can't let it happen. Maybe the ale that I've slugged down is helping. I shrug my shoulders back and lift up my head.

"My name's Jack," I say, in a loud voice that doesn't even seem like my own. "Jack the Giant-killer."

They're looking at me again now but I daren't look back. I stare at the wall above their heads. And all of a sudden I know what I have to do. I put one foot on the rung of Bent-nose's chair and bound onto the table, knocking several glasses sideways. There's cries of "Hold up, lad!" and "Steady on," but I take no notice. And Bent-nose is clearing the glasses to make room.

"The land's full of giants," I say, staring round. "Terrible plundering monsters, eating the sheep and the cattle, destroying the grain. Everyone's miserable, but they won't do owt about it—except for me. And I'm only ten years old."

I stare at their faces now, breathing hard. They're all listening.

"There's one giant," I say very low, "who's worse than all the others. So tall that he can walk from one hill to another in a stride, and make all the earth shake." I stamp on the table. "He's eaten up everything—all the sheep, all the cattle, and now he's started on the children. He lives in a cave on the hillside, and it's littered with bones. And one day, he eats one of my friends."

There's some good-humored jeering at this but I won't let it put me off. I'm making this up as I go along, for one thing I've learned is that you can't tell the same story twice.

"*That's it!* I think. He's gone far enough. And I lie awake that night thinking up a plan. And the next day I pick up a pickax and a shovel, a lantern and a horn, and I set off to the giant's cave. And when I get there, it's dark."

They're all listening now. Seems like the whole pub's gone quiet.

"I can hear the giant snoring—the hill's rumbling with it. And I can see bones scattered about in front of his lair. But I won't turn back now. I've come this far and there's no turning back. So I set to, digging a pit."

I can see their faces, raw and red or sallow in the light from the lamps, eyes glittering through the smoke. I can see the pub and everything around me, but more than that I can see the quaking hillside and the deep yawning cavern. I can feel how hard it is, digging that pit, and I go through the motions of showing them the *clunk* as the shovel hits hard earth, the strain in my shoulders and back.

"I dig all night long," I tell them. "And I drag sticks and branches across the hole, and wet clods of earth, till I make it look like solid ground. And then, just as day's dawning, I put the horn to my lips and blow the loudest blast I can manage, once, twice, thrice. And the giant wakes up."

You could hear a pin drop in the pub.

"There's a horrible roaring and snorting as he comes to," I tell them. "And the blast of a giant cough, so loud that I'm flung to the earth," and I fling myself down on the table. "Giant comes out with his great thudding footsteps, rubbing his eyes, but he can't see a thing.

" '*Fee fi fo fum,*' says he. '*I smell the blood of an Englishman!*' "

There's scattered clapping and cheering at this, but I carry on.

" '*Be he alive or be he dead, I'll grind his bones to make his bread!*' And he stomps out further. 'Where are you?' he roars. 'Come out—I'm hungry for my breakfast.' And he steps forward, and forward again, and suddenly— *CRASH!*"

Everyone jumps, and I leap off the table. "He thunders down into the pit—*BANG! KERBOOM!* Everything goes deadly quiet. Then I can hear him groaning from the bottom, and I go right up to the edge.

" 'You see, Mr. Giant,' I say. 'Sometimes it's a bad thing to be in too much of a hurry for breakfast.' "

There's laughter and clapping as I climb back onto the table.

" 'Kind sir,' says he, very respectful, 'I'd be grateful if you'd lend me a hand, for I seem to have fell into a hole.'

" 'Oh, I'll lend you a hand all right,' says I. 'Just clamber up the side a little way.' And he starts climbing out and—*VUMMM! SPLAT!* I bring the pickax down on his head, splitting it wide open, and leave it there, buried to the hilt. And the giant's eyes roll right back in his head and he falls— *PHEEEEEW, THUD, THUD, BANG!* like an earthquake, so I'm flung to the floor, but he's dead. Dead as a doornail!"

I finish my tale, grinning broadly round. There's a second's silence then a burst of applause. People are drumming their jugs on the tables. I can hardly believe it. Seems like I could go on standing there forever with the applause like a fire in my chest and belly. I bow low as I can, in one direction then another, and there's a chorus of voices asking for more, but just as I'm rising from a third bow, one voice sounds above all the others.

"That were a fine tale, young'un," it says. "But I've a tale worth two of that." And I look up, and up, and through the smoke looms the one face I hoped I'd never see. Long and bald, with but three teeth in its head, and a grubby bandage round the crown where I hit it.

"I'm glad I've run into you," says Old Bert.

9

Wagon

Old Bert lunges toward me but, quick as a wink, I dive off the table and start scrambling on my hands and knees among chair legs and big mud-stained boots. The next few minutes there's a right row. There's shouts of "Catch him!" and "There he is!"; people flinging their chairs back, pewter jugs tumbling to the floor. When one table's overturned I dive under another.

"Eh! Mind me pots!" shouts the landlord—but too late, as they all crash to the floor. My heart's in my mouth and I don't even know where I'm going. I can't see the door, just a lot of kicking, shuffling feet.

Bent-nose's voice rises above the others. "What's the lad done to you?"

"He's a thief!" growls Old Bert and the cry's taken up, "Stop, thief!" but in the darkness and confusion no one can see. Someone knocks ale out of someone else's hand and in no time there's a fight brewing. Hands grasp at me but I shake them off. All I can think is, *I'm not going back, I'm not going back!* and the thought hammers with the blood in my head.

Finally I see the door. I head toward it on my hands and knees but someone grasps me by the collar and hauls me up, kicking. My hands grab a tankard of ale and I dash it upward into the man's face and he lets go, bellowing a curse. Then I'm running for the door but there's a pot-boy and a scullery maid in my way, looking scunnered at all the noise. I point behind them and yell, "There he is!" and when they turn I dive at the door and I'm out of it and into the yard, with half the pub following.

I've never run so hard, not even when we ran from Bent Edge Farm. I turn round long enough to shove a pile of barrels over in the path of the landlord and Old Bert. It holds them up but it doesn't stop them. My feet are flying faster, faster, over the cobbles of the yard toward the outhouse where I left Annie. I can see her standing in front of it, white-faced at all the row.

"Run, Annie!" I yell, and without waiting she turns and runs behind the outhouse and through the gate to where the horses are tethered. I dash round with her and suddenly I'm caught, hoisted upward, yelling and kicking.

"Hold your noise," says Bent-nose, lifting the cover of his wagon and thrusting me in. "Two of you!" he says, thrusting Annie in besides. He barely has time to pull the cover over before there's the thudding steps of the men from the pub.

"Have you seen them?" says one and, "Where did they go?" says another.

"Straight on, that way," Bent-nose says, calmly unhitching his horse. Then again, "They went that way—you can't miss 'em," and when someone else comes running up, "By 'eck, Seth—your pub's a bit rowdy for me. I'll be on my way."

"He's smashed all my pots!" the landlord complains and Bent-nose sighs sympathetically, climbing into his seat.

"You can't be too careful these days," he says.

"I knew he was trouble—soon as I laid eyes on him," says the landlord. "I'll skin him alive when I catch him! Did you see where he went?"

"Down by the byre," says Bent-nose. "There's a great crowd chasing him—you can be sure he'll be caught. Well, I'm on my way. I'll be seeing you." And he flicks the horse's reins and we set off, jigging and rolling down the hill.

All this time I've laid low, trying not to breathe too loud. Annie's lying next to me, clenched like a knot. The cart's full of a jumble of things—hard wooden stuff and one or two great wheels that slide about as we get going. We grip on to the sides and say nowt.

The cart rattles and jolts and soon picks up speed. Slowly I loosen my grip and shift round to sit with my back against the side. I can't help laughing to myself as we pull away from the pub. All those men chasing after, and me in this cart all the time! Seems like luck's on the side of the brave. Then I stop laughing, for I'm still hungry and I didn't get fed.

In the front of the wagon Bent-nose is starting to sing.

> *Oh, threedy-wheel, threedy wheel,*
> *Dan dol din doe . . .*

And Annie's uncurling now, and tugging my arm. She jerks her head toward the front of the wagon, meaning, *Who's he?*

"I don't know," I whisper. "He's from the pub."

She's not happy but I don't want her carrying on, so I tell her about my amazing deeds.

"I had all the pub hanging on to my every word," I tell her. "You should've seen me. It were great."

Annie's not even listening. She makes signs like she wants to get out of the wagon.

"Don't talk daft," I tell her. Then I lift the edge of the cover and peer out. All I can see is white rolling hills and a pale moon, out with the sun. Far off there's smoke from two or three cottages. Annie thrusts her head out next to mine.

"I'd keep hidden if I were you," Bent-nose says, breaking off his song. "Turnpike's coming up."

We duck down again, but in the darkness Annie pinches me.

"*Ow!*" I say, and, "What?"

She doesn't answer. She's skittering about a bit, afraid, and rolling with the motion of the cart. I grab hold of her and wedge her between a wheel and a bracket. Her teeth are chattering.

"Don't be feared," I tell her. "We're safe now." Then, "Sssh," for the cart's pulling up. We hear Bent-nose exchange a few words with the man at the turnpike.

"To market," he says, "fixing wheels."

The turnpike man lets us through. I can hear the drag of the gate, and I start to breathe again. Some time later I poke my head out of the wagon again.

It's a rutted road, neither straight nor crooked, and the wagon's making slow progress. On either side there's a bank: bare hedges just putting out leaves. Beyond that there's fields bordered by low stone walls, and I can make out painted signs near the gate. I wish again that I'd worked harder at reading.

"Mister," I say after a while, "what's them signs say?"

"Keep out, mostly," Bent-nose says without turning round. "Get lost. Be off, and such. Anyone found trespassing will be handed over to the magistrate. Didn't you know that all the leaves and grass in these parts are private property? Some places, trespassing's a hanging offense."

I didn't know that and I sit back down feeling worried. Don't want to be hung because I can't read. It's stuffy in the wagon, though, and after a bit I poke my head out again. "Where are you taking us, mister?"

"Whoa, girl, steady," says Bent-nose as the cart gives a terrific jolt and I bang my chin on the side. "My name's Barnaby the wainwright," he says after a moment. "Fixing wheels is my trade. What are your names?"

"Jack," I say, remembering in time. "And this is my sister—"

"Jill," he finishes for me, with a low grunt like a laugh. "Well, Jack and Jill, we're approaching the town now, where I'll spend the night, and in the morning I set up stall on the market. Now, I'll be stopping at an inn, but you're welcome to sleep in the cart, unless you've anywhere else in mind."

I haven't of course, so I say nothing to this, but Barnaby seems to feel like talking. "Road goes on, all the way to Manchester," he says. "That where you're going?"

"That's right," I tell him.

"Well, I can take you as far as this next town," he says. "Then we'll part company."

He stops talking and starts whistling. I can see now that some of the fields have tumbledown cottages in them, mostly boarded up, some part pulled down. There's a faint echo of a memory in me, of my mother's voice saying, "We've lost our home now, but we've got each other," and I feel the familiar, bitter pang.

Still, at least he's taking us where we want to go. And at no cost to us. I can't think why he's doing us such a favor, but I'm not minded to ask. My stomach growls and I wonder if it's too much to hope that he'll feed us.

I can see more and more houses clustered together, and I feel a knot of excitement. As we get nearer, the noise of the town increases. There's bells ringing and people crying through the streets, the sound of carts unloading, children yelling, babies crying—and it's evening! A smoky stench rises.

"You'd best duck down again," Barnaby says. "There's a tollbooth coming up. I've got to pay yet more money for the pleasure of traveling on the king's highway."

I crouch back down in the wagon, pulling the cover across. Just before I do I can see that Annie's eyes are rolled back in her head and she's muttering to herself. I kick her and she stops.

I mean, what's she griping on about, eh? We've got a lift all the way to town *and* a place to stay for the night. We've come through river and forest, field and inn, and at any one of them we could have been caught and turned in. But we're still here, thanks to me—free, just like Travis said. What more can she want?

Then it occurs to me why she's so feared. The houses. Annie's never been anywhere before where the houses press so closely in on every side, where there's so many people and so much noise. She's not used to anything but the workhouse. When I peep out it's strange to me an' all, the gas and lights smoking through the gloom, pigs nosing through the muck on the streets, and everywhere the din and clatter of people shutting up shop or calling their children in.

It's strange to me but I like it, and Annie doesn't.

Soon after the tollbooth we come to the inn. The Coach and Horses—

a white building with a gabled end. Barnaby steers us in through the gate. Light streams from the windows and there's the sound of singing inside. He leads the cart into a covered shelter and pays the ostler to stable the horse. All this time we're lying quiet in the bottom of the cart, but once we're in the shelter he lifts the cover.

"You'll be all right, staying here," he says. "No one checks the carts. I'll be up crack of dawn to fetch you out. Here." He passes us a water bottle and some bread. The inside of the bread's been scooped out and there's a big wodge of ham inside.

"Thanks, mister," I say with feeling, and tear into it straightaway. I don't say, *Why are you doing this for us?*

"If you want to go," he says, "feel free. No one's stopping you. I just thought you'd be better under cover than on the streets."

"Yes, thanks," I say again. "We'll be fine."

He smiles, showing broken yellow teeth with big gaps between. "Market tomorrow, eh?" he says, then he flings us a rug for a blanket and pulls the cover back over the cart.

"Hold on a bit, I'm coming," he calls to someone I can't see, then I hear his footsteps fading away.

All's quiet, or at least as quiet as a town can be, which is to say that there's a low roar of noise that never quite fades. There's dogs barking, the bellowing of oxen, the grunting of pigs, the cries of hawkers and beggars still, and every few minutes the ringing of bells. There's the stench of smoke and rotten vegetables, ale and swill, loud yells and singing from the pub. And a never-ending tramp of footsteps to the inn or past the yard, voices loud as they pass, then fading.

"Bessie's Brew, that were a good horse."

"So I said to him, I told him straight—"

"She'll not have no more now, not with the littl'un being took poorly."

Even under the cover there's a bit of light from the inn. It's a bit cramped in the cart, though, and I want to stretch my legs, but there's nowhere to go. I sigh and shift and wonder if I'll ever get to sleep. Annie's all hunched up and shaking, so I tuck the rug round us both. Then, just as I'm turning over and closing my eyes, she sets up a high mewling wail that near frits me to death.

"Shut your 'ole!" I gasp, leaping round and shaking her. "What's up with you? Do you want to get us caught?"

I shake her shoulder but she pays me no heed, rocking back and forth.

"Annie, shut it!" I say, desperate now, and she stops wailing but carries on rocking. I break up her share of the bread, which she hasn't touched, and give it her, but she turns her face away. There's a loud burst of laughter from the pub.

"Annie, it'll be all right," I whisper. "I'll take care of you."

Annie shakes her head.

"I *will*," I insist, and I lift the cover so that I can look at her face. "Haven't I always before?"

Then Annie sits up, bolt upright, eyes staring. Her throat works strangely. And she says, in a husky, hoarse voice that's not her own, "Leave."

I'm pressed back against the ridge of a wheel, too scared to speak.

"Leave now."

"Annie—" I manage to say finally, "cut it out," and the thing that's in Annie looks at me through her eyes.

"Go," it says.

I've had enough. Ignoring the danger of being seen I scramble to my feet, pushing the cover back completely. I lift a trembling finger and point at Annie.

"Eh, you in there—whatever you are—get out of my sister. Now. Do you hear? Get out."

I don't suppose I'm very frightening, but to my surprise Annie gives a long shudder and her head slumps forward. Neither of us says anything. Then, mindful of being seen, I pull the cover back across and sit down warily. I grab Annie's shoulder. "Annie, what's going on?" I whisper. "What was that?"

Even in the gloom under the cover of the cart, I can tell that she hasn't a clue.

I think of questioning her, then think better of it. As for leaving—I'm not going anywhere because some boggart or long-dead thing tells us to. That's how Jinny Green-teeth works, luring littl'uns to a watery grave. It's how Owd Nick works too by all accounts. Anyway, where would we go? The only place I want to get to is market, and that's where we're headed tomorrow.

Feeling a bit stiff and cold, I pull the rug back over us and try to settle down. Annie's already slumped over. I can hear her breathing but I can tell she's not asleep. Maybe she's as bothered as I am by what just happened. More even.

There's more singing and laughter from the pub, and I can't help but wonder what it'd be like to sleep in a nice comfortable room in that inn. Still, I've slept in worse places. I turn over and shut my eyes. I can hear the whickering of horses and the bleat of a sheep; someone shouting for the barrels to be cleared. I remember Travis, and try to let my head fill with the silence of the moor. Instead I'm thinking, *What would he do now?*

> *Don't know, don't care,*
> *Make a wish, catch a hare.*

10

Market

Well, I must've slept, because I'm waking up. There's a great din and clatter in the yard; someone's tugging back the cover of the cart. I sit up quick, but it's only Barnaby.

"Why, it's Jack and Jill!" he booms. "Good to see you this fine morning. Are we awake yet?"

Annie wakes up and scrambles backward, pressing herself against a wheel. I grab her hand and poke my head out. There's splashes of sunlight in the yard.

"We are now," I say, scratching.

"Good, good," he says, still loud. I shrink back.

"Come on," he bellows. "No need to hide now. It's a fine morning and we're off to market. You can ride in the front if you like."

"We can?" I say, but he's already off fetching the horse. I'm tired of hiding in the wagon, so I take him at his word and climb out. The air's cool on my face. Annie holds back, but I pull her out with a bit of a struggle, and she lands beside me on the muddy cobbles.

"That's the way," Barnaby says, returning with the dappled mare. "No one's going to ask questions here. We're just like any other traders. Man and littl'uns."

His face is all mottled with drink, his eyes shot through with red, but he seems in a fine mood. He hitches up the horse and hoists us onto the wooden seat. I pray that Annie won't start playing up, but she seems to have gone numb and quiet.

It's a fine thing, riding on the front of a wagon. Barnaby steers us through the gate and we're out in the narrow streets of the town.

The houses are all crowded in on one another, so close that there's no sunlight here. No snow either, though the wheels sink deep in slush and mire. *The town stinks*, I'm thinking. There's all kinds of rubbish piled in the street, pigs and dogs nosing around. There's a bunch of children throwing a stone in a courtyard and hopping after it. One house has a wooden pole with a bunch of gorse strapped to it and a sign in the window. I feel excited by the noise and dirt, but Annie cowers back.

There's some great clamor that we're traveling toward, and suddenly the narrow street ends in an open space, already full. There are so many people that for a moment I can't see anything else. Men and women and children, setting up stalls, leading animals into pens. Men standing on wooden boxes, shouting out their wares.

"Fine apples for sale!"

"Pots and pans, brushes and brooms!"

"A side of lamb, fresh from the field!"

There's women with fish baskets on their heads and donkey carts laden with vegetables, bigger carts with livestock or whole carcasses of meat, milkmaids with pails, stalls with bales of cloth, and a swelling roar of sound.

Barnaby gets down to pay another toll and I stand up on the wooden seat to get a better view. The ground's covered ankle-deep with filth and mire, hoofprints sunk deep in it and women's skirts sweeping it about. A thick steam rises from the stinking cows. There's a big tent with a sign outside, and a smaller, stripy one. On the far side of the market the ground rises toward a great hall and the parish church, windows glinting in the sun. On the other side there's a sight that makes me stare. Scaffolding and a gibbet, and a body swaying slowly in the breeze, a group of people clustered below. I've never seen a man hanged before, and right away I know I want a closer look.

I sit back down again as Barnaby climbs back in and we steer our way into the crowd. There's more and more people arriving every minute—farmers, drovers, butchers, vagabonds, thieves, mingled together in a thick stew. Tollbooths are making a fortune, and you never heard a noise like it. Drovers whistling, dogs barking, sheep bleating, pigs grunting and squealing, bells ringing and a roar of voices shouting oaths and quarreling on all sides. Crowd's churning like a monster, pushing and shoving, driving, beating, whooping and yelling. I have to clap my hands over my ears before I can start to hear.

"Look, Annie—there's players—juggling!" I bellow, for there's three men on a platform throwing balls about and as I watch, one of them leaps onto his hands and starts juggling the balls with his feet.

That's a neat trick! I turn to see if Annie's looking, but she's pressed back against the wagon with her eyes shut and her hands clamped over her ears. I grab her elbow and feel her bones rattling through her skin. I start to shout at her to look around, but it's no use, so I let her go.

Fat lot of good she'll be here.

Well, I can't wait to look around.

Barnaby pulls up the wagon into a space beside other wagons, gets down and starts unhitching the horse, Meg. Right away Annie leaps off and darts underneath it, out of reach of the crowd. Barnaby jerks his thumb toward her.

"She all right?"

"Right as she'll ever be," I bellow back. "Is this our pitch then?"

Barnaby shouts back to watch over the wagon while he sees to Meg, and he starts leading her slowly, slowly through the crowd. I glance under the wagon at Annie, who's all hunched up with her hands still clamped over her ears, then I climb back up—master of my own wagon!

The sun's flaring out in fits over the crowd. I can see littl'uns flitting about, nicking apples and anything else they can finger. All along the edges of the crowd and in a big space in the middle there are pens filled with sheep. Either side of us there's one wagon filled with carcasses and another with bales of cloth. There's a bloke selling meat puddings from a stall. Makes your mouth water just to look at them.

Soon as Barnaby returns I leap down. I help him set up stall. Seems like the wagon *is* his stall, so we just drag some of the wheels and brackets out and stand them all round the sides. Annie's penned in underneath, which probably makes her feel better. She's weird like that.

Barnaby drives a post into the ground and props up his sign beside it. Then he nods at me. "There'll be nothing doing here for a while," he shouts. "Go and have a look around, if you like."

"What about . . . Jill?" I shout back.

He shrugs. "She'll be all right there," he shouts. Then someone comes up to him, and he motions to me to be off.

I don't need telling twice. Off I go, pushing into the arms and legs of the crowd. I can just about hear Barnaby yelling at me not to get lost then, next minute, I already am, carried along in the press.

There's a man selling a potion that'll cure backache, foot rot, fever, and even mend your roof. There's another selling dyes, and a woman with a sign round her, selling milk.

What I want first is the stalls with food. I've seen them beggar children snatching apples quick as a wink and I want a go. But I'm passing stalls with pitchforks, stalls with saddles, stalls with horseshoes, anything but food.

I pass one stall piled high with books and papers, sheets with ballads on them pinned to the posts. The man's singing one of them as I pass.

> *Mother wept and father sighed,*
> *With delight aglow*
> *Cried the lad, "Tomorrow," cried,*
> *"To the pit I go."*

No time to stop. Past the pens I'm pushed and here at last there's stalls with rabbits hung from them, stalls with cabbages and turnips and great round cheeses hung from hooks.

This is more like it. I find a stall piled high with apples: yellow, green and red. Makes my mouth water, though I've never tried one. Close by I can smell the sweetness of them. Just as I'm looking at those sweet heaps, shining like gold, I realize I'm not on my own. A little tow-haired young'un darts up while the woman's serving someone and nicks two of them quick as wink. He bolts off without anyone seeing, and luck must be on my side because he drops one of them as he's running. And I'm faster than him. Before he can dart back I leap forward and stuff it into my shirt. He stares at me and I think I may be in for a fight, but then he winks and says, "Finders keepers"—and disappears!

I can't believe my luck. I look all around and no one's coming after me. Crowd's so thick, they'd never see me anyway. I take out that apple, smell it and sink my teeth into it as far as they'll go. Tastes like a chunk of heaven— like the apple in the Garden of Eden must've tasted. The juice runs over my hand and I lick it off. Then, after a bit, it tastes bitter. It's brown in the middle and there's the end of a maggot pointing out. I look at it twice then eat it anyway. No sense in waste.

I'm milling around with the crowd, going nowhere much, and I can't see for all the people, but I want to catch a look at that hanged man. Seems like I'm not on my own, for there's a big press gathering that way. When I get near I can't see but I can hear. The group that's gathered near him are ballad singers, singing his story to the eager crowd.

> *He's stopped her riding through the town*
> *With ribbons in her hair*
> *Her heart's blood stains her wedding gown*
> *And she has grown so fair.*

Singing's fine but I can't see, even when I jump up. All I can catch sight of is the man's feet swinging to and fro. So after a bit I pass on, munching my apple.

"Gather round, ladies, gather round, men," a voice booms. "Cloth'll fade, food comes and goes, but a good story'll last forever!" There's a barrel-chested man with a red beard ringing a bell and housewives with children gathering round, so I gather round with them. It's the story of Tom Tit Tot, and he tells it grand, doing all the voices and gurning like a goblin, and when he finishes there's much laughter and clapping and he grins round in a good-humored way. "Come on, ladies," he shouts. "You've heard the tale—now you can have it for your very own, a penny a time. Come on, now, it'll keep your childer happy through a long wet night!" And he brandishes a little book with a picture on the front of the little black imp and the maiden, and so many people cluster round that I can't see. He's selling them all a copy of that story! And I wish, not for the first time, that I'd learned how to read. But this time the wishing turns into a longing that's like a pain. I wait till the crowd's thinned a bit and push my way through.

There's hundreds of them on the stall, little books, each with a picture on the front. I try and work out what they are from the pictures, but most of them I don't know. I pick them up and feel the rough paper with my fingers. I turn the pages but the lines are like black twigs on winter trees and I can't make head or tail of them, though I turn the book about.

Then suddenly the stallholder's voice booms out. "Eh, lad, don't go fingering if you're not buying."

He comes over and I shrink back, because he's big. "I were only looking," I mutter.

"Then look, don't touch," he says, and starts shuffling the books into lines, so that all the ones with the same picture are lined up.

I can't help myself, I have to say something. "Eh, mister," I say. "That were a grand tale."

He grunts. Not friendly now.

"I can tell a tale," I say.

"Can you now?"

"I can," I say, warming to my theme. "About Jinny Green-teeth and the miller's wife."

He shakes his head. "Never heard of it."

"Or Jack the Giant-killer. You must've heard of that one."

But he's turned away again, selling another copy to an ancient woman like a crone, with a babby tucked under her arm.

I should give up and go away. But I want one of them books for my very own. So much, it's killing me. I pick one up with a picture of a dragon on the front, but he plucks it from my hands and cuffs me smartly round the head.

"*Ow!*" I say.

"Get on with you," says he. Then, as more people mill round, he starts telling them the story of the dragon. Everyone's laughing and cheering by the end and, once again, Red-beard's selling all the copies.

That's the life for me! I'm thinking. *I'd love to live like that—selling little books, telling stories.* I'm clapping and cheering with the rest of them, and when the crowd disappears I'm still there. Red-beard's back's turned, and I hang back a bit, but then I step forward.

"Eh, mister," I say. "If I tell you a tale, will you give me a book?"

"Clear off," says he over his shoulder.

"Well—what will you give me one for?"

He turns round then, hands on hips. "Have you got a penny?"

"No," I say. "But"—and I fumble at the rope that holds my trousers up—"I've got a tinderbox."

Red-beard puts back his head and laughs. I can see all the holes in his teeth. "I'm not wanting a tinderbox, lad," he says. I feel foolish and my face is bright red. But he's looking at me in a considering way. "What do they call you?"

"Tom," I say, remembering.

"Tom," he says. "What tales do you know?"

"Hundreds of 'em," I say. "Jack the Giant-killer, Jinny Green-teeth, the Giants of Boulder Hill, the . . . the angels who came to earth," I say, thinking of Travis's story and racking my brains for more.

Red-beard shakes his head. "How about the Black Dog of the Wild Forest?"

I shake my head.

"Well, read it then," he says, handing it to me, and I feel more foolish than ever.

"I can't read," I say.

That stops him in his tracks. "You can't read, but you want a book?" he says. I stare at my feet.

"I've heard everything now," he says. "Well, look. Seeing as you're a red-haired chap like myself, I'm thinking I'll give you a chance."

I flick the hair from my eyes. I suppose you could call it red.

"If you can tell me any of the tales on this stall," he says, "I'll give you a copy of the book. Now then, I can't say fairer than that. Tell it and sell it, and you can have one of your very own."

Is he having me on? I can't tell, but there's a crowd gathering again. I look at all the pictures on the front covers, trying to make them out. There's one with a picture of a fox and a goose, and another with a blacksmith shoeing the devil. "What's this one?" I say, pointing to a picture of a man with a bow and arrow, and a big tree spreading behind.

"That's the True Tale of Robin Hood," says Red-beard. "Have you heard it?"

I shake my head. *This was a daft idea*, I'm thinking. There's cries of "Tell us a tale" and "Get on with it" and "Give the lad a chance" from the crowd, and I'm thinking it'll be difficult to slink off, when suddenly I see it—a picture of a giant man with a little old lady tucked into his arm.

"Is that Tom Hickathrift?" I say, grabbing it.

"It is," says Red-beard.

"I know this one!" I say, and Red-beard bows mockingly.

"Well then," he says, and he turns to the crowd. "Ladies and gentlemen," he says. "Today we have a special treat. My young . . . *apprentice* here is going to tell you a tale for the first time himself. The good tale of Tom Hickathrift!"

There's scattered clapping. I look round at the faces of the crowd, which is always a bad idea. Some look curious and others sour. I stare at my feet, willing myself to remember.

"Come on, then," someone says. I clear my throat.

But I can't do it. Something's wrong. I can't tell the tale—not like I did in the pub. I'm stuttering and losing my way, and it feels like all the eyes are boring me full of holes like a colander. Someone shouts, "Spit it out, lad," and I'm blushing like a girl. The crowd start moaning and drifting off and Red-beard bats me across the head with one of the books.

"Learn to read," he says. "Then you'll tell the story as it should be told."

I back off, shamed. Why couldn't I tell that story? I can remember it all now. Why could I hold a crowd in the pub and not here? Was it only the ale?

I'm still going through in my head how I couldn't tell that tale when I pass the meat-pudding man again, and I'm starving. No way of nicking one of these, though, because there's two lads older than me looking on.

All I need's a penny. My hand brushes Travis's tinderbox. I look around. Everywhere there's buying and selling—all kinds of things. A few stalls away there's a man selling iron goods and hardware. I walk up to him, brave as I can.

"Eh, mister—how much'll you give me for this?" And it works! He turns it over in his long yellow hands and offers me halfpence.

"Sixpence," I say, and he laughs in my face.

"That's a good'un," he says, but I stare at him, not backing down.

"Tell you what," he says. "I'll give you a ha'pence for t'box, and ha'pence for t'joke."

A penny, then. I can't help staring as he drops it into my palm. Bright copper, with the king's head on. The first I've ever owned—the very first. I've lost the tinderbox, and the shovel, but the coin's brighter, winking in the sun. I turn it this way and that, making it glint. Then I think someone might snatch it off me, so I close my fingers round it tight.

I walk away with a swagger as though I've been doing this all my life. Man of trade. And I go up to the meat-pudding stall and buy a steaming great pudding and sink my teeth into it, and it's the best thing I've ever tasted.

It's a magic place, this, I see that now. A place where a tinderbox turns into a coin, and a coin to a pudding. Anything's possible here. Don't matter if you're a king or a pot-boy—all that matters is your money.

I pass the jugglers again, and this time they're doing tricks. One of them's eating a huge, knotted rope. Down and down his throat it goes, farther than you'd ever think, and all the crowd gasp. Then he turns round and you can see it, coming out of his back end, under his coat. A right laugh. I wish I could do tricks.

But mainly what's going on is buying and selling, buying and selling. I walk around for ages, watching them all at it.

Sun's gone now and there's a gray soaking mizzle. All this time I've forgotten Annie, but it finally comes to me that I should get back. I walk all over without seeing Barnaby's cart. *Annie'll be hungry*, I'm thinking, and just as I'm thinking that, I have a stroke of luck.

I'm watching two kids—a dark-haired, scraggy boy and an older girl. I'm wondering where they've come from and if they've got homes to go to. They're standing near a woman who's selling vegetables; then, while I'm watching, the older girl starts begging for some of the veg that's not quite whole—a carrot end or half a turnip. She's begging but not getting anywhere. The woman's trying to shoo her off.

I could have told her that, of course, that begging'll get you nowhere. But while she's begging round the front of the stall, the lad's round the back stuffing his jerkin with whatever he can get his hands on.

Then a man nearby shouts, "EH!" and they're both off, quick as wink. The man runs after them, and the woman takes two or three steps forward, shouting, "Stop, thief!" And while they're not looking I grab some turnips and stuff them into my shirt, before making off myself.

Told you—it's magic, this place! I run as far as I can into the crowd, then slow down because no one's following. The turnips bump against my ribs and I'm thinking that this should cheer Annie up. And that it'd be grand to get her working with me like that, in a team, but somehow I can't see that happening. And I feel annoyed at her, because you can't get Annie to do owt.

I pass a tall young man with pink cheeks who's addressing a crowd. "How many good weavers have been sent to their graves?" he's saying, and the crowd all nod and mutter. "Who among you here remembers when all this land was in common—it belonged to no fat lord? They put walls up around your land, then they accuse you of thieving and trespass!"

More angry muttering and cries of "Aye!"

I walk on past, still looking for Barnaby, left and right. Then, just when I'm getting worried, I see the wagon. There's another cart in front of it and Barnaby's fixing the axle.

"Where's Ann . . . Jill?" I say, running up.

"She's still under there, lad," Barnaby says, nodding toward the wagon. "She won't come out. I've tried."

I sink to my knees in the mud and crawl under the cart. There's Annie all right, with her head tucked into her knees, rocking herself. She smells. She's wet herself, I notice. Disgusting. All because she wouldn't come out.

I feel a bit bad that I've been gone so long. "Annie, I'm back," I say, but she doesn't look up. "It's grand out there," I say. "You should have come with me."

This time she does look at me, all hollow eyes and pale face. "I brought you these," I say, holding out a turnip. She grabs it and starts chewing in a fury. She's not got much in the way of teeth, Annie, but she can't half chew. Like, her legs are a bit bandy but she can run when she wants to, fast as a hare. I sit with her a bit to make her feel better and start telling her everything I've done.

"You should have heard me telling a tale, Annie—there were a massive great crowd. And when I finished, bloke says, 'That were grand. Best tale-telling I've ever heard. You've done so well, lad, you can have a penny!' " But Annie's not listening, she just goes on champing on the turnips.

After a while Barnaby pokes his head under the wagon.

"Is there a party going on?" he says, and, "Can anyone join in?"

I scramble to the edge of the cart and look out. Seems like the light's going and the rain's all soaked into the ground, making it muddier than ever. Crowd's got a lot thinner and Barnaby's pulling the cover over the wagon. "What's going on?" I ask.

"Market's over," he says. "Thought it might be time for a bit of refreshment." I crawl out farther at this and he jerks his head toward the big tent. "Thought we might've earned ourselves a bowl of furmety," he says.

Never heard of it, I'm thinking. But if it's food, it'll do. Seems like I'm always hungry these days. Much hungrier than I was in the workhouse. I crawl back to Annie. "Come on out," I say. "We're going to get fed."

All her back hunches up. "Come on," I tell her. "You can't stay under here all your life, eating turnips."

When she still won't come I grab her arm and pull. It's not easy but I'm feeling strong. Tom Hickathrift's got nothing on me. Soon I tug her out into the mud.

"Are we ready then?" Barnaby says. Annie just stands by me, glowering. If she had any fur it'd be lifted right up.

There's a lot of noise from the tent and I hold Annie's arm tight to stop her bolting as we follow him in. *This* is where everyone's got to! There's loads of people inside, standing around, or sitting at long tables that run along the sides of the tent. At the top end there's a stove over a charcoal fire, and a huge crock hanging over it. A withered old woman's stirring it—looks about a hundred years old. You can hear the *scrape, scrape* of the spoon and the steam rises. Smells a bit like damp bread. Barnaby goes right up to her and we follow on, hanging back a bit, like, because of the racket. Next minute he's handing us a steaming bowl with two spoons.

"Try your teeth out on that," he says, turning back to the woman.

I look down. There's a kind of slop in the bowl, with grains floating about in it like pips. I drag up a spare stool and sit on it. Annie stands beside me and we both tuck in.

It's not half bad. Bit chewy, though, and the grains get stuck between your teeth. I'm in a race with Annie to see who can shovel down the most. When I glance up at Barnaby I see he's slipping the woman a few extra pence, and she pours something into his bowl. I recognize the smell—the old hag who called herself Nurse at the workhouse used to drink rum all the time. He finishes that bowl quick and gets another, without looking round to see if we might want some. Then he gets talking with a group of men.

I can feel my eyelids starting to close. Don't know why I'm so tired, I haven't done much. I'm beginning to wonder what Barnaby's plans are for the night, when one of the men says loudly, "Are these your littl'uns?" looking at us.

"Nay," says Barnaby. "Just some waifs and strays I picked up."

"And you're feeding them?" he says. "I hope they're good workers."

I look at him. He's a big man with a big bald head. His nose is all red from the rum. I don't like him.

The talk moves on to the cost of wagons, but the big man keeps looking our way. "Lad looks wiry," he says. Barnaby's helping himself to more furmety-rum.

"Aye, he'll do," he says. His face is all flushed now, like Baldy-head's nose.

Baldy-head gives me a long look, from my head to my toes. I glower back.

"He's a bit small for his size, innee?" he says.

Barnaby says, "It's not size you need, but strength and willingness to work."

"True," says Baldy-head. "And the littl'uns take less feeding."

I don't like the way this is going. I look round the tent, wondering whether to leave, then Barnaby's next words make my hair prick up.

"Sounds like you're looking to buy some labor."

"I might be," says Baldy-head.

"Are you buying?" says Barnaby.

"Are you selling?" says Baldy-head.

"Eh," I say, getting up, but Barnaby pulls me to him.

"He might be small, but feel his arms," he says, and next minute Baldy-head's prodding me with his big, meaty paws.

"What's going on?" I say, trying to twist away.

"What's your price?" says Baldy-head.

"Ten shillings apiece," says Barnaby, and Baldy-head laughs, a short, hard laugh. "Pull the other one," he says. "It's got bells on."

I'm staring at Barnaby, trying to catch his eye, but it's like some change has come over him. He's looking at me and through me, but not as though he can see me. Then a man with a long, bony face says, "I'll give you ten bob for the pair."

"No way, man," Barnaby says. "Ten shillings apiece is my last word."

I try to wrench my arm away, but he holds fast. "Give over," I cry, and all the men laugh. I look at Annie and she hasn't moved. She's staring at me like a frit rabbit. Then Barnaby gets up and seizes us both, hauling us to the middle of the floor.

"Listen up!" he bellows. "Market's not done yet. I've got these two fine workers to sell. Lad's a real workhorse—tough as they come. Littl'un's wiry too. Now, who'll give me ten bob apiece?"

There's a general murmur at this, and I hear someone cry, "Shame!" and look round to see who it might be. But someone else is saying, "I'll give you five."

"Gents," Barnaby cries, "do me a favor. The lad's trainable—you can get any amount of work out of him. And the lass'll cook and sew and clean. Ten shillings apiece is a giveaway price. Daylight robbery!"

"Aye, but who's robbing who?" one man says, and they all laugh.

I've had enough of this. I wrench my arm back and cry, "Give over, mister. We're not for sale!"

"Lad's got spirit," says a thin man with a goat beard.

Suddenly there's a pile of men crowding round, and I'm stuck like a runt in a litter. The words Annie spoke last night come back to me sharp and clear and hard. *Leave*, she'd said. *Leave now.*

I wish I'd listened. This is the worst mess yet. Men and women are prodding and poking us now.

"You could sell 'em separate," says a sharp-faced woman, and she lifts Annie's hair, looking for marks and scars. Annie twists round and spits, and there's cries of "Watch it!" and "Eh—the little witch!"

"I'll give you six bob for the lad," someone says.

I yell at them, "Are you deaf? We're not for sale!"

"Needs a good whipping, that one," says Baldy-head.

They're all crowding round me so close, I can hardly breathe. Annie's eyes are rolling like she might have a fit. I wish she would—that'd make them back off.

But they're not backing off. They're crowding closer yet, poking and tugging. I kick out at the nearest one and get my ears boxed in payment.

"Six shillings!" says one and, "Seven and six!" another.

Then suddenly one voice rises above the others.

"I heard slavery's been banned."

Some of the racket dies down and a young man pushes himself through the crowd. He stands in front of Barnaby, who glares up at him. "The buying and selling of all persons," he says, "is no longer lawful."

I recognize him now. It's the same man that was speaking to the crowd earlier, about handloom weavers. His cheeks are very pink but he stands facing Barnaby, and he's a good six inches taller.

"If you don't like it," says Barnaby, "you know where the door is."

The young man doesn't stir. "I don't like it," he says, "and I'll not stand by and watch it happen."

There's some yelling and jeering at this, but I'm staring up at him.

"Don't let him sell us, mister," I cry. "We're not his to sell."

"I can see that," says the young man.

But Barnaby says, "What's it to do with you? Get you back where you came from!"

In a moment things turn nasty. "Mind your own business," someone cries, and, "What's it to you?" But then someone else says, "He's got no business, selling childer," and the voice of the woman selling furmety rises above all the others.

"I'll have no fighting in my tent," she says. "Clear off, or I'll have the law on you!"

"Officers are coming round anyway," says the young man. "They always do at market close. So I'd let the lad and lass go, if I were you."

Barnaby glares up at him, breathing hard. But he can tell that the mood in the tent's changing at the mention of the law. Folk are already turning back to their own business. For a minute I think he will let us go, but then his face turns ugly.

"What'll you give me for 'em?" he snarls, then quick, without warning, he picks up one of the lamps from the tables and dashes it at the young man, who staggers back. The lamp crashes behind him, catching the skirts of a woman who screams, and the next minutes are all confusion. Barnaby's let go of me but he's dragging Annie, so I make a dive for his feet and trip him up. The woman's skirts and one of the tablecloths are on fire and everyone's stamping and roaring. Barnaby lets go of Annie and she scuttles away before I can get to her. Someone knocks over a long table in the general dash for the door.

"Annie!" I cry. "Annie!" And then, with a great heave and a creak, part of the tent comes crashing down.

The next moment's a blur of tramping feet and crashing things and swearing. I'm swearing myself as more than one boot kicks me or stands on my hand, yet somehow I make it through what was once the door of the tent, out into the wet blue evening.

"ANNIE!" I roar at the top of my lungs, then suddenly I see her, disappearing round the back of the striped tent. But she's not alone—someone's pulling her along.

"ANNIE!" I bellow, and I take off after them, fast as I can go. "ANNIE!"

And she turns, tugging backward on the arm that's pulling her, and whoever it is turns too, and I see with a stab of relief that it's the young man who spoke up for us in the tent.

"We were wondering where you were," he says, and all I can do is pant.

11

Alan of Hirst

We thought we'd best be leaving," Pink-cheeks says, his stride lengthening as we trot along. "No use hanging around trouble. Officers'll sort that rabble out." And in fact we can see them arriving now, on horseback and foot.

Well, I'm in no rush to meet officers of the law, and it seems like Pink-cheeks isn't either, for he's striding fast. He leads us over some wooden planks across a ditch, then through a stile, and then cuts through a field.

"Right," he says, on the other side of a copse of trees. "I suppose it's too much to hope that you've got a home to go to?"

I look at Annie, Annie looks at the ground. "Thought not," says Pink-cheeks. "So. Where are you heading?"

I can answer that one. "Manchester," I say, looking up, and Pink-cheeks puts his hands on his hips, considering.

"Are you now?" he says. "Have you got folk to go to?"

I shrug. Seems like I'm all out of stories.

Pink-cheeks shakes his head. "Well," he says. "You'd best follow me."

I hang back. Right at this minute I'm not keen on following anyone. I mean—I *thought* I could trust Barnaby Bent-nose. Seems like you can't trust anyone. Travis was right about that. I think of Travis walking the roads of England in freedom, and here we are, falling into one trap after another. *It's because we're kids*, I think, and I wish with all my heart I was grown, tall as this feller standing here.

"What's up?" he says, then a bit awkwardly, "It's all right—I won't harm you."

I look at Annie again. Pink-cheeks sinks down onto a fallen branch.

"My name's Alan," he says. "Alan of Hirst. What are your names?"

Here we go again. "Jack," I say, rubbing my forehead. "And—"

"Annie," says Alan, before I can say Julie or Jill. "Well, Jack and Annie," he says. "What's your plan for the night?"

I don't answer. *Plan?* I'm thinking. *That's a good one.*

"I can't just leave you in a field," he says, and I shrug again. "Look," he says. "A little way from here there's a traveling fair. I know the man who runs it, and he's all right. And they happen to be traveling to Manchester. And if I ask him nicely, then maybe he'll take you along."

My ears prick up at this. I've always wanted to see a traveling fair.

"I don't suppose either of you have any skills or trade?" Alan asks without much hope.

But I say, "I can tell a story," with my chin lifted up. I nearly add, "And Annie here can see the dead," but don't.

For the first time Alan smiles. "I dare say that's better than nothing," he says. "We'll have to see what Honest Bob has to say."

Honest Bob? I'm thinking. *Who'd trust a man with a name like that?* But we follow Alan anyway, since we've no other ideas, and he takes us across this field and over a wooden bridge that spans the river, and round the side of the hill. And I can see the fair already—a small huddle of painted vans.

As we get closer I can see that there's little men feeding the horses. Men only just bigger than Annie, but with big heads and hands. *Dwarves,* I think. *Creatures from folktales.* And my heart starts to beat a bit faster.

"Hi there," Alan calls as we draw near, and I'm staring now. "Is Honest Bob around?"

The nearest little man looks up and I want to laugh. Everything's too big for him—big nose, big mouth and teeth, big eyes like a dog. I nudge Annie but she's got that blank look on her, like she's not looking at anything.

"He's in his tent, same as ever," the little man says, waving toward a small green tent propped up by sticks. His voice is higher than a man's—more like a duck quacking—and I want to laugh again, but then I see that the other little man's actually a little woman dressed like a man and I'm staring again.

"Horse'll need shoeing again, Balthasar," she says.

He ignores her. "He's a bit worse for wear if you ask me," he calls after us as we stride toward the tent. At least, Alan strides and we trot behind. He lifts the flap of the tent and calls Honest Bob's name. There's a deep groan from within.

"Honest Bob," Alan calls again. "I've brought someone to see you."

"If it's the beadle, I'm not in."

"It's not," says Alan. "It's Alan of Hirst. And two children."

More groaning, then shuffling, and finally a head pokes out. A bleary, grizzled head. The eyelids are red and swollen shut, one of them more swollen than the other, with a darkening bruise.

"What time is it?" he growls.

"Nighttime," says Alan, holding the flap up for him. "You've got two guests."

The reddish, grizzled face swivels toward us, though the eyelids barely open. "I hope they're paying guests," he says.

"Well," says Alan, "not as such."

The grizzled head disappears again.

"Wait!" Alan says, poking his own head in through the gap. "They need to get to Manchester, that's all. And they can work for their keep."

Silence. Alan pokes his head in farther. "You owe me one," he says, into the tent. "Or shall I speak to the beadle?"

There's a kind of growl from inside, then Honest Bob's head appears again, looking fierce. "Christ almighty," he says. "What does a bloke have to do to get some sleep around here?"

Alan is unmoved. "Is it a deal then?" he says.

Honest Bob waves a hand at him. It's a very grubby hand, fingernails even blacker than mine. "Flo'll deal with it," he says. "Go talk to Flo." And he disappears again, this time pulling the flap to behind him.

We stare up at Alan and he smiles encouragingly at us. "Flo's all right," he says. "Wait here a bit." And he walks over to the two dwarves.

I stare round at the wooden wagons, just three of them in all. They're all brightly painted and carved, with strange faces and masks, some laughing, some crying, animal heads round the borders. The rain's let up now but I'm soaked through and cold. I look at Annie but she's looking at the ground. She seems calm, though, not like in the market.

It seems like a long time before Alan comes back, and he's got the little woman with him. I try not to stare. She's got breeches on her, and braces and a check shirt, just like the man and, same as him, her head and hands are too big for her. She's not like him, though. She's got brown, curling hair and wide gray eyes, a bit like Miss Julie. If it didn't sound daft to say it, I'd say she was beautiful. And she smiles at us, very kind.

"Alan tells me you're traveling with us awhile," she says in a kind voice. Annie says nothing; I mumble something and shuffle a bit.

"Well, you're very welcome, I'm sure," she says. "We can always do with an extra hand. Is this the little maid?" she says, looking at Annie.

Little maid? I'm thinking. *She's near as big as you.*

"What's your name?" she says to Annie, and when Annie doesn't speak she reaches over and takes her hand. To my surprise Annie doesn't snatch it back.

"Her name's Annie," I say, and add, "she doesn't talk much."

"That'll give her more time for thinking," the woman says. "Well, my name's Flo and I work with Balthasar over there, and tonight the two of you can sleep in our wagon."

She leads Annie off by the hand but I stay where I am, looking back at Alan.

"You'll be all right with Flo," he says. "I'll have to be going now." And he starts walking away.

"You're leaving us? Here?" I say, but he doesn't turn round. "Well—thanks," I say, thinking somewhere else we're being dumped. But if Alan catches the tone in my voice he doesn't let on; just lifts a hand as he walks away into the night.

I hurry to catch up with Flo and Annie. What else can I do?

"These two'll be wanting a bed for the night," she says to Balthasar. "They're staying with us."

Balthasar straightens up and stares. "With us?" he quacks. "There's no room."

"We can pull the table out," Flo says. "And you can sleep on the floor." She turns to us. "It'll be fine," she says. "I'll just introduce you to everyone first."

The nearest wagon is painted yellow and blue, but she hops up the steps to the next wagon, painted orange and purple. "Cora, dear," she calls. "We've got new people staying with us. Come and see!"

Then over to the last wagon, red and green. "Come on out, boys!" she calls. "I want you to meet someone!"

The wagons rock and creak, there's calls of "Who is it?" and "What's going on?"

And then the doors open—and now I'm really staring.

First off comes out a blue, green and orange man, all bald, with scales and fish crawling all over his skin. Next there's a great rumbling creak from the orange-and-purple wagon, and the door bursts open and I'm hard put to it not to yell—for there's a monstrous, great woman inside, big as all the giants Jack ever had to kill. She comes down them wooden steps and, by some miracle, they hold. Taller than Old Bert and near five times as wide; more of a mountain than a woman, with great shaggy hair hanging in plaits and just one tooth in her head. And I'm sweating and praying that there's only one head, for I hardly dare look. Then, from the same wagon as the blue-green-orange man, the jugglers from the market come tumbling out. They cartwheel across the grass and one of them leaps onto the shoulders of the others. And I can see now what I didn't notice at the market, that they all look exactly the same—like three peas from a pod. They've all got black, glittering eyes, pointy noses and wide, wide mouths. The one on top leaps down, turning like a wheel in midair, and lands in front of me, moving his head this way and that.

"Leave him alone, Vito," says Flo. "Now don't fret, dearie," she says to me. "He takes a bit of getting used to—but then we all do, don't we, dears?"

At this the horrible blue-green-orange man next to me gives a great snort, and the giantess grunts, and suddenly they're all laughing, with me stood among them not knowing which way to look. *What've we got into now?* I'm thinking, and words about frying pans and fires come to mind. I think about Alan bringing us here, and how he seemed like a friend, and remind myself not to trust no one, ever again. For it feels like we've wandered into some horrible folktale, and I don't know what the end'll be. I hope it's not *So the two poor children were et up for breakfast, and never seen again. . . .*

Flo's speaking again. "Let me introduce us all," she says. "You've met Vito, and his brothers are Pepe and Luigi. The large lady's Cora. The colored gentleman's Ivan—all the way from Russia. And your name is?" But I still can't say anything.

"He don't know his name," Vito says, and I shoot him a look, and mumble, "Jack."

"And the little maid's Annie," says Flo, then she takes my hand. "You look dead beat," she says, and suddenly I know I am. I feel kind of achy and shivery too, but I don't know if that's cold or fright.

"It's too wet for standing around, Flo," says Balthasar.

Flo says, "You're right, pet; you usually are. Help me fix up the wagon. Come with me," she says to me and Annie. "You'll be sleeping with us tonight."

Wonderful, I'm thinking, though I suppose I'm glad I'm not sleeping with the giant lady. And because I can't think of anything else to do, I follow her up the steps of the blue-and-yellow wagon.

Inside there's a big jumble of pots and pans, costumes and props. There's a huge bear's head hanging from a hook. The van smells funny. Old food and something else—like the mothballs the mistress used to keep in her cupboard. There are wooden ledges along the walls with blankets on them and a rolled-up blanket for a pillow. Balthasar unfolds a table on long wooden legs.

"You can have Balthasar's bed," Flo says, pointing, "and the little maid can sleep on the table, when I've made it up."

"Where'm I sleeping?" says Balthasar, not best pleased.

"I'll do you up a bed on the floor."

"Why do I have to sleep on the floor?"

Flo sighs, tugging his blanket up. "Serve up some stew, can't you?"

"Pot's empty," says Balthasar, looking in a large crock. "Shall I cook up some more?"

Flo hesitates. "Are you very hungry, dears?"

Neither of us is that hungry after the furmety, and I get the feeling that there isn't much to go round, so I shake my head. Flo looks relieved.

"There's a bit of bread left," Balthasar says.

"And I'll make us some tea," says Flo. "Sit you down, dears."

We perch together on the edge of one of the ledges, wedged between that and the table. There's food stains all over the table and I pick at them with my thumb while Flo pulls blankets down from a cupboard. It's not very high up, but she has to stand on the table to do it. Balthasar says, "Scuse me," and goes to sit on the steps with a hammer and some boots. Soon he's banging away, fixing the soles back on.

"Your clothes are dripping wet," says Flo. That they are, and hanging off. She rummages about a bit in a chest and finds us some that look like they're costumes—yellow breeches and a striped shirt for me, and a blue dress with the lace all frayed for Annie.

She holds the dress out to Annie. "This should fit you lovely," she says, and for a moment there's a tremor in her voice. But she hands the clothes over and then goes to the steps with Balthasar. She hangs up our old clothes on hooks over the door, talking all the time about the show they'll put on tomorrow, somewhere called Auden Shaw.

Annie looks different in the blue dress, like a big doll. I feel a right ninny in the yellow breeches, but I don't like to say no. And at least they're dry and warm and cleanish, though they've got that funny mothball smell. They're too big round the middle and short at the ends, but they've got red braces on that I slip over my shoulders. And pockets so I can drop in Travis's sling.

When we've finished, Flo turns round. It's like she can't take her eyes off Annie.

"Well," she says after a moment. "I'll just make us that tea." And she brews up, moving easily around the crowded wagon. Soon we're chewing on a chunk of bread and sipping sweet tea like the master used to. It's not real tea—more like hot water with a bit of milk and honey, but it goes down well. And Flo starts telling us about the traveling fair, with Balthasar chiming in and interrupting all the time.

Seems like it used to be much bigger than it is now. "Oh, much bigger, much," says Balthasar.

They had a unicorn once, Flo tells us fondly.

"I used to polish his horn," says Balthasar.

"He used to eat lumps of sugar," says Flo.

"He were terrible for sugar," says Balthasar. "You had to hide it away in a big tin."

"And the mermaid," says Flo, "she was a lovely lady."

"My favorite was the goose with the human face," says Balthasar. "And the Siamese twins, don't forget them. Joined at the hip they were, but they were rare dancers."

I'm so caught up in this tale of wonderful creatures that I forget to be shy. "What happened to them?" I ask, and both Balthasar and Flo look very sad.

"They've gone now," says Flo.

"All gone," Balthasar says.

Seems like the fair's fallen on hard times. Once Honest Bob owned as many as twenty wagons, and wherever they went there was feasting and fun.

"Now, with all the fencing off, there's hardly anywhere *to* go," Balthasar says, getting up. "It's all private property, and rents and fines."

They were fined in Wakefield, for public disturbance. "Dancing—that were all!" says Balthasar. Moved on in Rochdale for breach of the peace. "That were Bob trying to outdrink Ivan," Balthasar says. And when they tried to camp in Oldham they found that the rates had tripled.

"So there's hardly anywhere left," says Flo, and they both shake their heads, so that although it's a sad enough tale, I want to laugh, and manage to cough instead.

"But listen to us talking," cries Flo, "when these two childer are tired to death! And we've got an early start in the morning."

She scoops the crumbs off the table, scattering them to the floor, and Balthasar clears the pots. Then Flo starts making up a bed for Annie, and I lie down on the ledge, with a blanket over me, one under me, and a rolled-up one for a pillow.

It's strange trying to sleep in the crowded wagon. Balthasar and Flo seem to manage it right away and, cripes, how them little folk can snore! Enough to rattle the wagon and all the pots inside. Wind's building up outside, and my thoughts are all jumbled with the memories of the past days; of Dog-woman and Travis and Barnaby, Old Bert and Alan. And now this lot. So, in all, it's hardly possible to sleep.

12

Show

Morning comes and everything's blurred. I've got a right headache and soon as I move I'm sneezing.

Someone's yelling outside. "Move your arses! Come on—up! What am I paying you for, eh?"

"He's not paying us at all," Balthasar mutters, hauling the big crock down the steps.

"Come on, *shift*, you lazy sods!" the voice goes on. I wipe my nose on my sleeve and poke my head out of the van. There's Honest Bob, ranting and raving and banging on the doors of each van with a stick. When he sees me he stops in his tracks, looks as if he might set about me with the stick, then thinks again and goes back to banging on the door of Cora's van. Then, when we're up and shivering, he disappears into his tent again.

We all gather round the crock in the blue morning light while Flo doles out porridge. No one says much, we're too busy shivering; though I catch Vito smirking at my new gear as if he thinks I look funny. *You can talk*, I think. If he says owt I'll have him. But there's no time for fighting. Soon as we're finished we have to hitch up and get moving.

I help clear away the pots, but when it comes to hitching up horses I'm not much use, so I stay in the van, looking at the props. A golden wig, a red cloak and a tasseled hat, a big cardboard bush. Everyone else runs around saying nowt. What's clear is they do all the work while Honest Bob sits in his tent.

"He weren't always this bad-tempered," Balthasar says, rolling up the wig in the cloak.

"He's a good man at heart," agrees Flo, wiping pots. "He's just going sour, like milk."

"Like bad ale, you mean," says Balthasar. "He's slowly pickling himself."

That's all they say about that because Honest Bob comes roaring by again.

"Are we setting off this year or next?" he thunders on, and Flo and Balthasar shoot one another a look and scramble out to the front of the van. And we're off, creaking and rocking, on our way to the next town.

Sun's whitish in a white sky, but there's neither snow nor rain. Flo asks if I want to ride in the front with Balthasar, and she sits in the van with Annie. The town's a smoky smudge on the right and we pass it and go on through fields and trees and straggling cottages. Every time we pass a cottage, children run out and point. I can't say I blame them. We're the only bright-colored thing on the whole of this gray earth.

All the time we're riding, Balthasar's talking. "Time was we traveled all over England and Scotland and Wales," he says. "Now we just stick to this area. Farthest we've been for years is Liverpool."

After a bit he says, "Do you want to hold the reins?" and he shows me how to hang on to them—not too tight—and he sits back, making himself comfortable, and lights a pipe.

"I can tell stories," I tell him, and right then and there I tell him the story of Tom Hickathrift. At least I *can* tell it now, but not as good as I'd like, and he keeps having to help me out.

"Very good, lad," he says when I'm finished, though I get the feeling he's being kind.

"I know other stories," I say.

"Telling stories's not much use to you, lad," Balthasar says. "You'd do better at a hiring fair, picking up a trade."

But I don't want a trade, I'm about to tell him, when suddenly there's a great crack and a crash, and cries from the van behind. I jump near out of my skin but Balthasar doesn't move.

"It's Cora," he says calmly and, reaching over, he takes the reins from me and brings the van to a halt. I leap down to see what's going on. The orange-and-purple van's leaning over, and Honest Bob's flown into a rage.

"You're not worth your keep, woman," he roars at Cora, who gazes down at him steadily. The wheel of her van's gone into a rut, and the van's lopsided so she can't get out without tipping the whole thing over, and everyone has to pitch in, struggling and straining, to set it to rights. Then we see that the shaft's broken, so we're all held up while the brothers and Ivan set about mending it.

Back in Balthasar's van, Flo's showing Annie how to spin using a distaff made from a forked birch branch, and a fir cone for a spindle. Annie's wrapping the wool round a piece of card and they both look strangely content, so that I feel like I can't interrupt. I pet the horses for a bit, then wander down to a stream and watch a heron flapping upward with a fish in its beak. Drops of water spray from its breast and you can almost hear the creak of its wings.

When I get back, first person I see is the giantess. She's got out of the van somehow and is sitting with a feather pen in her great hand, making scratching noises on a sheet of paper. I can't help it; I stare so hard that she looks up.

"What's the matter?" she says in her odd, grunting voice. "Did you think big and ugly's the same as stupid?"

"No," I say, though of course that's exactly what I thought.

I step closer. "What are you writing?" I ask.

She shuffles round so I can't see. "What's it to you?"

"Nothing," I say. Then, "It's all right, I can't read."

The giant lady stares at me and I can't help thinking how fearsomely ugly she is. *Whoever gave birth to that?* I'm thinking. *Midwife must've smacked the mother when she were born. All the same, she's clever.*

I step closer again. "Will you teach us?" I say.

I've surprised her now. "I'm no teacher," she says, then she turns back to her writing. It's all curly, like a lot of string.

"What does that say?" I ask when she's finished a word. She sighs.

"I'm writing something for the show," she says, "when I'm not being interrupted." And she turns her back on me.

For the show? I'm thinking. *Like a play?* But she won't say any more, so after a bit I walk off whistling.

Seems like the van's all set now. The brothers are practicing juggling. Vito's got three balls in the air, then four, then he drops one. He catches sight of me and throws two of them my way. I drop them right away and Vito grins, flips over into a handstand and bats them upward with his feet.

"I wish I could do that," I say.

"What can you do?" says Vito.

"I can tell a story," I say, but he snorts.

"Stories!" he says, and he walks off, still juggling. I can't think of anything rude to say back. Seems like everyone here can do something I can't. I go back to Balthasar's van and Flo's packing the wool away.

"We're setting off now," she says. "Only another mile to go."

I climb back in. "Cora's writing something for the show," I say, and Flo beams.

"Yes, she told us," Flo says. "She's writing in an extra part for Annie here."

For Annie? I think, openmouthed. *Not for me?* I look at my sister but her face gives nothing away.

"We'll have a little practice when we get there," Flo says, beaming tenderly at Annie. *And what will I do?* I'm thinking.

I go to the front to sit with Balthasar again as we set off. "Annie's got a part in the show," I tell him.

"Yes, Flo were saying," says Balthasar.

"Can I be in it?"

Balthasar flicks the reins. "Well, we'll have to see," he says. "What were you thinking of? Can you do any tricks?"

I can't but then neither can Annie. Annie can't do owt.

"Well, now," says Balthasar kindly. "Can you play an instrument?"

I'm not even sure what he means. "I don't think so," I say.

"Well, we've got enough stories for now, lad," he says, "but I tell you what. You watch the show, and then after you can tell us all a story and we'll see if it's one we can use."

I'm not that happy about this but when I ask him again, all he'll say is, "We'll see what Honest Bob has to say," and I can't get any more out of him.

"What's in the show anyway?" I say a bit sulkily.

"Oh, lots of things, lad. You'll see when we get to the field. We'll have a bit of a rehearsal."

"But what will I do?"

"Oh, there's lots to do, lad, lots to do. You can help us shift props."

That sounds dead boring but I can't think of anything else to say, so I keep my mouth shut, and drum my heels against the seat.

The road's full of people straggling by. There's a woman sat in a ditch, trying to feed her baby. Her face is covered in sores. Then we pass a whole family trudging along as though tired to death. The man tries to run after us, begging for bread, but Honest Bob drives him off.

"Ah, poor souls," says Flo, poking her head out of the van.

Soon we come to a tollbooth and Honest Bob gets down to pay. He exchanges a few cross words with the man inside, then we all pull into a wide open space. It looks like all the other fields around, except it's deeply rutted with wagon wheels. In the distance there are a few cottages and not much else.

Ivan and the brothers are unfolding a huge tent from the brown wagon at the rear. We start unloading props from our wagon—the green bushes and three bears' heads, a blue backdrop with fishes and reeds painted on, and lots of rope. Then there's another backdrop, painted to look like the inside of a cottage, and a table and chairs. I'm amazed at how much comes out of that wagon.

Honest Bob runs around barking orders then he disappears back into his tent.

Flo turns to Annie and hands her a bundle of clothes. "Put these on, dear," she says, then to me, "give us a hand with this cradle," and between us we tug out a large wooden box on rockers. We carry this into the tent and set it up in front of the cottage scene. "There," says Flo.

I step out of the tent and look around. The field's wide and empty. "Where's the audience?" I say.

"People come," says the giantess. "Word gets round. Now we rehearse."

Tale's called Black Annis and the Missing Bairn. Flo brings Annie out and I have to laugh, for she's all got up like a babby, wrapped in a blanket, with a bonnet on her head and a pacifier in her mouth. And she's small enough to fit in the cradle, with a bit of a squeeze. They help her in and rock the cradle and she sits in it looking for all the world like an infant. Except for her eyes. Annie's eyes are about a hundred years old.

"Close your eyes, dearie," Flo says. "Just pretend you're asleep."

So she closes her eyes and looks well enough, then Honest Bob starts to tell the tale, holding the sheets of paper that the giant lady was writing on before. He speaks in a big, booming way, not like his usual voice. It's all about an honest laborer and his wife, who have their babby stolen by Black Annis, a fearsome monster with a great blue face and one huge tooth. There's a great storm, with thunder and lightning, and when it's over, the babby's disappeared and the poor folk are grief-struck. They look everywhere for her, then the goodwife promises her soul to whoever brings the babby back, and a horrible demon appears, with horns and a tail. And the demon and Black Annis fight it out all over the stage, until the demon chases Black Annis off, then tries to claim the soul of the goodwife. But the husband's too quick. He throws a phial of holy water at the demon and it disappears in a cloud of stinking smoke. And when all that happens, the babby's back in her cradle, blinking through the smoke.

That's it, folks—show's over. Clear off and tell your friends," says Honest Bob in his usual snapping voice, and the few children and farmhands who'd gathered around to watch move slowly off.

"Tell your parents, tell your friends," Honest Bob calls after them. "Tell your neighbors, your uncles and your aunts! Tell them to come back here in an hour's time."

There's plenty to do in the next hour, for there's more than one play, and music and dancing at the end. I help clear away some props and put up others, and by the end of an hour there's quite a group of people gathered on the field, and the show begins with the brothers, juggling and playing tricks, leaping onto one another's shoulders while keeping all the balls in the air. And after, Cora plays her fiddle and the audience are stamping and clapping to the music, and I have to run in and out of them, offering a hat for coins. The brothers play the tambourine and Honest Bob's got a pipe. Everyone joins in. Even the giantess is dancing with a farmer. I look around at the audience and see how their sallow faces are all lit up as they dance, how it makes them forget everything else, and I feel a peculiar kind of ache. Because I want to be part of it but I've got nothing to do.

Too soon it's over and the people are straggling away. Then I have to help take everything down again. It's hard work but I don't mind, so long as I get a go next time. Traveling about the country, playing and singing, that's what I want to do. And if I ask Cora, maybe she'll write something for me. Maybe one day I'll run my own fair!

Everything's cleared away except for the big tent, because now it's raining, so we all sit under it while Flo dishes out meat stew.

"Do you remember the dancer with the wooden legs?" says Flo.

And Balthasar says, "Aye, what a racket!" and they all laugh. "The one I remember," he says, "is that man with the hole in his chest—you could put your hand in and feel his heart, actually feel his heart beating!"

"Yuk," says Flo.

"I remember the dancers in Russia," says Ivan, staring into the shadows. "So light. They flew through the air like many colored birds. But the war comes and—*pouf!* They are gone now. All gone."

And the talk goes on like this, a kind of sadness flowing through all the laughter like water. And I sit in the middle of it all, feeling strange. It's not just the strangeness of the faces, because I'm getting used to that now. It's the firelight maybe, and all the shadows flickering over the tent.

I start yawning, then after a bit I get up to stretch my legs. I walk round the vans, tracing some of the pictures with my finger. The vans form a circle, and it's like in that circle is one kind of world, and outside it is the other. The world of cottages and fields and laborers.

I stand for a bit, looking out across the fields to where I think Manchester must be. *That's where I'm going*, I think. *Manchester*. I say it aloud to remind myself that I am someone and I've got somewhere to go. Then even though the grass is wet I fling myself down and look at the world another way, through the strands of grass. There's another kind of world down here, and I'm moving it just with my breath. Right nostril's blocked with my cold, but the left one's working, and I open my mouth. Strands of grass flicker and quiver. Everything looks different. I wonder what it'd be like to be a field mouse, or a beetle. It comes to me then that there's not just one world, but millions of them. Like the workhouse. That was a whole other world. Then I lie on my back and look at the moon. There's no moon really, just a patch of brighter cloud where it's trying to shine through. I wonder what it'd be like to be up there, looking down.

I can't help thinking what it'd be like to stay with these players, if they'd have us. And I wonder if it's the right time to go back and ask Honest Bob if I can have an act of my own.

13

Annie

Sometimes, at the workhouse, I'd find I couldn't speak. Oh, I were fine at night, when it were just me and the other kids, and I'd keep them up all night telling stories. But when the beadle came and the master said, "Come on then, speak up! What have you got to say for yourself?" I'd find I couldn't speak at all, and generally I'd get drubbed. Or when I was sent for by the board for fighting. I'd try and try, and all that'd come out'd be a little stuttering sound like a hammer makes when it's bouncing off a nail, or a chicken makes, pecking the ground. I'd get beaten then too.

So now, when I try to tell Honest Bob my stories, it's just like then.

"You see—Jack—he were no one—he were just a kid—but he thought—he thought—and he went—he took a shovel—and—"

I hate myself. Why won't it come out?

Honest Bob listens to all this with a look of bleary amazement on his face. Like I'm some kind of boggart he's dreamed up through drink. And eventually he says, "Chrissakes, lad—isn't my beard long enough?"

And he goes off then, to shout at Ivan. And I'm left feeling stupid and kicking a stone.

Is it because I'm a bit scared of him? Because I still expect him to turf us out? But it can't only be that, because I can't do it right for Balthasar either. And before that, on the market, I was hopeless. Seems like the only time I really told a good tale was in that pub. It must have been the ale.

Well, whatever it was, I can't do it now. And I hate myself for it. I hate myself and I want to thrash Annie. Because Annie's doing all right—and she never even wanted to be in a show.

Flo can't get enough of her. They're always together, like they're joined at the hip. Whenever I look up Flo's combing her hair, or showing her how to sew, or dressing her up in some new frilly gear from that chest. And now, whenever we're all together, Annie's eyes are on Flo, not me. Which you'd think'd be a good thing, but somehow it makes me mad as a hen. Because I'm not really needed around here. Oh, I help out—feeding the horses and such, and Balthasar shows me how to mend a crooked wheel, but it's not like he needs the help. At least Annie used to need me.

Apart from this, everything's fine. A lot of the time there's nothing to do, and I never thought I'd complain about that, but sometimes I feel like a spare part. What I do is, I practice using the sling Travis gave me. I practice and practice and I get quite good. One day I manage to knock a pheasant out and bring it back for the stew. That were good.

Everyone's kind enough to me. And the fair goes on, taking the long way round to Manchester, through Denton and Gorton and Openshaw and Clayton. Sheep get dirtier and the buildings get bigger. One day I see my first factory. It's huge—hundreds of windows and a great chimney belching out smoke. *Wouldn't fancy cleaning that*, I think, remembering the workhouse sweeps.

And wherever we go, a few people come to watch, except now they're factory hands rather than laborers, and they get more ragged and dirty-looking as we get nearer to Manchester.

First time I saw it I didn't know what it was.

"What's that?" I asked Balthasar, pointing to a big black smudge in the sky.

"Why, Manchester, of course," says Balthasar, and I stare hard. It's like the sky ends in blackness, and there's smoke and flame. I can just make out more big chimneys in the black welt, belching out smoke. They must be huge. I stare out at it all the time we travel toward it, and the blackness and the smoke increase. It's like a big coal pit in the sky.

"Wait till we get to Ancoats," Balthasar says, after we've done one performance to about ten people. "That's when the crowds really start coming. We always stay in Ancoats for a while."

The houses change from cottages to rows and rows of redbrick terraces all piled closely on one another in narrow streets, so narrow that when you stand at one end of them you can't see the other end. All the light disappears. And there are more and more children playing out in the filth of the streets, seemingly without parents, some of them without clothes. Only little children, mind, smaller than Annie. All the older ones are in the factories. Though sometimes I see older ones flitting about like they've got nowhere to go. They run after the vans, throwing stones at the horses. Honest Bob calls them thieving scavengers and sets me on lookout in case any of them nick our stuff. Though what I'm supposed to do if I catch any of them, I don't know.

The night before we get to Ancoats something weird happens. We're all sitting out in a field after a performance. There's been even fewer people than usual. We sit in a circle, eating stew, feeling depressed. At least the rain's packed in.

Then Balthasar says, "Wait till we get to Ancoats, things'll look up then," which is the kind of thing he's always saying to cheer us up, only I'm not sure how many of us believe it.

"Ancoats, Liverpool, Salford—is all the same," says Ivan. "People no want us anymore."

"Now, there's no use talking like that," says Balthasar.

Honest Bob says nothing. He stares at the fire with red-rimmed eyes. No one else says anything either.

Annie sits between me and Flo. I can tell she's in a peculiar mood. Don't ask me how I know—she's as quiet as she always is—I just do.

After a bit, Balthasar and Flo start talking about how things used to be, like they usually do, to keep some kind of conversation going.

"It was all fields around here once," Balthasar says. "Fields and forest."

"The lord of the manor used to come and watch," says Flo.

"Do you remember that Christmas when he asked us back to the Hall?"

"That was the last really big fair," Flo says. "We still had . . ." Her voice trails off, and Balthasar looks choked up. I look at them curiously.

"Who?" I ask.

But Balthasar says, "Never mind."

Flo says, "She was such a lovely little dancer." And I can tell she's near to tears. I'm about to ask who again when Annie starts swaying back and forth and humming, a funny little tune I don't know.

"What is it?" Flo says to her, then she gives a little start and a cry, holding her mouth. Still humming and swaying, Annie rises to her feet. Everyone stares as she dips and bobs, then turns round slowly. Her eyes are glassy and pale.

"Give over," I say, uneasily. All we need is for Annie to start freaking everyone out.

She starts to spin, turning round and round on her little bandy legs, humming more loudly now. I want to laugh, but it isn't funny.

Balthasar's watching her with his mouth and eyes wide open. And Flo's clutching her face with both hands now.

I consider pulling Annie back down but suddenly she speaks, looking at Flo and not looking at her—just like that night we spent in Barnaby's wagon in town.

"Look at me, Mammy," she says in a high, unnatural voice, and Flo makes a little sound like a sob. "Like this." She whirls round faster and faster.

Everyone's staring now. "What the blazes—" says Honest Bob, knocking over his tin beaker as Annie dances by. The brothers start murmuring to one another in their own language.

Then Annie sinks down, facing Flo. "Did I do it good, Mammy?" she says.

Flo's hands are trembling as they leave her face and reach for Annie. "Ida?" she says in a strangled voice.

"Nay, lass—" says Balthasar, but he doesn't seem to know what to say next.

Annie turns to him. "Daddy story," she says, and rising upward again she totters toward him, then flings herself onto his chest, clasping her scrawny arms round his neck.

Balthasar's eyes close and he lifts his great hands as if he doesn't know what to do with them, then, as if he can hardly believe it, he strokes her hair. And then Flo's with them, and they're all clasping one another and rocking and Annie goes on humming that weird little lullaby.

Honest Bob says, "Well, I'll be damned," and he takes a long swig from the bottle of rum he keeps close to his chest.

Ivan crosses himself and so do all the brothers. "Your sister, she is a—" and he says a funny word that I don't understand.

"A medium," says Honest Bob. "As I live and breathe."

"Who's Ida?" I say.

But Flo says, "Oh, my own sweet baby, my little girl," clearing that one up. Tears are running down her face, into Annie's hair.

"Ida's dead," says Cora, and I'd worked that much out for myself. "She died before her sixth birthday. In their van."

That's where the clothes came from then, I'm thinking, and I glance at the giantess. Of all of us she seems unmoved, like a mountain, but leaning forward slightly, with an expression of great interest in her eyes.

"Is no good," says one of the brothers. "Is witchcraft."

"She ever done this before?" says Honest Bob, and I manage a hollow laugh.

"All the time," I say. "Try stopping her."

"Mammy, Mammy," Annie says, pulling herself away. "Watch me." And she's up and dancing again, like a little doll. And one thing I know for sure is, Annie can't dance. She never learned how. Yet here she is, skipping and twirling, and Balthasar's reaching for his accordion, and with the tears rolling down his face he strikes up the tune Annie was humming, and Flo starts to clap.

"Oh, that's right, that's right, my darling," she cries as Annie leaps and hops. "That's right, my baby girl!"

Then as suddenly as it started, it's finished. Annie sinks down with a shuddering sigh, and her head nods onto her chest.

"Ida!" Flo cries, clasping her, but it's plain that Ida's gone. Balthasar stops playing on a horrible twang and sits with his head bowed, breathing hard.

Honest Bob seems worked up about it all. He takes another swig, then wipes his mouth on the back of his hand. "Can she do that for anyone?" he says.

"Oh, aye," I say, sullenly. "Anyone, anywhere, anytime."

One of the brothers leans forward and clasps my arm. "Can you ask her about our sister?" he says in a shaking voice.

I see then where all this is leading. To Annie being the star of some weird show. "Ask her yourself," I say, getting up.

Annie's looking at me now, from Flo's arms, and it is Annie again, not some dead thing.

"Go on—ask her," says Honest Bob. I glare at Annie, and she seems to shrink back into Flo.

"I can't *ask* her," I start to say.

And Flo says, "Hush, my baby, Mammy's here." And Annie's staring at me again with huge, bewildered eyes. Another mess I have to get her out of.

"It's not your baby," I point out. "It's Annie."

And Flo's eyes flare up angrily but Balthasar says, "He's right, Flo. Whatever it is, it's gone now." He puts a shaking hand on her shoulder and Flo sighs a long, trembling sigh.

"Well, by God, lad," says Honest Bob. "I've never seen anything like that before. That child's a gold mine, a living gold mine!" His eyes are like two bright coins. And for some reason this makes me mad.

"It's not a show!" I shout at him. "It—it's like some bloody madness—or sickness she's got. She can't help it!"

And at that moment I look round at Cora and Ivan, Balthasar and Flo, and realize what I'm saying. That Annie's just another kind of freak. She'll probably do well here. Flo will treat her like her daughter. It'll be like home. Only not for me. I can see that now. This place'll never be my home.

Honest Bob looks like he's about to say something, to command Annie to do something else, but Flo says, "She's so tired," in a soft voice, still stroking Annie's hair.

"We all are," says Balthasar. "It's time for bed." Cora starts to gather up the pots. Honest Bob starts to speak again but Balthasar holds his hand up. "Whatever's next, it'll wait till the morning."

Flo stands up, still holding Annie, and looks at me, pleadingly but with a kind of challenge in her eyes too, and with a bad grace I help her to lead Annie back toward the van.

Flo and Balthasar whisper together for a long time, glancing over at Annie, who doesn't move. Then, when they're finally asleep, rattling the van like usual with their snoring, I lie awake and my thoughts are all sour. What's Annie doing, drawing attention to herself like that? They all think she's God's gift now. Honest Bob thinks she'll make his fortune. People'll come looking for us; people we don't want to see. I lie there, my thoughts churning over like sour milk and suddenly I can't stand it anymore.

I scramble round so that my top end's near Annie and whisper at her in the dark. "You think you're something now, don't you, eh? You think you're so clever."

I stop, breathing hard, and suddenly I know Annie's not asleep either. She's lying there, listening. It doesn't stop me, it makes me worse.

"You think you're so special—little Annie from the workhouse, the star of every show. Well, you're not. You're nothing special, Annie, you're nowt. You think these people care about you—you're wrong. They'll pick you up and leave you behind like everyone else. Soon as they realize what you are—

nothing. Dead weight. No one's going to carry dead weight around like I've been doing. And I'm not doing it anymore, I'll tell you that much."

My voice runs on, spilling out all the poison in my brain, until I'm wore out and I can't think of any more bad things to say. "No one wants you, Annie. No one ever did. And I don't want you anymore either. Soon as I can—I'm off."

And Annie says nowt, just lies there. I can hear her breathing. She's not even crying and somehow that makes me even more mad. But in the end my voice just runs out all on its own, and I scramble back round and lie on my back, staring at the jumble of masks and pots dangling from the ceiling. It's hard to know why I'm so miserable, but I am. My thoughts chase themselves round and round until they come back to this one big thought—that Annie's found her place now and I haven't. She's got something that she can do and I haven't.

So what use am I? I keep asking myself, staring upward. *What use am I?*

14

Thief

What use are you, lad?" thunders Honest Bob. "If you can't even keep an eye on our stuff?"

Street kids have broken into the van with all the props while we were performing, and nicked it all—loads of stuff. Costumes, masks, scenery, tools. God knows what they think they'll do with it.

"Not my fault," I say sulkily, kicking at the wheel of a van. Wrong.

"Not your fault?" he explodes, and all the veins in his neck stand out. "Not your fault? Well, whose is it then? Mine? I mean, where were you?" he raves on. "What were you doing?"

I say nothing. I was watching the show from the sides.

"You've been hanging around with us—eating our food, drinking our drink, sleeping in our van. . . . What do you do for it all, eh? What do you do for your keep?"

I hate him. I wish I was bigger and I'd kill him. I mean, what does he do, eh? Stays in his tent, drinking all day.

"Leave the lad alone," Balthasar says. "I can make more props."

I hate him too. And everyone else. They're all listening.

"Make more?" bellows Honest Bob. "How long's that going to take? And what do we do while we're waiting?"

Good questions. No one answers.

"We've got enough for the next show," says Balthasar, "if we cut out the puppets."

But Honest Bob isn't going to calm down. He pushes his face right up to mine. I can smell his stinking breath.

"I took you on," he says, "as a favor to a friend. Well. You've got one more chance, laddie," he says. "One more. Anything like this happens again and you're out. Got it? Out!" He stares round at everyone. "What are you lot staring at, eh?" he barks. "Haven't you got work to do?"

He stalks off and everyone else shuffles off too. They don't look at me and I don't look at them. Except for Annie, who's staring so that I want to kick her.

I wish I could tell Honest Bob to stuff his traveling show but somehow I can't. I can't say anything, and that makes it worse.

Balthasar walks by me, carrying a saddle. If he says something sharp I'll hit him. But all he says is, "Don't worry about him. He's all blow and no bellows."

Somehow it doesn't make me feel any better. Everyone's gutted—I can see that from the way they're all moving around like they're carrying something heavy. I stay where I am, staring at the ground. I wish I could run away but somehow I can't. Anyway, where would I go?

We're in Ancoats now and there's a kind of fog hanging over the fields. We can hear the din of the town—the groan and whirring of great factories, the bells calling the workers in, the blasts of heat from the chimneys. All around us the earth's bare, like it's been scorched.

We've given one performance in the afternoon, and there's another this evening. That's when I lie in wait.

First off I sit on the steps of the props van. Then I realize that no one's going to come near with me sitting there, so I skulk down behind the wheels. Because what I want to do is catch the little devils. Catch them and thrash 'em, and drag their bleeding bodies to Honest Bob, to make him eat his words.

From where I am I've got a view of all the vans. I can't hear much, though, because of all the racket from the tent.

It's a cold night with a damp mist. The smoke in the air's sunk down to meet the steam rising from the earth. I lie beneath the van with my hands tucked under my armpits to keep them warm, and all I can think is, *Please come back, come back now. Just one more time.*

They will come back, now they've found they can nick stuff. "There you are, sir," I'll say to Honest Bob when I fling down the bloody corpse. "Don't trouble yourself to thank me. Glad to have been of service. But now I'm off." And I'll walk away without a care, though Annie and Flo'll beg me to stay. And Honest Bob'll shake his head and say, "I misjudged that lad—and now I don't know what we'll do without him."

I'm so busy thinking that I almost miss my chance when it happens. I'm cold and stiff under the van and am just thinking of moving when I see a kind of flicker from the corner of my eye. There it is again! Only when I look for it directly, it disappears.

Slowly I edge out between the wheels. There it is—a movement by Cora's van. I crawl on my stomach over wet earth. I don't give a thought to how many of them there might be. All I can think is I'll catch them, and prove Honest Bob wrong.

I can see him now—a little, whey-faced young'un, and I'm in luck because he's smaller than me. He's picking at the lock with something sharp. I haul myself along and when a twig snaps I duck right down behind a tuft of grass, not breathing. But I'm in luck again. He's concentrating so hard, he doesn't look up. Then the door creaks open and swings wide and he's in.

Quick as a ferret I'm up and in after him. "Gotcha!" I say.

He whips round, all eyes. All eye I should say, because I've just got time to see that he's only got half a face—half a face and one eye—then he bowls into me so fast I'm flung backward down the steps. There's the thud of his foot on my chest as he leaps over me, and bounds off down the field like a jackrabbit.

I leap up, cursing and clutching my chest, and hoof it after him. I don't even shout for help—I want to catch this one myself. But he can run! He's only little but he moves like a hare. Over a stile at the bottom of the field, through a ditch and out toward the houses that press in round the edge of the field. I'm cursing even harder now, because all he's got to do is disappear into one of them houses and I'm stuck. But he doesn't. Right along the narrow street he runs, the mire splashing up round his feet, and I follow and soon we're in a maze of alleys and houses, and he's diving down one alleyway and then another, and it's all I can do to keep him in sight.

Soon we're on a broad street with stalls and vegetables strewn all over the road, my nose is full of the stench of old cabbage, and the kidney-pie man shouts, "Hoy!" as we barge past. It isn't raining but there's water everywhere. There's a burst pipe gushing out onto the street; dirty water drips from the eaves and gutters, and spills into the pipe water. It's like the whole place is dissolving into an ooze.

Twice I nearly have him. Once as he crashes into barrels, sending the whole lot spinning over, and once as he darts round a corner only to find a big gate swung to. But that doesn't stop him and over he goes, and I just about grab the ripped end of his jacket and pull, yelling in triumph, but he yanks himself out of it and bounds over the gate. I've got a stitch in my side that feels like a knife, but there's nothing else for it, so over I go.

Now we're in like a courtyard with alleys running off and folk lying drunk in the doorways. The stench gets worse and the fog thickens into a soup. I can hardly see. There's the sound of crying and moaning from underground rooms, all the glass of the windows is broken. But the fog muffles all and soon I can only hear my own ragged breathing and the *drip-drip-drip* of water.

I wish I'd never set off after him. I wish I'd just scared him off. While I'm here giving chase, there could be ten more of them breaking into the vans. But I can't give up now. I can't just go back.

Out of the alley, back onto the broad street which curves and goes steeply down so that we're hurtling downhill, skidding on cabbage skins. I wish I knew where the hell I was. Turn left and the houses crowd in thick and fast. It's so narrow, there's no light left. I feel like I've been following him for miles. I don't even know my way back. How will I get back, dragging him?

Then this alley ends in a broad open space with a great warehouse at one end, and I can't see him—I can't see a thing. All my mad hot temper changes to despair.

"OI!" I cry. "Come out!"

"It's no good!" I yell, and my voice falls muffled, like shouting into a pillow. "I'll get you! I'll find you wherever you are!"

And I swear I hear a tittering laugh, like a scattering of tiny stones.

That makes me mad all over again. "Come out now, you coward!" I roar. "Too scared to show yourself, are you?" And I run toward the warehouse but the door's locked.

Then I hear it again—thin ghostly laughter through the fog—and all my hair stands on end and I know this is not where I want to be. Annie'd like it, but not me.

"Show yourself!" I cry, and my voice sounds thin and high as well.

Then suddenly I can see them; shapes in the fog, as though the fog itself is swirling into human form. Here and there, then all around me on all sides, ghostly forms closing in, and suddenly I've no breath left to speak. There's dozens of them, and only the closest ones have eyes. There's a roaring in my ears and I can hardly breathe. The closest face has long straggly hair, jug ears and a wide thin mouth. As they press in on me I see that they're all carrying weapons—sticks and jagged bottles, raised high. And Jug-ears has a length of metal pipe.

"Wh-who are you?" I stutter, and Jug-ears smiles. It's a girl. There are big gaps where her teeth should be, and the metal pipe gleams.

"We're the Little Angels of Angel Meadow," she says. "Who are you?"

15

Angel Meadow

Right at this minute I can't remember, so I say nowt. The girl with the pipe steps closer. I recognize the shawl she's wearing, from one of the vans, and a stripy skirt.

"Get him, boys," she says.

"Stop!" I yell as they dart forward and I leap backward onto a crate. "I'm not on my own. There's more people coming after!"

The girl's smile doesn't even flicker.

"He seem like he was on his own to you, Half-moon?" she says, talking to the lad I chased. I can see him more clearly now, and he looks for all the world like someone took a trowel and smudged half his face out. He nods.

"He's on his own all right," he says, in a high, raspy voice. "Rest of 'em's back at the fair."

"And he followed you all the way here?" she says.

"Tore my jacket off."

"Did he?" And they all close in some more.

Oddest bunch I've ever seen. One looks like she's got a horrible, monstrous head until I realize it's an enormous bonnet with feathers curling from the top. Then there's one with no fingers, several with no teeth, one black as a coal shovel, so I can't help but stare. They're near enough their own freak show. But I can tell they mean business. I can either scream blue murder or think—fast. Behind the crate there's a wall with builders' rubble all along the top.

"Eh," I say. "I only wanted to meet you."

This pulls them up a bit. "You what?"

"Everyone's heard of the Little Angels," I say, my heart beating thick and fast. "You're famous. I wanted to come and . . . and join."

Jug-ears pushes her face close to mine. Gray-brown eyes, with crescent moons of white beneath. "You?" she says. "Wanted to join us?"

"Beat his brains out, Queenie," one of them says.

"Straight up," I say quickly. "Or I'd never have followed . . . Half-moon there. I'd have just shouted for help when I caught him."

Never knew I could think this fast. Surprising what a murderous gang with lead piping'll do for your brainpower. Queenie looks like she's considering, but I can see it's only an act. She's playing with me and I'm playing for time.

"You want us," she says, "but why would we want you?" And she turns on her heels and flounces off. "He's all yours, boys," she says.

Quick as lightning I scramble up from the crate to the wall behind, sending rubble and sharp stones flying in all directions. Before you can say *Watchit* I've got Travis's sling out and I'm firing stones at them faster than a pea-shooter, thankful for all those hours I had nothing to do at the fair but practice.

Whirr! Whizz! Splat! There goes the last tooth one of them's got. *Pheeew! Bonk!* Got another one right between the eyes. I catch one after another of them as they try to scramble up the wall after me, and I run along it, still firing stones. One of them slings his stick up at me, catching me on the shin. There's a blinding pain so that I nearly fall off, but I manage to stay, and next moment he's nursing a bloody nose.

There's no way off this wall except over rooftops, so I carry on, running and firing. One of them's clambering up again and I stamp on one of the two fingers he's got, and he falls back with a roar of pain. Now they're getting mad. More and more of them attack the wall at once and it's getting harder to keep firing and stamping. Plus the wall comes to a dead end and I'm nowhere near the alley. I can only go over the rooftops, or else jump straight into the thick of them and hope to scramble away.

Just as I'm thinking this, Queenie Jug-ears speaks. "Stop!" she says. "Hold off!"

Gradually they all fall back, and stand surrounding me like a pack of dogs. "There's no way out," she says. "He'll have to come down sometime."

"I can keep this up as long as you can," I say.

"No you can't," she says, and she might be right. But there's always the roof. I glance over my shoulder at a steep roof with missing tiles. Never tried scrambling over one of them before.

"Tell you what," she says. "Hand over that sling and I'll grant you safe passage."

I laugh at her. "No way."

She steps closer. "Up to you," she says. "We can wait."

I lick my lips but my tongue's drier than they are. Seems like a week since I had food or drink. Why doesn't someone come into this yard and see what they're up to?

"I tell you what," I say. "You let me down and I'll teach you how to make your own slings."

There's jeering and catcalls at this, but Queenie seems to be considering.

"If you had slings," I say, "you'd have had me off this wall by now. Slings are the best weapon there is," I say above the heckling. "You can break a shop window, nick all the stuff and knock the hat off the policeman who comes for you."

There's a bit of a laugh at this, so I go on. "I've seen six policemen in a row knocked out by a single stone," I say.

"Give over!"

"Pull the other one!"

"It's true!" I say, and I believe it. "Let me off this wall and I'll show you."

Queenie steps even closer and I stare down into her white-rimmed eyes. "Go on then," she says. "Step down."

"How do I know you'll stand off?"

Queenie smiles. "You don't," she says.

This is the crunch. "Step back," I tell them, but no one moves until Queenie nods, then they shuffle back about an inch.

"Farther," I say, and glaring, they move farther away. Not very far, though. Close enough to have me when I jump down. Still, it's my best hope. I fit two stones into my sling and jump down from the wall, springing upward at once, ready to strike. No one moves.

"Now," I say, staring hard at Queenie. "Get them to line up some bottles on that wall."

Queenie stares back at me a minute, then nods. A few of the gang run up and place the broken bottles they were carrying in a row along the wall. When they've finished I nod.

"Now stand back," I order, and everyone moves.

Right, Travis, I'm thinking, and it's like a prayer. I'm remembering the time he showed me how to knock a row of pinecones off a gate. I've practiced, like he said, but the truth is, I've never managed it.

Not the right time to mention that.

I take the first stone out of the sling and fit it in again. Everyone watches; no one moves. The air's thick with the sound of their openmouthed breathing.

There's six bottles on that wall, placed far enough apart so that they can't just knock one another over. I step forward, then back, running finger and thumb along the length of the sling, measuring the distance with my thumb outstretched.

"Get on with it," says Queenie.

I lift my sling high and whizz it round. *Phhtt! Plink!* The first bottle falls, no problem—*crash!* Then to my surprise the second one follows it. The third one wobbles a bit but stays firm, and the other three don't even move.

I look at Queenie. "See?" I say.

"You said six," says she.

"Well, that's how it's done," I say, and make to go.

"Oh, no, you don't," she says, and the others all press round. "You said six!"

Before I can answer there's a loud noise from outside the yard.

"Give it up now, lad," snarls a man's voice, "or you'll join the cripples in Hanging Ditch!"

And a lad's voice answers, "I told you I don't know where they are, Mr. Weeks, sir—I don't! You're breaking my arm, sir, you are!"

The next minute a foul-faced man strides in, dragging a red-haired lad with him, and there's two henchmen with big clubs behind. I glance round at the gang and they're all shrinking back in terror. Not so murderous now.

"Well, well, well," says Foul-face Weeks. "Here you all are." He spreads his arms wide.

"Arty—you snitch!" spits Queenie.

"He were killing me!" squeaks Arty.

"Not at all," says Weeks. "Just a friendly jog." And he gives Arty's arm a final jerk so that the lad howls in pain, then lets him go. "I could get a lot less friendly," he says, striding toward Queenie, "if you don't pay what you owe."

I don't stop to think. I have the second stone in the sling and whizzing toward him. It hits him, *clunk!* right between the eyes, and he keels over with a look of surprise on his face. The gang stare at him, aghast, and the henchmen come bounding forward.

Next few minutes are chaos. I'm slinging all the stones I can find and the kids are charging forward with their sticks and bottles. One henchman falls, then Queenie's shouting, *"Run!"* and we're bounding down a narrow passage I hadn't even noticed before, between two yards.

On and on we run, though I don't think anyone's following, through a maze of alleys and courtyards where there's more bodies lying in doorways and little kids and babies playing in the dirt.

Soon we come to the banks of a river. At least it once was a river with proper water—now it's a great churning mess of purples and browns, solid particles floating on the surface and birds walking over them, pecking. There's some great chemical works on the banks, spilling out dyes, and the stench is horrible. Under a bridge we go and into a tunnel that seems to go on forever with the sound of water roaring above, and suddenly I realize we're *under* the river.

Here, finally, we slow down, panting, and wait for the rest of the gang to catch up. There's Queenie and Half-moon with me, and two or three others, then the dark lad comes running, then Bonnet; and finally a girl with sores on her mouth and a long yellow plait staggers toward us, half carrying a little lad with a bent leg.

"Have they gone?" Queenie asks the girl.

"They'll not follow us here," the girl says, then to me, "you got him all right."

And I start to grin, proud of myself, but Queenie says, "Yes—and what happens when he comes to? He'll never let that go, not Weeks. He'll hunt us down and kill us all!"

She glares at me and I stop grinning. "You've brought trouble on us," she says.

"Looked like you were already in trouble," I say, but Queenie's mad.

She paces up and down restlessly and strikes the tunnel wall, but Plaits says, "He's right—he'd have had you then."

"Give over, Pigeon," Queenie says. "He'll have us now, when he finds us."

Pigeon? I'm thinking. *Don't any of this lot have proper names?*

"We'll have to move territory," Dark-boy says.

But another says, "We'd have had to anyway. We're always moving."

"Who is he anyway?" I say.

"What's it to you?" says Queenie.

"Well, I hit him, din't I? Suppose he comes looking for me?"

There's a pause, then Pigeon starts talking, helped out by one or two others.

Seems like this Weeks guy is a bad lot—as if I hadn't guessed. Gangs of kids live on the streets, by thieving mostly, and whatever they take they have to give him half. He's their codger—whatever that means—and he's got a gang of his own. He mainly works the streets around Strangeways, the big workhouse in Angel Meadow, but his territory extends all the way to Hanging Ditch. Beyond that there's another codger who looks after the Rookeries of Deansgate. Bailey, he's called, because he takes charge of them going into and out of the New Bailey prison. He bails them off and then they owe him, and he presses them that come out into working for him, because they can't get work anywhere else. Weeks does the same with the workhouse.

"So there are more street gangs then?" I say, and Queenie looks at me as though I'm daft.

But Pigeon says, "Hundreds."

There are the Toads of Toad Lane, the Rooks of Deansgate, the Cocks of Cock Pit Hill and the Shambles, who don't sound like much, but they're all older and hard as nails. Weeks controls the Little Angels and the Toads and another gang called the Shude Hill Mob; Bailey runs the others. From time to time they raid one another, or meet up at Cock Gates and fight for territory.

This is a whole new world. "But where do you all live?" I ask, realizing as I say it that it's a daft question.

"In a palace, of course," says Queenie, sharp. "That's how I got my name."

Then Pigeon does a passable imitation of a queen walking with her train. "Just look at my castle," she says, pointing at the dripping tunnel. "And the throne, and the four-poster bed."

They're all laughing now—except for Queenie—and I laugh with them.

"But how do you eat?" I say. "And who tells you what to do?"

"No one tells us what to do," says Bonnet. "We fend for usselves. Free as birds." She spreads her ragged skirts wide.

"That's enough questions," Queenie says. "This is getting us nowhere. What'll we do?"

Then there's a conference, one after another of them putting forward ideas.

"Go to Bailey."

"Move right out—miles away."

"Join up with another gang."

I stare round at them all in the half-light from the tunnel mouth. There's only ten or twelve of them, not hundreds like I first thought.

"Aren't there any more of you?" I say, interrupting, and Queenie glares.

But Bonnet says, "There's enough of us to look after usselves, that's all. Too many and there's nowhere to hide."

That makes sense. I go back to nursing my shin, where one of them clouted it. But I can't help wondering what it'd be like to live in a gang, with no grown-ups telling you what to do. In spite of the dirt and the fact that some of them have no fingers, or only half a face, in spite of the dangers, or maybe because of them, it seems like an exciting life to me. Living free, like Travis said.

"So are we going to Bailey then?" one of the lads asks.

But Queenie says, "No!" very sharp, then adds, "He'll only trade us in."

"Come off it," says Pigeon. "Bailey'd do anything to spite Weeks."

"You were thinking of going to him anyroad," says Half-moon. "Weeks kept upping the stakes."

"I'm not going to Bailey!" Queenie says.

"So, anyway," I say into the pause, "when are we leaving?" Truth is, I'm tired of them discussing stuff and I want to know how I'll get back.

"You can leave anytime you like," says she. "We don't want you."

"I'm gutted," I say.

"And you won't be coming back here neither," she says, turning nasty now.

"Hold off, Queenie," says one.

"He knows too much," she says. "He could bring people to us."

I manage a hollow laugh. I've just been set upon, hit with a stick and had to run for my life down a stinking sewer. "Why would I want to?" I say.

There's a pause. I get the feeling that no one speaks to her like this and she doesn't know what to make of it. She looks me up and down.

"He helped us out," Pigeon says and the others chime in. "Safe passage," one of the lads says and the others agree.

Queenie rubs her forehead. "I can't think—too much has happened. . . . Look," she says. "You don't know us and we don't know you. Maybe we can keep it that way."

"Suits me," I tell her.

Grudgingly Queenie nods. "Safe passage," she says.

As she says it she makes a little sign with two fingers, pointing to her heart, mouth and away to the opening of the tunnel. "Where is it you've come from?"

"Ancoats," I say. "The fair."

"Digger," says Queenie. "Ors'n'cart." Dark-boy steps forward, and the one with no teeth.

"Go with him—the back route, through the tunnels. And make it fast. And you—" she says to me. "Don't try to come back or bring anyone with you or it'll be the worse for them—and you." She pushes her face close to mine. "You'll never find us, but we'll find you. See?"

I believe her. No choice.

"Right," she says. "What are you waiting for?" And with the two big lads pressing in on me, I set off downward, into the dripping tunnel.

16

Free

The tunnels are like a stinking maze, one turn after another. Neither Digger nor Ors'n'cart speak as we pound along. They could be taking me somewhere to do me in for all I know. At least they seem to know which way to go to avoid the water—I can hear it crashing and roaring overhead. And faintly above that, the noise of the city. Don't know how I'd ever find my way back here.

At last Digger stops and crouches, and Ors'n'cart climbs onto his shoulders. He's pushing at something metal, like a grate, then he hoists himself upward, and Digger nods at me and I climb up the same.

Ors'n'cart hauls me out, into a ginnel between two houses, then he lowers his arm in for Digger. My ears are roaring from being in the tunnel so long. Digger leads me to the end of the ginnel and there's a long, narrow street, gas lamps flickering and flaring like there's wind in the pipes.

"End of this street," Digger says, "turn left, and right again. Then you'll be in fields."

He makes the funny sign with two fingers, on his chest, lips and away. Then he turns to go. I'm surprised that they haven't attacked me—I'm still alive.

"Er, right," I say to his retreating back. "Safe passage." But he doesn't look round as he disappears into the ginnel.

I make my way along the street, limping. My shin's hurting and my heels where my boots rub. All's quiet, though here and there a lamp shines from a window. Feels like I've been gone hours. I turn the corner and there's more houses and a dirt track to the right, which I follow, and soon I can see open fields and the huddle of vans.

Nothing's changed; it's as though I've never left. They're all eating stew round the fire. I'm glad I've not missed food, for I'm starving.

No one even looks up as I approach. It's like they've not even noticed I've gone and come back. Then I see that one of the brothers is sobbing in another brother's arms, and Flo's holding Annie in hers. Flo says, "Hush now," to Annie, stroking her hair. Everyone looks scunnered.

Straightaway I know what's been going on.

"What's up?" I say, hanging back. I've been here before, but right now I don't want to know.

"Can I have some stew?" I say, and Balthasar gets up to get me a bowl. His face is pale and his hands shaking. *Don't want to know*, I'm thinking.

Then Honest Bob lifts his head, as though stirring out of a dream, and notices me for the first time. "Where've you been, lad?" he asks sharply, then, as I sit down, "Faugh! You stink to high heaven!"

That's the thanks I get. "You'd stink too," I say, "if you'd been where I've been."

"Where's that then, lad?" says Honest Bob. "In a midden?" He turns to Flo. "It's a rare gift that lass has got. We've got to put her on show."

"Nay, Bob, never," says Flo. "Look at how it takes her! She's ill—shaking!"

Nobody's even listening to me. And Annie's got her face buried in Flo's chest.

"I've been chasing gangs of thieves," I say. "They were breaking into your precious vans."

"She'll get used to it," says Honest Bob. "A bit of training—and a proper show. We can do it so she's well prepared. She wouldn't even have that much to do for the punters."

"I'm not listening," Flo says. "I'm getting this child to bed."

Am I talking to myself? I think. "They were stealing our stuff," I say.

"And you chased them off," says Balthasar, placing a hand on my shoulder. "Well done, lad. Now, have you finished with that bowl?"

"They'll come from far and wide," says Honest Bob, his eyes glittering. But Cora stands and sweeps Annie into her arms, carrying her back to the van. The weeping brother's led away by the other two, and Ivan helps Balthasar clear up.

"There were hundreds of them," I say, to no one in particular.

It's no use. No one's interested. Yet I got into all that trouble when they did break into the vans!

I lie awake that night, listening to Flo and Balthasar whispering about Annie, and how Vito, Pepe and Luigi's sister had spoken through her, in a language only they could understand.

I feel sore in my heart. I let my thoughts run on, over everything that's happened to me in the past few hours, and suddenly I'm wondering what it'd be like to be one of them; the street kids, leader of my own gang. I can see myself now—the bravest and fastest of them all, cock of the gang, just like I were cock of the workhouse. I'd lead them into war on the rival gangs and win. My gang'd be the strongest and best. Queenie'd have to step down.

If I wanted to go and find them, though, I'd have to act fast, before they move on.

Soon as I think this, my thoughts turn to Annie. I can't see her there, living off her wits in a gang. Just like always, she's holding me back.

It's daft, thinking like this. I'm not going to go running off with that gang. Besides, they wouldn't have me. Yet even when I finally sleep I dream of running along alleyways and across walls, over rooftops and bridges. There's dozens of children with me, paint on their faces and feathers in their hair. They're carrying pan lids as weapons and they beat them with ladles. Rooks are gathering on the rooftops and below us there's the angry faces of Old Bert and Barnaby and Honest Bob and Weeks, looking up and shaking their fists. Because they're stuck on the ground and trapped in the gutter, and we're up high, flying free.

In the morning things go from bad to worse. First off I'm told to feed the horses, and I spill a whole sack of grain on the ground.

Course Honest Bob's there, watching. "Are you daft or useless, boy?" he roars. "Get that picked up!"

So I'm there scooping up grains out of the grass and beating the birds off, and when I turn round Annie's watching. For the first time in days, Flo's not with her.

"What?" I say as she stares at me, then I take a step or two toward her. "What game are you playing?" I ask her but she says nowt, only tucks a strand of hair behind her ear. "I mean, what is it, Annie, can't you stop showing off?"

No answer. I feel like shoving her. "What about going to Manchester? They're not going to want to let you go at this rate."

Annie hangs her head.

"Annie, Annie," calls Flo. "Come and try this costume on."

"Go on then," I say. "Run off to your new friends."

Annie doesn't move. She's staring beyond me and when I look there's a whole flock of blackbirds pecking at the grain. I run at them, swearing, and right at that minute Honest Bob reappears.

"Haven't you picked that up yet?" he bellows. "Are you feeding the birds?"

"Drop dead," I mutter, and next moment he's grabbed the front of my shirt, shaking me.

"You've outstayed your welcome, lad," he says, very low, then he lets me go. "Get it picked up—every grain. Then take them to water." He stomps off and when I look round Annie's scuttled off too.

With the best will in the world I can only fill half a sack with the spilled grain. So the horses get just a bit each and the birds do very well. Even filling it that much takes forever, so I'm late leading the horses to the spring. I stand by watching them lap at the water, which even here is a murky brown, quite different from the springs we passed with Travis. It makes me think of the river last night, churning all different colors, and from that to the street gang, wondering where they are now and what they're doing. What would it be like, to be their leader? I'd make the rules, give the orders. They'd bring me their booty, so I wouldn't have to do much, but I'd still go out raiding from time to time to show them how it's done. We'd outraid all the others and win all the fights—because we'd all have slings. And all the other gangs'd want to join us. . . .

When I look up again, one of the horses has gone. It's Fanny, the whitish-gray mare who's always a bit skittish. She's jumped the stream, and a small wall. I can just see her munching away at the far end of the next field.

Cursing mightily, I run after her, jumping the stream, climbing over the wall. She lifts her head, still munching as I run up, her tail flicking from side to side. Then, just as I get near, she makes a funny whickering noise and canters off.

This is how we spend the next half hour—her waiting for me to catch up, then galloping off again when I do. I'm sweating like a pig and calling her all the names under the sun, but I daren't go back without her. I just hope to heaven all the other horses are still where I left them.

Then finally I see that she's galloping toward a great ditch with a thick hedge of briars on the far side. If she jumps that she'll really hurt herself, and I'll never be able to follow. I'm about to give up in despair when I remember my sling. I fit a stone in it and aim for the far side of Fanny.

Have you ever tried aiming for the far side of a galloping horse? I daren't hit her, so the shot goes wide but still she veers off, taken by surprise. Then I fire another and another. It's working! She's veering back to me.

The next stone hits her on the leg. I didn't mean to, but she stumbles, then trots on, limping. If I've lamed her, Honest Bob'll kill me. Still, it slows her down long enough for me to catch her by the bridle.

"Sorry, Fanny," I mutter as she hobbles along. "What did you want to do that for?"

I'm vastly relieved to find that the other horses are still there. My knees are shaking from all the running around, but I manage to lead them back to the vans.

"Where've you been?" yells Honest Bob, and, "What've you done to that horse?"

"She ran off," I say. I daren't say I was firing stones at her. "She must've stumbled."

Honest Bob utters a string of foul oaths such as I haven't heard since Bent Edge Farm, but Balthasar's got Fanny and is feeling tenderly down her leg.

"If that horse is lamed I'll lame you," Honest Bob says, but Balthasar looks up.

"It's not broken," he says, "just bruised." He's giving me a peculiar look but all I can think is, *I'm starving*.

"You've missed breakfast," Flo says.

Great. "Isn't there any left?" I ask.

But Honest Bob says, "You haven't earned any." Then he takes Fanny from Balthasar and leads her up and down a bit.

Balthasar's still looking at me with that searching, peculiar look. "What?" I say.

"Doesn't feel like she stumbled," says he. "Feels like she's been hit with a stone."

Suddenly I can see what he's thinking, and I stare at him, openmouthed. "I never!" I say.

Balthasar shrugs and turns away. "Horses don't run off for no reason," he says.

This is too much. "I din't throw stones at her!" I shout, but he's walking off. I start to run after him, to try to explain, but Honest Bob catches me.

"Go and get that tent set up," he orders. "And look sharp!"

There's a look in his eye I daren't argue with. I hold back a bit, then go to help Ivan drive the tent pegs in. Balthasar'll have to wait.

My hands are shaking as I tie the ropes, and my mind's elsewhere. I'm fuming inside. All that effort and now they think I lamed that horse on purpose. Plus I'm still starving. I don't know if my hands are shaking more because I'm angry or hungry. Result's the same, though. The knots don't work. First blast of wind and the tent collapses.

Honest Bob's hopping mad. "Can't you even tie a knot, lad?" he roars.

I pick up a rope to start again and he skelps me across the back of the head. "Go and sit in the van!" he barks. "You're neither use nor ornament!"

I fling the tent peg down, not quite daring to fling it at him, and storm off. I sit in the van, bursting with rage. No one's knocked me about for a long time, and what I'm thinking is, *No one'll do that again.*

When I look up Annie's peering in.

"What are you staring at?" I snap at her and she disappears again, leaving me alone with my thoughts. And there's a lot of them; I've got a lot to think about. All the things that have happened today are helping me make up my mind.

Then Flo comes. "Won't you join us for some food?" she says, and though I'm starving I can't stand the pity in her voice. I shake my head sharply, once.

"But you've not had breakfast," she says, and I look away. Flo sighs. "Wait there," she says, and she comes back a minute later with some broth and bread. Part of me still wants to hold off but I can't help myself. I fall on the food like a ravening wolf.

Flo watches me, clucking and tutting. "You don't want to mind Honest Bob," she says. "We all have our bad days."

Good of her to say it, and the food's good too, but I still don't want to talk. Sighing, she takes my bowl away.

A bit later, Honest Bob himself comes by. "I want a word with you," he says, and I glare at him sullenly, then shift myself out of the van. He's looking at me like he's got something to say but he can't think how to say it. I look up at him warily, in case he's thinking of hitting me again. He rubs his fingers through the bristles on his chin.

"As I understand it, you're planning to leave."

I stare up at him. Has he read my mind?

"Speak up, lad," he says. "I thought you were only traveling with us to Manchester."

I nod, looking away.

"Well, we're here now," he says. "And what I want to know is—are you taking the little lass with you?"

"She's my sister," I mutter.

"What?" he barks.

"I said, she's my sister," I say loudly.

"She's no use to you," he says. "But I can use her. You can leave her here."

So that's it. I'm not even surprised.

"Annie won't stay without me," I say, but he waves a hand.

"She'll be looked after here," he says. "Better than you can. I mean, where are you going, eh? What are your plans?"

There's that word again—*plans*. Makes me nervous.

"Speak up," he says again.

And I say, "I haven't got any."

Well, I have, I suppose, but I'm not telling him.

He nods. "Thought not," he says. "Well, if you've no plans and nowhere to go, what kind of life can you offer her, eh?"

I'm not answering this, so he goes on. "Well, that's what I'm saying. Leave her here. Flo loves her and she'll go down a storm with the crowds. You'll be better off on your own. So . . . how about it?"

How about it. Free at last. No one to look out for but myself. He's waiting for an answer and I don't know what to say. So I say, "What's it worth to you?"

Honest Bob's eyes open wide, then narrow, and he gives a short, barking laugh. "Well, well, I thought it might come down to that in the end," he says, with a smirk on his face that makes me want to kill him all over again.

"What's it worth to me?" he says, and he studies my face carefully then reaches into his back pocket and draws out a shiny coin. Looks valuable. "It's worth this much to me, lad—take it or leave it."

Clear as a bell I hear my mother's voice saying, *Take care of your sister, Joe.*

"Make it two," I say. Honest Bob laughs more harshly this time.

"Don't push your luck, lad," he says, and I back down from the look in his eyes. I reach out my hand and pocket the coin, wondering how much it's worth.

"But I'm telling you, she'll not stay if she knows I'm going."

Honest Bob nods. "Then she'll not have to know that you're going, lad."

I stare at him. He sits down on the steps of the van. "You can go tonight, when the performance starts. No one need know. And by the time she realizes, you'll have been gone too long to follow."

No one need know. No explanations, no good-byes. Not to Balthasar or Flo. Not to Annie. I just disappear like a rat in the night. Well, it would be easier. Because how do you explain to your sister that you're leaving without her, and not coming back?

Honest Bob's waiting, half a smile playing about his lips.

"Done," I say, and it sounds in my ears like the single tolling of a bell.

"Grand!" says Bob heartily. "Sorted then. Now, if you'll excuse me, I've a show to put on." And he strides off whistling.

Slowly I climb back into the van. My head's all mizzy and my thoughts are whirling like a snowstorm. I put my hand in my pocket and feel the coin, all the little ridges round its edge. Maybe it's a sovereign. I never in all my life thought I'd own one of them. And I'm lucky, because I was planning to leave anyway. So the joke's on Honest Bob, because if he'd known he needn't've offered me anything.

But even that thought only makes me feel a bit better. I sit in the van as the light fades, trying to sort out my head, think what I'll do next. Another thought strikes me and I search around the van and find a square of cotton. I fold this up, knotting the corners into a kind of sack, and hunt around for things to stuff into it—brassware, pretend jewels from the chest, even a wig. Booty. You never know what you might need to bargain with. A hunk of bread goes in next and I hunt around a bit for more food. I tie a spotted neckerchief round my shirt and find a cap for my head.

When I turn round again, there's Annie. My stomach flips over, then falls. "What are you doing?" I say. "You're on in a minute."

She says nothing, just stands very white and still, watching me.

"Go on," I say. "You'll miss the show."

Nothing. I give a snort of impatience and carry on scouting around.

Then she says to me, "Don't go."

"What?" I say, whipping round. "Who told you?"—realizing too late I've just given myself away.

Annie looks up at me with her luminous eyes. "Don't go," she whispers.

I spot a tasseled scarf with tiny mirrors sewn on, and stuff that in my sack as well.

"It's too late, Annie," I say.

"No."

"What do you mean, no?"

I glare at her, but she steps forward, putting her hands on my shirt. "Take me."

I shake her off. "What good'd that do? You're better off here."

"No."

"Stop saying that. Look, I'll know where you are and they like you here . . . it'll be your home. And you'll be a star, on stage every night. And Flo'll look after you like you're her own."

She shakes her head. "No."

"Well, you can't come with me. I don't want you."

She stumbles toward me, clutching my shirt again, and I'm horrified to see there's tears in her eyes. I don't cry, and neither does Annie.

"Give over," I say gruffly. Then she's on me, her fingers clutching my shirt.

"Take me," she says.

One by one I prise her fingers off my shirt and shake her off. But she flings herself at me again and harsh, dry sobs come bursting out of her. My head feels like it's bursting and I have this nightmare feeling like I'll never get rid of her. So I tear her off me so hard, she falls over, grab my sack and run down the steps of the van.

"Get lost," I say. "Don't you come following me. It's over." And I make a sign with my hands like I'm cutting through the air. "Do you hear?"

Even so, as I turn my back I hear her following with her snuffling breath.

Desperate now, I quicken my pace, and when I still can't shake her I stoop and pick up a stone. "Get back," I say, "or I'll stone you!"

And the next step she takes I fit the stone in my sling and aim it. It whirs past her feet and she holds back. "I mean it, Annie," I say. "Next one'll hit."

I'm as good as my word and the next one hits her shoulder. She stumbles and the next thing I know she's crying loudly, bawling like a calf.

I turn and run before everyone hears. Faster and faster I go, leaping over the ditch, jumping the stile, racing toward the houses at the end of the field. My own eyes are hot and wet and I rub them angrily. *You won't stop me, Annie*, I'm thinking. *Not this time you won't.*

I can still hear the noise of her crying as I turn into the street—the sound I've not heard since our mother left us at the workhouse. When I look back I can just make out her blurred shape, unmoving, by the vans.

I don't like it, of course I don't, but she'll get over it, I tell myself—and as I round the corner another kind of feeling takes over me. A kind of fierce joy. *I'm free!* I tell myself in time to the pounding of my feet, and I jump up onto a low wall and run along it. *Free, free, free!*

PART II

Lost and Found

17

Graveyard

I don't stop running till I get to the end of the long street and turn off into the little ginnel where the grid was. I'm going so fast, I almost miss the grid, then my foot slips on it and I bend over and haul it up. Before I can stop and change my mind I drop my sack into it so that I have to follow. I lower myself into it, clinging to the edges of the hole with my fingertips, then I let go. It's farther than I thought and the drop hurts my feet. I pick up my sack and limp off into the darkness.

Soon the darkness is total. Like I wave my hand in front of my face and I can't see owt. Still I stumble on, trusting to memory, my nose full of the stench of rotting things.

It's not long before I realize I'm lost. The tunnel twists and turns and there's smaller tunnels leading off to either side. I'm sure I should go along one of these, but I'm blasted if I can remember which. Everything's different in the dark. There's the stench and the eerie noises rumbling around.

How much farther? I think, and I can hear Digger's voice saying, *There's tunnels everywhere under Manchester.*

Course they might not be in the tunnels anymore. They said they had to move territory. A small part of me wonders why they couldn't just stay in the tunnels. I mean, I don't like them, but they're a grand place to hide. Weeks and Bailey or anyone could come looking and not find you down here, not if they looked for a hundred years. Why didn't the Little Angels just set up camp in the tunnels?

Doesn't take me long to find out. There's another twist in the tunnel and the rumbling noise gets louder, building to a roar. I don't know what it is, so I carry on, and then, with a gushing noise, the water comes. Not just water neither—filthy, stinking slime, and I'm up to my waist in it, gagging from the stench.

Panicking, I grab the tunnel wall and hold on fast, my sack between my teeth. There's dead animals in the water and hair and something hard that knocks my arm and drifts away. I cling to the side of the tunnel for dear life and the next gush almost sweeps me along. Worst thing would be to fall over in this lot, floating facedown in the filthy slutch.

I hang on and on, digging my fingers into the cracks between bricks, only breathing when my head feels like it's bursting. If the water doesn't knock me over, the smell of it might knock me out. Either way I'm done for.

Slowly the gushing dies down and I'm able to take a step or two forward, wading through the filth, still clinging to the tunnel wall and fearful of slipping. I plow on, determined to haul myself out at the next sign of a grid. But when I do find a grid it's way above my head, and the walls are too slippery to climb.

Cursing myself, I wade on, wonder when the next tidal wave'll come my way. Why didn't I just try the streets? I could have found my way to Angel Meadow and tried to remember the way we'd run. And hope I didn't run into Weeks, of course. But right now Weeks is looking like the least of two evils. By a long way.

Have you ever tried wading your way through waist-high slutch in the pitch-dark, carrying a sack in your teeth? It's not long before I'm totally wore out. The next grid I find is lower and I can jump up and reach it—but not lift it up, of course. However did I think I'd lift it from the underside? Either I was born stupid or I've gradually lost my brains as I've got older.

Things go on like this and the water won't have to knock me over—I'll just lie down in it and let it carry me away.

Finally, when I'm all out of ideas and hope, I see a light. Someone's left the lid off a grid! I stagger toward it, hope flaring in me like one of them gaslights with the wind in its pipe.

Have you ever tried getting out of a wet tunnel? Clambering up and slithering down, banging elbows and knees. If I wasn't so desperate I'd give up.

Anyway, what seems like hours later I'm lying facedown in the mud. To one side of me there's a clump of nettles, to the other a large stone. But at least I'm in the open air.

That's all I do for a while—lie down and breathe. Then I realize I've lost the sack, and I close my eyes in despair. Because I'm not going back down again. No way.

I push my hand into my pocket and find the coin. That's still there at least. Maybe I'm not being punished for selling Annie.

When I look up again the first thing I see is a stone. It's covered in moss but someone's carved lettering on it—them funny sticks and swirls that make up words. If I could read, it might tell me something I need to know.

Slowly I get to my knees. There's not just one stone but hundreds of 'em, all with markings. Mist swirls round and clings to my face and with the mist comes a silence, though it's not like the silence of the open moor. My hand tightens on my coin. I know what this place is. A graveyard!

Well, I'm not staying here to be spooked. I get to my feet, feeling sick and wobbly after all that swirling muck. My leg hurts but I hobble on as fast as I can. Where there's a graveyard there's usually a church. Maybe I can shelter a bit in the doorway. I hurry past the stones and dripping thorns, try-ing not to think of all them stories where the devil appears in churchyards to steal your soul.

I'm not very good at not thinking about it and before long I'm clammy with fear, teeth chattering like magpies, and very sorry for myself. I'm sor-rier still when a stone rises up in front of me and grabs me by the neck.

"Who goes there?" it cries in a terrible voice. "Hold still or I'll cut your throat!"

18

Mad Pat

I start praying in earnest, like I never did at the workhouse. A fearful shape—man, not stone, but all in coarse gray, with a rag tied round his head and one milky, staring eye—looms over me. I shut my eyes.

"What are you? Demon?" he roars, shaking me so I can't answer.

"Speak!" he bellows, but my teeth are chattering too hard. "What do they call you?"

"Jack—Joe—Tom," I stutter.

"Jackjotom," he mutters, and grinds his teeth. "What kind of demon are you?"

There's a note of fear in his voice that surprises me, and I open one eye. I take in his clothes, which are nearly as soaked as mine. Muddy, ripped by briars. His great bare feet are cut all over, and he's shivering as much as me.

"You come out of the ground," he mutters, "but you'll not take me with you!" And he seizes my shirt and lifts me clear off the ground.

"I'm no demon, sir!" I cry. "I came from the tunnel, not the . . . other place. I wasn't looking for you, I swear! I was looking for my friends!"

"Friends?" he bellows.

"The . . . Little Angels," I gasp, and he gives such a roar, I nearly pass out from fright.

"Angels? Angels? What would a demon want with angels? You see that spire?" he swings me round so that I can see, dimly, a tall spire through the yellow mist.

"Ye-yes."

"That's where the angels come from," he whispers hoarsely. "Swooping down from their steeple to peck out your eyes!"

He's mad, I think sadly, for while it's better than him being Owd Nick, it's not a comfort. But if there's one rule I live by, it's never annoy a mad-man who's got you by the throat.

"Sir, not those angels, sir," I say, trying to free my throat. "The Little Angels are just boys and girls. They wouldn't peck out your eyes."

"How do you think I got this then?" he says, pointing to his glaring, milky eye. "No angels—but demons did this!"

"I'm not a demon, sir," I say. "I'm a boy. Jack's the name. If you'd put me down, sir, we could maybe talk."

He shakes me so hard, I can't think, never mind talk, then suddenly lets me go so that I collapse at his feet. "What's your business with the Little Angels?" he says, a cunning look in his evil eye.

"The Little Angels, sir?" I say, picking myself up cautiously. "Do you know them?" For something in his look makes me think that he might.

"What's it to you?"

"They're my friends, sir, I told you I was looking for them."

It's stretching it a bit to say that the Little Angels are my friends. And it's come to something when the best friends you've got are a gang that tried to beat you to death with lead pipes—but there you go.

He knits his brow and glares at me with his good eye. "Friends?" he spits.

"I lost them," I say, and I must have looked as forlorn as I felt, for he shakes his massive head.

"You're better off without friends," he says. "Friends'll not help. Not when the poor rate comes and the paving tax and the lighting rates and the rates for water and the window tax . . . Where are your friends then?"

He's off then, up on his feet again, swinging his arms around, and the spit flies from his mouth. "When the beadle comes to cart you off to the poor-house, where are your friends? When they come to tax the air you breathe and the cuts on your feet, where—are—your—friends?" And he shakes his massive fist with each word.

"I don't know, sir," I say after a long pause. "But . . . will you help me find them?"

He sits down on a stone then and all his anger subsides. "I had friends once," he says. "Now I'm on my own—like a lone wolf," and he puts back his head and howls.

"Sir!" I gasp. "Don't excite yourself, sir."

"Do you know who I am?"

I shake my head. Not a clue.

"Name's Patrick McGann," he says, thumping his chest. Then he leers at me with his milky eye. "They call me Mad Pat," he says.

Can't imagine why, I'm thinking, but I say nothing, and he looks at me again, sharp.

"You want a house by the church," he says, cocking his head toward the steeple. "Twenty-two Half Street."

I'm taken aback by this. "A house, sir?"

He waves his hand, dismissing me. "It's where they all end up, sooner or later. Woman there'll know who you want. Tell her Pat the Irishman sent you."

"Right . . ." I say, still stumped. There's something in his manner I can't work out, but at least it looks like he's letting me go. "Er, thanks." And I step backward and turn, anxious to be off.

"You tell Beelzebub from me," he roars after me as I quicken my pace, "if he wants Pat the Irishman he can come for me himself!"

I hurry away, grateful for my escape, over the low wall of the burial ground, round by the side of the church.

I find Half Street easy enough, a row of crazy, tumbledown old houses, each one a different size and shape, some of them leaning forward so far, it looks like they're listening to the sermons in the church. Windows are narrow and high off the ground. No numbers on the doors. Then I find one with 17 carved in oak lettering with leaves entwined round. There's a narrow passage next to this, barely wider than me, and the next house says 23.

Stumped by this, I stare at the ginnel. There's a pool of yellowish water where the ground ought to be, and the sound of poultry squawking beyond. No choice but to splash my way through.

The ginnel opens into a yard. There's hens, even sadder and scraggier than the ones in the farm, and a tethered pig. Sure enough, the houses on Half Street have other houses attached to the backs. Maybe that's why it's called Half Street, because only half of it faces the front.

Some of the doors are hanging off and all the paintwork's peeling. Windows are higher up and narrower than at the front, and most of them broken. Some of the highest ones have bars on them. I look from door to door, and the last one I come to has two number twos scratched on it with a knife.

Luckily I paid more attention to numbers than letters in the workhouse. Satisfied I've found the place, I rap smartly on the door, and when no one comes, rap again.

There's the sound of shuffling and swearing, then the door opens about an inch. "Who is it?" growls a voice. It's a woman's growl, and I can see long, shaggy hair hanging down.

"My name's Jack," I say. "I'm looking for someone and a friend of mine told me to come here."

The door opens wider. I see a big, shapeless woman, tied up like a sack in the middle. Shaggy black hair hangs around her face and black eyes peer at me suspiciously. "What friend?" she says.

"Pat the Irishman," I say, and her eyes open wide. Next thing I know, door's flung open and out comes a volley of curses, the likes of which I've never heard before. I back off hastily as she lumbers toward me, brandishing a stick.

If I thought Cora was the ugliest woman I'd ever seen I was wrong. This one's teeth are like tombstones, long and curving and all standing apart from one another. I back off so far, I crash into some bins and the stick comes crashing down beside me.

"He's not really my friend!" I cry. "I just met him . . . in the grave-yard . . . I told him I was looking for the Little Angels and he said to come here. And to give you his name," I add bitterly, realizing I've been had.

I see her give a start when I mention the Little Angels, then her eyes narrow.

"Give me his name?" she thunders. "I'll give you something to remember me by. Take this back to him!" and she raises the stick again. Just in time I dodge to one side as it comes crashing onto the bin behind. At the same time I fancy I see a face appear quickly at the topmost window of the house. I only catch a glimpse of it through bars, then it disappears.

"Beg pardon if I've given offense!" I say, dodging the stick again. "I only came to ask if you'd seen them but seeing as you haven't, I'll be on my way!" and I skip toward the ginnel as Madam brings her stick down yet again.

To my surprise she doesn't follow. Probably too fat to fit down the passage. When I realize she's not following I stop on Half Street then, remembering the face at the window, go back to take another look at the ginnel. She's not there. Peering at my feet in the yellow water I spy something I'd not noticed before—a single white feather, long and plumy.

No hen dropped that, but I do know where I've seen one just like it—on the hat of the Little Angel they called Bonnet.

Course, there might be any number of hats like that in Manchester. Still, I pick it up, twirling it thoughtfully in my fingers and, as if by magic, when I look up Queenie's there.

"Well, well," she says, "if it isn't the Sling."

"Queenie!" I say, managing a grin. For close behind her there's Digger and Ors'n'cart.

"What are you doing here?"

"Looking for you," I tell her.

"Looks like you've found me."

"So it does. Who are you looking for?"

She frowns and I see she's staring at the feather. I give it a twirl. "Soon as I saw this," I say, "I said to myself, 'Something's up. If that feather's not Bonnet's,' I say, 'then I'll eat her hat.' "

Queenie's eyes narrow suspiciously. "What are you up to?" she says.

"Me?" say I, all wide-eyed. "What should I be up to? I've come to see you, that's all—to see if I can join."

There's muttering behind Queenie at this, but Queenie says, "Why would we want you?"

"Well," say I, twirling the feather again, "I know something you don't."

Queenie gives a sharp look at me and the feather. "Such as?"

"I know where Bonnet is."

"Is that all?" says Queenie, and the others laugh.

"We know where Bonnet is," says Pigeon, pushing her way through. "Question is, how do we get her out?"

"Maybe I can help."

"How?" says Queenie. Course, I haven't got that far yet.

"Well . . ." I say. "You tell me who's got her and why she's got, and I'll tell you how I'll help. But only if I can join your gang."

Queenie's not impressed. "Push off," she says, and makes as if to push past.

"Wait!" I tell her. "Don't go knocking at that door. She'll chase you off with a big stick."

Queenie finally looks impressed. "You mean to say that you knocked on the Tally-woman's door?"

"So what?"

"And lived?" says Pigeon.

"Last lad who did that," says Digger, "had his head split in two."

Thanks a lot, Pat, I think. "Well, she chased after me," I say, "but I dodged her. Who is she anyway?"

We've crowded back into the yard by this time and are whispering behind the bins. The pig snuffles and grunts at us suspiciously, like we're after his food.

The Tally-woman's sometimes known as Mother Sprike. As far as the church knows she looks after orphans and street children, giving them a bed for the night and soup. She gets an allowance from the church for helping them "relieve the poor." Really what she does is set them to work for her. She lives in that house with her five enormous daughters. They walk the streets for a living, Queenie says, looking at me as if I'd know what that meant, and I nod wisely. They pick up orphans, especially girls, and make them work for them in the house. Once the Tally-woman's got you she doesn't let you go, unless someone comes along and pays a big ransom. You pay her, supposedly for board and lodgings in that hole, and she keeps tally.

"She's been after Bonnet for a while," Pigeon says, "because she's pretty." And again I nod as though I know what she means.

"Well," I say when she's finished, "how much money does she want?"

Everyone answers at once. "Too much!"

"Loads!"

"She's dearer than the best hotel in Manchester."

"I see," I say, fingering the coin, which is still in my pocket. I'm not ready to let it go just yet and besides, it might not be enough. "Well . . ." I say again, to give myself time to think, and just then the pig snorts and sneezes and loads of muck flies up. And I have my big idea.

19
Pig

Have any of you lot," I ask, "got a knife?"

Digger has, a short brown one with a folding blade. Might not be sharp enough.

"We need to cut the pig loose," I explain, and they all look blank. I've ridden a pig before, on Bent Edge Farm. Main challenge is to get it to go in the right direction. "When I get on the pig, cut it loose," I say to Pigeon and Ors'n'cart. "Make as much noise as you can behind, on them bins. Queenie and Digger can knock on the Tally-woman's door, loud as you can. Rest of you try and make sure the pig goes forward. Use your sticks if it looks like swerving."

"What'll you be doing?" says Queenie.

"Riding the pig," I say, and some of them laugh. "I'm going in," I tell them. "Tally-woman won't know what's hit her—you lot can come in after and get Bonnet."

"How will we know where she is?" asks Pigeon, wide-eyed.

I squint up toward the top of the house. "I saw a face up there," I say, pointing to a tiny window below the roof. "Just go in shouting her name."

Queenie doesn't seem too happy about all this but no one else has a better plan. I can see they're a bit nervous of the pig, which snorts and glares at us as we approach, but I walk right up to it, holding out some cabbage leaves from the ground.

"Just keep feeding her these," I say, and I grab her ears and swing my legs over.

Digger's slow cutting that rope. The pig rears and bucks and I lie flat as I can, gripping hard with my knees. Pigeon and Ors'n'cart set up an unholy racket, banging on the bin lids with their sticks, and the pig breaks the last strand itself.

Pig goes wild, rearing and lunging. It runs every which way round the yard, squealing like it's being slaughtered, and by some miracle I hang on. Soon the other kids get the hang of driving it forward with sticks and Queenie bangs on the Tally-woman's door.

Out flies the Tally-woman, roused by the racket, and the pig charges forward.

"What—?" she says, and it's as far as she gets, for she's bowled over by the charging pig. It carries her along a narrow passage that stinks worse than the yard outside. I'm clinging for dear life to its back and she's on its front— I'm right up against her horror-struck face. The others pile in behind and it all goes much better than I hoped, for the pig skids to a halt in front of the wall and sits down squarely on the Tally-woman. I slide off its back and follow the others up the narrow twisting stairs.

"Bonnet!" we yell. "Bonnet!"

Just as I thought, she's in the topmost room. "In here, in here!" she squawks, and we fly up the last lot of rickety, rotten stairs.

The door's locked but luckily the wood's as rotten as the stairs. A few kicks send it flying open and Bonnet runs forward, feathers flying from her hat.

Back down the stairs we go, hardly pausing to laugh at the Tally-woman, who's still stuck under the pig, roaring and swearing. Pig's still screaming and Pigeon and Ors'n'cart are still banging away on the bins, but as soon as they see us they leave off and we all charge into the ginnel.

"Which way?" I shout, and Queenie swings round and stops dead in her tracks. Lumbering toward us up Half Street are five of the biggest women I've ever seen, all decked out in frills and furbelows, each one more brightly painted than the last. When they see us the biggest one lets out a roar and they all gather up their skirts and charge forward. "This way!" I yell, hoofing it in the opposite direction.

Though I haven't a clue where we're going, I'm leading the way. Past a long line of rickety houses, through a ginnel into a yard, and out again onto a broad thoroughfare where the gas lamps and the lights from shop windows shine as bright as day and carriages and hackney cabs roll past with rich people inside. Still the five enormous daughters of Mother Sprike gallop after us like carnival figures, so everywhere we run people and children point and laugh and stare. I grab one barrow off a lad hardly older than me and tumble it into their path, him shouting in surprise—but nothing stops them and it's getting desperate.

I turn off down an alleyway that leads to yet another yard where women and drunks sit in doorways, and little kids play in the dirt with no clothes. We shoot out the other end and double back on usselves and it works. The five enormous daughters grind to a halt and can't work out which way we've gone. Then Queenie pulls my sleeve and takes the lead. We head back along the street and duck into another ginnel, and by some miracle we're back where we started. Two, three ginnels more and we're by the church and the burial yard. Mad Pat sees us and sets up a howl and I shake my fist at him as we run past. Round another corner, through an alley and we're on the banks of the river itself.

Tall houses lean over like they're about to fall in. Some of them seem like they've already slid partway down the bank. In front there's a narrow path, so narrow you can only go along it sideways, and an iron rail that's rusting and falls off toward the end. Below us the river heaves and churns, brown and purple with dye, and the great factory opposite belches out colored smoke, and lets out a stink that's worse than the sewers. But just as the broken rail gives way we come to a door, painted blue, hanging off its hinges.

Queenie and Digger push the door aside and we're in. A dark square room like a cellar with one tiny window, high up and barred. It must have flooded at one time and the water just covers our feet. There's no roof either, just planks of wood where the ceiling must have been. We stand around, panting, and start to laugh.

"We did it!"

"Did you see them?"

"All them apples from the barrow!"

"The look on their faces!"

"Do you think she's still under that pig?"

"Are we all here?" Queenie says, and I try to get my breath back while she counts. There's Digger, Ors'n'cart, Half-moon, Pigeon, Bonnet, the little lad with the bent leg—Lookout, and another lad I don't know called Pickings. There were more of them in Angel Meadow.

"Where are the others?" I say.

Queenie says nothing, but Pigeon says, "They've gone to join Bailey."

After I left them in the tunnels there was a big row. Some of them wanted to go straight to Bailey but Queenie wasn't having it, and the rest of them said that'd be just swapping one bad codger for another and, anyroad, Bailey might just hand them over to Weeks. So the ones who wanted to go left and the rest found this cellar, where they slept last night on the wooden boxes piled round the walls.

"We don't want a codger no more," Half-moon says. "Everything we take's ours."

Sounds good to me. "So are we all here then?" I say.

"Eight," says Queenie.

"Nine now," I say, pointing to my chest, and Queenie shoots me a look. "I'm with you," I say. "I want to join."

"I've told you before," says Queenie. "We don't want you." But the others chip in.

"Let him!"

"He rescued Bonnet, din't he?"

"He saved us from Weeks."

"We need more numbers."

Even in the dark I can feel Queenie looking at me. There's a long pause, then she says, "Anyone who joins the Little Angels has to do a special task for the gang."

"I just did," I say, and the others agree.

"They have to have our mark cut into them." She flashes her arm in front of me but it's too dark to see.

I lick my lips but my tongue's dry from all the running. "Suits me," I say.

"And they have to be loyal forever to the gang—to share their takings and help their brothers and sisters of the gang and to fight all other gangs and anyone else who harms us, in the name of the Little Angels."

"Suits me," I say again, and it's like an oath.

Digger gets his knife out. I can hear rats squeaking up above.

"You'll need a name," says Queenie, and I'm about to say I've got one, when the rest of them join in, making suggestions.

"Slingshot."

"Pig-boy."

"Dodger."

"Dodger," I say firmly. I'm not being called Pig-boy.

Digger takes my wrist and leads me toward the weak light from the tiny window. I don't see what he's carving because I shut my eyes until he's finished, but it takes forever. My eyes sting and my knees start to tremble, but I'm not crying because I never do. I'm still chuffed at my own cleverness and success, so I can stand the pain. When he stops he cuts his own arm and joins his blood to mine and holds my arm up.

"The new Angel, Dodger!" he says.

And they all cry, "Dodger!"

"You're one of us now," Pigeon says.

I hold my arm up to the light and I can just make out, through the blood, the shape of angels' wings. I stare round at them all and manage a grin. I'm up to my toes in water in a leaking cellar where the rats run, but for the first time ever it feels like home. The start of my new life.

"Right," I say. "What'll we eat?"

2 0

Gang

First day with the gang I have to learn my way around the streets of Manchester. And there's a lot of them. We all go together, running through a maze of alleys and courts. They show me around; I teach them to use the sling.

We hide round a corner of Market Street and I send a volley of stones over toward a meat-pie stall. Pie man comes running and Pigeon and Ors'n'cart nick enough pies for us all. Then we climb onto a shed roof up Back Piccadilly and sit eating them, and a police officer comes chasing a thief. We crouch down low and I fire stones at him so that he runs this way and that. Then back to the fish market near the burial ground and Digger uses the sling while Half-moon snatches a bag of oysters.

Course, they all want one of their own then, and we tear strips off our clothing to make them, and go and practice on Mad Pat, who stamps and shakes his fist at the spire.

"Angels from hell!" he shrieks, finally cowering behind one of the gravestones.

All day we work the crowds and alleys till we make our way back to the cellar, to count our booty.

We've got apples from the apple market, boots from a shoemaker's stall, a woman's purse nicked by Queenie and, best of all, a flagon of porter. We uncork this and pass it round, drinking a toast.

"Here's to staying away from Bailey!" Queenie says.

"Here's to me!" I say, wiping my lips, for after all, I've shown them a new weapon.

Queenie pulls it off me. "We drink to the gang," she says. And she hands the boots to Pickings, who's barefoot, though I could do with a new pair.

Digger takes it next.

"To freedom," he says, and we all drink to that. Then we act out some of the things we've seen, the policeman running round in circles, and Mad Pat shaking his fist at the spire. Finally we lie down on the wooden crates.

It's hard to sleep with all the noise of the town. Hard enough to sleep on wooden crates standing in a pool of water anyway, but there are drunks singing, a fight breaking out somewhere, a fire bell ringing and farther along the river a babby crying on and on, and through it all the noise of the river slapping and sucking at its banks.

There's an hour or two when even the town sleeps and the streets are empty except for the last drunk staggering home and roaring out his drinking song. Tramps curl their chilly limbs in doorways. Even in April the snowflakes fall and melt as soon as they touch the mud. A thick yellowish mist hides the stars and the few streetlamps left lit look like the eyes of a sick man. In the crowded cellars people sleep piled onto one another; their breathing hoarse and bubbling like thick water.

Then, though the light doesn't change, as if there's been some signal, the bustling of the streets begins. Market carts and wagons roll slowly along. The knocker-up comes banging on doors, and the first factory bells ring. Women wrapped in shawls and men with heavy clogs trudge toward the factories; women carrying baskets on their heads parade to market. The apple market and the fish market are full of wagons and the pavement strewn with vegetables. Sheep and pigs are driven through the streets to Smithydoor market. There are boys fighting, pie men calling out their wares and donkeys braying. Maids with milk jugs open the doors as the milk cart passes. Soon there's all the noise of bakers' shops and pawnbrokers and booksellers opening, and men carrying briefcases make their way to the exchange. Beadles and aldermen ride by in rich carriages, small office boys in big hats run along in pairs. The baked-potato man sets up his tin stove and the kidney-pie man his stall. All day long the streets get greasy and the muffin boy rings his bell.

There's a hundred factories in Manchester, rearing above the other buildings like giant beasts, roaring, belching and grinding their many teeth, hungry for cotton. Bales of cotton arrive on the river for spinning and dyeing, and in hundreds of backstreet workshops seamstresses sew the cotton into shirts and sheets and aprons and tablecloths, workmen's trousers and a thousand other things. Everywhere there's the whirring and buzzing of machines turning raw cotton into something else. A black smoke covers the whole town and through it the sun is a pale smudge. And the noise! The crunch and grind of machinery, the ringing of factory bells, the pumping of pistons, the whistle of steam, the noise of houses and shops being torn down and streets widened, the cries of street sellers, the thunder of clogs and boots . . .

But for those few weeks in the spring and summer, the streets were ours. We ran through them like rats, thieving, begging and always bringing our takings back to the cellar by the river. Picking pockets, of course, which was how Pickings had got his name, him being the best. And scavenging down the sewers. It were amazing what you picked up there—rings and bracelets, coins.

I had my pick of the office boys. There were one who always ran behind the others, and never had a mate. I'd see him every morning running up Shude Hill, hanging on to his hat, which were nearly as big as the rest of him. He couldn't go too fast, on account of the hat and him being too pudgy. So I'd catch up with him, going barely faster than a walk . . .

How're you doing," I say, very polite. "Where are you going in such a rush?"

He carries on huffing and puffing, looking neither to the right nor left.

"Let me help you with them parcels," I say, taking them off him easily enough.

"Give them back!"

"Only trying to help," I tell him, opening one, but there's only books inside, with numbers in, not pictures.

"I need them!" And his face gets all red and puckery.

"Now don't you take on," I tell him. "You can have your parcel back—but what'll you give me for it?"

"Nothing!" says he, so I catch him by the ear and he twists and squawks. Then, because he's trying to kick me, quick as wink I turn him upside down and shake until the coins fall out, and a wodge of bread with some ham tucked inside. Then I set him on his feet again, thank him kindly and give him his parcel, taking his hat in return . . .

Thing is, all the time I knew him, he never learned to go a different way, which were just stupid, if you ask me. Or even start off early. He'd see me coming and go pale and red by turns, but carry on chuffing desperately up the hill. One time, when he had no money, I took his trousers, which were better than mine. That's how I got the look I came to be known by—I was the Dodger in the big hat and corduroy breeches.

I wasn't the leader, of course, but with me the Little Angels went farther and did more than they'd ever done before. I remembered the upturned carriages I'd seen with the fair and we'd go along London Road and Oxford Street, leaving stones for the wheels to run up against. Then, when the carriages fell, I'd run up and offer help and in all the confusion of skirts and crumpled limbs, Pickings and Half-moon'd get away with a fair few silk purses. Or Pigeon'd carry Lookout, the little lad with the lame legs, to beg from a pastry stall, and while they were being driven off Digger'd be round the back, nicking pies.

Then there was coshing. Queenie and Bonnet had worked this one before, where a gent, looking as fine and dandy as you'd like, 'ud follow a young girl into the darker courts and the rest of us'd be waiting there with sticks. *Bam, splat!* And thanks for the pocket watch, kind sir, and the wallet.

There were other gangs, the Toads of Toad Lane, the Rooks of

Deansgate and the Shude Hill Mob. All of them bigger than we were, in size and numbers. And if they caught you, they'd take all your day's earnings off you, and more besides—for they'd send a tracker out following you till you'd earned even more for them. And if you were really unlucky, they'd sling you off Hanging Bridge when they'd finished with you. So, of course, you had to avoid the gangs as best you could.

Except on Sundays. On Sundays the whole of Manchester ground to a halt. The factories lay like big beasts panting in the sun, and only the occasional carriage carrying toffs'd roll slowly along Oxford Street toward the fields. There was nowhere for the poor to go outside of work except the gin shops. So Sundays we made our own entertainment. Soon as the bells rang for the end of church, the gangs'd come out, all fired up with gin, and run riot through the empty streets. It was warfare—the Toads charging at the Shambles and the Shude Hill Mob pitching into the Rooks with iron bars and bottles. Up Clock Alley and Cock Gates, Toad Lane and Old Millgate, the battle'd rage; men, women and children pouring out of the courts and ginnels to shout them on. Once or twice they'd get carried away and pour up Market Street, smashing all the windows, and only then did the police appear, looking very ginger about it, and if it got too bad they'd ride them down with horses. But mainly the ones who went near made themselves comfortable in a gin shop and watched.

We'd watch too, not joining in. Queenie never let us, though I argued with her about that. There were few enough of us as it was, she said, without losing any more. And she had a point—for when it was all over there were always bodies left unmoving in the rubble. If they carried on long enough, she said, we'd soon be the biggest gang. So we'd climb up steps onto the high railings or low rooftops and cheer for whoever it was we wanted to win that week. Sometimes I really wanted to join in with all the fists flying and broken glass. But we had to watch from a safe distance.

Because we had to hide from so many people—police, Mother Sprike and the gangs—I came up with the idea of us going out in pairs, one of us always looking out for the other. Queenie and Bonnet went around together, Digger and Ors'n'cart or Pickings, Pigeon with Lookout, and Half-moon always stuck by me. Seems like he felt there was a special bond, ever since I chased him all the way from Ancoats. At first I looked out for him while I learned the tricks of the trade, but I soon got better and faster than he was, and he was a good lookout, in spite of only having one eye. We got to be the best team, bringing home the most brass. He never stopped asking questions in his funny, rasping voice.

"Why are we going this way?"

"What are they fighting about?"

"Why am I always lookout?"

"Where'll we go next, Dodger?"

"Can I have a go?"

It was just like being followed around by Annie, with more noise. Still I got used to him, and it wasn't a good idea to travel alone.

The main people we had to look out for were Weeks and Bailey. And they were always around. You'd catch glimpses of Weeks in the crowds or in a gin shop. Weeks was a short, thick-built man with blue stubble on his chin and a stained overcoat that he never took off. And he was never without his minders—two charmers called Catcher and Carver. Bailey was much bigger, almost a giant, with red hair and tattoos. We saw much less of him because he had so many people working for him he had no need to go out—he just sat in his den off Deansgate. And, of course, there were three or four of Queenie's angels who now worked for him, and knew all about us. And about me and my sling, and the shot that felled Weeks in Angel Meadow. Queenie didn't know if they'd spill on us or not. But Pigeon ran right into one of them one day—a stringy lad called Tippings on account of him being found in Tippings Court. He was running off Market Street into Swan Yard, carrying half a brick in his hand. He was brought up short by the sight of Pigeon carrying Lookout and for a moment she thought he'd set up a yell.

But then his eyes glazed over and he ran past just as if he'd never seen her, and not a word was exchanged. So Pigeon said we probably could trust them.

"Trust no one," Queenie said, which was Queenie's motto and religion all rolled into one. That and, "Ask me no questions and I'll tell you no lies."

Queenie was a bit older than me, by my reckoning, and a bit taller, but not much. I don't know how she came by her name but I do know she ruled the gang with a rod of iron, and it's hard to say how. Except that you didn't mess with Queenie. If you argued with her over anything she'd look at you with those crescent-moon eyes and say, "Because I say so," quiet-like, and that was the end of it. And she was clever, Queenie, in the sense of picking the right person to scam—sauntering into a shop, looking almost respectable and getting a conversation going, and coming out with not only the goods but the money she'd started with *and* extra, having fooled the shopkeeper into giving her more change. She never lost her cool, which made her seem older than she was, I reckon. Certainly plenty of men followed her down Long Millgate—where we had 'em.

That first week or two I had plenty of run-ins with Queenie—about where we were going that day for instance, and who with. I couldn't see how it was that a girl ruled the gang—my gang, as I came to think of it. Both Digger and Pickings were bigger than she was and most of us had days when we brought home more booty.

It came to a head one night when we were sharing out our spoils and doing our own entertainment—acting out the scrapes we'd got in that day. Pigeon imitated the posh woman she'd begged off and followed down the road, nose held high, train sweeping down the pavement.

"Be off with you, you dirty little girl. I'll report you to the police."

"Oh, ma'am" (simpering), "you'd never report a *orphan*? With a crippled brother? And a father in the asylum? Dribbling and drooling into his bowl?" And the woman had hurried away so fast, she'd fallen over her own skirts.

Then Pickings showed how he'd stood in front of a vegetable barrow, juggling the fruit so that most of it ended up in his own pockets, until the man caught on and chased him all up Withy Grove. Great fun.

Queenie sat watching with half a smile on her face, while the rest of us laughed. She never went so far as a laugh, her eyes only relaxed a bit into a heavy-lidded smile.

I laughed, watching her all the while, then I said, "Seems to me we could use a better name." No one said anything to this, so I added, "The Little Angels—that's a girl's name, innit?" I looked round for support. Digger and Pickings were smiling, but they hid their smiles from Queenie.

"It's our name," she said.

"Yes, but we're not in Angel Meadow no more."

"He's right, Queenie," said Half-moon, but stopped under Queenie's glare.

A rat ran over the beams of wood above. "We could call usselves the River Rats," I said, glancing up. "Like the Toads, or the Rooks."

"I'm not changing the name," she said.

"Well—you can keep it," I told her. "The rest of us could be known as the River Rats."

She said nothing to this and everything went quiet, so I laughed to ease the strain. Then that night, after I'd fallen asleep dreaming about my gang, the River Rats, I woke up choking . . .

Queenie has me by the throat—two fingers under the jaw—and I can hardly move or breathe. I lie there spluttering and she says, "Who runs this gang?" very low. I splutter something and she jerks my head back sharp. "*Who?*" she hisses.

"You do," I manage to gurgle.

"Can't hear you."

"And I—can't—breathe," I choke out, kicking feebly. Her grip on my throat tightens and orange stars swim in front of me.

"I—run—this—gang," she says, stabbing into my throat with each word. I can feel the blood bursting into my head. "Don't you ever forget it. Or you'll end up back in the sewer where you came from." And she jerks my head back so far, I feel a spasm of pain. Then she lets go, and I lie gasping for air like a fish. She stands over me, glaring down.

"Blimey, Queenie," I say when I can speak again. "You know how to make a point."

"Just so long as I have made it," she says. I struggle into a sitting position.

"You're the queen, Queenie," I say, and that strange half smile passes across her face. "I'm your man." I rub my neck, wondering if she's burst anything. "Never meant to give offense," I say. Queenie says nothing and she doesn't move either, a ray of light from the window moving across her face. I glance up at her.

"So," I say. "You don't like the name River Rats then?"

And for the first and last time in our acquaintance, Queenie laughs—a short, harsh sound but still she's laughing, and I'm laughing with her. And I'm all right with Queenie after that.

She never said a thing about herself, where she came from or how she'd ended up there, and she never asked me either. In fact, if I was to name the main law of the gang it was this—don't ask. In the poorest courts and alleys no one ever asked about anyone else. Mainly they were all sunk in their gin-soaked dreams.

In the cellar next to us, for instance, there was a family of about fifteen all piled together, white and thin. There were some day workers from the tanning factory in the next hut, then a man and wife with two littl'uns and another on the way—her getting grayer by the day. They never thought to ask how we, a gang of children, came to be living in the next cellar along, though it was as big as theirs and if anything, slightly less wet. That was one thing I got to know about the poor—that hopelessness that followed them around like the smell. They could have slung us out and claimed an extra cellar for themselves. As it was, they barely looked up when we went past. No one asked us anything, which was just as well, and we didn't ask each other either. All I knew about any of the Little Angels was how they got their names, and I didn't even know that about Queenie.

Digger got his name because at one time he'd had a job digging up newly buried corpses from the pauper's graveyard for two medical students, who'd later been caught doing it and sent down. Don't know where he came from, but he once said his mother had been a slave. That's someone who has to work all the time for no money, like in the workhouse. Ors'n'cart had been named by Queenie, who'd seen a horse and cart pull up on Cross Street in the early hours of a Sunday morning and dump a bundle near the chapel, and when she got close up that bundle turned into a boy staring at her with unwinking eyes, and she took him back with her to Angel Meadow. Pigeon had been named because she scratted and pecked about on the ground looking for food droppings. Lookout because that were his most useful role, Half-moon because of his face, Bonnet because she was never without her hat, Pickings because he was the best pickpocket around in spite of having just two fingers on each hand. He'd lift money from the inside of a gentleman's vest and the gent wouldn't even know he'd been hit.

So there we all were, living like kings off cabbages and fish. We drank porter and gin when we could get it, and ale when we couldn't, and only if we were desperate would we try the water from the nearest pump, which came out in a brownish trickle and was nearly as thick as the river. I'd only been with the gang a short time when it began to seem like forever, as though I'd had no other life, and even Annie seemed a long time ago and far away.

There was no reason, it seemed to me, why my new life wouldn't go on forever more. But then things took a different turn.

21

Heatwave

The snow passed and the warm weather came. The city stank and broiled in its own sweat. Fueled by the factory furnaces, the air turned to a reeking oven. No rain fell and the river ran slowly then stopped. But great bubbles welled from beneath the surface and burst, discharging their stinking breath. The rich rode by in open carriages, fanning themselves with silk handkerchiefs pressed over their noses, while in the alleys and courtyards people lay on the cobbles, passed out with drink, and flies crawled into their open mouths.

The heat made every one of us ill. Half-moon came out in a rash that ruined his face even more; Ors'n'cart couldn't breathe for catarrh in his throat. I'd got used to the stinging and burning of my flesh that came from living so near chemical works. The insides of my nostrils were scorched and the flesh on the palms of my hands tingled while my eyes stung and ran. But I'd cut my foot one day, running without shoes, and it got swollen and painful. My breathing was hoarse and thick, like some of the river water had got into my lungs . . .

Then the vomiting starts.

Lookout's the first—heaving up so violently, it comes down his nose and bursts the little vessels in his eyes. None of us'll sit with him except Pigeon. She says he'd drunk some of the thick brown water from the nearest pump.

"I told you about the water," says Queenie, but Pigeon just says they were desperate. She sits with him all night while the rest of us try to sleep on the concrete ledge with its broken rail. I must have got some sleep, because the next thing I know I'm waking up to the sound of wild weeping. I scramble up and back into the cellar and Queenie's got her arms round Pigeon. And lying in a pool of his own blood and filth is Lookout, eyes wide open like he's still trying to look out for us all.

I cover my nose with my hands, but nothing shuts out that smell.

"I told him he'd be all right," Pigeon sobs. " 'Lookout, dear,' I says, 'your mam's watching over you—she won't let nothing bad happen.' But he started shaking—and the blood came and—and I told him he'd get better!" she wails, her face turned into Queenie's shoulder.

I can't stop looking at him, like I've never seen anyone dead before.

"What'll we do with him?" Digger says, and Queenie nods toward the river.

The river's not moving, of course, and we don't want him staring up at us all summer, turning black, so Pickings and Digger run to fetch sacks and me and Digger, Pickings and Half-moon carry Lookout downstream toward Hanging Bridge while the others stay back to clean up the mess.

The moon glows reddish through a haze. Seems like everything's back to front—the sun a white glare by day and the moon blood-orange at night. I can't think of a single thing to say. I'm thinking about Lookout, thrown away as a babby and thrown away now, scarcely more than a babby still. There's people around, shuffling along the streets with downturned eyes. No one asks us owt. We climb up the steps to the bridge, hoist him up and roll him over. There's a thick splash from below, then the river's ooze covers him up.

No one says anything. Seems like someone should say a prayer, but none of us can remember how. "Be seeing you, Lookout," I mutter, and that sounds daft, but no one laughs.

We make our way slowly back along Millgate. I've got my hands in my pockets, fingering my coin, that in all this time I've never let on about nor used. When we get back, Pigeon's quiet, staring at the floor with red-rimmed eyes. No one says anything. We lie down and try to sleep.

I didn't think I would sleep in all the heat, moths and spiders flitting across my face and the rats squeaking and nipping, but I must've, because

soon I'm dreaming of Annie. It's a dream I've had before, where I'm pris-
ing her fingers off my coat, but this time I'm dropping her off the bridge
into the river, and I wake with a start and a shudder.

Pigeon's still sitting where I left her, rocking herself and crooning. I pick
myself up and join her, sitting on a crate.

"Can't sleep?" I whisper, and she shakes her head. I try to think of saying something like "He'll be in heaven now" or "He's out of his misery," but
I can't. Instead I say, "At least you were with him, all the time," and she nods
at that, just a small movement of her head.

"I were with someone once who died," I say, and I start telling her about
this kid in the workhouse, the year we all got scarlet fever, and she's listening but she doesn't stop rocking. "It's hard the first time," I say, and she
shoots me a look. Not the first time then. "Who else?" I ask, though I'm
not sure I want to know.

"Spider," she says, her eyes fixed on some distant past. "Fingers, Trapper,
Hare'n'hounds, Stagecoach." She counts them off on her hands.

"How many of you were there?"

She holds up the fingers of her hands, once, twice, then shakes her head.
Can't count.

"What happened?" I say nervously, but she shakes her head again. Even
in the thin light of the moon I can see her face is greenish. I change the sub-
ject.

"I knew a man once," I say, "earned his living telling stories. Well, he sold
skins as well, but wherever he went he told a story and got food for it. He
told us—I mean me, one about angels. Shall I tell it to you?"

No answer. Her breathing sounds hoarse and the shaft of moonlight's
gone so I can't see her face. I start telling her anyway, about the shepherd
on the hills and the crowd of angels bright and fierce, and I can tell she's listening. As I tell it I'm thinking about Travis and wondering what he's up to
now, but soon all I can see is Dog-woman running down the side of that hill,
finding her pack, like I've found mine. I come to the bit where she's living

in the forest, and the pack she lives with gets old and dies but she outlives them all, when I feel the touch of Pigeon's hand on my sleeve.

"Dodger," she says, swaying a bit, and then it happens. She's sick, all over my feet.

I leap up shouting, "Help! Doctor! Help!" and soon everyone's stirring. Pigeon's on the floor now, retching and spewing, and all I can think is, *Who's next?*

"We need a doctor!" I shout.

"Don't talk daft," snaps Queenie. "There's no doctor comes down here."

"Then we have to take her to one," I snap back. "We can't just sit here waiting for her to die!"

Pigeon groans and spews up brown water into the water she's lying in.

"Get her onto the crates," says Queenie, her face all creased with worry.

We pick her up and she's light as though even her bones are empty, but she's racked and heaving. *Just like Lookout*, I'm thinking, and cold dread sits on my stomach.

"Queenie, listen," I say. "We've got to at least tell a doctor. We've got to try. I'll go. I'll be as fast as I can. And if he won't come, well then—"

I can't think what we'll do if he won't come.

"We've got no money for doctors," Queenie says, and without thinking my hand goes to my pocket, where the coin is. I say nowt, but Queenie's sharp eyes take this in.

"There's doctors on King Street," Digger says, and just then Pigeon gives a groan that comes right from her feet, and throws up clear across the room.

"I'm going," I say. "I'll be back as fast as I can." And without waiting for argument, I set off at a trot, up onto Long Millgate, take a left onto Toad Lane, which turns into Hanging Ditch, and follow that all the way to Deansgate, where King Street joins. It's a fair trot of over a mile, but I don't want to cut through the alleys and courts at this hour. I keep my head down and trot fast and no one bothers me.

The houses on King Street have brass plaques and there's a special sign that means doctor that Queenie pointed out to me once when we were begging. First one I come to I pull the bell rope hard as I can and keep pulling until a manservant comes, looking out, then down at me. He steps forward with an oath and I step back quick.

"Please, sir, I need the doctor."

"Clear off, you scally."

"But it's my friend—I need him to come."

"Doctor's sleeping. He'll not come out for the likes of you."

"But I can pay!" I say, holding out the bright silver coin, not without a pang.

He steps forward then, raising his stick. "Be off with you, you little thief!" He brandishes his stick and I retreat, then he goes back in and slams the door. I glance upward and see the curtains twitch and a head in a nightcap look out, then quickly withdraw.

The next house I come to no one answers, swing on the rope though I do, and the next there's the sound of dogs barking and snarling and someone shouts through the door, "Clear off or I'll set them on you."

"But I need a doctor!" I shout, driving the dogs to a frenzy, but the door stays shut.

There's four doctors on King Street. When the last door opens I fall to my knees. An old woman's standing there in her nightdress, with a shawl and nightcap, holding a lantern and peering out as though even with the lantern she can't see.

"Who is it?" she says.

"Ma'am," I say, desperate, "don't shut the door, ma'am, please."

She holds the lantern higher and squints down. "What do you want?" she says sharpish.

"A doctor, ma'am, please . . . I need the doctor."

"At this time?" She starts to close the door.

"No, ma'am, please—look, I can pay!" And I hold out the coin again.

The lantern sways and bobs. "What is it?"

"A—a sovereign, ma'am . . . I think."

"A shilling more like. Be off!"

I gape at her. *A shilling?* I'm thinking, and I feel a murderous rage toward Honest Bob. Queenie handled all the money so I never knew.

But she's closing the door again and I lurch forward and grasp the hem of her nightdress. "It's not for me, ma'am—please . . . my friend's sick, sick to death."

She twitches the nightdress away. "What ails him?"

"Her, ma'am—she's not here, I couldn't bring her, she's too sick. Oh, ma'am, tell the doctor, please. He has to come!"

"Where is your friend?"

At least she's not shutting the door in my face, but she's not getting the doctor either, and when I tell her where Pigeon is she steps back immediately and starts to close the door again.

"No, ma'am, *please* . . . She keeps spewing and no one can stop her. She'll die if the doctor won't come!"

She steps back, twitching her nightdress away. "Is it the cholera?" she says, a note of fear in her voice.

I haven't a clue but I nod my head vigorously. "That's it, ma'am, that's it—and we don't know what to do. Oh, please tell the doctor. Please!"

"The doctor's out, child," she says, but her voice isn't unkind. "And if it's the cholera there's not much he can do. Keep her warm and clean and give her sips of good clean water."

What country's she living in? "There's no clean water by the river, ma'am. When will the doctor be back?"

She sighs. "I don't know, child. Look, there are special hospitals for the worst cases—it's them you want, not the doctor."

I seize this. "Where, ma'am, where?"

She gives me three addresses, one at the back of Piccadilly, one near Strangeways in Angel Meadow, and one not too far from where we are, on Balloon Street. "They'll give her a bed for the night," she says.

I thank her several times as she shuts the door. Then I hare back toward the river.

Just like last time, the gang's sitting on the concrete ledge outside the cellar, while Pigeon spews her guts up inside. I tell them about the hospital and there's a furious row, because Queenie doesn't think she should leave.

"She'll die if we keep her here!" I shout, hearing all the time the terrible retching and heaving from inside.

In the end me and Digger say we'll take her, and Half-moon insists on coming along. Pigeon can't walk, so we make a chair with our hands and carry her, Half-moon propping her up behind. It's hard going. Up Long Millgate in the other direction, turn right up Balloon Street, stopping every few yards so that Pigeon can spew. And we've gone the length of Balloon Street without seeing no hospital. Half-moon runs ahead of us, checking the alleys. Finally he says, "There's a warehouse in Tanner's Yard and someone's in."

We're out of ideas, so we follow him. Sure enough there's a warehouse and a light shining beneath the door. We bang on it, loud as we can, and to my relief a woman comes out in a nurse's uniform, carrying a lantern.

"You'll wake the patients," she says very sharp.

"Please, ma'am—it's our friend . . . she needs the doctor."

The nurse takes one look at Pigeon, all greenish pale and lolling, and steps forward to help her in. I'm so relieved, my knees are trembling and my mouth dry and Digger has to explain.

The warehouse is a single, huge room, no windows, lined end to end with bodies sprawled on blankets—no beds. Two other nurses pass between them, carrying lanterns and jugs. There's a moaning and groaning as from souls in hell.

"Mary," says the first nurse. "Make up another bed."

More blankets are brought. "Where's the doctor?" I say.

"Dr. Kay'll be here in the morning," she tells us. "You can come back then." And she ushers us toward the door.

I feel a huge wrench, leaving Pigeon there, crumpled on a blanket. None of us have ever been parted before. But the door closes on us firmly.

"Doctor'll be here around eight," she says through it, and we stand around outside, not knowing what to do.

"We could wait here," Half-moon says, but Digger says there's no use waiting, we should come back in the morning like the nurse said. Then a church clock strikes three and we realize it's already morning, and we make our way back through the deserted streets toward the river.

We trudge on through the silent streets, and neither me nor Digger says anything. Only Half-moon trots behind, asking questions.

"What'll we tell Queenie?"

"What'll we tell the doctor?"

"Suppose he asks us where she's come from?"

"Shut up, can't you?" Digger says because, obviously, we don't know the answer to any of these questions, and Half-moon falls silent. We carry on without speaking, conscious that Queenie'll be furious, feeling like we've given Pigeon up to the enemy. And soon we pass the bridge where, only a couple of hours earlier, we ditched Lookout's body. Seems like we've hardly had time to think about him, but now we pause on the bridge, looking down, wondering if we'll see an arm or leg.

I can't see anything, but suddenly Digger catches my arm. "Look!"

To the far side of the bridge the bank slopes less steeply and there's a kind of ledge. Above it the pavement's collapsed. It's a famous place, this, for people losing their step and falling in—tramps on a winter night or young toffs who've had a few too many, they all meet their end in the grimy water. Many's the time me, Digger and Pickings have hauled a body out and rummaged through its pockets. Dredging, we call it, and we get some of our best booty that way. Now I see that Digger's pointing to a body sprawled out on the side. It's too big to be Lookout and it's in a man's coat. I glance at Digger and Half-moon, and I can tell we're all thinking the same thing. If we find a wallet or a gold chain, it'll help to pay for Pigeon's medicine.

Cautiously we go down the steps at the side of the bridge, which are covered in green slime. Even more cautiously we approach the body, in case he's not dead, only dead drunk. But he's facedown and doesn't seem to be moving.

Digger goes a little way ahead, on lookout. Me and Half-moon crouch beside the body. I hear the *slap slap* of the water's edge.

The coat's soaked, though how the water lifted him onto the ledge I don't know—there's been no rain for days and the river's shrunk. I push my hand right into the one pocket I can find. Nothing. I tug the coat back and push my hand farther, beneath his ribs, looking for other pockets, and motion to Half-moon to try to turn him over.

At the same time I notice two things. One that the body's not cold, and two, as I press his ribs, there's a heartbeat. . . .

Next thing I know he's rearing upward, the whites of his eyes all yellow in the moon. He turns, spewing a spout of filthy water right into my face.

Weeks!

22

Killer

Weeks's arms thrash out wildly and he's got Half-moon by the neck, and he's up and dragging him backward, roaring in triumph.

"I've got you, you little scally!" he says.

My head's whirling so fast, I can't think, but I can see the knife.

"Help, help!" I roar, and I can hear Digger's footsteps—but they're running away!

"Shut your noise or this one gets it," snarls Weeks, and he presses the blade right up against Half-moon's neck.

I see Half-moon's eyes rolling in terror and clamp my jaws shut.

"How long did you think you could hide from me?" sneers Weeks. "Your little lot owe me money and I'm not a man to let that go. Now, you tell me where Queenie is or I'll string you up and use your own guts as a rope."

"We're not with Queenie—" I begin, but he starts forward, cursing, and the knife presses into Half-moon's throat so that there's a small spurt of blood and a helpless whimper from Half-moon.

"Don't kill him!" I beg. "I'll tell you—I'll tell you where she is!"

And I tell him, describing exactly where the cellar is. Because for all I know he'll make us both go with him.

"Now, that's better," he says. "See how much better it is when we can talk? Queenie never understood that. But here's a message she will understand."

And before I can say or do anything, or even think, the knife flashes and a red line appears on Half-moon's throat. His eyes look at me, surprised, then roll back and he's hanging limp and Weeks just tosses him into the river. I stare at Weeks like I've lost my mind, then I'm shouting, "NOOOO!" till my lungs are bursting, and his fist whips out and he has me by the throat, shaking me till my teeth rattle.

"You're the little geezer that knocked me out, aincha?" he yells, and it feels like I'm looking my own death in the face. His other arm holding the knife lifts and he opens his mouth again, then I hear a thudding noise on his back and he stops with a look of concern on his face like he can't quite remember what he was going to say. Then he's falling forward, on top of me, but I wrench myself sideways as he lands.

And behind him stands Digger, and Digger's knife is stuck in Weeks, right between the shoulder blades.

We don't need telling that it's time to run. We bound back up the steps to the bridge, but just as we start to cross, a shadowy figure steps onto it on the other side. Catcher. We turn, and heading toward Weeks's body on the bank is Carver. He looks up at us and roars when he sees the knife.

We clear the bridge just as Catcher and Carver crash into one another behind us. I'm legging it behind Digger along Chapel Street, when he swings round and pulls me into an alley.

"Got—to split—up," he gasps. I don't want to be on my own, but I can see the sense in it. The whites of Digger's eyes flash in the dark. "Don't—go back," he says. "Don't—take them—to Queenie." I shake my head.

The sound of heavy footsteps pounds toward us. Then, without warning, Digger launches himself at the opening just as Catcher and Carver catch up.

They must be right on top of him and I hear one of them yell. Next moment the other's diving into the alley just as I'm diving out the other side.

I come to a narrow footpath above the river and I run along it, praying it won't suddenly collapse. Soon as I can, I dive back into another alley that winds and twists. Digger must be in Salford now, if he isn't caught.

The alley leads to a court that leads to another alley and soon I'm out on Blackfriars Bridge. I'm heading back into Manchester, but away from the cellar where the rest of the gang are huddled. And still he's following, going faster now, catching up. Light from a gas lamp strikes his bald head and I see it's Carver.

Over the bridge we go, back into the alleys off Market Place, where the great bins overflow and I can hide. My ribs hurt and blood's pounding in my ears. All around me there's rubbish from the market and human rubbish lying in doorways or on the street. But all I can see is Weeks drawing that thin red line across Half-moon's throat. And the sound of Lookout's body hitting the river. And my chest hurts worse than before and my breath comes tearing out of my throat painful-like. But I'm dry-eyed—not crying—because I never do.

23

Bin

I spend all that night in a reeking bin, and I'm near chewed to death by rats. Gives me plenty of time for thinking, though, and all my thoughts are grim. Digger's gone, and he'll not be back in a hurry. Lookout and Half-moon are dead. Pigeon's in the hospital. That leaves Queenie, Pickings, Bonnet and Ors'n'cart. I need to get a message to Queenie, but I daren't go back to the cellars. I have to hope she turns up at the hospital.

Somehow I get some sleep, and when I wake up it's the full glare of day and the heat's simmering. I feel sick, which is hardly surprising given the stink. Very carefully I poke my head out of the bin, half expecting to find Carver's ugly face leering down. But there's no one in the alley except for a few starved cats flitting about.

I hoist myself out of the bin. *Doctor'll be here at eight*, the nurse said. I haven't a clue what time it is now, except that the sun's been up awhile and I can hear all the sounds of the market and, beyond that, the great mills steaming and grinding away.

I nick some fruit from the market to keep me going, then head back up Hanging Ditch toward Balloon Street, staying in the thick of the crowd, looking around me all the time to right and left. Though I can't read the names of the streets it's like I've got a map of the whole city in my head. I know this city better than anywhere, better than the workhouse, because there I couldn't run about.

When I reach Tanner's Yard a nurse is throwing the slops into the street. I stay well back, crouching behind a low wall, bite into my apple and wait. Church clocks strike for the half hour but I don't know which one.

While I'm waiting I try to think what we might do next, but I'm out of ideas. I'm stiff and aching and though I'm eating the apple to keep my strength up, I'm not that hungry. Lots of things flit backward and forward in my brain—Old Bert, Young Bert, Barnaby, Dog-woman, Travis. I think about the traveling fair and Annie, but they must be miles away by now. Remembering Annie makes me feel worse, like I'm being punished for selling her. Then I think about Digger and wonder if he's safe and managing to hide. I won't think about Half-moon, or Lookout, but it's like there's a painful place in the back of my mind.

Church clocks strike nine and I curse softly, for I've missed the doctor arriving. If I'd seen him I might have tried to have a word. I shift position, wipe the sweat from my eyes. Feel like going back to sleep.

Then I see her, Queenie, and she's on her own. I wait till she's passing then grab hold of her and pull her down.

One thing I like about Queenie—she'll never yell. She whips round like a fury, though, two fingers jabbing toward my eyes. Just in time I duck, hissing, "Queenie—it's me," and she grabs my arm.

"Dodger! What's happened?"

I tell her everything. There's no easy way to say any of it, and her shoulders slump so that I think she might fall, but she doesn't cry. I expect her to tear strips off me for leading them all into trouble, but all she says is, "Right," and presses her hands to her eyes.

The silence goes on for so long, I get worried. "Queenie," I say. "What'll we do?"

More silence. She takes her hands away from her eyes. We watch another nurse chucking out slops. Then she says, "We'll have to go to Bailey."

But you didn't want another codger, I think, *especially not him.* But I don't say anything and she goes on.

"Bailey won't care that Weeks is dead—he should be pleased. We'll go to him and . . . and promise all our takings if he'll take us on. He'll be chief now. . . . He's the only one that can offer protection."

Still I don't say anything. I know Catcher and Carver'll hunt us down if we don't get protection.

"We'll have to get word to Pigeon, though," she says, and we both look toward the door of the warehouse.

"Have you heard—?" she says, and I shake my head. Queenie sighs. "Well, one of us'll have to wait here, and I need to tell the gang what's happened."

"I'll wait," I say, and Queenie nods. Neither of us wants to go in because of the questions they'll ask. After a minute I say, "How'll we find Bailey?"

She looks at me with those heavy eyes. "Dodger—you can't come," she says.

"What are you saying?" I say, catching her arm, but she only goes on looking at me sorrowful-like. I close my eyes. I know what she's saying. Bailey might take the others on but he'll never take me or Digger, not if the word's out that we were involved in Weeks's killing. Catcher and Carver'll be after us, and if I go to Bailey he'll hand me over as a gesture of goodwill. Something like that.

I swallow hard, still not opening my eyes. I can feel Queenie's gaze on me.

"I'm sorry, Dodger," she says, low, then she's off, slipping away at a great pace to tell the others. I watch her go, without so much as a good-bye, and I sink down again behind the wall. My head feels hot and cold by turns and I rest it against the brick. I try to think what it might mean, being without the gang. It means I'm not Dodger anymore. I can't be Dodger without Digger and Pickings and Ors'n'cart and the others.

I don't know where I'll go or what to do. It's one thing living on the streets with the Little Angels, and another trying to get by without them, hunted and alone. I don't hate Queenie, for I know what she's thinking. While I'm with them I'm a danger to them all.

Somehow or other I fall into a sleep, but it's a sleep in which lots of voices are jumbled up in my head. Queenie's voice and Honest Bob's, and my mother's. I wake up with a start when my mother says, *But where's your sister, Joe—where's Annie?*

I've got a raging thirst and it takes me a minute to work out where I am. Then I hear a man's voice saying, "That's all I can do for now, I'll be back at two," and I raise my head above the wall.

It's a young, fresh-faced man, his shirtsleeves rolled up past his elbows. And the nurse with him is saying, "But, Doctor, are you sure I shouldn't bleed him?"

He's the doctor then. Somehow I thought all doctors were gray and fat.

Almost before I know what I'm doing, I'm standing up. There's two thoughts in my head, *Pigeon* and *water*, though water comes first. I lumber toward them and my legs feel like wool, and they look at me in surprise. The fresh-faced man looks like he'd normally be smiling, but there's a frown between his eyes. I start to speak, but my tongue's all thick and swollen.

"Pigeon—" I say, and the frown deepens.

"What's that?" he asks, and I try to explain, but even I can hear I'm not making any sense. I'm nearly up to them now, wobbling like a newborn calf.

"What is it, boy?" he says, but not unkindly, and I open my mouth for one last effort.

"Water," I say, and sink down into the darkness where his feet should be.

24

Bath

When I open my eyes, there's a china bowl staring back at me. I say staring, because the front of it's carved into a head, like the head of a babby, with wings behind. Something white's fluttering in the background. *Nah*, I think, and shut them again.

I keep them closed for a long time. Sometimes I hear voices, speaking low. I keep my eyes closed so whoever it is thinks I'm asleep, but I still can't catch what they're saying. Everything around me feels soft, softer than anything I've felt before. When I open them again there's that painted babby, leering back.

Have I died and gone to heaven? No one told me the angels were made out of pot. And whenever anyone told us about heaven in the workhouse it seemed clear that none of us were going.

There's footsteps and I shut my eyes again quick. A woman's voice says, "I only hope the master knows what he's doing," quite close to my head. Then she sets something down and moves off.

When the room's quiet I shift my head and open my eyes again. This time I'm looking at a window. It's partly open and the fluttering thing's curtains, white as snow. The light hurts my eyes and when I close them there's an orange square burning my eyelids.

I can't work any of this out, so I give up trying and go back to sleep.

My dreams are jumbled, full of Queenie and Digger and Annie. Half-moon's there and when I see him I feel a gladness that's almost a pain, but I can't remember why. And somewhere in the background, Dog-woman's prowling.

Half-moon says, "Can you sit up?" and when I don't answer he says it again. I open my eyes and see gray trousers and a green waistcoat. Not Half-moon's gear. Whoever it is has his hands behind my shoulders, propping me up. I see a face bending down, and it's a face I've seen before, young, with a crease between the eyebrows. Something stirs in my memory and instinctively I cover my face.

"Put your hands down," he says, and, "open your mouth."

I'm too weak to do anything other than what he says. He peers into my mouth like he's looking for my lunch. *You're out of luck there*, I think, realizing how hungry I am. Then he sticks something cold onto my chest and listens. What's he listening for?

"That's a lot better," he says, letting me go so that I sink back into the softness of what I now realize is a bed. Never slept in one before, or at least not one like this. I sink down into it, and farther down, like it might close above my head.

"Do you know where you are, boy?" he asks, and I shake my head. "This is the house of Sheridan Mosley, of Mosley Street. A very kind gentleman who's taken you in."

The name sounds important, as if I should know it, but I don't. The voice is coming back to me, though—a pleasant voice though he talks funny. *The doctor*, I think, and suddenly I can see the warehouse where we took Pigeon. It hurts to think about it, so I stop thinking and close my eyes.

When I open them again the doctor's gone but a woman's there. A very stout woman, nearly as broad as tall, gray curls slipping out from her cap.

"You're alive, I see," she says, leaning over me to plump up my pillow. Well I knew that much, but there's a lot more I don't know. Next thing, though, she's pulling at the neck of the gown thing I've got on and scrubbing at me with something rough and wet.

"Eh—stop that!" I say, batting at her feebly.

"Oh, you've got a tongue in your head, have you?" she says. She doesn't stop scrubbing, though, round my face and ears. I cough and spit, but she carries on, muttering to herself.

"Never seen so much filth in all my days," she says, scouring my neck. "Look—you've stained the pillows. Mr. Mosley's best linen!" She picks up the china bowl. "Look at the state of that water!" she says, showing me a grimy pool before taking it away.

Shouldn't've washed me then, I think of saying, but she's already gone. I never did hold much with all this washing. The workhouse nurse used to say, when she'd delivered a baby, *They get washed when they're born, and when they die, and that's good enough for them*, and that's the one thing we ever agreed on. If we were meant to get wet, we'd have scales.

Nothing happens for ages after that. I go back to sleep and in my sleep it seems I can sense someone bending over me, not doing anything, just breathing. Even with my eyes shut I can feel the gaze on my face. I don't like it and I twist away, but I don't wake up.

Next thing I know, food's coming. *Hurrah!* I think, trying to sit up and failing. I can hear the rattle of wheels outside the door and the smell of something delicious wafts in. Then the maid comes in. She's very young—not much older than me—and ugly, with a pockmarked face, but she smiles at me as she pushes the trolley near and I think she's probably all right.

"Can you sit up?" she says, and I try but I still can't manage. She lifts the lid off a bowl and the smell of rabbit wafts up, reminding me painfully of Travis. It's soup, though, and I can see her thinking it'll end up all over Mr. Mosley's best linen.

"I'll just go and get someone," she says, and disappears, calling, "Mr. Bung?" down the stairs. I strain toward that soup, cursing my own weakness.

There's heavy footsteps and the maid reappears with a jowly man who has heavy-lidded eyes and a hairline that's retreating toward the top of his skull. He tramps over without words, looking very ill-pleased about it, and hoists me up. The little maid feeds me herself from a silver spoon, smiling and winking encouragement each time I manage to swallow.

That soup tastes grand! It's so good, I want to hold on to the taste for-ever. I'm sure I could down the full tureen, but in fact after only a few mouthfuls I've had enough. Then the little maid feeds me something crisp and sweet that melts away on my tongue. "Meringue," she calls it.

Now I really have had enough and I feel a wave of sickness. I sink back, close my eyes, and the next thing I know it's all coming back, wave after wave of it, all over the silk sheets.

The little maid leaps back with a cry and Mr. Bung curses like a trooper, and I cower, expecting to be beaten half to death, but though his face is black as thunder all he says is, "Fetch Mrs. Quivel," and disappears, mopping at his trousers with a napkin.

In comes the stout housekeeper with a steaming bowl and some fresh linen and I'm made to lie on a long chair while the little maid changes the sheets. Mrs. Quivel hands me a clean nightgown, then says, "Look at the state of you! You need a bath."

"I don't then," I say, and she looks as though she'd like to box my ears but daren't quite.

"Go and fetch Mr. Bung," she says to the little maid.

Bung arrives with another fellow and they're carrying a tin bath between them. *How many servants are there?* I'm thinking, and, *You're not getting me in that.*

If I were any stronger he wouldn't've stood a chance. As it is he slings me over his shoulder and carries me, kicking, behind a screen that Mrs. Quivel and the maid pull across. Next thing I know he's dropped me in the tin bath, nightgown and all. Then he reaches into the water and drags the nightgown off me while I roar.

It's the shock of the water, that's all. I sit there gasping and not knowing what to do. Then I realize that he's staring at me. There's something in his eyes I don't like. He reaches out a hand.

"Excuse me," I say.

Then Quivel returns. "Mrs. Quivel!" he says, low. "Look at this!"

"Certainly not!" says Quivel.

"Do you mind?" say I.

"Come here!" he orders, and Quivel peers round the screen.

I feel a right prune, sitting there, and I don't know what they're staring at. If I wasn't stark naked I'd leave. Then Bung reaches out a finger and traces something on my back, and I realize what all the fuss is about. It's scars, innit, from when my back was opened time and again by the birch, in the workhouse and at Bent Edge Farm. I've never seen them, of course, but from the pattern his finger's making I can tell they're all over my back. They can't be a pretty sight, because Quivel's got her apron pressed to her face.

Good to know that the sight of you makes someone feel sick.

"Heaven preserve us," she says. I've had enough of this.

"If you've quite finished," I say, staring back, and Quivel's face disappears. There's a furious whispering behind the screen. I make out the words, "Master'll have to see," then there's silence. I move my legs in the water. Even the bits of me I can see aren't pretty. My legs and feet are bruised and scabby, one toenail's ripped off and my hands look like I've dug up a field without a shovel. Feels strange sitting in the water and I'm just wondering when to get out when Bung reappears and tips a jugful of water over my head, just like that!

"*OW!*" I roar.

"Does it hurt?" he says.

"No," I say, surprised.

"Well, this one might," he says, and another jugful comes pouring down.

I sit there, holding my breath with my eyes closed tight while they pour one jug after another over me. Feels like they're trying to wash me away. When it stops I say, "Can I get out now?" and Bung hands me a towel. I stand up carefully, draping it round me, and over the screen there's a clean nightgown.

My legs feel wobbly and weak, but somehow I pull the nightgown on and climb back into bed. All I want to do is sleep.

When I wake up it's dark, except for a little lamp shining in the corner. I can hear the sounds of the city through the window but they seem far away.

My skin feels different, soft. As I lie there memories come flooding back, of Queenie and Pigeon, Lookout and Half-moon. Not happy memories. And there's a gap in them because I don't know how I got here.

Then I hear another sound, a quiet *tap-tapping* along the hall outside. *Tap-tap-tap-tap*—coming my way. I glance round the room but there's nowhere to hide. Except under the bed, of course, and I'm just thinking about diving under when the door creaks open.

In comes a man I know instantly must be the master of the house. Dark blue waistcoat and silver hair. There's a watch chain from his pocket like many a one I've nicked in my time, and he carries a cane with a dog's head for a handle. He says nothing to me but crosses to the chair by the lamp and sits down, propping his stick on the chair arm. Then he pushes his gold-rimmed glasses farther up his nose.

"My name is Sheridan Mosley," he says. His voice is higher than I thought it would be and he talks funny, not like me. "What is your name?"

I think back over all the names I've had. "Dodger," I say.

He makes a noise that might have been a laugh. "That is not a name," he says. "Do you have no other?"

I shake my head, watching him. His eyes are a bright, light blue and his face pink and white despite the silver hair.

"Well then, I shall call you Nathaniel," he says, "Nat, if you prefer," and I think of objecting but then I think, so what? Just one more name to add to the list.

"How did I get here?" I ask.

"You were fortunate in that I ran into Dr. Kay, quite by chance. He told me there was a new child in the hospital who did not have cholera, and that he wasn't sure what to do with you. I said you could come here."

He pinches snuff delicately with his long fingers.

"Now I have to ask you the same question," he says, and I look at him blankly. "How *did* you get here? Tell me your story, Nat."

25

Doctor

Tell him my story? I've never told anyone my story. Suppose I tell him about the workhouse and he sends me right back? Yet somehow here, in his house, in his bed, I feel like I haven't a choice. He could send me there anyway, I realize. Besides, I'm too weak to make anything up. I'm all out of ideas.

So I start telling him, about being left at the workhouse, and sent from there to Bent Edge Farm. I make the escape as exciting as possible, and tell him about Travis showing me how to use a sling. Then I tell him about the forest and how creepy it was, and Dog-woman, and telling stories at the inn, and Barnaby trying to sell us at market, and about the traveling fair.

Of course, I dress some bits up and leave out others, but I make a grand tale of it and I've not even had any ale. My escapes are more heroic and I'm more of a star at the fair. I skip the bit about selling Annie and when I get to living on the streets, there's not much I can say at all. Don't want him calling the police on me.

"So one by one the others were falling sick," I tell him, "and I hit on the idea of taking Pigeon to hospital. I were just waiting around to see the doctor when I fell ill myself. And now . . . here I am."

I finish lamely, and even to my own ears the story sounds strange. But Mr. M.'s leaning back with his eyes closed and fingers still pressed together. He says nothing and I can't tell what he's thinking.

The silence goes on for so long, I'm about to speak, when there's a knock at the door and the little maid enters.

"If you please, sir, the doctor's here," she says, and Mr. M. gets up immediately.

"Show him in, show him in," he says.

In comes the doctor, smiling and looking worried at the same time.

"And how's our patient today?" he says, asking Mr. M., not me.

"Oh, very much better," says Mr. M. "He's just been telling me the story of his life. And a fascinating tale it is too. Told with flair." Then just as I'm feeling pleased with myself he adds in a lower voice, "I think the fever might have inflamed his imagination."

Well, I like that! I think. I tell the God's honest truth for the first time in my life and he doesn't believe me! I may have dressed it up a bit, but it all happened. *That'll teach me*, I'm thinking.

Doctor comes over and starts prodding me about and I say, "Ow," at intervals. Then he looks down my mouth again. Don't know what he thinks he'll find there. Maybe he's after my teeth. He puts the funny cold thing on my chest again and listens. I wasn't going to speak to either of them, since they won't believe me anyway, but there's something I need to know.

"Please, sir," I say, "how's Pigeon?"

He looks at me blankly.

"The girl we brought to the hospital," I say, and my heart's in my mouth in case he tells me she's died.

"The little white-haired girl?" he says. "She's gone now."

My stomach gives a great lurch and I think I might be sick again, but he says, "Her sisters came for her. She wasn't fully recovered but they insisted they had to take her home."

Her sisters? I think, and he must have seen the blank look on my face for he says, "One of them had a great hat on with feathers."

Bonnet, I think, *and Queenie*. I close my eyes.

"They assured me she'd be well looked after and that they'd moved from the place they were staying, which was just as well. These cellars aren't fit for rats. I sent the men round with some chloride of lime to get rid of any infection. . . . If only we could teach the poor about sanitation," he says to Mr. Mosley, "half the problems of Manchester would be solved."

I'm not listening. *So Pigeon's with Queenie and Bonnet now*, I think, *and they'll all be with Bailey. And I'm here.* I open my eyes.

"How long have I been here?" I ask, and the doctor looks at Mr. Mosley again.

"Best part of a week?" he says, and Mosley nods.

A week! I'm thinking. *They'll all have forgotten me by now. Moved on. And I can't join them.* But the doctor's talking again.

"I think the main thing is to get some food down you now," he says. "Are you hungry?"

"Starving," I say, and Mr. M. rings a bell. Soon Quivel appears, looking very bad tempered, and when the doctor tells her to prepare some food for me, she looks more bad tempered than ever.

"If you please, sir," she says. "He's not keeping anything down. I don't know how many times I've changed the sheets."

"Well, we have to keep trying," the doctor says mildly. Quivel doesn't move.

"I just hope what he's got's not catching," she says. "I can do without catching cholera at my time of life."

The doctor frowns. "Cholera isn't catching, as far as we know," he says. "And in any case, he hasn't got cholera. The worst you could catch from him is malnutrition. And," he says, eyeing her stout form, "you're unlikely to catch that."

Quivel stumps off grumpily. Mr. M. catches me smirking and I expect him to be cross, but he just smiles back. He chats to the doctor for a while about boring stuff like drains. Both of them seem to have forgotten I'm here.

I gaze round the room. There's a portrait on the wall of a stern-looking man, and silver candlesticks on a dresser with the china bowl. There's a vase with flowers and a gold clock with angels, and a black, carved statue of a foreign-looking gentleman with a fat stomach. *There's lots of stuff I could nick here*, I think, and then I think, *but where would I take it?*

When Quivel comes in she makes a great show of spreading towels all over the bed. She holds the spoon out to me, standing well back.

"Well, I think I'd better be going," the doctor says, and both he and Mr. M. stand.

"I'll leave you to it, Mrs. Quivel," Mr. M. says.

When they've gone, I half expect her to start beating me about the head with the ladle, but she just stands like a soldier at the side of my bed, staring angrily at some point above my head.

This time I keep it all down, and sink back exhausted as she clears it away. She leaves the towels, though, just in case, and pulls a bowl out from under the bed. More pot angels.

"Try and aim at that, will you?" she says crossly before stumping off. Then she leaves me to think my own thoughts and watch the shadows from the window flicker about the room. I've got a lot of thoughts, but none of them seem to lead anywhere. Seems like I'm safe here, for the time being, but soon I'll have to leave. And I don't know where I'll go, or what I'll do when I get there. Seems like I've lost everything I started out with, and I feel a bit sick when I think about it. I've lost Annie—I got rid of her to be with the gang, and now I've lost them, so what's next? That's the biggest thought I've got, and I don't know what to do with it. Keeps coming back, though, like the chiming of a bell. *What next?* it chimes. *What next, what next?*

26

Visitors

What do rich people do with their lives? Blowed if I know. On the streets there was always something to do, something to nick, someone to run away from. And the fighting, of course. Great fighting, with lots of blood.

There's none of that here. The little maid comes in maybe three or four times a day with food, which is good, of course, and more than I've ever eaten. Once or twice I try to get her to talk.

"What's your name?"

"Milly," she says.

"My name's Nat now," I say, and she nods and smiles. "How old are you?"

"Thirteen," she says, and looks at me shyly. "How old are you?"

"Fourteen," I say, and she shoots me a look. "Or thereabouts," I add. "Do you live here?" But she only nods and clears away the dishes quick.

Next time I ask her, "What's up with your eye?" because she's squinting, and she puts up a hand to her face. I feel sorry for her suddenly.

"Mrs. Quivel says it's a lazy eye," she says, and from the look on her face I know she doesn't like Quivel any more than I do.

"How long have you lived here?" I ask her, but there's Quivel's step on the stair and she disappears. It dawns on me that she's been told not to talk. I do find out, though, that her family live in a village a long way off. The last time she saw them she had seven younger brothers and sisters.

"Father's ill," she says, "from working in the mine. That's why we all had to look for work." Her chin trembles and I feel sorry for her again. Don't know why. It's not like I'm better off.

Her younger brother's in the mine as well, and there's another sister in service. That's all there's time to say, though, because Quivel's always hanging about, like she's got nothing better to do. Sometimes she comes in, looking about like she'd like to bite something, but she only swats at a fly and leaves again.

In between times the clock ticks by slowly, slowly, and I just lie back, thinking about leaving, wondering where I'll go. I wonder what Digger's doing now. And Annie.

There's too much time to think, if you ask me. Good job I don't cry.

In the evening Mr. M. pays a visit.

"Please, sir," I say, "where are my clothes?"

He arches an eyebrow. Good trick that.

"Clothes?" he says.

I pluck at the nightgown. "Well, I din't come here in this."

"If you're referring to the rags that you were wearing, I'm afraid they had to be burned. We couldn't be sure, you see, that you weren't carrying any infection."

I stare at him, horrified. "Them were good trousers," I say. "And the hat were nearly new!"

"We kept the hat," he says, "though I had it cleaned."

That's not much comfort. I'll look a right wally on the streets in a nightgown and hat. "But sir," I say. "How will I leave?"

There goes the eyebrow again. "Leave?" he says. "Is there somewhere you need to go?"

"No, but—"

"But?"

"Well . . . I can't stay here forever, can I?"

Mr. M. smiles, settling himself back in his chair. "I wouldn't worry about that, if I were you. You can stay here for as long as it takes."

I shake my head. "What takes?"

"For you to get better of course. You're still very weak. But if you're worried about clothes, I'll have my tailor measure you up in the morning."

"How much'll that cost?" I ask, and he makes the small sound that passes with him for a laugh.

"I wouldn't worry about that," he says again, and he takes out a newspaper and starts to read to me.

Conversation over. I lie back and stare at the ceiling as he starts reading about something called a Reform Bill, and a Factory Act, but I'm not listening.

I'm trapped, I'm thinking. No money, nowhere to go and no clothes, not even my trousers. *I had a coin in them pockets*, I think, giving him a hard stare, but somehow I can't bring myself to say it. After all, I probably owe him that much and more.

He sees I'm not listening and folds the paper. "Shall I leave it with you?" he asks.

I shake my head. "Can't read," I tell him, and for no reason there's a gleam in his eye.

"Would you like to learn?" he says.

Would I? I'm speechless and can only nod.

"Well, I think that can be arranged," he says.

"What . . . you mean it?"

Steady on, Dodger, I tell myself. *No need to go falling all over him.*

He gets up. "That's something else that can be arranged in the morning," he says. "But I think you've had enough excitement for one day."

Yeah, sure. It's thrilling, lying here.

He smiles, as if he knows what I'm thinking. "I'll tell Milly to put out the lamp," he says, and leaves.

Like you couldn't do it yourself, I'm thinking. That's the thing about rich folk—they never do owt for themselves.

"Oh," he says at the door, "there may be one or two visitors for you as well," and he vanishes—but it's as if his smile's still hovering in the room, waiting to pounce.

Now why should I think of it like that? I mean, I owe the man my life. He's taken me in, fed me, and even if he did burn my clothes he's having more made. And reading! I'm finally going to learn to read! That's enough to keep me here without complaining. That's a reason to stay, if ever there was one.

Yet still underneath all these happy thoughts, there's a small worried one buzzing away. I try stamping on it but it just comes back like a fly round the big bin that's my brain. *Don't trust him*, it says. And why it should say that, I don't know. Because nobody in my life has ever been this good to me—not even Travis.

That night I dream about Dog-woman again, prowling restlessly through all the rooms of the house. And I follow her but I can't speak. And when I get to the kitchen, there's Travis, sitting at the table. There's food spread in front of him, but on the table itself, not on a plate, and he looks as if he doesn't know what to do with it. Somewhere in the background there's Quivel, humming like a great fat bee.

Travis picks up a knife and puts it down again. Then he picks up a fork. He doesn't know what to do and I can't tell him. He can't even see me. He drops the fork and his head sinks into his hands. Then I wake up.

It's morning and my head aches. Milly's pulling back the curtains. "Mrs. Quivel says you have to have a wash," she says.

"*Again?*" I'm outraged. But Quivel comes in and sets about me herself, with the bowl and a little towel, scrubbing hard behind my ears. I mean—how dirty can they have got since my bath?

All the same, I put up with it, because today's the day I might start learning to read.

Milly brings breakfast. An egg in a silver cup. I pick it up.

"*Use the spoon, boy!*" Quivel thunders, and timidly Milly shows me how to tap the top of it, then take the top off.

I eat while Milly dusts and Quivel glares. That seems to be the main thing she's good at, glaring.

Then after breakfast, a visitor's announced. Mr. M. brings him up himself. "Mr. Silver, my tailor," he says.

Little man, big nose. I have to get out of bed while he measures my height (four foot six) and round my chest (nineteen inches) and up my legs. "Watchit," I say.

"The young sir would like me to make a suit for an elephant, maybe?" he says. "Or a dancing bear?" He fixes me with eyes hardly higher than my own.

"No," I say, and let him get on with it. Though it doesn't seem dignified. Can't believe Mr. M. has to go through all this palaver for his clothes. Fact is, I can't believe any of it at all. Feels like I'll wake up soon, back in the den with Queenie.

He takes a lot of measurements while I try not to sigh and shift about. He writes them all down, muttering to himself. Mr. M. watches me with half a smile on his face. Glad I'm good for something, if only to keep him amused.

"Now for the cloth," he says, picking up a book full of material. He shows Mr. M. the samples, rather than me, while I stand there like a dummy. Mr. M.'s wearing purple with a waistcoat in like a pale pink silk, and he seems to be picking the same for me. *No way*, I'm thinking.

"The cerise," says Mr. Silver, "and a coral lining."

"Excuse me," I say. I put my hand out and Silver snatches the book away. "Now just hold on," I say. "I'm the one who's going to be wearing this getup, right?"

Silver stares at me like an offended hen. Mr. M.'s eyebrow shoots up, but he says, "No, no, the boy is right." He waves his hand at Silver, who can hardly believe his ears, and sits himself down in the chair.

"Right," I say. "Hand it over."

Silver looks like he knows what he'd like to do with the book and me, but he says, "I will handle the samples, please." And still looking outraged, he holds the book up toward me and turns the pages.

"That'll do," I say, when he comes to one that's dark green, like the forest.

"And the waistcoat?"

For the waistcoat I'm torn between gold and a pale blue-green, finally settling on the last.

"Very good," says Mr. Silver, after Mr. M. nods at him. "Tomorrow we make a fitting, yes?"

Mr. M. shows the tailor out. And I'm tired already, though I've done nowt, so I crawl back into bed. But I've hardly closed my eyes, or so it seems, when I hear voices outside my door again.

"Mr. Mosley, you are too too kind!" says the voice, and then the door opens.

Come right in, I'm thinking. *Don't mind me.*

A plump woman comes in and I have to stare. She's all done up in pale blue silk, with ruffles at the neck and blue ribbons gathering up her ringlets into big bunches. Her face is pink and white, like a doll's, but as she gets closer I see that it's painted on and there are lots of lines beneath the paint, like cracks in a pot.

"More than kind," she's still saying. "Kindness itself." She comes right up to me and peers down with her watery blue eyes. "And how is our little patient today?" She beams, nodding so that all the ringlets quiver and bob.

I mutter something, looking away. I wish I had my clothes.

"This is Miss Chitters," says Mr. M., looking pleased with himself. "She teaches the Sunday school at the Cross Street Chapel, and has graciously consented to teach you for one hour every morning."

"In return for a very handsome donation to our Little Helpers of the Poor," Miss Chitters puts in, beaming and wagging her head. Then from her large flowery bag she draws out a book with a picture on the front, and despite myself I'm craning to see. Mr. M. draws up a chair, then goes and sits in his usual place, watching us.

"And have you had any kind of instruction before?" Miss Chitters asks. She speaks slowly and clearly as though I might be deaf. I shake my head. Don't want to go into all that stuff about the workhouse.

She holds the book up, but away from me. "And what would you say the true purpose of learning to read is?" she says, wagging her head again.

That throws me. I think back to all the books I've seen that I haven't been able to read, to the stories about giants and dragons, then to Barnaby Bentnose telling us about how you can be hanged for trespassing.

She's still waiting.

"So I won't be hanged?" I say. She looks a bit shocked by this, then laughs merrily and Mr. M. smiles. I feel myself going red.

"Goodness," she says. "I hope it hasn't come to that yet. A lack of education may cost you many things, but in this country at least one cannot be hanged for it."

Not what I've heard. But she lowers her jiggling ringlets toward me and raises her eyebrows. "Shall I tell you the true purpose of reading?" she says.

How old does she think I am?

"The true purpose of learning to read," she says solemnly when I don't reply, "is so that you can receive the Word of the Lord. Now, can you say that after me?"

I'm blushing scarlet now, glaring down at the bedspread. But she's waiting and something tells me she can wait a long time. There's something unbending in her, in spite of the ribbons and frills, and I groan inwardly but mutter the words.

"That's right," she says, satisfied. "I think we're going to get along famously. Now—" She puts the book down on the bed and turns to the first page. There's a picture of an angel on it, but not like the ones I imagined when Travis told his tale. Don't look much like Queenie's gang neither.

This one's got golden curls like Miss Chitters and a flowing nightgown like me. He holds a book in one hand but he's not looking at it—his eyes are raised to the sky. *Perhaps he's bored with it*, I'm thinking, but Chitters says, "Notice how the book is open but his eyes are raised heavenward, because he receives the Word of the Lord direct."

If you say so, I'm thinking.

"You can hear the sound of the letter in the word—*A* and *angel*, but here"—she turns the page and there's a picture of a man, a woman and a snake—"*a* makes the sound *a* in *apple*. Like the apple in the Garden of Eden. You know that story, surely?"

I nod, just to stop her telling it to me.

"Good," she says. "Now, can you think of any words that you might know that begin with *a* as in *angel*, or *a* as in *apple*?"

Is this a trick question? I have to think for a bit. " '*Anging*?" I say, though I know what the response'll be.

Mr. M. coughs and Miss C. looks at me reprovingly.

"The poor boy has had his head filled with the lowest kind of knowledge," she says to Mr. M. "It is high time indeed that he learned of higher things."

Mr. M. looks grave, yet I thought I caught him smiling. "But do you think you can teach him?" he says.

"I'm sure of it," she cries. "Miss Amelia Chitters is not one to take things on lightly, but when she does, she does not give them up. And not even the hardest heart is immune to the purest knowledge. Why, I've known even hardened criminals to weep when I read to them from this book!"

No doubt, I'm thinking.

"But, if I could ask one thing, my dear, kind Mr. Mosley?"

"Anything."

"Might we take our lessons unaccompanied? I feel sure that we would make more progress that way—and you must have other, more urgent business?"

Mr. M. looks as though he might disagree, but thinks better of it.

"Very well then, Miss Chitters. I'll leave the boy in your capable hands. But I should like to know how he's getting on."

"Depend upon it," Miss C. says. "After each session I shall make you a full report."

"Did you hear that, Nat?" Mr. M. says, getting up. "I hope to hear that you've been a model student—dutiful, industrious and grateful." He gives me a look.

"No doubt of it!" replies Miss C., saving me the trouble. "We'll work through the next half hour, and I'll come to you directly."

"Very well then," Mr. M. says, though he still shuffles about a bit, not wanting to leave. I'm not sure whether I'll prefer her without him or what. The minute he's gone she draws her chair up closer to the bed.

"*B* is for *Bible*," she says. "And *blessing*, which is what little children receive when they are brought to the Lord at *baptism*. Can you say *baptism*?"

"Miss Chitters," I say.

"You can call me ma'am."

"Ma'am," I say, "I don't know if you've had a word with the doctor, or owt, and I don't know what he's told you—but I've not gone daft."

She looks astonished at this, so I try to explain. "My body might be ill but there's nowt wrong with my head."

Miss Chitters takes a deep breath and closes her eyes. She picks up the book and for a second I think she might hit me with it, but she just says, "Nathaniel, have you ever tried to learn anything before?"

I think back to practicing with my sling. "Yes . . . ma'am."

"Good. Then you'll know all about starting at the beginning. Learning to walk before you can run?"

"Yes, but—"

"Then I want to hear no more about it. And just for this once"—she fixes me with blue eyes that are no longer watery, but like steel—"I will overlook your rudeness. *Just this once*. Do you hear me?"

I stare at her, astonished. *I can be a lot ruder than that*, I'm thinking, but her chins are wobbling in anger and I don't want a scene. And I still do want to learn to read, so I say, "Yes, ma'am," and try to look as though I'm studying the book.

"Good," she says, more calmly, and turns the page. "*B* is also for *brimstone*," she says.

It takes a long time because for each letter she tells me a Bible story. So that first session we get all the way to *D*.

"*D* is for—"

"*Dinner*," I say, hearing the trolley, and she laughs.

"You've learned something today at any rate," she says, and she gets up, tousling my hair. "I'll be back again at the same time tomorrow."

I try to look pleased. And wonder what she'll report to Mr. M.

Still, I am learning something, and that makes the time go faster. Especially since Miss C.'s not the only visitor. There's a regular stream of them, every day, from the Provident Society, and the Literary Club, the Sanitation Society and the Statistical Association, whatever they are. There's even one from the *Daily Herald*, who draws a picture of me lying in bed, with Mr. M. leaning over in a concerned way.

They all come by to have a good look at me, the invalid from the streets. And one thing they're all agreed on is, Mr. M.'s doing a wonderful thing.

"Oh, it's a wonderful thing that you're doing for that poor dear boy," say the Misses Plum, holding their handkerchiefs to their eyes. "A wonderful, wonderful thing." And they have to be shown out, quite overcome.

Some of them speak to me; others don't.

One day a very grand lady comes to visit. Very grand, very tall. She's introduced to me as Lady Shadbury. She sits on one side of the bed and Mr. M. on the other, but she addresses all her questions to him. Just like I'm not there. The conversation wanders on for a bit while I pick at a thread on the bedspread.

"So you found him—?"

"Dr. Kay found him, madam, although strictly speaking, he found Dr. Kay. Brought one of his little friends to the hospital. She was suffering from cholera."

Lady S. shudders delicately. "I hear the new hospitals are teeming with the poor wretches. And more where they came from, I shouldn't wonder. That's the trouble with the poor. They're so terribly . . . incontinent."

Two red spots appear on her cheeks. "And if only they'd learn the basic principles of sanitation, so much trouble would be spared. That's why I came to see you today, Mr. Mosley. To ask if you'd like to contribute to our little scheme."

Lady S.'s little scheme is to dole out free soap to the poor. Mr. M. listens politely, then he leans over toward me.

"What do you think of that, eh, Nat? Free soap to every household?"

Thought they'd forgotten about me. "Can they eat it?" I say, not meaning to be funny, but Mr. M. laughs and Lady S. looks considerably put out.

"One has to think *round* the situation," she says, still talking to Mr. M. "The problems of the poor cannot be solved by food alone."

Then there's a thin gent with narrow eyes and a long black beard. He's from the Statistical Association, and he sits with Mr. M. at the back of the room, discussing river pollution for a long time. Then the talk turns to overcrowding.

"Do you know," says the thin gent, leaning forward, "that the last figures reveal that in the worst areas of the town there are as many as three thousand individuals crammed into ninety houses. That's an average of over thirty per house."

He sits back and Mr. M. looks at me. "What about that, Nat?" he says. "Does that back up your experience?"

I think back to the teeming cellars by the river, and the one-room shacks. "Sounds about right," I say.

"No wonder there's dirt and disease," the thin gent says. "What's needed is some form of population control."

"Or better houses," I say, and they both look at me.

"Is that your considered opinion, Nat?" says Mr. M. "If we carry on building more and better houses, will the poor not simply breed more?"

I shrug. Though it does seem to me that the poor have lots more children than the rich. And why that is, I don't know.

"They need to be educated," says the thin man, "to have fewer children."

In his view, if they stop the poor having children, they solve a whole barrowload of problems in one go. Don't know how he thinks he'll manage that, though.

"If you have kids," I say, "they earn money for you. And there's more chance of being looked after when you're old."

"True," says the thin gent, looking at me through narrowed eyes. "But how if you can't support them? And what does the money go on, eh? Food, or drink?"

Then there's a short discussion of the evils of drink, how it leads to riots, and the possibility of closing the gin shops.

"That would cause riots," I say, butting in, and they look at me again. Seems like I'm expected to say more.

"If you take the five-shillings-a-week men," I say, "living in shacks by the river—what've they got but gin? What'll five shillings buy you?" I say, warming to my theme. "Maybe four loaves of bread? Or rent and two loaves. But my guess is, they skip the bread and the rent, and just buy gin."

"Exactly," says the thin man, as if I've just proved his point, which I haven't at all.

"But if you take the gin off them," I say, "what've they got then? Stone cold sober, they'll just realize what a bad deal they've got."

The thin man sucks in his cheeks and Mr. M. looks at me with a gleam in his eye. "I hadn't suspected you of being a radical philosopher, Nat."

"What's one of them?" I ask, and they both laugh, in a relieved kind of way, it seems to me.

I've had enough of them and I'm glad to see them go. But I am getting better. Between visitors I practice walking round the room, picking things up, a jeweled casket, the little fat man carved in black—heavier than I thought. And I look out of the window, onto Mosley Street, as I've been told this place is. Named after Mr. Mosley's family, no less.

It's a broad street, and fine carriages parade up and down it all day. At night the Blue Locusts patrol it—several of them, not just one. Which is funny, if you ask me, because in the streets by the river, or the rookeries, or the courts off Angel Meadow, where all the trouble is, you'd never catch one. Yet here they are in droves where there's no trouble at all. Protecting the rich from the poor.

Almost opposite the window is a grand building with great pillars and letters on the front: P-O-R-T-I-C-O. I asked Miss C. to spell it out for me, and she said it was a great library, full of books. That whole building, full of books! And that's something that Mr. M. does in the day. Every morning around ten he crosses the street and goes into the library, and sits reading for a couple of hours at least.

That's something the rich are good at, reading. That and sitting around discussing the poor. Hard to believe, really. When you think of all the poor going about their business, with no idea of how interesting they are. And just as poor as they ever were.

One day two gents come to visit: one tall and thin and fair, and the other one round and red-faced, with black eyes. Mr. M. introduces them as the brothers Grant, lawyers who have offices farther up Mosley Street. The little round red-faced one does all the talking, and each time he says something he laughs loudly, whether anyone else laughs or not.

"That's the spirit, Mosley—regenerate the urban poor, what? Ha ha!"

"More policing, that's what we need, more of the boys in blue, ha ha ha!"

I say nothing at all this time, even when he leans over and pinches my cheek and says, "Soon be up and joining the hunt, eh? Ha ha ha ha ha!"

As soon as they've gone I get up to stretch my legs. Then I hear them talking in lowered tones outside the door.

"So what's the scheme then, Mosley? Are you planning to adopt the lad?" And I prick up my ears, creeping closer.

"Not at all," says Mr. M. "I merely want to satisfy myself on a few points."

"Conducting an investigation, eh? Well, you want to be careful." And he says something else I can't hear, finishing with, "You can take the boy out of the workhouse, but can you take the workhouse out of the boy, eh? Never mind, Mosley, ha ha ha!"

Then they all go down the stairs, and I'm left wondering what they're going on about and why Mr. M. is keeping me here. I crane out of the window, watching them leave in a carriage, though they're only going farther up the street.

Time I was going too, I'm thinking. I've been here long enough, prodded and poked about and discussed. Time I was off, though I don't know where to. And I can't get far in my nightgown.

Then right on cue my new clothes arrive.

They're quality, I can tell that much. The feel of the cloth is like nothing I've felt before, the green dark and velvety, the blue shining like a peacock's tail. Before I can put them on I'm made to have a bath, which is mad, since I've already had one. Then Bung cuts my hair with a very bad grace, dragging the comb through it while I roar. He has to cut great chunks out of it that are matted, and when he's finally through Mr. Silver comes in and fusses and clucks over the fastenings and hems.

"Do you like them?" asks Mr. M.

"Can't see them, can I?" I say, and Mr. M. nods at Bung, who disappears then comes back, wheeling a long mirror.

This is the first time I've ever seen myself—apart from looking at my face in brasses and such. I've never seen the full picture, though, and now I can.

I don't recognize myself. I look small and white, with ginger stubble on my head. The fine clothes make me look like someone else. Like a sparrow in a peacock's clothes.

"Well?" says Mr. M.

I reach out a hand and touch my face in the mirror. *Whose are those small, scared eyes?* I'm thinking. *I don't look much like Jack the Giant-killer now.*

"Don't put your paws on the glass," says Bung, and I take my hand away.

"Will the clothes do?" says Mr. M., and I nod at him, speechless.

"Aren't you going to thank the master?" says Bung, and I do thank him, stumbling over my words. But they take that for me being overwhelmed. Which is true in a way, but not the way they think.

"Well," says Mr. M., looking satisfied, "I think it's about time we went out, don't you?"

27

Carriage

We go out in a big black carriage. Never been in one of these before and at first I'm nervous, remembering what we used to do to carriages in the gang.

But nothing like that happens. And it's nothing like the workhouse van, I can tell you that much. After the first rush of air on my face, which makes me feel weak, I'm helped up by a man all done up in livery. Then Mr. M.'s helped up too, because of his bad leg. We sit facing one another on seats covered in velvet, and the carriage gives a little jerk and we're off.

I hang out of the window, looking at all the buildings. Then the street opens out onto a broad field with a church in the middle.

"St. Peter's Church," says Mr. M. "It's best not to lean out too far," he adds, as I nearly catch my head on the gates. I sit back in, and he looks at me with that half smile on his face, both hands clasped round his cane.

"Where are we going?" I ask, and he tells me we're just taking the air.

"What happened to your leg?" I say, and the smile slips, as I meant it to.

He raises the eyebrow. "A childhood illness," he says, and it's clear he's not going to discuss it. That's one thing I've learned. The rich don't like you asking questions—though they ask enough themselves.

We travel along Oxford Street and apart from a few great houses it's as though we're in open country. Yet I know that behind the great houses there's Little Ireland, one of the poorest areas of all. Then we turn back, returning from a different direction past the new town hall, along King Street and toward the great Royal Exchange. I lean out again, foolishly thinking I might see someone I know.

Everything looks different from this angle. You're looking down on people for a start, and the crowds part in front of you. Not like being down there, pushing and shoving. And I can see right into the shops. There are governesses pushing prams and market traders shouting, and men with briefcases heading into the Exchange.

"My grandfather built that," says Mr. M., nodding toward the huge building.

"No way!" I say. "He must have been an important bloke then."

Mr. M. looks amused again. "You could say that," he says, and he starts telling me about his family.

Seems like the Mosleys *own* Manchester. That's how important they are. It was a Nicholas Mosley who bought it in 1596. I whistle, and Mr. M. looks stern. But I'm looking at him with new eyes.

"So, do you own it then?" I say, but he says his cousin Oswald owns most of it, and he lives in Ancoats Hall. Near where the fair was.

"I am really a very minor branch of the family," he says. And yet he owns that big house.

"Don't you have no children, sir?" I say, and again he shoots me a look.

"I never married," he says, and that's the end of that.

There must be two Manchesters, I'm thinking. *This one, with its broad streets and grand buildings and carriages, and the one where I used to live.*

Can't get the two of them to come together. Seems like the rich can travel around Manchester all they like, without ever seeing the poor. And I fall quiet for a while thinking, *I don't know my way around here. And even if I did, where could I go, dressed like this? People notice you in gear like this. You're expected to belong somewhere.*

That night we eat in the same room, at opposite ends of a great polished table.

He shakes out his napkin and lays it across his knee, then waits while I do the same. "Now, Nat," he says. "Let's see how well your reasoning and deduction can be applied to food."

He teaches me about knives and forks, which ones for which course, where the drink is poured and how to think of my plate as a perfect circle, divided between meat and three kinds of veg. I can't help thinking that the rich make it hard for themselves, when they could just pick up the plate and slurp, but I do as I'm told. *The better I behave the sooner I'll be out of here*, I think, and then I ask him straight. "Why are you keeping me here?"

He unfolds his napkin before he replies and dabbles his fingers in a dish of water. "Don't you like being here?"

"I'm just wondering, that's all."

Mr. M. gives a thin smile. Then he leans forward. "Nathaniel," says he. "What in your opinion is the worst problem facing the poor?"

That's easy. "Poverty," I say right off.

He doesn't laugh. "But there are those who say that drink causes poverty."

"No," I say doggedly. "Not having money causes poverty."

"What about education?" he says, wiping his mouth.

"What about it?"

"Do people not need to be educated before having money? So that they spend it more wisely?"

Still I say nothing. Seems to me there's a hole in the argument somewhere, but I can't see where.

He sits back and raises his glass. "Of course there are people," he says, "who believe that you cannot educate the poor—that they will always revert to a brutish condition. There are, even now, scientific papers that suggest that the ancestors of mankind may not be Adam and Eve, but a little lower. Animals, for instance."

He's talking with his mouth full again. Full of big words. But I get the idea and laugh at him. "That's crazy!"

He smiles. "Certainly I do not think it could be applied to *all* members of the human race," he says.

"You mean, not to you," I say, but he doesn't answer that one.

"The difference between man and animals is that mankind can be educated," he says. "If the poor can be educated, then something can be done for them. It would be the moral duty of the wealthy classes to do it."

Suddenly I see what he's getting at. "What am I then? Your big experiment?"

"I wouldn't put it quite like that."

"Sounds like it to me."

He sighs, not looking at me. "Children who are left to fend for themselves grow into feckless adults. Who in turn produce more children."

I give up trying to understand him. "So what have you got in mind then? For me, I mean?"

"I haven't decided quite what to do with you yet."

Don't like the sound of that.

"So, you're not going to send me to the workhouse then?"

"The workhouses are already teeming. Other solutions have to be found. There is a great deal of interest in Manchester in the problem of the poor. Different bodies and charitable concerns have put forward different proposals. It remains to draw all these together and come up with a single, workable solution, if possible."

"The problem of the poor," I say, as if chewing it over.

"Pardon?"

"You said the *problem* of the poor. Not the *problems*."

Mr. M. looks a bit ruffled by this.

"Semantics," he says, carving himself an extra piece of meat, and since I don't know what he means, I can't argue.

When I leave him that night I think to myself, *I'm not staying here to play your game, mister. I can leave anytime I like!* But quick as wink the thought comes, *Not in these clothes, you can't.*

28

Hat

All the days go by exactly the same. Miss C. moves me off the alphabet and on to *Little Lessons for Little People*, spelling out words, and putting words into sentences, like *T-H-E P-O-O-R A-R-E A-L-W-A-Y-S W-I-T-H U-S*.

At the end of the lesson she says, "Now I want you to sit there awhile, Nathaniel, and reflect upon your sins."

"What for?" I say, thinking, *How much time does she think I've got?*

Miss C. looks disapproving. "Because it is something that the well-brought-up child must do, Nathaniel. It is an important part of a moral ed-ucation."

I know better than to argue by now, so I stare at the little table and try to look guilty while I think about food, and Miss C. mutters a prayer.

"Very well, Nathaniel," she says, like she knows what I'm thinking about. "I will return in the morning."

Thing is, I do feel bad, but not about anything she'd understand. I feel bad about Annie. Sometimes I dream that I'm carrying her, and her arms are round my neck. One night I dream that she's staring at me from the win-dow of Mother Sprike's house. I wake up and lie with my cheek pressed against the pillow, thinking of all the times we lay together. If I close my eyes I can feel her hair on my face. Sometimes I just stare out of the window, at the rain making circles on the pavement, and wonder what she's doing now. But even if I went back and found her, the problem's the same. Where would we go?

Once I start thinking about Annie, though, there's no stopping. So I try not to start. There's other things to think about.

Why am I still here? There's nothing keeping me here, I'm not a prisoner. And I'm fed up with lessons. I should leave, and try to find Queenie, or Digger.

But they don't want you, my thoughts say, and *You're learning to read* and *You're getting good food.*

Feels like I've handcuffed myself to good food and a bed.

Mr. M. teaches me numbers himself, and I get on all right, better than with reading and better than Mr. M. expects. I can add up well enough, and divide. In the workhouse, I used to have this scam going, that the littl'uns gave me a portion of their food in return for protection from some of the older lads and some of the men, and if they were good or did me a favor, I'd give them a portion back. So that way I learned adding, subtracting and division.

Even so, it's hard going because we work right through till tea, and by the end of the lesson I'm completely cheesed off and my head's aching.

"Perhaps you'd like another drive out?" Mr. M. says as we eat, and I look at him sullenly.

"Where's my hat?" I ask.

Up goes the eyebrow. "Your hat?" he says.

"Yeah, you know. Thing that goes on top of your head." And when he doesn't answer I say, "You said you'd kept it, remember?"

"Yes, of course," he says. "But I hardly think it'll go with those clothes."

"I want it back," I tell him.

For a minute I think he'll tell me off for being rude or ungrateful, but he only shrugs and says, "Very well, I'll have it sent up to you in the morning."

And in the morning, there it is! Mrs. Quivel hands it to me like it's something she's just stepped in. "Master said you wanted this," she says, wrinkling her nose. I seize it in delight. It's all been cleaned up brand-new, though there are still shiny, greenish patches on it.

Soon as she's gone I put it on and strut about, feeling like Dodger again. Then I put my new clothes on and turn about, trying to see myself in the polished wood of the wardrobe.

Milly comes in with tea on a tray. "Hey, Mil, what do you think?" I say, and she nods and smiles, but I notice that her eyes are red.

"What's up?" I ask, and at first she won't tell me.

Then she says, "Father's ill again, really poorly. And I can't go to see him."

"Have you asked?"

"Of course I've asked," she says hotly. "But Mrs. Quivel says—" She stops and presses her lips together as Quivel herself appears, arms folded.

"Laundry's waiting," Quivel says, and shuts her mouth up like a trap.

Milly goes, but reappears an hour later. "Mil," I say. "How can I get out?"

"Out?" she says, looking scared.

"Out on the streets," I say. "Just for a walk around."

Milly plumps up the pillows on my bed. "All the doors are locked," she says.

"What—all the time?" She doesn't say anything to this, so I ask her, "Don't you ever go out?"

Milly shakes her head, and there, like magic, is Quivel again.

"I don't recall saying as there'd be time for idle chat," she says.

I glare at her, thinking, *I'll not be taking orders from you for much longer, you old hag.* But Milly goes with her meekly.

Then Miss C. arrives but I can't concentrate on my lessons. All the time I'm thinking, *All the doors locked!* And I get quite snappy with her, so that she makes me copy out *T-H-E M-E-E-K S-H-A-L-L I-N-H-E-R-I-T T-H-E E-A-R-T-H* ten times.

Over tea I ask Mr. M., "Don't you ever go for a stroll about?"

"How do you mean?"

"You know, a walk. Stretch your legs." As I say it I remember he's got one leg lame.

I could kick myself, but all he says is, "If I want to take the air I go out in my carriage."

"Yeah, I know, but . . . it's not the same, is it?"

"Why not?"

"I miss having a walk."

"Do you?"

"Perhaps I could go out one time, on my own?"

"I hardly think that would be wise."

"You can't keep me here—I'm not your prisoner."

"Certainly you are not," says Mr. M. "But wandering about the streets led to the mess you were in when you were brought here. You of all people should know that the streets aren't safe."

I go on at him then, about how it'd be different now, but all he'll say is, "Perhaps when you are well enough, we'll see." And he won't be budged.

That night we go out in the carriage again. Past St. Peter's Church we go, turning right along Peter Street to Deansgate. I'm working out the street signs as we go, and I can actually read them! Doesn't help, though. In some funny way it's distracting. Seems like I knew the area better when I couldn't read the names of the streets.

I keep peering out of the window, hoping to catch sight of someone, anyone, I know. There's a flash of striped material on a corner, but it isn't Queenie. Even the street sellers look different, like the whole world's changed while I've been cooped up with Mr. M. And I think to myself, *I could push the door open now and jump out and run*, but still the thought comes to me, *Where to, in these clothes?* Scallies'd have me stripped to the bones before you could say "cravat." So I sit back and drum my heels on the wood.

"See anyone you know?" says Mr. M., like he's been reading my mind.

"No," I say shortly, and for the rest of the journey he doesn't talk and I don't either. We just glide through the streets, and I have a funny feeling, like I'm dead and traveling in a hearse. *That's it*, I tell myself, loosening my collar. *I'm getting out.*

That night I get into bed in my clothes, and wait until the house is silent, then open the door of my room. All's quiet as I creep downstairs, and I nearly jump out of my skin when the clock chimes. But no one comes, and the carpet's so thick that the stairs don't even creak when I go past.

There's four floors to this house, and a long line of portraits going down with the stairs. I can tell they're all Mr. M.'s family, because they look just like him and their eyes follow you just like his.

Mr. M.'s study is two floors down. I put my ear to the door. All's silent, so I try the handle. Locked.

Just out of curiosity I try the next handle along. That's locked as well.

A hard house to nick stuff from, I'm thinking, and it comes to me that maybe that's what they're thinking, that I'll nick stuff, and even though I was going to have a bit of a look about for something I could take with me, I feel insulted.

I go all the way to the ground floor without trying any more doors, because I don't know who sleeps where. There's a curtain across the main door, and when I pull it back I feel a furious disappointment. It's bolted, of course, top and bottom, but I could pull those back. Problem is, there's three big locks—the door's locked outside *and* inside as well!

Down more stairs and along a passage to the kitchen. You have to cross the kitchen to get to the scullery door, but even the kitchen door's locked. With a sigh that comes from the bottom of my toes I turn round and head back up the stairs.

Second floor up I hear a noise, like a door clicking open, and I freeze, pressing myself back into the shadows. Footsteps draw near then go away

222 The Whispering Road

again. Slowly I unfreeze. Bung probably, doing a last check. My ears strain for further sounds. Nothing, but I know I've got to get back to my room fast.

I pull off my clothes and climb into bed, feeling the vastness of the room all around me. When I close my eyes I swear Annie's in the corner, not saying anything, just looking, and it comes to me then that I'm a prisoner, and I've not seen it before.

29

Woman

The next day I do badly again at all my lessons. I get a long sermon from Miss C., and when Mr. M. tries to teach me something about algebra, I throw my pen on the floor and sit hunched, waiting for him to beat me. But all he says is, "Dear me," and looks at me thoughtfully, with that eyebrow of his.

"Perhaps we should take some air," he says when I don't apologize, and out we go again, round Piccadilly Gardens.

It's a quiet, murky night, not dark yet, but seeming so because of the murk. Gas lamps blink their bleary eyes in the wind. In the big square that's Piccadilly a huge infirmary stands, which doubles as a madhouse, and the howls and shrieks from the back of this building are fearful to hear. All along the side of it there's stalls and barrows. One man selling little circles of black pudding, another herring, and an old woman wheeling a barrowful of oranges very slowly. There's posters up on the hospital walls: *100 shirt hands wanted. Ninepence a dozen for men's shirts, fourpence a dozen for boys'*.

We pass a woman who's walking with her head down and shawl wrapped round her. Light brown curls fly out from it as we make a breeze going past, then suddenly, from behind, there's a deafening howl.

"STOP!"

It's the woman. She's let go of her shawl and the light brown curls are whipping everywhere in the wind. She lifts up her finger and points.

"Where are my babies?" she howls. *"What have you done with them?"* And next thing she's loping toward us while everyone stops and stares.

Mr. M. bangs with his cane on the wall of the cab. "Drive on!" he barks. *"Drive!"*

And the driver pulls off at a cracking pace with the young woman still running behind.

"YOU STOLE MY CHILDREN!" she yells, still running after us, and I crane my head out of the window just in time to see a man coming out from the doorway of a shop and catching her. She's pulling away from him, but he's holding her back, trying to talk to her. There's a sign above the shop he came out of: ABEL HEYWOOD PRINTERS. That's all I have time to see before Mr. M. raps sharply on my knees with the cane.

"*Ow!*"

"Sit back in!" he says, more sharply than I've ever heard him speak before.

I stare at him. "What were all that about?"

Mr. M.'s lips are pressed together so tightly, they almost disappear. "I haven't the faintest idea."

He's lying.

"What was she saying about her children?" I ask him, and he purses his lips even tighter than before.

Then he says, "The woman is obviously deranged."

We pull past the front of the big splendid building that's the infirmary and asylum. Dome and pillars—you'd never guess what it housed.

"She's probably escaped from the asylum," he says more calmly as we leave the square.

No, she's not, I'm thinking. *She came out of the shirtmaker's.* A bit later I say to him, "What's that shop, where the man came out of?"

"What shop?"

"Abel Heywood—printers," I say, and he looks crosser than ever.

"That man," he says, "is a low-born criminal and thief." I look blank.

"He is the purveyor of scurrilous material," he says, and when I look blank again, adds, "he trades in scandal and blasphemy. He's been imprisoned in the New Bailey before now and will be again. He is a dangerous criminal, and the so-called paper he distributes is wholly illegal." And he snaps his mouth shut and won't say another word.

Well, I'm thinking as we pull up outside his house, *what's rattled your cage?*

Mil," I say, next time I see her. "You've got to help me."

She gives me a worried look. "Why?"

I sit down on the bed. "Is there any way out of the house?"

Milly looks more worried than ever. "I can't say." She gives the pillow a shake and makes to leave.

"Milly," I say. "I need to get out."

"What for?"

I can't tell her, can I? That I want to go to that printer's shop, and ask about that woman, and Mr. M.

"I just . . . I just want to meet someone."

She shakes her head. "Doors are locked."

"Who has the keys?"

"Mrs. Quivel."

"Can you get them?"

She looks really frightened now. "I dursn't!"

"Just for one night."

She shakes her head and picks up the jug and bowl.

"Milly," I say, desperate now. "You know how you feel, about not being able to see your father?"

Her eyes brighten with tears. I take a deep breath. "Well . . . the person I need to see is looking for her children. And . . . well, since the workhouse, I've been looking for my mother."

She draws in her breath sharply. It's not really a lie. As I say it, suddenly I believe it. I realize that it might, it just might, be true. Suppose she *is* my mother—in Manchester, making shirts, looking for her children? But the thought's too much for me, banging upward from my chest to my throat, and my knees feel weak, so I'm glad I'm sitting. I tell Milly about the woman who ran after the cab. I try to picture her face, to see if it looks like mine, or Annie's.

It's funny how you think you don't want a thing, then suddenly you know you do, more than anything.

Milly's eyes are open wide. I tell her a bit of my story and she sits on the bed next to me. I don't know how much she knows already—news travels through servants like a dose of salts—but she listens anyway and sits down on the bed next to me as she takes it in.

"So you see," I say to her, "I have to go."

Milly nods slowly.

From downstairs we hear Quivel's voice. "Milly?" Milly doesn't move.

"If I could just get out one time," I say. "I'd be back before anyone'd know it." *Or not*, I'm thinking, but I can't say that to her.

"Mil-ly!" says Quivel's voice again, and Milly starts to get up.

"Milly—please!"

"Tomorrow night," she says slowly. "After supper, I put the slops out at the scullery door."

I let all my breath out at once. "Thank you."

"At eight," she says, "but you mustn't be long."

"I won't be," I tell her.

Then Quivel's voice comes again. "*Milly!* Where've you got to, girl?" and Milly turns as we hear footsteps on the stairs.

Just in time I remember. I can't wear this posh gear on the streets. "Milly?" I say, and she turns again. "Suppose it's raining?"

It's been raining every night, and she takes the point. I can't get these clothes wringing wet. They'd never dry by the morning. Her eyes flicker up and down me once, then she nods. "I'll sort it," she says, and slips out of the room.

"Thank you," I whisper at her back.

All that night and all the next day, I'm on hot bricks. I get another sermon and a rap across the knuckles from Miss C., and fortunately Mr. M.'s out so

I eat tea in my room and don't have to do any maths. In the long hours after tea I pace up and down and stare out of the window, trying to remember the face of the woman on the street, trying to imagine that she looked like me or Annie, though I know how daft that is. But if she did, and she was our mum, then there'd be somewhere to take Annie. I'd go back to the traveling fair and say, "Sorry I've kept you waiting, Annie, but there's someone I'd like you to meet." And her face'd go all shiny with joy.

Soon as the little clock's striking eight I sneak downstairs, past the study, where I can hear Mr. M. moving about, down again, and down once more till I'm standing near the kitchen. And I can hear Bung and Quivel inside.

"Put your feet up, Mr. Bung," Quivel's saying, in quite a different tone from the one she uses for Milly. "Try some of this. If you don't want it, work'ouse'll have it." Then Bung says something and they laugh.

The only way to the scullery that I know of is through the kitchen.

Just as I'm thinking I'm trapped, a door I hadn't noticed before opens and Milly's face appears, white as a ghost. She beckons and I follow, down another short flight of stairs to a narrow, cluttered passage with a door at the end.

Milly puts her hand on the latch and turns to me. "You won't be long, will you?"

"I'll be back before you know it."

She hesitates then passes me a bundle. "This was in the laundry," she says. It's an old coat, big and brown and stained. I slip it on and it falls to the floor, just covering my boots. I roll the sleeves back.

"It's Bung's," she whispers. "He uses it for the dirty jobs. But I thought it'd cover you if it rains."

"Thanks, Mil," I say. With this and the hat I'm near perfectly covered, and disguised.

She puts her other hand on my arm. "You will come back, won't you?"

"Course I will," I say.

"I'll get into terrible trouble—" she says.

I don't want to come back but I can't leave Milly in trouble. I put my hand over hers. "Don't worry, no one'll notice I've gone."

She brushes away tears. "I'll leave the door—but I have to lock it last thing. Oh, don't be late!"

I try to comfort her the best I can, then slip out into the street.

Soon as I'm in all the bustle and scurry I feel better. My lungs swell up, taking in all the dirty air. I'm on my way through the backstreets to Piccadilly Gardens, and the shop on Oldham Street.

Just behind Piccadilly, which is as posh as can be, there's a maze of courts and alleys, like a rabbit warren. Each yard's a funnier shape than the last. And over all of them hangs a stinking smoke—a stink my nose recognizes right away, though having been out of it for so long, it seems overpowering. It's the stink of rotting things turfed out of houses, and burst sewers and fatty meat broiling. And it's dark here, because the houses are piled closely to. Yet there's no one in the first court except for two drunks, man and woman, lying senseless, and one old dame behind a broken window, stirring a filthy brew and adding to the general stink.

Next courtyard's empty too, except for some pigs and hens. A cow sticks its matted, knobbly head out of a window and blinks the flies away. Its eyes look terrible, reddish, sore. Haunted by the memory of grass.

Where've all the people gone? I'm thinking. They can't all be in the gin shops. Then I hear it—the sounds of a crowd—some yelling and broken cheers as I plow through the alley.

A clog fight. Two women circling each other, shouting out names. From time to time one of them strikes out with the clogs on her feet, and the crowd roars them on. Time was I'd've hung around to watch, but now I've got a job to do. Into the next yard, where people are passing through and a little girl on a step is clasping a babby in her arms and asking everyone who passes, "Have you seen my ma?"

She looks no more than six or seven, very thin, with sores on her face and blank eyes. Makes me feel queasy somehow, like I've never seen it before. Living at Mr. M.'s has made me soft, I think, and I shrug my coat back on, because it keeps slipping off my shoulders, and plow on.

I tramp through the mire of the courts onto Oldham Street, and there, sure enough, is the shop. There are boards across the window and it looks shut. I glance round, then nip into the nearest alleyway, looking for the back of the shop.

The backyard gate's open a chink, though boxes are propped against it. I put my shoulder to it and push. The yard's full of crates and boxes, and the boxes are stuffed full of papers. I pick one up and hold it toward the light, which is fading fast. *T-H-E P-O-O-R M-A-N-S G-U* it says, and I can't read the rest of it. But there's lots more, closer print I can't read either. I can hear the noise of machinery inside, so I go right up to the door, which is painted a dull red, and give it a shove, and to my surprise it creaks open. There's no one here either. The noise of some kind of machinery's coming from below, somehow. There must be a cellar somewhere beneath my feet.

But in this room there's stacks and stacks of newspaper.

I'm peering so closely at the print, I don't hear anyone come up behind me, so I all but drop dead with fright when I'm grabbed and thrust farther into the shop and the door slams shut and I can hear the sound of bolts drawing. Then a voice speaks right in my ear.

"Who are you and what do you want?"

30

Caught

I say nowt, for it seems like the safest bet.

"Speak up—what's your name?"

Still I say nothing, and there's the sound of a match, then a lamp flares, lighting a long, bony face with a dark, raggedy beard and black, glittering eyes.

Dangerous criminal, I'm thinking.

"I'll not ask again," he says roughly. "State your name, and your business."

He sets the lamp down on the table. His fingers are covered in ink and he's wearing a printer's apron that's also stained with ink.

"Now, I can wait all night," he says in soft, dangerous tones. "But I'd just as soon not. So let's get this over and done with, shall we? Are you spying?"

"S-spying?" I say. I've got my stammer back.

"Who sent you here?"

"N-n-no one," I say, cursing myself. "P-please, sir, I s-saw you last night."

"Last night?" he says, frowning fiercely.

"Yes, sir—with a woman. She was running after a cab and crying out something—about her children."

I think it best at this point not to mention that I was in the cab. I can see from his face that he knows what I'm talking about, but he gives no other sign.

"Well? What of it?"

"I thought . . . I thought I might have . . . some information."

Don't know what makes me say that. Must be crazy. I'm staring down at my shoes now, wishing I hadn't spoken, wishing I was anywhere but here.

"Information? You?" he says, then when I say nothing he leans forward and says very softly, "What kind of information?"

"Sir," I say, looking up at him, then up again, for he's a tall, rangy kind of a fellow. "How many children has she lost? Were there . . ." And I pause and lick my lips, hardly willing to go on. "Two of them?"

I can see by his face that I'm right, and he nods slowly. "Boy and girl?" I say, and my heart starts thudding like a piston, and I look away, feared that he'll read all my hopes and fears on my face.

"How did you know that, boy?" he says, more gently now.

Seems like there's no choice but to tell him the foolishness of the thought that flared in my mind and has kept me awake ever since.

"Sir . . ." I say, and I can hardly get the words out. I stare down at my feet and try again. "She lost her children and I—we—lost a mother."

"But there's only one of you."

I shake my head. "I have a sister—but I've lost her as well."

I look up at him defiantly, half expecting him to laugh. *Bit careless, aren't you?* he could say but he doesn't, and he's not laughing.

"Older or younger?"

"Younger," I say, and he nods slowly and sits back on the edge of the table.

"What's your name, boy?"

I take a deep breath. "Joe," I say. "Joe—Sowerby." It's so long since I've said that name, it sounds strange in my ears.

But he's shaking his head. "That's not the name she told me," he says.

My stomach turns over and for a moment I feel the floor rushing toward me. He grabs my shoulder and sits me on a crate. "Steady on, lad," he says, not unkindly. "Have you eaten?"

I nod, speechless.

"Drink then," he says, looking round.

I wait while he finds a glass and fills it with water from a jug. For a moment I think of all the names I've ever given, and maybe she's not given her true name either, but I brush that thought away as daft. *Not if she's looking for her children*, I'm thinking.

I gulp the water down, and the shock of it clears my head. "What's her name?" I ask.

He's watching me with a thoughtful look on his face, like he doesn't know whether to tell me or not. Finally he says, "Nell," and my heartbeat quickens again. *Ellen—Nell*, I'm thinking. One of the women in the workhouse was called Ellen, but everyone called her Nelly.

"Sir?" I say.

"Abel," he says.

"Abel," I say. "The woman I saw—Nell—she was running after a cab—and shouting. She said that the man inside had stolen her children."

Abel's face darkens. "It's a long story, lad."

"Can I meet her?" I say.

The silence between us grows in the dark. I'm thinking, *No, he'll not let me.* Daft idea anyhow.

Then he picks up one of his own papers. "Do you know what this is?" he says, holding the paper up.

"The Poor Man's . . ."

"Guardian," he says, and he carries on from where I left off. " 'A Weekly Paper for the People, Published in Defiance of Law to Try the Power of Right Against Might.' Do you know what that means?"

I shake my head.

"It means that by the law of this country, this paper is illegal. Do you know why?"

More head shaking.

"Because the law of this country says a printed paper has to have a tax on it of fourpence or it can't be sold. Fourpence a copy! Then it has to be licensed and printed on a certain kind of paper. And you know what that means?"

I shrug.

"It means, Joe, lad, that working people, the very people I want to reach, can't afford it. It's a tax on knowledge, Joe, lad—a war on words!"

His face is lit up now and he shakes the paper at me. "Whereas if I print it myself, in secret, on the poorest paper, and distribute it myself, I can sell it at just a penny a time. So that's what I do, all in secret. And that's why my greeting was a little . . . rough. Do you understand?"

I nod slowly, looking at the paper. There aren't any pictures. "Do you print stories?" I ask suddenly, and he looks surprised.

"It's a newspaper, lad. Of course I print stories." He reads, *"Mr. Owen on the Distribution of Property. Immediate Extension of the Suffrage."*

"I mean, like Jack the Giant-killer and such. Tom Hickathrift."

He puts back his head and laughs suddenly, a short laugh, making me jump.

"Nay, lad, not those kind of stories. Real stories. About anything that affects the working man."

Not interesting ones, I'm thinking.

I drain the glass and remember Milly. "I'd best be getting back," I say, standing. He doesn't move.

"Maybe she can tell you herself," he says, and my stomach lurches all over again. "Come back here tomorrow evening and I'll see what I can do. I'm not promising anything, mind."

"I don't know if I can come back tomorrow," I say, and there's another silence. I want, more than anything, to see her now. Before I lose heart.

Abel sighs, then stands. "Wait here," he says, and my heart leaps up all over again. "I'll be two minutes," he says—and leaves me in the shop! Not that there's much worth pinching.

I put my hand out to one of the boxes, and snatch it back again, because it's shaking. *She'll recognize me from the cab*, I'm thinking, then I think that I don't care. I want to know what's going on. How Mr. M.'s involved, if at all. And to see her face again, up close.

Inside's much darker than out, because of the small window. I peer into the shadows of the yard, and sure enough I hear a noise. My stomach's hurting, worse than when I was sick. Abel pushes the gate open and I see a figure behind him, draped in a shawl. I stand back from the window, rubbing my sweating hands on my coat as the door opens.

"Joe Sowerby," he says, "this is Nell Dawkins."

The figure steps forward, pushing her shawl back, and a quantity of fair, curly hair falls out. My chest is so tight, I can hardly breathe. She steps right up to me, gazing earnestly into my face, and I stare back. Everything about her's pale—pale hair, pale eyes, pale skin—like she's been washed and all the colors have run. She's got a square chin and a small, hooked nose. She looks nothing like me. Or Annie.

And I can see the same thought flickering in her eyes; yearning and disappointment. She shakes her head, the slightest motion. "No," she breathes. Then suddenly her look turns sharp. "But I do know you," she says, and my heart gives a leap then goes on falling. "You were the lad . . . with him!" She stares at Abel and he looks back blankly. "He was in the cab with Mosley!"

On an impulse she tugs at my coat and it falls open, revealing all my finery. Light dawns on Abel's face, then swiftly darkens.

"He's no workhouse child!" says Nell, her voice turning shrill. "He's Mosley's spy!"

31

Nell

In the silence that follows I can count my heartbeats. Before I've got to three Abel's crossed the room and bolted the door. He turns, leaning against it with his arms folded. "You've got some explaining to do," he says.

As usual, when I need to, I can't say a thing.

"What's there to explain?" says Nell fiercely. "He's Mosley's boy!"

"I'm not!" I say.

"Well, what were you doing with him then? In these clothes?" She tugs at my waistcoat and I brush her hand away. "He'll report back to Mosley about the paper!"

"No, I won't!" This is like a nightmare where I can't get out what I want to say. "It's not what you think!"

"What is it then, lad?" says Abel, and his bony face is stern. "Speak up. We're listening."

I've no choice but to tell them then. I sink down onto a chair and I tell them everything. The most complete story so far. It includes Annie, though not the bit about selling her, and life on the streets, even the thieving. Then the cholera, and being taken in by Mr. Mosley. They're listening but I can't tell if they believe me or not.

"I don't believe you," says Nell when I've finished, and I drop my head onto my hand, for I've no way of proving any of it. "Why would he take you in? You come here, asking questions about me and Abel—you're his spy!"

"NO!" I say, too loudly.

Abel says, "Why do you think he took you in?"

"I don't know," I say, rubbing my forehead. "He's got these . . . ideas about poor people and whether you can educate them or not. He says some kind of solution has to be found."

Nell and Abel exchange a look. Then Abel says, "I believe you." He sifts through a bundle of papers, finally fishing one out. He holds it out to me. "What do you think this is, eh?"

I try to read the headline. "*M-A-N-C-H-E-S-T-E-R T-H-E F-E-U—*"

"Feudal City," he finishes for me. "That's the main story we've been running for months now—about how Manchester's still run like a village, with a manorial lord. And you know who the lords of the manor are, don't you?"

I nod. "The Mosleys."

"Right. The Mosleys own Manchester—and what they say goes. Which was all right, maybe, in the Middle Ages, but not now we're a thriving industrial town! Why, there's a hundred thousand more workers living here since the start of this century, and they create the wealth of the whole nation—right here in Manchester! But do they have a say in how the place is run? No. The whole system's rotten and has to change. We need elected councillors. Parliamentary representation. But naturally enough the Mosleys don't want that."

He pauses for breath, then sits on the table, facing me.

"The Mosleys are big on charity," he says quietly. "They're not all a bad lot. Sir Oswald Mosley, the actual lord, is the most philanthropic fellow I know. But they think if they throw charity at the poor it'll solve the problem. Because the poor are the biggest problem they've got. Prison and workhouses teeming, disease spreading like fire through the courts and alleys, and a crime rate second to none. The poor are swelling in numbers day by day, and that's the biggest proof there is that the old system's got to go. So the Mosleys and others like them are bent on finding other solutions to the problem."

Different solutions have to be found, Mr. M.'s voice says in my head. *A single workable solution if possible.*

"What do you mean?" I ask.

"I mean," says Abel, "that if the children of the poor can be placed out of the parishes, it takes a great strain off the workhouses and prisons. And the manorial lords."

I don't know what to make of all this. My head's aching. And I'm late. "I'll have to go," I mutter, standing.

Immediately Abel moves in front of the doorway, blocking it.

"Let me out!" I yell at him, furious now.

"Let him go, Abel," Nell says unexpectedly. "Let him go back to his master—and find out for himself what kind of man he is. No man at all but a monster! Trading in children and the lives of the poor! Let him find out what plans are laid for him!"

"What are you talking about?" I say rudely.

Abel says, "Mind your manners, lad."

"No, leave him," says Nell, and she sinks down, covering her face with her hands. "All this is talk. *Talk!*" she bursts out suddenly. "How is it helping me find my babies? How do I know if I'll ever find them again?"

"Shouldn't have left them then, should you?" I shout, and Abel grips my shoulder and shakes me hard, crying, "Watch your tongue!" But Nell's hands slide down her face and she looks at me with such horror in her eyes that all my anger melts away and I just feel bad.

"He's right," she says to Abel. "I should never have left them. The Lord forgive me for that—but he won't; he never will!"

And she rocks herself on the chair, her terrible eyes staring.

Abel gives my shoulder a shove. "Perhaps you'll listen to her story before passing judgment," he says, very cold.

"Let him go," says Nell.

"No," says Abel. "He can hear the full story before going back. Then he can make up his own mind."

For a long time no one says anything and Nell goes on rocking. Then she says, "I had a home once, and a family. My husband, Robert, he was a handloom weaver—but the big mills started replacing the handlooms and the weavers went down to two pence a day . . . two pence!" She stares at me as I take that in. "And soon there was no work at all. Poor Bob went out every day looking. And one day he went out with others, breaking the machines that took their livelihoods, and he never came back. The police charged at them and hacked them down." She stares at us again, dry-eyed. "That same winter we lost the cottage. I couldn't pay the rent. So I took myself and the babies into a barn and waited for death—that was all I wanted. But the farmer found us and took us to the workhouse."

Another silence. But she's not looking at either of us now, just staring ahead, her eyes full of darkness. "They split us up, me and the children. I could only see them through a grille in the door. But I watched them wasting away."

She's crying now and the tears run freely down her cheeks.

"Then one day I'm sent before the board. And who should be there but Mr. Sheridan Mosley"—she spits the name out—"himself. I didn't know him then. But he was the one who said a place had been found for me, in a big house, to work as maid. And I asked about the children but he said they had to stay where they were—the lord and lady didn't want dependents. And I cried and begged them, but all he'd say was that I'd been given a great opportunity, and if I worked hard and saved my wages I could come back for my children. So I did!" she cries, looking at us. "I believed him and that's what I did. I worked myself to a bone and they kept not giving me wages, so I left that place and took piecework where I could—all the time heading back toward the workhouse, forty miles away! It took me the best part of a year to get back and when I did, you know what?"

She looks at us, nodding, and I feel like there's a knife twisted in my stomach.

"They said my children had gone—long since, and they wouldn't say where. They said Mr. Sheridan Mosley had found them a place. I should let them go, they said, and be grateful they were now useful members of society. And when I wouldn't go, they set the dogs on me."

She holds out her arm and it's badly scarred.

"So I followed that name," she says, nodding and rocking again. "It's a well-known one and I followed it all the way to Manchester. And I found his house but they wouldn't let me speak to him. So I waited for when he went out and he couldn't shake me off. I knew he recognized me but his eyes went blank and he said, 'I haven't the faintest idea what you're talking about.'"

She looks up then and her face is all twisted with crying. "I didn't give up," she says, "of course I didn't. I followed him everywhere, crying out after him in the streets. But when I went to his house he had the police on me, and finally I was sent to the New Bailey for four months. And it was there"—she looks up again, her face softer this time—"that I met Abel. And he has helped me to find work and lodgings—and he puts their names in his paper. Sarah and Ned, see."

Abel shows me the advertisement.

All this time I feel like there's a howling in my head that's not the wind, and it's not dogs either. Because Nell's story could be my mother's and Sarah and Ned's my own. Even as she said "handloom weaver" I could see a wheel turning in a humble room, and hear a soft voice humming.

"But why . . . ? Why would he do such a thing?" I burst out finally, and Abel shakes his head.

"Who knows?" he says. "Poverty's the worst problem in all the big towns. It's the biggest threat to the manorial lords—that the poor'll combine and grow strong and rise up together. And you've seen the state they're in now. So you'll know that it's too much for the coffers of any one family—even the Mosleys."

He looks at me, his dark eyes glittering. "Slavery's over, so they say. But slavery was a profitable game. What happens to all the children of the poor that are placed out in mills and farms? They're not paid—they barely get food and keep—but maybe someone is. And they're not shipping slaves to America anymore, but they ship the poor to Australia and Canada by the thousands. Who profits there? The least you can say is it gets rid of them— thousands of beggars who'd be stretching the poor rates, taking up space in the workhouses and gaols, and costing good money for rope to hang them with."

My head feels like it's bursting. I hold it at the sides, trying to keep it all in. All I want to do is go home. Yet I have no home—only a bed that belongs to Sheridan Mosley.

I clench both my fists at the side of my head. "It's not true," I say. "I don't believe you."

Neither of them says anything, and even in my own ears my words sound false. It is true—I know it. But I can't stand it.

"Can I go now?" I say, and Abel steps to one side, drawing the bolt.

"Make your own mind up," he says. "Find out for yourself."

I can't bear to look at him. Or her. Feels like a year's just passed in that room. I get up slowly, half expecting him to stop me. None of us speaks, and I can hear him breathing as I pass. Still no one says anything. I push past all the boxes in the yard and tug open the gate. Then I start to run.

The last thing I want to do is enter Mosley's house again. But there are things I have to know. And for Milly's sake I have to go back.

She's pitifully grateful to see me. "Oh, Master Nat!" she says. "Oh, where have you been?"

But I'm in no mood to talk. I go upstairs, hardly caring if I'm seen, and all the house looks strange to me. I pull my clothes off and climb into bed and lie awake, staring, too many thoughts thundering through my head like trains.

32

Revenge

Then when I do sleep, I have this dream. I'm following Queenie—or is it Annie?—down this passageway, and I try to call out to her but my mouth makes no sound and I can't catch up to her because my legs won't move fast enough. The passage is deserted and full of mist. It's like moving through soup. She disappears ahead of me and suddenly I don't know where I am. Then there's this sound, a *tap-tap-tap* behind me, like water dripping, only sharper, clearer, and getting closer. My ears strain toward it and I know what it is—not water but the sound of a cane on the pavement. *Tap-tap-tap* drawing nearer, and I'm more afraid than I've ever been in my life. But my legs are like lead, going slower and slower while the man with the cane catches up.

With a great effort I wrench myself awake. I lie still, trembling and sweating. Everything that Abel and Nell told me hits me again with force, but it's different now. Instead of hundreds of thoughts chasing themselves like rats around my head, there's just one: *I have to leave.*

But I want to have it out with Sheridan Mosley.

This thought keeps me awake till morning light moves across my bedspread. Then, just as I close my eyes again, breakfast arrives. I pull myself into a sitting position, but I've hardly started when Miss C. comes in.

"My goodness," she says. "What kind of hour is this for breakfast?"

I glance at her darkly. "I couldn't sleep," I say.

She tuts and clucks. "I hope it was not your conscience keeping you awake?"

I ignore her, digging away at my egg.

"Come now," she says. "Put away the tray."

"Can I eat my breakfast?"

"*An idle soul shall suffer hunger,*" she says. "A little fasting might help you to concentrate."

She nods at Milly, who lifts the tray. Just in time I cram more toast into my mouth. Then she has me going over to the table just as I am, in my nightgown, because she's wasted enough time already, she says.

"We'll begin with Proverbs," she says, and makes me copy out *The sluggard will not plow, therefore shall he beg in harvest, and have nothing.* Bible stuff—I've heard it all before in the workhouse. But when we get to *In all labor is there profit but the talk of the lips tendeth only to penury,* I can't help myself.

"If that were true, you'd be on the streets," I say.

Miss C. looks like she can hardly believe her ears. "I beg your pardon," she says.

"And so would a lot of other people," I mutter, thinking of all Mr. M.'s friends.

Miss C. couldn't look more shocked if the angel on the chamber pot had flown right up her nose. She turns very pink, then white, then a deep dark red. I watch with interest, but suddenly the ruler comes whistling down through the air, landing with a crack on the table, and I only just whisk my fingers out of the way in time.

"Watchit!" I say, and she splutters in rage.

"How dare you!" she says in a voice turned deep. "You will apologize at once!"

But I'm still annoyed about breakfast. "What for?" I say. "It's true, innit?" And suddenly I'm getting up, pushing back my chair. "I'd like to get dressed, if you don't mind," I say.

Miss C.'s mouth is so far open, you could wedge a book in it. "I never— in all my—such—*insolence*!" And she picks up the bell and rings it for all she's worth.

Quivel comes running. "Bring Mr. Mosley at once," Miss C. cries in a terrible voice, and Quivel flies off. Miss C. follows her out onto the landing. "Mr. Mosley!" she calls over the banister, and I tug my breeches on quick.

My heart's racing now, for I've never in all my life answered back like that. *He'll throw you back in the workhouse*, I'm thinking, but I can't dwell on that now. I tug my nightgown off, keeping one eye on Miss C., who's still hanging over the balcony. I step back sharpish when I hear Mr. M. hurrying up the stairs. *I'm in for it now*, I'm thinking.

Mr. M. and Miss C. come back in the room together.

"This—*ingrate*!" she says. "Tell Mr. Mosley what you said!"

Mr. M.'s in the doorway, looking from one to the other of us in alarm. "Nathaniel," he says, "what is going on?"

"Tell him!" thunders Miss C.

"All I said was that she talks more than I do," I tell him, "which is true enough. And then she went mad."

Miss C.'s face turns from red to purple.

"You see?" she cries. *"How like vipers are the tongues of men!"*

"Miss Chitters, please!" says Mr. M. "Nathaniel, tell me properly what happened."

"I'm sick of lessons!" I tell him.

Miss C. cries, "After all my time and effort. This *ingratitude*! You must beat him, Mr. Mosley, and beat him well. Kindness has had no impact. *Spare the rod and spoil the child.*"

"Try it!" I say. I'm losing my fear and beginning to enjoy myself.

"Now, calm down, please," Mr. M. says, trying to be severe, but squeaking a bit. "There'll be no beating in this house. Nathaniel, you can stay in your room without food until you apologize. Miss Chitters, come with me, please."

Miss C. looks as if she's about to ignore him and lunge at me, but Mr. M. takes her arm and steers her out. A minute later there's the sound of the door being locked.

"Kindly reflect on your behavior," Mr. M. calls through the lock. "I shall be back to speak to you later."

Left on my own again, I fling myself down on the bed. This isn't a punishment. Not like the ones you got in the workhouse, where they'd take the skin off your back. And if I'd spoken to Mistress on the farm like that, I'd've been killed and fed to the pigs. I stare at the ceiling, thinking, *Mr. M. can't have done all them bad things.*

Hours later, though, it definitely feels like punishment. I'm bored, almost to tears, when he opens the door again. And hungry too.

"Well, Nathaniel," he says, his lips looking pinched. "What have you to say for yourself?"

My heartbeat quickens but I take my time, looking up at the ceiling then round the room. "Nowt," I tell him finally.

His pale face goes a little paler, but all he says is, "Very well. I'll have Mrs. Quivel bring you some broth. And then I want you to take a little walk with me."

He closes the door again. I'm thrown by this. I thought the least he'd do would be to starve me but, no, here comes the broth and some bread, and I down it in one because I've not eaten since breakfast.

When I've finished, Mr. M.'s at the door. "When you're ready," he says, without smiling.

I'm thinking I'll get to the door with him and run off, but I still want to hear what he has to say, so I follow him down the stairs and through the front door.

We set off walking, and the evening's fine. Birds rise and settle on the eaves of the houses. He places one hand on my shoulder and the other holds his stick.

"All these fine old houses are being sold as warehouses now," he says as we pass a boarded-up terrace. "Everywhere you look people are moving out of town. Why do you suppose that is, Nat?"

I don't answer and he sighs gently. "The old days are coming to an end," he says. "We live in a different world. When you look around this town, Nathaniel, what do you see?"

"Too many people," I say, and he pounces on that.

"Exactly. But what can be done?" And when I don't answer again, he says, "Shall I tell you what I see? I see a town at a turning point. Part manorial village, part sprawling industrial city. All the filth, all the misery and poverty, has come with the industry. It never used to be like this. My family would look after the poor people in times of famine. My grandfather would share out his grain at the doors of the Collegiate Church, and take everyone into his halls in time of threat. That was the way things were done around here for hundreds of years. But the new lords of Manchester are the factory owners, and they do not care for the people. They have created a perpetual famine. And a new class of people come pouring into Manchester every day from all over England. A new class, more depraved than the old, swarming into the courts and alleys, and bringing with them crime and disease."

"Is that what you mean by *the problem of the poor*?" I ask him, and there's a sharp edge to my voice.

"The old ways have gone forever," he says, as if he hadn't heard. "And we shall go too. There is no place for us in our own land."

He takes off his spectacles and wipes them, and for a moment I feel almost sorry for him. But then I remember what Abel and Nell said.

"Is that why you're so keen to get rid of them?" I say. "Before they get rid of you?"

He stops polishing his glasses. "Get rid of whom?" he asks.

"All the poor people," I say. "Isn't that what you mean by *a workable solution*?"

He looks taken aback by this, but not thrown. "Who have you been speaking to?" he says.

So it's true, I'm thinking.

He waits for a while and then says, "Well, what do you think, Nathaniel? What would you do? What's the best way to relieve the suffering of the poor? Should we leave them in their misery, or try to find them useful, pro-ductive work? Where they can live indoors rather than on the streets? What do the poor need most? Laws about sanitation, perhaps—or the gin shops? What would you do?"

"I wouldn't take them from their families."

He's shaken by this, but he laughs. "But how would it be possible to place the whole family in employment? And what is the alternative? To move the whole tribe into the workhouse? Or maybe transport them to Australia? The real problem is that the poor breed so many of their own kind."

"No," I say sharpish. "The real problem is that the rich live in houses like yours, and the poor live like pigs in pens."

We're turning a corner now, into a street where the houses are boarded up and new signs nailed to the fronts of them.

Mr. M. stops. "Ah," he says, and his spectacles gleam down at me. "But perhaps the question is, whether it is in the *nature* of the poor to live in the way they do. Bred in the bone as it were."

I'm speechless, and he carries on walking. Then I find my tongue. "You think the poor are like animals, don't you?" I say, feeling my face burn with wrath. "And that makes it all right to herd them into pens!"

"Keep your voice down," he says. "You are talking in ignorance. Of course the poor are inbred, as are the rich—they have been for centuries. It is an essential way of preserving the finer traits—intelligence, aesthetics, judgment, restraint—in the ruling classes. In the poorer classes, of course, rather less fortunate attributes are reproduced."

He thinks I won't be able to argue with all them big words, but I've heard them all before, from Miss C.

"Such as?" I say, hopping mad now and showing it.

He smiles. "I hardly think you need telling."

"No—go on."

"Well, the opposite traits of course. A certain dullness and brutishness. A lack of control. Intelligence replaced by a low animal cunning that makes crime the natural outlet."

He shoots me a look as he says this, but I'm past caring. "That must make you feel a lot better then," I hiss at him.

"Not at all," he says, raising the eyebrow. "Indeed, when I took you on I had hoped for great things. And you showed some initial promise—you learned your lessons quickly, for instance, and demonstrated the ability to be trained. Above all you showed a capacity to *appreciate*, which is one of the highest faculties we possess. But now it seems that the improvement has run its course. You are becoming boorish and inattentive again. Miss Chitters has commented on a regrettable lack of respect, and an inability to take in new information. We have concluded that your ability has reached its natural limit and it would be a mistake to press you further. Cruel, in fact."

I can hardly believe my ears. "What are you saying?"

"I'm saying, my dear boy, that the experiment has proved to be rather disappointing. That, fed and clothed and educated as one of the most privileged, you are still reverting to your natural condition—a rather low condition that finds its natural outlet in deceit and material dishonesty."

He bends toward me. "Don't think I haven't heard you creeping around my house at night," he says. "What were you looking for? Money? Or things you could sell on the street?"

So many thoughts are charging through my head that I can only gape at him, looking, I daresay, as low and oafish as he thinks me.

Then he says, *"You can take the boy out of the workhouse, but can you take the workhouse out of the boy? . . .* That was well said, I think."

I find my voice. "Well, if you think you're sending me back there, you've got another think coming. That's what you'd like, innit? To play God with me—and with the lives of all the other poor children you pretend to be interested in; taking them off their parents and getting rid of them . . . 'Oh, we must take care of the children,' " I say in a high voice, " 'because the parents aren't fit.' But what happens to them then, eh, Mr. Mosley? And what happens to the poor parents?"

For a second his eyes bulge, then he laughs in a high-pitched horrible way.

"The poor parents?" he says. "Why, they're a danger to their own kind. You know what they spend their time doing at the Wood Street Mission? Trying to save the babies their parents have dropped into the river! If we weren't *getting rid* of the children as you so delicately put it, their parents would be doing the job in another, far more brutal way. But you know all this, Nathaniel. I took you in, hoping to prove that the way forward lay in kindness and education and care. I was wrong, of course."

"You think you're so clever, don't you?" I yell at him, spit flying from my mouth. "You don't know nowt! But I'll tell you this much. You may think you're some kind of organ-grinder, Mr. Mosley—*but I ain't no monkey!*"

I take a step toward him, hardly knowing what I'm doing, my head full of the wrongs of Nell and my mother. Mr. M. raises his cane, stepping backward, but before he can bring it crashing down I've seized it and wrenched it off him. Then I strike out at him with it and catch him across the jaw. He staggers back and I just keep hitting out.

"I'll—tell—you—what—the—poor—need—shall—I?" I yell at him, striking out with each word so that he collapses under the blows. "Some—RIGHTS—that's all!"

I finish and throw his cane a long way behind me. Then I see what I've done.

He's struggling to get up, his face all bloody. "You—fool!" he gasps, sinking down again.

Horror washes over me like cold water. I take a step or two back, then suddenly I'm running, fast as my legs'll carry me, in any direction that's away from him. Don't know where I'm going but I've no choice but to run—faster and faster, like all the hounds of hell are following.

33

Refuge

I spend that night in one of the boarded-up houses that's being converted to a warehouse. One of the boards over the window is loose, and the others rotting. I pull them away with shaking hands and climb through.

Don't get much sleep, though. Can't stop thinking about everything that's happened. *It's all true*, I'm thinking. *Everything that Nell and Abel said.*

All over the country poor kids are taken from their parents and never see them again—all for the sake of getting them out of the parish. And even though my mother gave us up, seemingly of her own accord, I can't help but wonder what happened to her after, and whether or not she ended up in the kind of place she couldn't get back from.

Soon I've got other things to think of. I've left Mr. M.'s, like I intended, but I've left with nothing—nothing I could have nicked to sell on the streets; nothing but the clothes I'm wearing, that mark me out as a target for anyone who's looking. And the police'll be looking, sure as eggs are eggs. Folk like me can't set about folk like him.

Looks like all my plans have gone wrong. Just for a change.

Hold up, Dodger, I tell myself. *It's not long since you were in the workhouse, but you got out of there and you stayed out. No one'd've given much for your chances when you left that farm, but here you still are.*

I tell myself this and try to keep my chin up, but inside I'm shaking. And thinking, *From the workhouse to the gaol, that's where you're going.*

In the morning, because I can't think of anything else to do, I make my way to Abel's shop. I stick to the backstreets, passing pigs, hens and littl'uns all foraging in the muck. This time the front door of the shop's open, propped by a brick. There's a young man with a mass of fizzy black hair standing behind a wooden counter and behind him the walls are lined with books. The front of the shop's so different from the back that I wonder if I've got the right place.

Still, I go up to the counter. "Can I speak to Abel Heywood, please?"

A change flickers over the young man's face, then it straightens again. "There's no one of that name here."

I stare at him. "Well, he were here the other night."

"Can I interest you in a romance, madam?" he says clearly, to a woman who's just entered the shop behind me.

But he's not getting rid of me that fast. "If he's not here," I say, "how come his name's over the front door?"

"*Mabel the Mildewed,*" he says to the woman, just like he hasn't heard, and he opens a cabinet for her. "A rural romance—love and madness, knights and castles, dungeons, suicide and a wedding."

"It says 'Abel Heywood, Printers' on the front," I point out, and he looks at me like I'm an annoying fly.

"It was a printers, indeed, at one time," he says. "Now, as you can see, it's a penny reading room."

Suddenly it dawns on me that the press has to be kept secret. So at the front of the shop is a reading room and at the back is the printers.

"Well, maybe I'll just stay here and read then," I say, thumbing through a magazine.

"Do you have a penny?" he says.

I'm getting nowhere this way. And now he's off talking to an old man.

"Look," I say to him in lowered tones when he comes back. "I was here the other night, right? Talking to Abel. I know all about *The Poor Man's Guardian*. And Abel's expecting to see me. So just tell me when he's coming back, and I'll go away and leave you alone."

He doesn't look best pleased by any of this.

"No, the shop closes at eight in the evening," he says clearly as another woman comes up behind me. "There'll be no one here after that. You can try again later, if you like," he says, and she gives him a funny look. Because he's looking at her but talking to me. And he adds as the woman moves away, "So clear off, before I say something to the officer outside."

I whip round and indeed there is a police officer, just passing the shop. I think of saying something sharp like, "He's just as likely to arrest you as me," but the last thing I want to do right now is call his bluff. So I wait till the officer's well past and nip out.

I spend a weary day on the streets. Nowhere to go, nothing to do. No sight of anyone I know, which is probably a good thing. Plus I'm starving. This is the first day in weeks I've been without food. And I'm losing my touch. I try nicking a pie and get chased by a little man with a big dog. Finally I see a little lad carrying a bag of black pudding. I stick my foot out as he walks past and he obliges me by falling over it. I pick up his bag and leg it, leaving him howling.

Course, he's eaten half of it. Still, it's better than nothing. But that's all I have to eat all day—that and a handful of cherries I nick from a stall. I spend the day avoiding people as best I can, which isn't easy, since there's masses of them, and none of them seem to be alone, like me.

You can get lost in a crowd, but it's no place to be alone. Around about midafternoon I begin to feel like I don't exist. Course, I don't want to be seen but still, it's a funny feeling. If you're going to live on the streets, you need a gang.

Around about seven I make my way back to the shop. I know it's early, but my feet hurt. I go straight round the back this time. Gate's closed but it's not too hard climbing over the top. And the back door's shut so I sit on the step, pull my hat down over my face and sleep.

I'm woken when the back door scrapes open. It's Abel, coming in with his back to me, and refastening the gate.

"You took your time," I say to him, and he jumps violently.

"How did you get in?" he asks.

I laugh. "Security's not your strong point," I tell him, "considering this is supposed to be a secret press."

I stand aside to let him open the door. "You'd best come in," he says over his shoulder.

Once again we sit in the little back room with all the boxes. "So," he says, "you've come back."

"I have," I agree.

"Been thinking about things, have you?"

"That's right," I say.

"Come to any conclusions?"

I take my hat off, put it on the table and rub my grubby fingers across my forehead. "Look," I say. "I'm in trouble."

And I tell him everything—even about battering Mr. M. with his own cane. I don't lie because he has to see how much trouble I'm in. When I've finished he gives a long, low whistle, then stares at his inky fingers on the table.

The longer the silence goes on, the farther my heart sinks. He's going to tell me to stay away from him because he's in enough trouble already.

Then, just when I think I can't take the silence any longer, he says, "How well do you know the city?"

I stare at him. "Like the back of my hand. Why?"

"First thing is—we'd better get you some new clothes." And as I go on staring, he adds, "You stand out a mile in that gear. I daresay that was the point."

"You mean . . . you're not turning me in?" I say, hardly believing it.

"Turn you in?" he says, frowning. "You'd not be able to work for me if I did that."

"Work? For you?" I say.

"I want help with distributing the paper," he says. "I can't pay you—but you can sleep in the cellar. It'll depend on you being honest, mind. And staying out of trouble."

"You mean it?" I say then, as a thought strikes me. "But . . . the police'll be looking out for me."

"There's been nothing in the papers," he says, surprising me. I'd've thought it'd be everywhere by now—*Charity Boy Assaults Benefactor* and such. They'd love it.

"I'll keep my eyes open, of course," he says. "But so long as we get you out of that gear and you stick to your job, you should be fine."

I stutter out some thanks and Abel strokes his beard. "We'll have to sort something out about food," he says. "I can't have you nicking stuff. Is that clear?"

"As if!" I say, grinning broadly. I can hardly believe my luck. "You won't regret it, Mr. Heywood sir, you never will! I'll work hard for you—day and night. I'll do any job you want. I'll sweep the cellar if you like. I'll . . . well, what *is* my job, exactly?"

34

Queenie

This is how it works. All day long, while the front of the shop operates as a penny reading room, Abel writes his paper and prints up articles from famous people like William Cobbett and Richard Cobden. Then all night—for the man never sleeps as far as I can see—he runs the copies off in his cellar, and I help him box them up. We use hatboxes, shoe boxes, cake boxes, in fact, any kind of box that doesn't look as if it might have newspapers in it. One time I carried a dozen that had *Caldwell's Pies* on the front. As soon as they're boxed up I take them to different places in the city—the Mechanics Institute, and the Co-operative Society, and to the back rooms of about a dozen pubs where people meet who're not supposed to, under the law. Not criminals like Weeks, but workers who want to form themselves into something called a union. The shoemakers' union's one, and the woodworkers' another.

"If what you want to do's against the law," Abel says, "easiest way is to break it. The hard thing is to change it."

I follow him about the town for the first few days while he shows me the workshops where plasterers and painters, bricklayers and toolmakers take the paper and read it aloud to one another in their lunch breaks. Plus, there's some private people who take them. There's a grocer in Tib Street, for instance, that parcels several of them up in chests of tea and has them sent with the rest of his stuff to London. There's a baker's shop on Lizard Street who takes a box, and—this is a bit embarrassing—the man at the meat-pie stall in Piccadilly, who I tried to nick a pie off. He has several.

He doesn't recognize me, though, because of my new gear. Abel brought it the first morning. Corduroy trousers and a pale brown shirt, a printer's apron, just like his only smaller, and a cap that covers my hair, which is growing fast.

Abel has a long conversation with him about thieves and the police while I stand by, trying to look scarce. "It's a terrible thing, thieving," says Abel, laying a hand on my shoulder. "Does everyone down in the end. What do you think, Joe?"

I think, *What's he playing at?* And nod, while bending over to hide my face and pat the dog, which snarls.

I trot after him because his legs are so much longer than mine, and he talks at me, but he's not boring like Miss C. He makes it all seem like one of the old tales. Like the rich are all giants, and the poor are like Jack.

"The factory owners think themselves the gods of this town," says he, as a carriage rolls past, spattering mud our way. "But we've a different religion now."

"Hark at that noise," he says outside a factory where there must be a thousand wheels whirring. "You know what's being made, Joe?"

"Aprons?" I say.

"History," says he. "Not so long ago only the lords made history, and the kings and queens. But now it's the people of this town.

"It's a great town, this, Joe," he says. He's standing in the filthiest court I've ever seen, so that I have to wonder if we're talking about the same place. "Perhaps the greatest there's ever been. It's changing the face of the world. And its own face is changing, Joe—it's starting to smile!"

That's Abel for you, carried along by hopes and dreams. His lean inky fingers work faster than any I've ever seen, and I work fast for him, and hard. And soon I'm taking all the boxes around myself.

It's a different town again, now I'm working and moving among working people. Even the streets seem different, now that I'm using them for a different purpose—like there's one world layered over another. I have to be careful not to stumble into Mr. M.'s world, of course, or back into the world of crime. But it's not difficult. I just stick to the routes I know, moving quickly and quietly, troubling no one, and soon it's as if those other worlds never existed.

Best of all, when I take boxes to these places, they always slip me something—a pie here, some biscuits there, an orange off the old woman with her orange barrow. *We'll sort something out about food*, Abel told me, and he did. And every night he brings back bread and cheese to see us through the working hours.

One night he's printing an article by William Cobbett . . .

> The Daily Diet of Children in the Workhouse
> 1/2 pt milk gruel
> 7 oz rice pudding
> 1/2 pt of soup

"Is that right?" he asks me.

"Sounds about right," I say. "Except for the rice pudding. And the soup. We only had soup on a Sunday."

And he changes the article as we speak.

Soon I start to feel like a different person. Different clothes, different name, different job. I haven't forgotten about Annie, but it seems like I couldn't go back now if I tried.

Then one day I see Queenie.

I've just made a delivery in Blackfriars. I'm staring up at the pigeons as they dip and swoop, and wondering what it would be like to be a bird, when she walks right past me, not looking. And it's so long since I've looked for her that I have to look again to make sure. She's wearing different clothes as well. A woman's fancy gown, pink and lacy, though soiled at the hem and frayed. And a bright green hat with a small feather—not like Bonnet's. She's carrying a little bag and walking with dainty steps. Not like Queenie. Yet it is Queenie and I take a big breath, about to bellow her name, when I realize there's a man following. In his middle years, not as old as Mr. M., dressed smartly, with a thick black mustache.

I know what you're up to, I'm thinking, and I grin to myself. She'll lead him into one of the courts and a whole gang of little blaggers'll leap out and cosh him and rob him blind.

Well, I'm not about to blow her cover. I follow them round the corner, keeping my distance. They pass through one alley, then a court, and no one jumps him. Then when they get to the alley that leads to St. Mary's Church they stop and I stop too, dodging quickly back into the courtyard.

The man says something and I hear him laugh. Then there's another kind of noise.

I know what they're doing—I've heard it before, in the workhouse. I didn't like it then and I don't now. I move farther away then back again, because I don't want to lose her.

It only takes a minute then I'm dodging back into a doorway as the man reappears, looking shifty. I have to wait while he crosses the yard. Then I nip into the alleyway and bump right into Queenie, who's straightening her dress, and she gives a little gasp of fear.

"Hello, Queenie," I say.

Her eyes look glazed over somehow, then they focus.

"Dodger!" she says, and she starts to smile, but I pull her through the alley and out by the church.

"What are you doing?" I say, pulling her round to face me.

"Dodger," she says again, still smiling. "You've grown!"

And you've shrunk, I feel like saying, because that's what it looks like. Her face is pale and shrunken, her eyes enormous, with big bluish shadows beneath them. Then I realize I probably have grown, because my eyes are level with hers. All these weeks of good food.

"Nice dress," I tell her.

She puts out a hand and touches my face, still smiling, and I try not to flinch.

What's wrong with her eyes? I'm thinking. The pupils are huge.

"Hello, Dodger," she says, and her voice is funny. Kind of blurred.

I shake her arm. "Queenie, what's up?" I say, and she looks a bit self-conscious then.

"Nothing," she says.

"Where are all the others?" I ask her. "Pigeon, and Pickings. Ors'n'cart?"

She pulls away from me a bit and her eyelids droop. "We all work for Bailey now," she says slowly.

I thought as much. I wait for her to ask me what I've been doing all these weeks, where I've been, but she doesn't.

"Queenie," I say. "What are you doing?"

But she looks away from me, past the church. "Got to get back," she mumbles and moves away, but I catch her arm again.

"Queenie," I say, and I hardly know how to go on, then the words come tumbling out. "You don't have to go back, not if you don't want to—you don't have to do anything you don't want!"

The words sound daft even to my ears, but I'm thinking, *I'll take her to Abel—he'll know what to do. She can deliver papers with me.*

She pulls her arm away. "No time," she's saying.

"Queenie," I urge her. "Don't go back. Come with me. It'll be all right."

She looks at me properly then, her eyes look up and down over my new clothes. "I can't," she says flatly, and I feel her emptiness and despair.

"Why not? You don't have to live like this."

She shrugs. "It's my life now," she says, and I see her glance up at the church.

"It doesn't have to be," I tell her. "Come with me now!"

She shakes her head, still looking at the church. Then she looks at me again. "You're doing well, Dodger," she says. Only her lips are smiling.

"I've got another kind of life now," I say. "You come with me and bring the others. It can be your life too. We can start again."

"Too late," she murmurs.

"It's not too late!" I say, feeling desperate. "Look, just come with me. Don't go back there—to *him*!" I shake her shoulder, as if trying to shake some sense into her. She looks at me, smiling properly now, then she touches my face again.

"It never was your world, Dodger," she says. "Not really. You didn't belong. But it is mine. I can't change. I can't just move into your world—not now. Not after everything I've done."

"You *can*!" I say, shaking her again, and her eyes fill with tears.

"Look at me, Dodger," she says. "I'm not anyone. I walk the streets. Don't tell me I can just walk out of my world into yours, because I can't. The things I've done won't ever go away. And I'm sick, Dodger—you know." She nods at me. "I'm sick. I'll not get well again—"

"Don't say that!"

"I can't live with ordinary people. Wherever I go, they'll know what I am."

She glances at the church again and I know what she's thinking. Suddenly I can see it all the way she sees it, the way the church would see it. And Miss C. and Mr. M. and all the rest of that crew.

Queenie looks at me levelly enough, like she knows what I'm thinking, but I feel like I'm breaking up inside. And because I can see it all clearly, I can't speak. *But you're Queenie*, I'm thinking. *That's who you are.* Yet I don't say it.

"I'll have to go," she says finally, moving away, but I catch her hand as she moves and press it to my lips, and she looks at me, startled, and turns her face away as I kiss her again, so that I just catch the corner of her mouth. Never done that before, or since.

For a moment she clutches me and I can feel her crying without a sound, then she breaks away, almost running, turning into the next alleyway without looking back. And I know she doesn't want me to follow her, so I don't. I just stand where I am, arms falling uselessly at my sides, feeling like someone just carved a great hole in me. Then after a while of standing stupid-like, I set off, back toward Piccadilly.

All the birds are calling and crying, setting up their usual evening din, but I hardly hear them. I push my way through the crowds and the shiny streets. My chest hurts and I feel worse and worse inside.

I'm not looking where I'm going and on the corner of Oldham Street I walk smack into someone who's coming the other way. "Sorry," I mumble, without looking up. But the other person steps back.

"Joe?" she says. Then, catching sight of my face, "What is it? What's the matter?"

It's Nell, wrapped in her shawl. I can tell from her eyes how bad I look, but I just say, "Nothing," and start to press on toward the shop.

"Are you looking for Abel?" she says. "He'll be late tonight—but he's given me the key. Come on. We'll wait together."

Didn't want company. But I follow her round the back of the shop and into the back room, waiting while she lights the lamp.

"There, that's better," she says.

I say, "I'll be fine now. You go if you like."

But she stays looking at me as if she's really sorry, and I can't take it. I turn my face away.

"Joe," she says, very gentle. "What is it, Joe? Has something happened?"

"It's nothing," I say again. "Just . . . someone I used to know."

Then before I know it, I'm telling her everything, about Queenie and the gang, how I had to leave them to live with Mr. M. while they had to go to Bailey, and about Queenie now, how she looked, and what she said. And Nell doesn't say anything the whole time, but when I've finished she steps forward and takes me in her arms and presses my head into her shoulder. I feel myself going all stiff as she rocks me, and my breath comes in great gusts and bursts. But I'm not crying, because I never do.

"Oh, Joe, Joe," she mourns. "There are so many evils in this world."

I just stand and let her rock me. It's never happened before, not so long as I remember. Maybe my mother used to do it, long ago.

When she lets go we sit down on opposite sides of the table. "Eh, Joe," she sighs. "If only I could be sure the same thing hasn't happened to my own little girl."

I wipe my nose on my sleeve. "What did you say her name was?"

"Sarah," she says, like a sigh. "And my boy was Ned—Edward, after my father."

"How old were they?" I ask, happy to talk about something else.

"Sarah would be eleven now, and Edward coming up to thirteen. I haven't seen them for four years." Her mouth quivers, but she doesn't cry.

"Did they look like you?" I ask, for something to say, and she nods her head.

"A little. Sarah did. Edward took after his father, but fair, very fair."

"Which workhouse was it, where you left them?"

"Rochdale." She looks at me. "Why?"

"Oh, nothing." I shrug. "I just thought I might have seen them if they'd been where I was, that's all."

"Saddleworth?" she says, and I nod, but she shakes her head.

Then the next thing she says makes the hair on the back of my head stand on end.

"You'd remember my Ned if you'd seen him. He had a birthmark on his face. A little bluish pattern all over his left cheek and eye—like bilberries on the moor."

I just stare at her, and she looks back at me, wondering. But I'm saved from having to speak by Abel, who comes crashing in at the door.

"I've just been tipped off," he says. "There's going to be a raid!"

35

Raid

Now we're both staring at him.

"What will you do?" says Nell.

Abel runs his fingers through his hair till it all sticks up. "There's a bloke I know," he says, "owns a warehouse at the back of the Bridgewater Arms. He says we can move all the stock there. But we'll have to be quick."

We work all night, loading the boxes onto barrows and wheeling them through the backstreets to the warehouse. It starts to rain and the barrows are heavy, and soon we're slipping and sliding through the muck. I don't mind too much, since it gives me something else to think about. But the words Annie spoke to me in the forest keep coming back to me all the time.

Light hair, she said. *Like straw, the boy has . . . And a pattern like bilberries—here.*

I don't want to think about it, because I never believed her. But now my insides are stiff with dread and guilt. *Annie*, I'm thinking. *Where are you now?*

Soon, though, there's no time for thinking. I never knew there were so many boxes in the back room and the cellar. Abel works with Matt, the lad who runs the front of the shop in the daytime, to get the printer loaded onto a cart and covered up. Nell helps at first but then he sends her home.

"Things could get nasty," he says. "I don't want you running foul of the law again."

She protests a bit but she's already had a long day's work and looks worn-out. So I help her load some of the boxes onto another barrow and she wheels them off a bit unsteadily to her cellar room.

Then, just as we're loading the final lot onto my barrow, there's a thundering crash at the front door. Matt goes to answer it while Abel helps me tug the barrow into the yard.

"Don't go by Oldham Street," he hisses at me, and I nod to show I've understood.

I wheel that barrow fast as I can through the back alleys. It overturns twice on the uneven cobbles, and I have to pile all the boxes back on again. God knows what state the papers'll be in. I go up Back Piccadilly and onto Lever Street, my feet slipping in the mud and all my muscles straining. From Lever Street I turn onto Hilton Street, which crosses Oldham Street, and I pause at the corner to watch what's going on.

A crowd's gathered and I can just make out Abel, because he's half a head taller than the rest. There's lots of heckling and jeering.

"Have you got nowt better to do?"

"Call yourselves constables!"

Then Abel says something to one of the officers and gets himself struck across the face with the baton, and a cry goes up, "Traitor! Traitor!"

They're yelling at the police, not Abel. I hear the sound of glass smashing and pick up my barrow fast, wheeling it toward Market Street and the Bridgewater Arms.

Abel's friend, a burly bloke with a handlebar mustache, lets me into the warehouse and we unload the boxes. "Is that it?" he asks, and I nod.

"Best make yourself scarce then," he says, drawing the great doors to and bolting them. I've half a mind to ask if I can stay the night in the warehouse, because I don't know if it's safe to go back. How long do raids take? But the moment passes and he's hurrying off, drawing his collar up against the rain.

I loiter a bit, not sure what to do. Maybe I should go to Nell's place. And tell her, tell her everything Annie said. But it's already beginning to sound daft in my mind—the ravings of a mad littl'un. *Coincidence*, I tell myself, and wander round at the back of the pub, kicking a stone.

There's children waiting in the shadows at the corner, a girl holding the hand of a younger boy, three little boys pressed into a doorway, another girl holding a babby.

Waiting for their mam or dad, I think, giving the stone an extra kick. There's an old man bent over crutches with a rag tied over one eye, hobbling slowly down the steps from the pub. *He's had no luck there*, I'm thinking then, remembering the last pub I was in, consider going in and trying my own luck at telling a story.

Look where that got you, I think, and shrug, clutching my shirt at the chest, because it's cold now as well as wet. Then I remember the night I spent in a boarded-up house, after leaving Mr. M. Lots of the houses around here have been sold off as warehouses. And I can't stay here all night. I turn round and head into the shadows at the back of the pub.

And just as I'm passing, a hand grabs me by the scruff of the neck, hoisting me clear off my feet and dashing me into the wall.

"I've got nowt!" I yell, soon as I can speak, but he just keeps clobbering me into the wall. My hands and feet thrash about wildly because now he's got me by the throat and looks set to dash my brains out. I can't see a thing because there's no lights, but as soon as he speaks I know his voice.

"Thought you'd got away from me, eh?" he says.

Carver.

36

Knife

Next thing there's a knife up against my throat as he hauls me away from the pub. "Thought you'd given me the slip, dincha?" he growls, but I can't think anything. All I can see is Half-moon's face as the knife draws a red line across his throat, like another mouth.

Carver pushes me up against a door. "All these weeks I been looking for you," he spits. "I'm going to slit your belly and feed your guts to the birds!"

He raises his knife, and all I can do is shut my eyes tight and hope Miss C. was wrong about heaven and hell. Because I know where I'll be going.

Then all of a sudden there's another sound, like a *thunnk*, of someone bumping into Carver's arm. Carver staggers forward, driving the knife deep into the door, a gnat's whisker away from my ear. I open my eyes and there's the one-eyed tramp I saw before, clutching Carver's shoulder.

"Alms, s-s-sir," he quavers, and just for a second I think I might be going mad.

Carver curses horribly and wheels round, driving his fist into the old man's nose. It squashes like an overripe plum, and he staggers over. But in that split second I whip round the corner and crouch behind some bins.

I can just see Carver smashing the man's crutches over his head and kicking him, then he wrenches the knife out of the door and comes walking my way.

I don't know who's breathing louder, me or him. Closer and closer he gets and I want to shut my eyes but I can't. He kicks one bin over, then the next, then just as I'm thinking I'll have to run at him, head down, and butt his stomach like a goat, he turns off into the alley facing me, still cursing under his breath.

I daren't move. Seems like my knees have turned to water and I can't move. Seems like hours of listening to his footsteps fading away before I can bring myself to come out from behind that bin. And I should run, of course I should, but I have to make sure of one thing. I have to be sure I'd not gone mad when I heard that tramp speak. Trembling like water before it drips off a spout, I make my way over to the bundle of rags on the cobbles.

He's a pitiful sight—one leg ending in a bloody stump, the other foot twisted behind him, his nose smashed, his crutches broke and his good eye all shot with blood. He groans as I approach and spits out a bit of tooth. I sink down beside him and turn his face to mine. He smiles with what's left of his mouth.

"Hello, Tom," says Travis.

37

Crutch

Blimey, Travis," I say, when I can speak. "What happened to you?"

Travis makes a huge effort to get onto his knees, and sinks down again. "Help me up," he groans through clenched teeth. "Twisted—my—ankle."

And he's only got one foot.

I pull at his arms, he clutches my shoulders and somehow we get him into a kneeling position. Then, sweating and desperate in case Carver comes back, I brace myself against the wall while he puts his full weight on me and hauls himself up.

Good job I've got all these new muscles. Travis's face is creased in agony, and mine can't look any better, as he presses down and hops—one tiny shuffling step then another—out of the alley onto Market Street, me acting as his crutch. People glance up at us curiously then look away. They don't offer to help, and I daren't ask. *Got to get him to Nell's*, I'm thinking. The shop isn't safe, and Nell's is nearer.

Somehow we hobble across that road, me half dragging, half carrying Travis, him swearing like a trooper under his breath, which reeks of gin. We turn off into another alley and into a court, stumbling across the legs of people just lying in the yard. Then through another alley into the court where Nell lives.

Travis sinks down on the steps leading to Nell's cellar while I bang on the door. *Please, please be in*, I'm thinking, and soon I hear her voice, sounding fearful. "Who is it?"

"It's me, Nell—Joe. Let me in!"

A pause, then the door scrapes open. It's Nell pulling a skirt on over her nightgown, clutching her shawl. She claps a hand to her mouth when she sees Travis.

"It's all right," I tell her. "He's a friend. And he's hurt. Please let us in!"

She could say no, of course, but she doesn't. She opens the door wider and comes out. Travis shuffles down the steps on his backside and between us we haul him into Nell's room.

There's a thin mattress on the floor and Travis collapses onto it, moaning. Nell's room, if you can call it that, is only part of a cellar. A sheet draped over a rope divides it from the rest, and I know from what she's told me that a family live in the other half. Nell's bit is big enough for the mattress and a stool and the boxes she took from Abel, which are piled up in the corner. There's mold on the walls but the stone flags are only a bit damp. Nell presses her finger to her lips, meaning we've got to be quiet, then she crouches over Travis.

"It's his ankle," I whisper. "I think he's sprained it."

Nell unties the laces on his boot. *Travis never wore boots*, I'm thinking.

The ankle looks blue, even in this light, and swollen. She moves his foot a little and Travis tries not to groan. She tugs the boot off gently then looks round and tears a strip off the end of the cotton sheet. She pours some water on it from a cracked jug and places the cotton strip over his ankle like a poultice. She does all this without asking questions, while I sit on the stool and wipe the sweat from my forehead. Then, from the pocket of her skirt, she produces a small flask and when she opens it there's a strong smell of rum. She holds it to Travis's mouth and he gulps it down. "Thanks, miss," he says, and closes his eyes. Then she offers me a swig.

I don't think much of rum but I take it anyway, and it runs through me like fire. I can see why people take to it because, just for a few moments, it makes me feel strong and warm.

Nell drinks the last of it herself. "Sleep," she says, and props herself up against the boxes and the wall. She looks too exhausted to ask questions. I slump down on the floor, propping my aching head up on the stool. *I'll never sleep like this*, I'm thinking, then suddenly I do.

Morning light's slanting in at the cellar window when I wake up, stiff and cramped. Travis is still flat out with his mouth open; Nell's on her way out of the door. There's noises from the other side of the sheet.

"Where are you going?" I ask Nell.

"Work," she says shortly. "Where do you think?"

The sheet shifts behind me and a bleary face appears, takes the scene in openmouthed, and disappears again. Then they're all marching through, five or six of them with their boots or clogs, and the last of them: a fat, shape-less woman with a spiteful face.

"Landlord'll have something to say about this," is her parting shot to Nell as she leaves, and Nell shoots me a despairing look before hurrying after them.

"Wait!" I say, but she only hurries up the steps.

"I'll be back at noon," she calls over her shoulder.

Travis is stirring by now, and I shift myself onto the stool, stiffly, for my legs've gone dead. Travis stares at the wall, then round at me. His bandage has slipped and it's hard to know which of his eyes is in a worse mess.

"What place is this?" he says, hauling himself into a sitting position.

I try to explain, without making the story too long. He listens, closing his eyes again, and I'm not sure how much he's taking in. When he finally opens them he just says, "Water," and I pick up the jug and help him to drink from it. Then he turns over again and sleeps.

But I want to know what's gone on at the shop. When I'm sure he's asleep I slip out, running fast as I can toward Oldham Street. And there's Abel and Matt, putting the shop back to rights with a crowd of helpers. I'm so pleased to see him I shout aloud, and he turns to me, spreading his arms wide.

"Joe!" he says. "You're safe then. Good lad!"

He seems much happier than I thought he'd be.

"What happened?" I ask him.

"I spent the night in a cell. Matt here had a whip round to bail me out. But they had to let me go anyroad because—guess what?"

I shake my head.

"The Stamp Act's been repealed!"

I look blank.

"That means the paper's legal! We can run it as a proper newspaper and sell copies on the streets!"

He picks up a truncheon that's lying in the road and kicks it halfway down the street. "YES!" he cries, raising his fists to heaven.

"That's great!" I say, feeling as though I should say something, and he cuffs me playfully.

"We won, Joe! That's the last time my shop'll ever be raided. How d'you fancy being a street seller?"

Telling stories on the street, to crowds of people? That's all I ever wanted!

"But right now you can sweep up glass," he says, handing me a broom.

First I have to tell him what's happened. And about Travis. "And I think Nell's worried she'll be in trouble with the landlord," I tell him. "Only I couldn't just leave him. He's saved my life, twice now."

"We'll have to move him," he says right away. "He can come here for now. What time did you say Nell's coming back?"

"She said she'd be back at noon."

"Me and Matt'll be there. We'll see if we can rustle up a stretcher. Have you had breakfast?"

Of course I haven't.

"Well, go inside then!" Abel cries. "Matt's mother's making tea."

I have a small feast of weak tea and bread, then I spend the rest of the morning sweeping glass and putting bookshelves back up.

"Look at the state of these," Matt says. Several books are muddied, with pages ripped out. "It'll cost a fortune, this."

"We'll soon get the money when the paper's on the streets," says Abel. I've never seen him so cheery.

Just before noon we set off to Nell's. She's so pleased to see Abel that she falls on him, hugging and kissing, till you have to look the other way.

She lets us in and I half expect to see that Travis has gone, but he hasn't, of course, in his state. He's sitting up, though, dazed but awake.

"Tom, you've come back," says Travis. "And I thought I'd dreamed you."

"Who's Tom, Joe?" says Abel.

"Who's Joe?" says Travis.

It takes a long time to explain. And even longer to get Travis out of that cellar. I'd never have done it on my own. Matt's made a stretcher out of a canvas sack pulled over broom handles—and at last Travis is up the steps, and Abel and Matt carry him in a sitting position all the way back to the shop. Abel makes a rough bed up for him in the back room, which has been cleared.

Nell says she'll have to get back to work. "Not for long you won't," says Abel. "When we get this place sorted you can come and live and work with me."

Then Matt's mother brings us more bread and cheese and tea, and Travis eats like a ravening wolf. Then we're left alone again, while Abel goes after his stock.

Travis doesn't seem comfortable on the bed. He keeps shifting and wincing. Gingerly I touch his foot. "Does it hurt much?"

"Aye, lad," he says, frowning at the place where his other foot should be. "They both do."

"Travis," I say. "What happened?"

It's a short, horrible tale. Not long after he left us by the forest he had an accident, poaching. Not so much of an accident as a man-made trap that new landowners spring on folk who are passing, just in case they hadn't realized they were trespassing. Which Travis hadn't, for the land had been newly enclosed.

It was the kind of trap sometimes used by farmers on foxes, only man-sized. Great steel jaws on a spring, triggered by stepping on them, and well concealed. They're made to trap poachers, so they didn't take the foot off cleanly, but mangled it as he tried to get away. He was in luck, if you could call it that, because a cottager passed some time later with his son, and they helped him to free himself. Otherwise he could have been caught and hanged.

The cottager and his son hauled Travis back to their hut and sent for a man who set bones and pulled teeth for the rest of the village. This man gave Travis a long swig of rum and took the rest of his foot off with a hand-saw. I can feel my eyes water when he tells this bit. And the cottager, who was a joiner by trade, made Travis a crutch and gave him one of his own boots.

But what about listening to the road through the soles of your feet? I'm thinking. *How will you hear what the road's telling you now?*

Course, he couldn't get far after that, not like he had done before. There wasn't too much work he could do, and when he begged he was clapped in the workhouse. There he spent thirteen hours a day smashing stone in a cubicle, until a chip of stone flew up and put out his eye. Then he had to lie all day in the corner of the men's ward, dreaming of the open fields.

He was given a job clearing the slops. And one day, when the master of the workhouse stood with his back to Travis and his front to the open door, Travis raised his crutch and beat him senseless, making his way across the yard.

Then he was a wanted man, and he made his way to where every criminal seeks refuge, here in the big town, where he was less noticeable and could beg in peace. All this time I've been taking papers around the streets, Travis has been here as well, skulking in corners, begging for bread.

"It's not that bad, lad," he says, seeing my face. "Could have been worse. It could have been a spring gun."

Could have been better, I'm thinking. But a spring gun, hidden in bushes, has taken many a poacher to an early grave.

"You shouldn't have left us," I say, because I still feel a prickle of resentment about it, even now.

Travis sighs. "Aye," he says. "Happen not."

"You could have come with us, into the forest," I say. "We met Dogwoman, you know."

Travis smiles with his swollen mouth. "How is she?" he says.

"Horrible," I tell him. "You never said she was real."

Travis hitches himself up. "All stories are real, lad, one way or another."

"She's no angel, though. Or I'm St. George."

"Now, you can't go passing judgment on folk like that."

"How do you suppose she got there?"

"I don't know, lad," Travis says vaguely. "I wouldn't mind seeing her again, though." He pauses, looking round. "I don't suppose you've brought any of that rum with you?"

I haven't, and he seems sorry to hear it. I can't imagine the old Travis drinking, but the wreck he's become needs drink. He spreads his shaking fingers across the blanket.

"Travis," I say, almost whispering. "What will you do?"

He only looks vague again. "Oh, I do this and that."

I want to ask him if he's still got his stories, if he can still hear what the road's telling him through the sole of his one boot, but I don't like to, so I say nowt.

After a while he says, "Where's your sister? Where's the little maid?"

Another long story. I try to make light work of telling him everything that happened after he left. I tell him about Dog-woman guiding us to the edge of the forest. He listens intently when I tell him about my storytelling in the pub, and he seems to know all about Barnaby Bent-nose.

"Bent as a nine-bob note, that one," he says. "I hope you've learned by now you can't go trusting everyone you meet."

"You taught me that," I say pointedly, but he only grins his gap-toothed grin. Blowed if I know what he's so cheerful about.

I tell him about Barnaby trying to sell us at market, then being taken from the market to the fair and, of course, he knows Honest Bob.

"Known him for years," he says. "He's the only bloke I know who makes Barnaby look decent and true. But he's all right really," he says. "He let me do a day's work for him a few weeks back."

I lean forward. "Then you'll've seen Annie," I say.

"Annie—?"

"Julie, I mean—my sister. She stayed with the fair. She wanted to, I mean . . ." I trail off lamely, but Travis looks puzzled.

"You left her with Honest Bob?"

I scratch myself. "I wanted to leave the fair when we got to Ancoats—I'd had enough. But Annie . . . well, she wanted to stay. And they wanted to keep her." I shoot him a defiant look. Naturally I'm not going to tell him about selling her for a shilling.

"You left her then?" he says, leaning forward.

"She wanted to stay!" I tell him, and he sinks back.

"You shouldn't have left her," he says.

You can talk, I'm thinking, but he says, "When was this?"

"I dunno," I say. "Some weeks back."

"Only I was with Honest Bob three weeks ago, in Ashton. And she wasn't there then."

I stare at him. "What are you talking about?"

"She wasn't there. And no one said anything about her either."

"She *must've* been. She'd be skulking in one of the wagons."

Travis shakes his head. "We had to clear all the wagons out. Order of the lord of the manor. They're a bit suspicious about wool smuggling thereabouts."

I feel my head reeling as I take this in, then my face flushes.

"What's he done with her?" I say angrily, and I get up and pace about. He might have sold her like Barnaby Bent-nose tried to sell us. Honest Bob'd do anything to get his shilling back. Then I think, *Or maybe she ran off, looking for me*, and I sink down on a box with a groan and cover my face.

"Don't take on, lad," Travis says.

"Don't take on?" I say, looking at him sideways. "I don't know what's happened to my sister! I might never see her again!"

Suddenly I'm hit by the full awfulness of what I've done. It seems like the most important thing in the world to see Annie again.

Travis nods. "You'll have to find Honest Bob," he says.

I look at him blankly.

"Well . . ." he says. "They were heading for Ancoats, same as always. They'll be there now, I should think. For Lammas."

38

Lammas

He's hardly said the words when I'm out of the door. He calls something after me but I don't listen. Lammas is a big time for markets and fairs. It's not Lammas till the end of the week, but they'll all be gathering. I'll find Honest Bob and make him tell me what he's done with Annie.

It's a hot, wet day. Steam rises from puddles as I splash past and the streets are crowded. I bump into a bloke with a barrow and he shouts after me but I take no notice. All I can hear is my mother's words: *Take care of your sister, Joe.*

I will, I promise her. *I'll find her and take care of her forever.*

But I can't find Honest Bob. When I get to the field where the fair was there's a crowd, and wagons, and my hopes soar, only to be dashed again when I realize it's not the same one. There's a man on a box with long silver hair selling pills that'll cure horses and mend your love life. I elbow my way through the crowd, asking everyone if they've seen Honest Bob and his traveling fair. Some take no notice; others tell me to push off. When I try to ask the fair folk I'm chased off by two rough-looking men with clubs. Then I go up and down the streets of Ancoats, asking in all the inns and alehouses and gin shops if anyone's seen Honest Bob. One or two know of him, but they don't know when they saw him last, or where he might be. At last, as the light draws in, I make my way back, limping and footsore. Worn-out.

Nell and Abel are in the shop with Travis. Abel's found him a crutch and he's trying to walk. I go straight past them and fling myself down on a box in the corner.

"Where've you been?" says Abel.

Nell says, "What is it, Joe?"

I can't speak.

Travis asks, "Didn't you find him?" and I shake my head.

"Find who?" says Abel.

The whole painful tale comes out then. Travis tells them about Honest Bob and I tell them about looking everywhere for him, and Annie.

We all sit around looking at one another. "You mustn't give up, Joe," Nell says. "I've never given up on Sarah and Ned. We'll find her, won't we, Abel?"

Abel says nothing. I look at Nell. I have to tell her.

"If we find Annie," I say, "you'll find them too."

Fear and hope spring into her eyes. "What do you mean?"

It's a hard thing to say. I say it slowly. "Annie's not like . . . other folk. She could always . . . see things and . . . hear them."

They look at me blankly.

"In the workhouse—she could see . . . not just the people there but . . . the people they brought with them."

More blank looks. This is hopeless. I don't know how to explain.

"Once she saw a man with a girl clinging to his neck. Turns out he'd strangled his niece. And when we were all sick, she saw the ones who died."

Nell's pale face goes even paler, but no one speaks.

"When we left Bent Edge Farm she said there were two children following—boy and girl. The boy had light hair and a mark over his face—here."

I pass my hand over my face. Nell claps a hand to her mouth and moans.

"What's this nonsense, lad?" Abel says roughly.

"It's true," I say. "That's why Honest Bob wanted her. She could see folk round all the people at the fair. She could see their ghosts!"

There's a stunned silence. Even Travis looks shocked. Nell starts to rock herself. "Not Ned and Sarah," she says. "Not my babies!"

Abel puts his arms round her. "Watch what you're saying!" he says to me angrily.

"It's true," I say again, though I've learned by now that no one believes you when you're telling the truth. "She kept seeing them following us all the time—in the forest and at the market. They kept whispering to her— telling us where to go."

"That's enough!" says Abel.

But Nell whispers, "What did they say?"

I shake my head. I can hardly bear to look at her stricken face.

"I don't know," I say. "I didn't believe her. I didn't want to believe her." I shut my eyes. It comes to me that I'm just as bad as all the people who never believed me. *If I find you, Annie,* I'm thinking, *I'll never doubt you again.*

"If this is some cock-and-bull story—" Abel begins, then he tails off, comforting Nell, who's moaning now, tears running down her face. "See what you've done?" he barks at me. "With your superstitious nonsense and lies?"

He looks like he might strike me, but unexpectedly Travis says, "I believe him."

Abel stares at Travis. "Then you're a bigger fool than you look."

But Travis doesn't back down. "There was something strange about that little maid," he says slowly. "Oh, I saw nothing to say that she could see . . . what he says. But there was something about her . . . not quite there. Like she was one of the fairy folk."

Abel snorts.

"She had a way of looking at you," Travis goes on, "like she knew what you were thinking. Once or twice she definitely did know—read my thoughts before I spoke them." He looks at Abel levelly for a moment, then turns to me. "You say she wanted to stay with the fair?"

I shake my head, as miserable as I've ever been. "I left her there," I say very low. "She wanted to come with me."

Then, as I see the look in their eyes, I burst out, "You don't know what it's like—she was always weird, like nothing on this earth. We couldn't go anywhere—everywhere we went she scared folk to death. They all thought her a witch or a changeling or something worse. She didn't fit in. The fair was the one place where she seemed to fit! And I—I'd had enough!"

There. I've said it. I fling myself back against the wall and kick my heels on the floor.

Silence. Then Nell stretches out a trembling hand toward me. "Joe," she says. "If we find her—could she tell me what happened . . . to my babes?"

Abel makes an exasperated sound, but I nod. "Yes," I say heavily. "Yes. She could."

"Then we must find her. Oh, Abel, we *must*!"

There's a hard, cold look in Abel's eye that's hard to take. "Is that what you want, Joe?" he says.

I stare back at him. "I want to find Annie," I say.

Abel's eyes glitter. "And it suits you to have us all go off on this wild-goose chase?"

Suddenly I see what he's saying. I leap to my feet. "You think I'm making all this up to get you to help!" I shout at him. "I don't care if you help me or not! And I don't care what you think. I'm going!"

Travis catches my shoulder. "Hold on a minute, lad." He draws himself up and looks at Abel, and Abel looks back like they're measuring each other. "If you'll wait till the morning, when my foot's better, I'll come with you."

Still angry, I shake him off, but Nell says, "We'll all look."

She's standing too and her voice has gone cold and hard. "You've helped me before, Abel, and you've no cause to help me now. But if there's any chance—any at all—of finding out what happened to Sarah and Ned—I *have* to find out!"

And Travis says, "If we find the little maid you'll soon know whether the lad's lying or not."

Abel looks from one to the other of us. Suddenly his shoulders sag. "Well, if that's what you think," he says to Nell, "then I'll stand by you. I always will. But how do you expect to find her? She could be anywhere. It's like looking for a pin in a haystack."

Nell looks at me and I look down. If I knew the answer to that one I wouldn't be here.

Then Travis says, "Honest Bob's a drinking man—and I still say he's heading for Manchester. We should check all the pubs and inns hereabouts; wherever the fair's likely to go."

"Ardwick Green," says Nell. "Moss Brook."

"Harpurhey," says Travis.

"Collyhurst," says Nell.

I look from one to the other. Suddenly it seems there's a plan. "We could all take a different area," I say.

"And report back here," says Nell.

"Hold on a bit," Abel says. He sits down on the edge of the table and sighs. "Look," he says. "I'm not saying I go along with all this. But you can't go wandering off on your own through all these places at night. You'll get yourselves killed. You're not fit yet," he says to Travis, then to me, "You're too young," and, "God knows what'd happen to you," he says to Nell. "If we're going to do this, we do it in pairs. And," he adds, lifting a box of *The Poor Man's Guardian* to the table, "we can take these with us. I'll put an advert in about the girl if you like."

So that's what happens. Night after night we go selling the paper in all the darkest, dingiest inns around Manchester. Sometimes I go with Nell, sometimes with Abel. When Travis's ankle heals he comes out too. Everywhere we go we sell copies and no one stops us because it's legal now, but there's no news of Honest Bob or the fair. We try not to get discouraged, to think that the fair's gone to a different town altogether, but by the end of the week it's hard.

Then it's Lammas Eve. All the streets are lit up and there's banners and flags. People follow torch-lit processions to the nearest fair. There's a big fair off Deansgate and Nell and Travis want to try their luck there. But something keeps drawing me back to Ancoats, though the Blue Locusts are out in full and Abel's wary.

"There'll be trouble, lad," he says. "There's always trouble where the fairs are."

In the end, though, he agrees to come with me.

We follow a procession along the Rochdale canal. There's fiddlers playing and jugglers on a wagon, and a huge cart carrying a wicker man. It's a good job Abel's with me because I can't see a thing above the heads of the crowd, and we're pulled along with them. There's folk wearing masks and banging drums. On Union Street the procession divides, half of it going to Smithyfield Market and the other to the Great Croft. We go from one to the other, but though there's any number of performers and stalls, there's no sign of Honest Bob's fair.

Abel takes my arm and steers me toward the main road. It's not easy pushing through the press, and the smell of gin and sweat's overwhelming. But all the pubs are on the Oldham Road.

And there's a lot of them, all crowded. The Briton's Protection, the Cheshire Cheese, the Death of Nelson, the Dog and Partridge and the Wenlock Arms. The crowds spill out onto the street. Gangs of Irish heckle the passersby, there's a crowd of people round a cockfight, and children on the steps up to open doors or pushing their heads through the railings in front of cellar windows.

Abel's fearless, going right up to the gangs—even the ones that are throwing bottles and stones. Most of them are surprised by this and turn civil; none of them's heard of Honest Bob.

At last, worn-out, we come to the Crown and Kettle, at the corner of Great Ancoats Street. I'm parched by now and Abel says, "I could do with a drink."

I follow him inside. There's no benches free, so I sit squashed on a stool in the corner. In one corner there's a big group singing and laughing, in another a fight that the landlord's trying to break up. I crane my neck but it's too dark to see.

Abel makes his way over with the ale. "Cheer up, lad," he says. "There's always tomorrow."

Then just as I'm about to answer there's a voice raised above all the others. "So the fair's up and running again and you're all invited. We're a little late, owing to yours truly being detained at His Lordship's pleasure—but none the worse for that. Come and see marvels beyond your wildest dreams!"

I leap up so fast, I send my stool spinning and knock Abel's arm so that the ale slops. "It's *him*!" I shout. "It's Honest Bob!" And before Abel can say anything I'm scrambling past tables to reach him.

Even before I get to him he's turning his gray grizzled head toward me. He's in a fine old mood, raddled with drink, and he lifts his arms in greeting. "Why, it's Jack!" he exclaims. "The famous disappearing boy! How are you?"

"How many names have you got?" says Abel, behind, but I'm not listening.

"Honest Bob!" I yell, tripping over the leg of a stool and grabbing someone's coat to save me. "Where's the fair? Where's Annie? What have you done with my sister?"

Honest Bob laughs in my face. "Now, it's a little late for showing concern," he says.

"Where is she, you filthy blagger?" I yell.

His face changes. He turns and addresses the crowd. "This boy's so concerned for his poor sister, he sold her to me for a shilling!" he says, and everyone's eyes swivel toward me.

"I didn't know it was a shilling, you villain!" I shout, aiming a punch at his back, but Abel catches my arm.

"No need for that," he says, then he speaks to Honest Bob. "The lad's just trying to find his sister," he says. "We'd be grateful if you'd tell us what you know."

"What I know?" says Honest Bob, raising his arms again in mock surprise. "All I know is, she's gone."

"Gone where?" I yell at him. "If you've got rid of her I'll—" But Abel's holding me back again.

Honest Bob just looks at me with a sneering grin. "It's a terrible sad story," he says, suddenly solemn, and he presses his hands together as though in prayer. "And I'm awful sorry to be the one to tell it to you—but your sister's gone, lad. Gone"—and he raises his eyes to heaven—"to a better place than this."

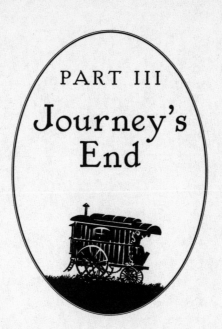

PART III

Journey's End

39

Fight

For a moment I can't speak, like I'm winded. Then I catch the look in his eye. "You lying git!" I howl, and launch myself at him. I lower my head and butt him in the stomach, driving all the air out of him, and he topples over, crashing into the table behind.

Next thing there's chaos. Table collapses and the tankards fly. Men leap up, swearing. A huge bloke with black shaggy hair rears over Honest Bob, who's sprawled across the broken table. He seems to know him.

"You!" he roars. "You stole my mule!" And he grabs Honest Bob by the throat and shakes him till he rattles. "I'll kill you, you thieving hound!"

"No—I will!" I yell, and grab his arm. Big bloke knocks me off like a fly. Then Abel taps him on the shoulder and he turns round, surprised, and Abel throws a beautiful punch, landing right on his jaw.

Then everyone's pitching in and the landlord's elbowing his way through. "What's going on?" he shouts, and someone lands him one as well.

Somehow, in all the confusion, Abel's hauling me off. "NO!" I yell, kicking. "Let me get at him!"

Then I see that he's shoving Honest Bob with the other arm, out the back door. We run across the yard together and turn the corner onto Great Ancoats Street, Honest Bob swearing like a trooper the whole time.

"What've you done with my sister?" I shout at him when we stop.

Honest Bob's surly, breathing hard. "By 'eck, lad," he growls. "I should leather you!"

"I think you've got a few questions to answer first," says Abel, very cool. "Or do you want to go back in there?"

Honest Bob growls and spits. Then he looks at me again. "Your sister's alive and well," he says grumpily. "Or alive at least, when I last saw her. I took her to the infirmary."

My mind races. "What—in Piccadilly?"

"We couldn't do anything with her," he says. "After you left she wouldn't speak or eat. She fell ill. Flo wouldn't leave her, but even she could see she needed help. She wouldn't come out of the wagon. Just turned her face to the wall."

Sounds like Annie.

"So you left her?" Abel says.

"What else was I supposed to do?" says Honest Bob. "I've a fair to run. She wasn't working—and Flo wouldn't work either, just sat by her side. And no one knew where you were," he says to me.

My anger boils away. It's my fault, not his.

"When was this?" Abel asks.

Honest Bob runs his fingers through his grizzled head. "Two . . . three weeks ago, maybe. I kept her all that time," he says as if that makes him a hero. "But she was pining away, wouldn't eat. She needed a doctor; even Flo could see that. So when we got back to Manchester I took her to the infirmary—and left her on the steps."

He glares at us defiantly.

"On the steps?" I say, mad all over again.

"Well, I couldn't pay for her, could I?" he shouts. "I'm not made of money. Costs a small fortune, keeping patients inside." Then, as I just stare at him, he says, "Look—they'll have taken her in. They don't just leave them there. And it seemed like a better place than the workhouse."

"But that's where she'll be now!" I say furiously. "They're not going to keep her there for nowt, are they?"

Honest Bob spreads his hands. "I did the best I could, lad. It's not as if you were there to look after her. Where were *you*?" he says pointedly, and all my arguments die away in my throat because he's right. I'm supposed to look after Annie, not him.

Abel puts his hand on my shoulder. "All right, mate," he says to Honest Bob. "Come on, lad," he adds to me, and I shake my head in disgust. For there's nothing else to do.

"You'll have to go and speak to them there," Honest Bob says as we turn to go. "And I hope you find her. Though what state she'll be in, I don't know."

Abel nods. Then he turns round. His arm moves so fast, I hardly see what's coming, and Honest Bob doesn't see it at all, but the next moment he's flying over backward as Abel's punch lands on his nose. We leave him there, spluttering in the mire.

Abel's strides lengthen and I trot after him.

"They'll have put her in the madhouse," I say desperately, because all I can think of is the dribbling lunatics roaming round the workhouse that had to be chained up when they took a fit. "We have to go there now."

"Not at this time, lad," Abel says without pausing. "It's past midnight."

"But I don't know what they're doing to her!" I say, and stop. I've heard fearful tales of what's done to lunatics—chains and whips, and bleeding by mad doctors who use them for experiments.

"It'll wait till the morning," Abel says, very calm.

"But I want to go now!"

"Look," says Abel, turning round. "They're not likely to let us in at this time. In fact, they don't allow visitors most of the time. But in the morning we'll go straight to the governor of the hospital. I know him. He was a friend of my father's."

We walk right by the hospital and I stare up at all the windows, hundreds of them, like I might see Annie's face. All this time she's been so near me, a couple of streets away, and I never knew. Just like Travis, and Nell. It's as though the road to Manchester's like a big tongue, licking everyone up.

Then we get to the shop and Nell hurries to meet us. "What?" she says fearfully, looking at my face. "Have you found her?"

"Let's go inside," says Abel, and we join Travis, who's sitting on the floor, nursing his foot.

Between us we tell them what's happened. And when we get to the part about the infirmary, Nell's hand flies to her mouth. "Oh, but they'll have put her in the madhouse," she says, just like me. "We have to get her out!"

Obviously, she's heard the stories as well.

"It's not a madhouse," says Abel, sitting down. "Not the kind you're thinking of, anyway. It's a proper hospital. I know the man who runs it."

Turns out the governor, John Sanderson, was a weaver, like Abel's father. A long time ago he had an accident weaving, and Abel's father took him to the infirmary. His right hand was mangled and he couldn't weave but they kept him on there, doing odd jobs. And he did well and worked his way up, and he's been governor there for the past twenty years.

"He treats his patients well," says Abel. "A more humane fellow never lived."

"But they'll have sent her to the workhouse," I say miserably, "if no one's paying."

"We don't know that," Abel says. "And either way, they won't let us in at this time. We should all get some sleep. In the morning, like I say, we'll go straight to John Sanderson's house."

"I'm coming with you," says Nell. She sinks down at the table and her eyes look huge and exhausted. "Oh, if only we can find her," she says. "If only she can tell me something—anything!" She breaks off, staring at the floor as if she can see awful things written there.

Abel puts his arm round her. "I'm walking you home," he says. "We'll all go together in the morning."

40

Governor

I'm left on my own with Travis, but I don't feel like sleeping. Don't feel like I'll ever sleep again till I see Annie.

"She'll be all right, lad," Travis says into the darkness. "Try and get some rest."

I can only sigh. "I've done everything wrong, Travis."

"No, you haven't," he says. Course, he would say that.

"I have," I say. "My life's a mess."

There's a little rumbling chuckle, but when he speaks he sounds serious. "Look," he says, "you've come a long way. You got away from those folk at the farm—and the workhouse. Nell told me about that. You got yourself into Manchester and you've survived on the streets. How many people can say that, eh?"

I only feel a bit better. "But Annie—" I say.

"We all make mistakes, Tom—Joe—whatever you're calling yourself. I made my mistake coming to the town. I knew it wasn't for me."

"Why did you?" I say. Seems like the old Travis would never have come near a place like Manchester.

He's silent for a while, then he says, "I had no plans to come here. But what happened . . . rocked me. I couldn't think straight. So I gave my freedom up. But I'm better now."

I crane toward him, trying to see in the darkness. "What will you do?"

"This place isn't for me, lad. I'd like to see the little maid again, to know she's all right. Then I'm off."

"But where will you go?" I say, thinking, *What will a one-eyed, one-legged tramp do in the country? At least he can beg in the town.*

Travis sighs and shuffles. "I need the open road," he says. "I'll head back toward the hills. Maybe I'll look up Dog-woman."

"What? Go back to the forest?" I say, feeling fear at the thought of it.

"Us angels have to stick together," he says, and even in the dark I can hear him smiling. *They say her bite will either kill or cure*, he told us, then I think of him trying to run with the pack. But I can see he'd rather die in the forest than live in the town.

"Let's hope you find her in the morning," he says, meaning Annie. "Try to get some sleep now, Tom."

And while I think I'll never sleep, suddenly I'm yawning fit to split my head in two. And I curl up on some sacking in the corner of the room.

In the morning Abel has to wake me up. "Sun's shining, Joe," he says. "Best set off early."

Nell's there already, looking pale and tense. My stomach's churning and all I can think about is Annie. We walk through the streets in silence. Lammas is a holiday and only a few people are up and about, though later they'll all be at the fairs.

The governor's house is in the hospital grounds. We have to cross a yard where people are walking round in a long line, for exercise, and my stomach churns even more when I see how they look: some empty-eyed, others bent and haggard. Bright sunlight doesn't improve them—most of this lot'd look better in the dark. Their mouths hang open and some of them are drooling. Annie's not with them.

From the hospital building there's the sound of someone crying on and on. We come to a bright green door with a brass knocker and Abel raps on it smartly. A manservant appears and he's dark, like Digger.

"Visitors for the governor," Abel says, but the manservant doesn't look impressed.

"Governor's busy," he says, but Abel stops him closing the door.

"Will you give him this card?" he says, and the manservant looks at it suspiciously, then nods.

Moments later there's the sound of someone clattering down the stairs.

"Why, it's Young Abe!" he says before he's got to the door. "Abel Heywood's son!"

Seems everyone in Abel's family has the same name. The door opens wide and an elderly gent with flowing gray hair stands beaming at us through silver spectacles, one hand on the door frame, the other in a leather glove by his side.

"Come in, come in!" he says, and we follow Young Abe through the door. The governor skips ahead of us.

"You'll have to excuse the mess—I'm preparing an audit and figures never were my strong point. Not like Albert here," he says, nodding at the manservant, who's still glowering at us suspiciously. But the governor shifts some papers from a seat.

"Sit down, sit down!" he cries. "To what do I owe this unusual pleasure?"

I look at Abel and Abel looks at me. Nell looks at us both.

"Mr. Sanderson," Abel begins.

But the old gent says, "John, please—your father and I were good friends. Call me John. Everyone else does."

"John, then," says Abel. "This is Joe."

John shakes my hand gravely. "How do you do?" he says.

Now I should say, "Fine, thank you," or something like that, but instead I just blurt out, "I'm looking for my sister!"

"Are you?" says the governor, shaking his head. "I'm sorry to hear it."

I look at Abel again. "I'm told she's here—with you."

"Is she?" he says, amazed. He pushes his glasses farther up his nose as between us we tell our tale. And at one point of it he says, "Ah," and I know he knows what we're talking about. I stop talking and he looks at us.

"Have you seen her?" I say.

The governor presses the tips of his fingers together. "A little girl was found here one night, yes. Nobody knew where she'd come from."

"Did you keep her? Is she here?"

"A problematic case," he says. "One of the most serious states of catatonia I've ever seen." He looks at Abel.

"But is she here?" I demand, and he carries on talking to Abel.

"The parish are supposed to pay seven shillings a week for the care of those who cannot pay," he says. "But of course they are denying responsibility. It cannot be proved, they say, that she is of this parish. The beadle said she would have to go to the workhouse."

My heart sinks. I never wanted to go near one of them places again.

"Is that where she is then?" says Abel.

"No, it is not," says the governor. "One of the doctors here is specially interested in catatonic states as opposed to dementia, and I thought he should be given the opportunity to examine her. She is here," he says, standing up and bringing out a large bunch of keys, and my heart flies up again.

"Can I see her?" I say, stepping forward.

He fingers the keys. "I don't suppose it would do any harm," he says, cautiously. "But in cases of catatonia you can never tell."

I start to speak again, but Abel interrupts. "What do you mean?"

The governor rocks on his feet. "Catatonia is a case of extreme withdrawal," he says, like he's reading from a book. "It sometimes occurs after severe shock. The patient will neither speak nor respond to outside stimuli. As though they have retreated, as it were, a long way inside themselves."

I look at Abel and Nell. "But that's just Annie!" I burst out. "She's always like that."

The governor looks surprised. "All evidence of normal consciousness is suppressed," he says. "There is no interest in the outside world at all; the sufferer lives completely in a world of his own. Very little research has been done in this area, so our doctors were most interested in her condition. I've seen one or two cases before, but nothing like this."

"But that's Annie!" I say again earnestly. "That's the way she is."

The governor looks at me over his glasses. "Do you mean to say," he says, "that if you stick a pin in her, she does not respond?"

"Have you been sticking pins all over my sister?" I say hotly.

Mr. Sanderson looks stern. "We have not 'been sticking pins all over her,' as you put it," he says reprovingly. "This is a humane hospital, run according to the principles of the great Dr. Ferriar. It is not an old-style asylum where patients were subjected to fear and shock in order to cure them. It is our belief that sickness of the mind can be cured as well as sickness of the body, by patience and rest and good diet. . . . But we did have to establish the degree of severity of catatonia. We pricked her with a single pin," he says, "and she did not respond."

That sounds a lot less like Annie. I'm worried now and I don't know what to say, but Nell steps forward. "Please, will you take us to see her?" she says.

She clasps her hands and the governor looks at her kindly. "Are you a relative?" he says.

She doesn't know how to answer that one, but Abel takes her hand. "Only the boy is a relative. We're looking after him."

"Well," says the governor, and pauses. "I suppose we have to establish first that she really is your sister. I'll take you to the nurse in charge."

We follow him out of the house and across the yard, which is quiet now, all the lunatics having been led back in. My stomach's all twisted into a knot. *Hold on in there, Annie*, I'm thinking. *I'm coming back for you.*

He opens the great doors with a huge key. "As I say, this hospital is run along the most humane principles that you will find anywhere in Europe," he says, leading us along a narrow passage that smells funny. "We are opposed to all forms of violence and use minimal restrictions when a patient becomes . . . excitable. Fresh air and kindness, that's what the good doctor used to say. But in the little girl's case we were thinking that we might have to resort to force-feeding," he says, opening another door. "We cannot allow her to starve to death in our care."

All the time he's talking I'm feeling worse. Annie's refusing food—that can't be good. We enter a large room with high ceilings. Several women patients are there. On the whole they look better than the ones in the yard. They're sitting quiet and sewing or knitting. A nurse is bending over one of them and helping her drink from a cup.

"Ah, here we are," says the governor as the nurse straightens. "Nurse Agnes Weir. She has particular charge of our little patient." And he explains to her who we are and why we've come.

Nurse Agnes Weir has a lot of white hair, red cheeks and the widest mouth I've ever seen. Green eyes far apart. Looks like a frog. She nods and clucks and makes sympathetic noises as the governor explains.

"Can you take them to identify the clothing first?" says Governor John.

Nurse Agnes leads the way and we all follow. We come to a room that's full of locked cupboards. "Now then," she says, "which one was it?" and I wait, hopping up and down while she opens one cupboard after another. Finally she brings out a small, pathetic-looking bundle, and I recognize the clothes Annie wore with the fair.

"Them's hers, all right," I say, clutching them, and something falls to the floor. Nurse Agnes bends down and picks it up and I can only stare. It's the necklace our mother gave Annie, the little beads and half of a coin that I now know is a threepenny bit.

"We take everything off and wash the things they come in with," Nurse Agnes says. "But we keep them all for them, for when they go out again."

I find my voice. "You mean she let you take the beads?" I ask, and Nurse Agnes looks a bit offended.

"We can't let them keep anything they might strangle themselves with," she says. "Them's the rules."

Now I really am worried. Annie never let anyone touch that necklace. She'd fly at anyone who tried.

"I think you can take them now," the governor says, and Nurse Agnes picks up a bundle of towels.

"Fresh linen," she says, "I almost forgot."

We follow her along one corridor and into another, and the voice we heard crying when we first came is louder now. A woman's voice crying, "Oh, what will I do, whatever will I do?" over and over again.

The next corridor's lined with doors. "These are the individual cells," Nurse Agnes says. "Any patient can come here to be quiet, if they're tired of the common room. And sometimes we bring 'em here to quiet 'em down, if you take my meaning. But mostly it's their choice."

"Do they eat in here?" Abel says, and he carries on asking her questions like he's doing research, which he probably is.

I'm hardly listening. I feel like hot coals are burning me up inside. It's a long, long corridor, and Nurse Agnes stops at each door to put a clean towel on each bed. All the doors are open, which surprises me, but in one room a man dashes toward us, snarling, and I see he's tethered by a long chain.

All this makes me feel worse and worse. I'm frightened of seeing Annie, and more frightened of not seeing her. Feels like a bad dream that won't end.

Then suddenly I can see a door at the very end of the corridor, and sure as if she's calling me, I know Annie's in that room. And I'm breaking free of the others and running ahead, and they're all calling after me but I can't hear. I charge into that room and see the little shrunken figure on the top of the bed, two pale feet pointing at the ceiling. And a groan bursts out of me like it's come all the way from my own feet, and I fall on her and scoop her up in my arms, crying, "Annie!" And for the first time in my life, I burst into tears.

41

Necklace

Seems like once you start crying there's no stopping. I hold on to Annie and cry till all the front of her gown's wet. She doesn't move. There isn't even a flicker in her pale eyes.

"Annie, Annie," I moan, rocking her. I don't even care that the others are watching from the doorway. This is the worst thing, out of all the bad things that have happened. And it's all my fault.

After a while Nell comes up to me and puts a hand on my shoulder. "Joe, dear," she says, and I can tell from her voice that she's nearly crying too, and she doesn't know what to say.

Then Nurse Agnes says, "Best leave them alone for a while," and they all tiptoe away.

I'm left with Annie. After a bit I prop her up on the pillow. I brush the hair away from her face and stare into her empty eyes. "Annie," I whisper. "It's Joe."

Nothing. But I have to keep on talking. I tuck another strand of hair behind her ear. "I left you," I say. "I shouldn't've left you and I'm sorry. And now you've left me. But I've come back, Annie—I'm here. It's me—Joe!"

She's so thin and small. Where the gown falls open I can see her heart beating, through her ribs. *She wasn't this small when I left her,* I'm thinking, then I remember I've grown.

I take her hand and rub it. "I've come back to you, Annie," I say. "Come back to me." But there's only the rise and fall of her ribs.

What'll I do if she won't come back? I can't stand the thought of leaving her in hospital. For a moment I think of trying to smuggle her out, but I can't see how. And what would I do with her when I'd got her away? Where would we go?

"Annie," I say, "don't you want to come away with me?"

My tears are still falling, splashing onto her gown. I lick one off the back of my hand. Never tasted tears before.

"I wanted my freedom, Annie," I tell her. "But I never found it. It wasn't freedom, leaving you." Then I lean forward over her, listening. Her hair gets in my eyes and mouth. "Where've you gone to, Annie?" I say, and just for a moment I can hear the silence in her head, like the silence on the empty moor.

How long we stay like this I don't know. Seems like forever, and no time at all.

Then the nurse comes back. "Time to try her with some food," she says. I watch, fascinated, as she tilts Annie's head back and pours a little gruel into her open mouth. Annie's throat moves all on its own, but her mouth stays open. When the nurse moves her back again, gruel runs out of the corner of it and down her chin, and the nurse scoops it up with a spoon.

"Just a bit at a time—keeps her strength up," she says to me.

I stare at her, hollow-eyed.

"Doctors'll be round soon," she says. "So you'll have to go. But you can come back again, tomorrow."

"I'm not leaving her," I say.

"You'll have to, dearie," she says, very kind. "You shouldn't be here at all by rights. Not without the doctor's say-so. But I'm sure Mr. Sanderson'll have a word, and they'll sign a visitor's pass."

"No," I say. "I'm not going."

Nurse Agnes looks at me like she's about to say something, then changes her mind. "I'll just have a word with your friends," she says, and hurries off.

She can have a word with the king if she likes, I'm thinking. *I'm not leaving Annie again.*

A minute later Abel appears.

"I'm not leaving," I say, before he starts.

He squats down beside the bed and touches Annie's hand. "You can't stay here, lad."

"I can then."

"Joe," he says more sternly. "John Sanderson let us in here in good faith. But he's got to ask the doctor for a proper pass. Now, if you don't behave he'll have us slung out and you won't get that pass."

I stare at him and my breath quivers in my throat.

"You've got to do what's best for her," he says gently, standing up.

"He's right," Nurse Agnes says behind him. "A bit at a time—like with her food. You don't want to overwhelm her, poor lass."

"Come back home, with me and Nell," Abel says.

I stare at them both, hating them. *Home?* I'm thinking. *Where's that then?* The only place I want to be is with Annie. If she won't come back to me, maybe I can join her, wherever she is, in the silent, empty places in her skull.

But they're both staring at me and I realize I've no choice.

Just for a change.

I turn back to Annie. Panic rises in my throat at the thought of leaving her there, so frail and still. "Annie, I have to go now," I tell her, my voice breaking. "But I'm not leaving you. I'll never leave you again, Annie, you've got to believe me." And I crush her to me again, burying my face in her neck. "I'll be back tomorrow, you'll see."

I put her down then, smoothing her hair, folding her hands, and somehow, though it feels like it's tearing me apart, I stand up. Abel doesn't speak but he nods and squeezes my shoulder, and I follow him out of that room, feeling like my heart's being wrenched out of me with every step.

We go back to the office where the locked cupboards are. Governor John's there with Nell, and she's all red-eyed from crying.

What's she crying for? I think, then I remember that she'd hoped to speak to Annie, to learn about her lost children.

The governor shuffles some papers about. "I'm sure the doctor will be more than happy to sign a pass," he says. "I'm sure he'll see it as fortuitous, you coming here. An aid to Annie's recovery."

I say nothing, but Abel says, "They do recover, then?"

"Oh, almost certainly," says the governor. "According to the evidence we have. Which isn't much, as I say. But there are definite indications that patients do recover. It's just that we can't say how, or when."

Abel and Nell look at me but I don't say anything. Somewhere inside me, though, I do feel just a little bit better. *Hope*, I'm thinking. *There's got to be hope.*

Abel and the governor exchange a few more words and then we're off.

"Come back anytime tomorrow," the governor says. "You can stay and see the doctor then."

He's kind enough—they all are. I suppose I've got to be glad that she isn't in the other kind of madhouse, with chains and whips. Or the workhouse.

Things could definitely be worse, I tell myself, trailing after Abel and Nell, but it doesn't stop me feeling terrible. Deserted somehow—the way I felt when our mother left us in the workhouse. I know it's mad but that's the way I feel. Seems like I always expected Annie to be there, where I left her, waiting for me to return.

When we get to the shop Travis is there, with Matt's mother and a panful of stew. He comes toward us, wiping his hands on his coat. "Did you find her?" he asks.

I fling myself down on the pile of sacks in the corner.

"We did," says Abel, and he explains in a few words what's happened. "But the doctor says there's every chance she'll recover."

Travis looks very serious. "That's good," he says uncertainly.

"It's not good!" I say. "She's lying there like a corpse—she doesn't move; her eyes don't even blink when you look at them. She's gone somewhere and I can't get her back!" Then I stop talking because I don't want to start crying again.

"But she's having the best care," Abel says, and he squeezes Nell's hand. "We have to hope."

"I saw people like that in the workhouse," Travis says. "Just turned their faces to the wall . . ." He trails off.

"You must all be starving," Matt's mother says into the silence. "Look— I brought some stew."

Supper's short and silent. The stew's good but I can hardly eat it, despite everyone telling me I have to keep my strength up. Nell hardly eats either, and afterward Abel says he'll walk her home.

"It's a working day tomorrow," he says. "But we'll come to the hospital later, and see the doctor with you."

Matt's mother goes too. "I'll leave the pot," she says, "in case you're hungry later."

Then it's just me and Travis. He doesn't say anything, just starts shifting the dishes.

"She's gone, Travis," I say very low.

"I know, lad."

"It's my fault."

"Don't start that again. Here." He sits down in front of me. "Finish this bread off."

I turn my face away. Feels like the first time in my life I've not been hungry.

Travis sighs. "Look," he says, "I know she's gone somewhere and you don't know where she is. But she might come back. That's what you've got to keep thinking."

I don't say anything. But I'm remembering the silence in Annie's head. "I do know where she is," I say.

Travis looks at me.

"She's on the moor—that time when we were with you. I . . . I heard it— I think."

Travis sits back, pulling his stumpy leg from under him. "Then you have to talk to her about it."

I stare at him. "And say what?"

"Talk to her about the moor, if that's where she is. About the sun rising and the birds calling. The hills changing color. Why do you think she's there?"

I remember it vividly. All the sounds of the earth waking up, but beyond that, beyond everything, a massive silence. "I think," I say slowly, "I think it was the last time she felt safe."

Travis nods. "That's what they do, lad. They go to a safe place in their mind. Where no one can get at them. Because the place they're in is too hard. It's a pity we can't get her out of that building," he says.

I think of taking her out. Back to the moors with Travis. Or the forest, even, to Dog-woman. Then I think of how hard it'd be, getting her out of the hospital. *I'm just taking my sister out*, I could say. *There's a wild woman in the forest who might bite her . . .*

Yes, that'd work, I think bitterly.

"But if you can't get her out," Travis is saying, "you have to go there with her. Show her you haven't left."

He's right, I'm thinking, and the small knot in my stomach tightens again. I shouldn't be here—I should be talking to Annie. "She always hated the town," I say.

"I hate it myself," says Travis, then he gets up clumsily and starts whistling an old tune. "Best get some sleep, lad," he says, breaking off. "Morning'll be here before you know it."

I lie down on the sacking, thinking of all the things I can say to Annie, thinking, *I'll reach her somehow, if it takes me all day*. And I roll over, but it's hard to sleep.

In the morning, first thing, I'm back at the hospital. The governor shows me in, but Nurse Agnes isn't there. There's a little dark nurse in the cells, making beds.

"Susan, this is Joe," he tells her. "He's come to visit our little ward in the end cell."

Nurse Susan stares at me and nods, before turning back to the beds. She's got bent legs, I notice, like Annie.

Annie's lying just as she was before. Shadows from the window flicker over her face, and it seems like she's staring at them but her eyes don't move, or blink.

I go to sit on the bed, but this time I don't burst into tears.

"I'll just leave you with her," says Governor John. "Stay as long as you like—the doctor seems to think it may be a good thing."

I hear his footsteps retreating but I don't look round. I take Annie's hand. "I'm back, Annie," I tell her. "I told you I'd come back."

It's hard talking to that empty stare. But talking's what I'm good at, so I close my eyes and begin. I tell her everything that's happened since I left her, and I don't miss out a thing—about Queenie and the gang, and Mr. M., and Abel and Nell. Annie's the only person who knows everything that's ever happened to me.

"Seems like you were right," I tell her, "about that boy and girl following us. They're Nell's children, Annie. She's hoping you'll tell her about them. She really wants you to, Annie—her heart's breaking. You were right, Annie," I tell her. "And I never believed you. I'm sorry."

I talk to her for hours and I'm concentrating so hard on what I'm saying that I nearly jump out of my skin when there's a small cough behind me. It's the little, dark, bandy-legged nurse in the doorway.

"Are you really her brother?" she asks, and I nod at her, thinking, *Go away*.

But she only steps forward. "Are you on your own?" she says.

I look around the room. "Looks like it," I say, and she steps forward again.

"Is your name Joe Sowerby?" she says.

I stare at her. "Who wants to know?" I say.

Then she reaches into the pocket of her apron and brings out the wooden beads. "Do you recognize this necklace?" she says.

I glance at it, then back to Annie. "It's Annie's," I tell her.

"No," she says. Then as I look back at her, she reaches into her other pocket and brings out another necklace that looks exactly the same. Only on the end of it is *the other half of the coin.*

42

Nurse

I stare at her as she brings the necklaces together. "They fit, you see," she says, nodding.

I hold out my hand. "Where did you get it?" I ask, in a strangled voice. I take the necklaces off her and stare at them.

She pulls up a stool and sits down. "I work in the hospital part as well," she says. "And a little while ago we had a patient come in wearing this round her neck. She was terribly ill, poor dear—consumption—but she wouldn't let us take it off her. And she kept talking all the time about her children— Joe and Annie, Annie and Joe—all the time. Then when she knew she was dying, she took the necklace off herself and gave it to me. 'Look after it,' she said, and I promised I'd keep it for her. She was afraid they'd just throw it away, you see. I think she thought that if someone had it, there was still a chance that its twin might be found, and that her children would learn what had happened to her and how she never gave up."

There's a huge jumble of voices in my head, like I've gone mad now, with Annie. I clench my fist round the necklaces. "She's dead then," I manage to say.

The little nurse looks terribly sad, like it's her very own tragedy. "I'm sorry to have to tell you," she says, and her lip's actually quivering. But I feel like laughing. Because it's all some big mad joke.

"When was this?" I ask her, and she says, "Well, that's the worst of it. It's not long ago. Three months maybe."

Three months, I'm thinking. *We've been on the road longer than that. I've been in Manchester longer . . .*

When we set off from Bent Edge Farm, our mother was still alive. When we met Travis and went through the forest, she was alive then. And I remember saying to Dog-woman that she was probably dead and Annie saying *No*, very definitely, and all of a sudden I know where Annie is.

Nurse Susan's talking again. "She was on her way to you," she says, and I do laugh then, short and loud, so that she blinks very quickly and looks worried. "She'd been all over the country doing laboring work—sent from one farm to another. She worked on those gangs where the women are all roped together and they go through the fields on their knees, picking taters. Each parish she came to she had to work for her keep, or go to the workhouse, so she couldn't get back to you. But that was all she wanted. 'If I could only see them again,' she said to me, 'I wouldn't mind dying.' She was on her way back to the workhouse where she'd left you."

And if she'd got there, we'd have gone, I'm thinking, *just like Nell*. And I don't feel like laughing anymore. Feels like there's a funeral inside my head, and a great bell clanging.

"I felt that sorry for her," says the nurse. "I took the beads like she asked, and didn't give them up like I was supposed to. And I didn't tell anyone about it. I wasn't here the night they brought your sister in, and I only saw the beads a few days ago. It gave me a terrible turn. I didn't know what to do. 'Susan,' I says, 'you've got to tell the governor right away.' But I couldn't be sure, you see. Because none of us knew her name. Then you came," she says, "and the name was the right one. And besides," she adds, "you look just like your mother."

That face, the face I could never see in my dreams, comes to me then, and it's my own. I shut my eyes and see it plain. I can hardly trust myself to speak, but I move my lips.

"Will you leave us alone now, please?" I say, and she looks sadder than ever.

She stops at the door. "Can I get you anything?" she asks, but I shake my head and she goes.

I lay my head on Annie's chest. "Annie," I whisper, but my head's full of my mother. "She died looking for us, Annie," I say, and I can't believe how sad I feel. I wasn't even looking for her. But maybe somewhere inside me, I was.

"It's just you and me now, Annie," I say. "It always was, just you and me."

After a while the little nurse comes back, bringing a jug of water and a mug. I don't say anything but I sit up, holding the necklaces out. "Look, Annie," I say. "The necklaces. They fit." And I press them to her heart. And a long quiver runs through Annie's body.

I jump back, startled. "Did you see that?" I ask the nurse.

"They do that sometimes," she says. "Move, without knowing it. It doesn't mean anything," she says, as if she's sorry to disappoint me. I look at Annie but her face hasn't changed.

But she moved when I gave her the necklaces.

I move Annie's hand so that her fingers curl round them. When the nurse goes again I lean forward, over Annie. "Mother," I whisper into her ear.

There it is again, the slightest tremor.

I sit up and cup Annie's face in my hands. "Mother," I say very low. "It's me, Joe."

I think I can see something in Annie's eyes, but maybe it's only a shadow.

"Mother," I say uncertainly. "I promised I'd take care of Annie, and I left her. I'm sorry I left her. But I've come back now and I'll never leave her again. So if you've got her, you have to let her go."

And the fingers holding the necklaces twitch.

"Mam," I say. My eyes are wet, but I'm not crying. "I know you had to leave us—you didn't have a choice. I know you must've broke your heart when you couldn't come back. I know I said you'd forgotten us and I'm sorry.

I know you loved us, more than anything. But if you've got Annie, you've got to let her come back to me. She doesn't belong with you—she isn't dead. She belongs with me."

Silence. There's only the sound of Annie breathing and my heart thudding.

I wipe my eyes on the back of my hand. "Give her back to me, Mam," I say miserably.

Then I remember the story I used to tell Annie when I needed her to listen. Our story. I put my hand over Annie's, and the necklaces, and take a long, quivering breath.

"It was cold," I say. "Colder than I've ever known. And you were tiny, you still couldn't walk properly. So our mam carried you, through the snow. She fell over twice but still she got up, carrying you, until we came to the workhouse on the hill. And she knocked at the door . . ."

I tell Annie the whole story, clasping her hand. And with my eyes shut I can see the whole thing. I can see my mother's face, crying. And when I get to the part where she says, *I'll have to leave thee now, but I'll come back for thee,* I swear I can hear her voice in the room, speaking with me. . . . She took the beads from her neck and put them round Annie's, who was clinging to her for all she was worth. *Look after your sister, Joe,* she said, just as the door slammed to.

"And I will, I will look after her," I say out loud, and I'm crying now. "I never meant to leave her. I love you, Mam," I say, and then it happens.

Annie shudders and goes stiff, like all her muscles are clenched. Then she takes a long, wheezing breath, and suddenly she's coughing fit to burst! I let her hand go and she curls her knees up, still coughing.

I run to the door. "Nurse, NURSE!" I'm yelling, and the little nurse comes running.

Then I run back to Annie and pick her up again, banging her on the back. "Annie, Annie, it's all right!" I tell her.

Her face is almost blue with coughing, then suddenly she stops. The nurse holds out a cup of water with trembling hands and Annie sputters into it, then manages to swallow. I hold her face and she looks at me, blinking, with her hollow eyes.

"Mother," she says, and sinks forward, into my arms.

43

Voices

The next couple of hours flash by, so many things are happening. Nurse sends for the governor, and he looks as if he can hardly believe his eyes.

"Well, well," he says. "Well, well, well!"

Apart from that, he's speechless.

I can't take my eyes off Annie, who looks like she doesn't know where she is, like she's just been born. The nurse fetches some soup and I help to feed her, because she'll only take it off me.

"Annie," I say, "do you know who I am?"

She nods, not looking at me, and I lean forward and she whispers, "Joe," and I hug her till she hasn't got any breath left.

"Careful, careful," says Governor John. "We must be careful."

He's in a right state, spectacles askew.

"The doctor will be arriving," he says. "I must go and tell him—" And he hurries away.

When we're on our own Annie looks at me, still blinking, like the light hurts. "You left," she says.

I start apologizing all over again but in no time there's footsteps approaching, several of them, and the governor's voice saying, "It's remarkable, really quite remarkable."

Then the door opens wide. I only half turn round, enough to see that Abel's there, and Nell. "Abel," I say. "Look at Annie!"

The doctor steps forward. "Nat!" he says. And I turn round fully then, seeing him for the first time. It's Dr. Kay.

My first thought is to bolt past them somehow. But I won't leave Annie. I shift backward on the bed, holding Annie's hand.

"I know this boy," says Dr. Kay. "He's a violent criminal."

This is all I need, I'm thinking, but Abel crosses the room and stands by me, putting his hand on my shoulder.

"Not this boy," he says. "His name's not Nat."

The doctor glares at Abel. "Can I see the patient?" he says. We move for him as he sits on the bed, but Annie's still clutching my fingers. He moves her head this way and that, gazes into her eyes, takes her pulse then, just as he did with me, looks down her mouth. Each time he tells her to do something Annie looks at me and I nod, and she does as she's told. All the time I'm thinking, *What now, what now?* Because for all I know, when he's finished, he'll call the police.

"How many fingers am I holding up, Annie?" he asks, and she doesn't speak but holds up four of her own, then three. He moves her leg and taps her on the knee with a tiny hammer, and her little foot flies up. When he's finished he smiles. "Well done, Annie," he says. Then he stands.

"It seems as though she's recovering nicely," he says. "If she carries on improving she can leave. Though there is the question, of course, of where she can go."

"She's staying with me," I tell him. He packs away his tools.

"What, in the New Bailey?" he says. My stomach gives a lurch, then goes on falling. "I treated Mr. Mosley," he says, "when you'd finished with him. And why he didn't take out a warrant for your arrest I'll never know. . . . His name was Nat then," he snaps as Abel starts to speak, and Abel backs down.

Then Abel says, "I think you'll find Joe had his reasons."

And Nell says, "That man took my children!"

"All he wanted me for," I say, "was to prove that the poor are like animals—that nothing can be done for them."

"Well, you helped him out there, didn't you?" the doctor says.

But Nell cuts in, "I was in the workhouse, and he saw to it that I was placed out and my children taken off me—taken where I could never find them. I still don't know where they are."

Dr. Kay raises his hand. "Watch what you're saying," he tells her.

But Abel says, "It's true—and I could find you a dozen other mothers with the same tale to tell. Poor children are being sent all over this country, and to other countries, and no one sees or hears of them ever again!"

"I don't need to hear this," says Dr. Kay. "All I know is that Mr. Mosley gave this boy a home—fed him, educated him—and was repaid by a vicious beating. The boy is dangerous. He belongs in prison!"

Annie scrambles across the bed toward me, and I hold on to her hard. Then the governor speaks nervously.

"I don't know the ins and outs of this," he says. "But I do know that it would be very unwise to separate the boy from his sister. By all accounts she fell into this state when he left her, and she has recovered on his return. That should tell us something, I think."

The doctor looks at us, and Abel says, "Look, sir. In his short lifetime the boy has seen and done more things than you or I could know. His sister too. They have survived difficulties and dangers we can't even imagine. You know, better than anyone, how the poor live—you wrote about it in your book. Small wonder if they go astray; more wonder if they don't. But I can say this—for the past few weeks the boy has worked for me, and he has worked hard and honestly and well. And he cares for his sister, sir. They are everything to one another."

"Their mother died in this very hospital," the little nurse puts in.

"What purpose would it serve, sending the lad to prison?" says Abel angrily. "He'd only be sent from there to some distant place, Canada even, or Australia, by people who think the poor have to be disposed of—like your Mr. Mosley."

Dr. Kay looks from one to the other of us, and swallows, then turns away. "I can't pretend to agree with all of Mr. Mosley's sentiments . . ." he begins, and then looks round. "But this is beside the point. I can't discharge the girl into her brother's care—he isn't fit. They have no home. Where will they go? Onto the streets, where they will revert to a savage state? They should go where they will be taken care of—if not to prison, then to the workhouse."

"NO!" I say, too loudly, but Abel looks at Nell, and she comes to stand by his side.

"They have a home, sir," Abel says, taking her hand. "With me and Nell. We plan to marry, and the children can stay with us. I can offer the boy honest employment, and I will see to it that they are both educated."

I look up at him, amazed, then at the doctor. I can see his mind's hanging in the balance. "You mean you will act as their moral and legal guardian?" he asks, and Abel nods. The doctor turns to Nell. "What do you say?"

"Oh, sir," she says. "I lost my own two children and I can't replace them. But if I can take care of these two—it's more than I could hope for!"

"Well," says the doctor, and he rubs his fingers across his forehead. "For whatever reason, Mr. Mosley did not seem interested in pressing charges and it is hardly my place to act for him. If you swear to me that they will be properly looked after, and kept out of trouble? Because if there *is* any trouble—"

"No fear of that, sir," says Abel, and I look up at him joyfully.

"Then maybe it is for the best," the doctor says.

"Oh, thank you, sir, thank you!" I say. "You won't regret it!"

"I hope not," he says, very serious. "Meanwhile, I think my patient has had quite enough excitement for one day. We should all leave her now."

"I can't leave her, sir," I say as Annie clutches me. "I said I'd never leave her again."

There's an argument about this but in the end Nurse Susan says, "I can make up a bed for him here, for the night."

And that's what we do. The doctor leaves, promising to come back the next day. Abel ruffles my hair. "I'll have to be going too," he says.

"Abel," I say, catching his hand. "Thanks."

Nell steps forward. "Good-bye, Annie," she says, touching her hair. Annie quivers but doesn't speak.

"We'll come back soon," Abel says. "Give Annie a chance to get to know us."

And they leave, Nell looking wistfully over her shoulder at Annie.

As soon as they go Annie scrabbles round to face me. "Flo?" she says, and I realize what a lot she's missed.

"You're in hospital now," I say gently, and start to tell her all over again about everything that's happened. In between, Nurse Susan comes in with bedding, and then warm milk.

"Does she know . . . about the necklace?" she asks in a hushed voice, but I haven't wanted to bring that up just yet, for fear of what the shock might do. I don't know how much Annie knows.

Then the nurse leaves and the noises of the hospital get louder, and along the corridor the woman's still ranting on. I don't like it any more than Annie. She stands on the bed and tries to see out of the window. I make her lie down again but she bobs up and goes to the door. "Go now," she says.

"We can't," I tell her. "Annie, come here."

Annie comes back to me, dragging her feet. I pick up her necklace that she's left lying on the bed, then I hold the other one to it.

"Do you know what this is?" I ask her. She leans forward so that her hair falls all over her face. "Look, Annie," I say. "The pieces fit."

She shudders but doesn't speak. Then she snatches the necklaces suddenly.

"Our mother was here," I tell her, my lips dry all of a sudden. "But she was very ill." Annie's fists tighten round the necklaces. "She never stopped looking for us, Annie. She loved us." I lie Annie down on the bed and she curls up toward me, still holding the necklaces.

I try a different tack. "Where were you, Annie? Where did you go?"

For a moment Annie doesn't answer, but her eyes film over, like she's trying to remember. Then she says, "Mother."

"You were with our mother?" I say, and she nods. "What was it like?"

"Dark," she says, helpfully. "And light."

I lick my lips. "What was she like?" I ask.

Annie's brow creases, like she wants to tell me something that's too big for words. "Angel," she says, and sighs and closes her eyes.

What, you mean like Dog-woman? I think of saying, but somehow I know that's all I'll get out of Annie. Her eyes flicker open again briefly, and I know that she knows, and she knows that I know, about our mother, and maybe that's all that matters. Her eyes close again, peacefully, and her breathing changes. And I lie down on my own made-up bed and try to get some sleep.

In the morning two doctors come with Dr. Kay and examine Annie for ages, and she hates it, curling up under the sheets, but somehow I convince her it has to be done before we can leave.

"Is she always this quiet?" they ask me.

"Yes," I tell them firmly.

"Can she speak for herself?" one of them asks, and I try to explain how it is with Annie; that she can speak but usually she won't. All the time I'm terrified that they'll find one of us unfit, and say she can't leave or we both have to go to the workhouse. Then Nurse Agnes brings breakfast and Annie eats like there's no tomorrow, while Dr. Kay looks on approvingly.

"Not much wrong with her appetite, anyway," he says, and the doctors prepare to go.

"If she carries on like this, there's no reason why she shouldn't leave," he says at the door, and my heart dances a little jig. I clasp Annie's hands and she smiles at me.

Apart from this, it's dead boring—nothing to do. Nurse Agnes talks to us a bit and wants to hear our story, and Annie submits to having her face and hands washed. I take her for a bit of a walk along the corridor, but she runs back when one of the chained-up lunatics roars. It's a long, long day.

But in the evening Abel comes with Nell.

"I've brought something for you," he says, holding his hand out to Annie. It's a little wooden bird. "Travis made it," he says.

Annie cups it in her hands. She doesn't say anything but she's smiling.

Abel sits on the corner of the bed and Nell sits on the stool. "I don't think he'll stay with us much longer," Abel says to me. "But he's hoping to see the 'little maid,' as he calls her, before he goes."

He talks to us then, about the shop and how well it's doing, and how he and Nell are renting a place in Ardwick Green. Nell says nothing, just sits looking at her hands, and picking at a thread in her dress.

"We're going to marry, last Sunday in the month," says Abel. "You're invited, of course—everyone is! Isn't that right, Nell?"

Nell looks up and nods, but she isn't smiling.

"What's the matter?" he asks her. "Don't tell me you've changed your mind!"

"Of course not," she says, looking back down at her fingers. Then she looks up again, at me. "I was hoping," she says, "that Annie would speak to me."

I look at Annie, Annie looks at the bird. I don't want her to try anything too soon that might send her back into that other world. On the other hand, there's Nell, desperate for news of her children, like our mother wanted news of us.

"Annie," I say.

No answer.

"Annie, this is Nell," I tell her. "She's looking for her son and daughter, just like our mother looked for us."

Nell gazes at her beseechingly. Annie looks up briefly, then turns her face into my shoulder.

"You remember when we left Bent Edge Farm?" I prompt her, and she's listening, with her face still turned away. "You said then that a girl and a boy were following us—right through the forest and into the town, remember?"

No answer. Her breathing's hoarse against my shirt.

"Well, where did they go, Annie? Where have they gone?"

Annie says something but her voice is muffled by my shirt.

"What?" I say, turning her chin with my fingers. "What did you say, Annie?"

"Not gone," she says more clearly. "Here, and here." She points to one side of Nell, then the other.

Nell gives a muffled cry, pressing her fingers to her mouth, then she looks to the left and right, as though she might see them. Abel swears under his breath.

"Are they . . . are they . . ." Nell gropes for what she's trying to say. "Are they saying anything to me?"

"Stop looking," Annie says. "You can't find them now."

Tears come into Nell's eyes. "Is it really Sarah—and Ned?"

Then Annie moves. She sits up in the bed, swaying lightly, and in her eyes is that strange, moony expression I used to hate.

"Mam-my," she says in a girl's voice that's not her own. "You look so tired."

Nell says, "Ohhh," on a long breath, as though all the air's leaving her.

"Mustn't look for us anymore," says the girl. "Too tired."

"Sarah?" says Nell, hardly able to speak.

Then a boy's voice comes. "We're with you now," he says. "You don't have to look. We'll always be with you."

Nell's crying freely now. "What happened? How . . . how did you . . ." she stumbles over the last word. "What happened?"

Then both voices speak together, from Annie's throat. "Hungry," they say. "No food, no water. Don't beat me again—can't work anymore."

Nell gives a great cry and falls from the stool to her knees. Her mouth's open but there's no sound. A strand of spit falls from her top to her bottom lip. Abel leaps forward and pulls her to him, but she struggles away, striking hard.

"NOOOO!" she howls, tearing herself away.

"Nell, Nell!" he cries. "You always knew it—in your heart."

"Mother," Annie says in two voices. "Come back to us." And all at once Nell's still, taking great sobbing breaths in Abel's arms. He sits her back on the stool.

"It's not dark anymore," the voices say. "We are with you now."

Nell bites her knuckles, her breath coming in long, shuddering gasps.

"We love you, Mammy," the voices say.

"I love you," Nell says, and she begins to sob in earnest. "I always loved you, I never stopped—I never gave up on you! I loved you and I always will." She's crying now in a high, keening wail.

Annie shudders, sinking downward, and grows limp. "It's all right, Annie," I whisper, stroking her hair, though I'm scunnered half to death. "Hush now, it's all right."

But Annie pulls herself away from me and slides off the bed. And on her own account she's tottering toward Nell. And a step or two away from her she opens up her arms, like she never has before in all her life, and says, "Mother."

And Nell scoops her up and holds on to her, like it's what her arms have needed all this time, and she rocks her backward and forward, crooning, tears rolling down her face and into Annie's hair.

44

Afterward

The next day two doctors say Annie can leave. It's all we can do to get her out of the hospital and onto the streets. She clings on to me all the way and hides her face, and I hear again as though for the first time how noisy and crowded the town is, bells ringing and people crying. We lift her into the cab and she scrambles onto my knee and digs her fingers into my arm, and her knuckles are white.

But when she sees Travis it's a different story. Her face lights up and she lets go of me and runs to him, and he picks her up and she touches his face. "Little bird came back," he says.

That night we all stay in the shop, drinking porter and celebrating the start of a new life while Annie sleeps. Then in the morning a horse and cart pulls up on Oldham Street, and we load it with boxes full of *The Poor Man's Guardian* to take to Huddersfield. And Travis is going with them.

"You can stop when we get to the moors and let me off," he says as Abel helps him up. He blows a kiss to Annie. "My special girl," he says, and she hides her face.

Then he reaches forward and shakes my hand. "Keep telling your good stories," he says, and I say I will.

"Give Dog-woman a pat on the head from me," I tell him, and he smiles and waves. And the cart pulls away and Travis gets smaller and smaller. I hope he finds Dog-woman, and her bite heals him and that he stays with her, running wild through the forest with her pack. I wish it so hard, I can almost see it, Travis and Dog-woman bent low, her on four limbs, him on three, the dogs wreathing and flowing like smoke around them.

I stare after him as he travels out of our story, and into his own.

Later we all go to see the house in Ardwick Green. We walk there, Annie clinging tightly to my hand and Nell's, and I wonder whether she'll ever get used to the noise. But Ardwick's better, and the house does overlook a green, with a few trees beyond. This is where we'll stay with Nell, until the wedding.

But what about the others? you're thinking.

What about Queenie and Digger and Pigeon and the rest of the gang, and Milly?

What about Mr. M., and Bailey, and the farmer and his wife at Bent Edge Farm, and Old Bert and his idiot son? They're all brought to justice, right?

Wrong. I wish I could say they were put on trial and hanged for what they've done, but it never happened. Oh, there was an investigation, all right, Abel saw to that. He ran a series of articles in his paper till more and more people spoke up, and in the end a special commission was set up to investigate the deaths of workhouse children that had been placed out in apprenticeship.

The first place they went to was Bent Edge Farm. But they never found owt. *Evidence inconclusive*, they wrote on their important-looking papers. For though they found that for years the farmer had been taking a girl and boy from different workhouses thereabouts, and that more than one pair of children had gone missing, it was hard to prove that they weren't already ill and starving when they got them. They were charged with neglect, and prevented from ever taking children on in that way again. And we had to be satisfied with that. Though when you consider that you can still be hanged for stealing bread, or wandering into the wrong field, it hardly seems good enough.

And Mr. M.? No case was ever brought against him. There was no evidence, except from the dead, and it was hard even to know what to charge him with.

And there was no news of Queenie and the others. Once, Abel's paper ran a story about a young black boy who was hanged for thieving at the New Bailey, and all day a great heaviness weighed me down, in case it were Digger.

Abel took me out on a walk that evening to try to cheer me up. When I saw that we were walking by Mosley Street I tried to twist away, but his hand held firm on my shoulder.

"Don't take it to heart, lad," Abel says as we walk right by Mr. M.'s house, toward St. Peter's Fields. "You never know what might happen yet. Life's a funny thing, happening all around us without anyone seeing. Look around you," he says. "What do you see?"

I look around the broad open space. "Nothing," I say.

"Do you know what happened in this very field, not twenty years ago?"

I shake my head. Haven't a clue.

And he tells me then the story of Peterloo. How when he was a little lad of nine he went with his mother to join a great crowd that had come to hear orator Hunt speak about reform. It was a fine day in August and the crowd was festive; that is, until someone gave an order and the military charged at them, sealing off all the exits and lashing out with sabers. Everyone was crying and screaming and the field was full of blood. Abel lost his mother and ran about in a panic, and a horse reared above him and a saber flashed—he shut his eyes but the man next to him fell dead. By some miracle neither he nor his mother was hurt.

"They said only eleven people died that day," he says, looking around as if he can still see it. "But hundreds more were injured and some died later.

My father's friend had his fingers trampled by a horse, and he never worked again. And that's a slower kind of death."

He looks at me and I can see it all through his eyes, the little lad fighting his way through the bloody crowds, crying, "Mam, Mam!"

"And do you know," he says, "how many ever got compensation for their injuries?"

I shake my head again.

"None of them," he says.

"That stinks," say I.

"Oh, they tried," he says. "But the cases just kept being dismissed. Or delayed for so long everyone lost heart and hope. So there was no justice in the usual way. And nothing left to tell you what went on. But just because you can't see a thing," Abel says, "doesn't mean it isn't there. Or that things won't change. Change comes in by the back door, and leaves by the window. There's never been another Peterloo, at least, and maybe one day there won't even be a workhouse. You have to take the long view. A hundred years from now," he says, looking around the open field, "the world'll be a different place—even as we speak it's changing."

That's Abel for you—always looking on the sunny side when everyone else is in the dark. But things did change. Soon after, the Charter for Incorporation was passed by Parliament. Manchester became a municipal town and then a city, and gradually the Mosleys lost power and moved out of the center. I heard that Milly didn't go with Mr. M. when he left; she went back to her family home.

At the end of the month Nell and Abel got married in the church in Ardwick Green. Annie got over her fear of crowds far enough to walk behind them with a basket of flowers. And crowds there were. Everyone Abel's ever known through the paper, which is hundreds, and all Nell's shirtmaking friends came out to see them and throw rose petals in front of them.

And from that day on we've lived together, as family, in the house in Ardwick Green. Abel's paper goes on thriving, and I help him sell it on street corners.

"Come and hear how the giants of industry will fall!" I shout. "Make the dragons fall and distribute their wealth through the land! The vote is your sword!"

Abel tells me I'm a great asset. And I love it—I'm doing what I love to do.

Sometimes I feel the past dragging me back. When I've had a bad day at work, or seen something I don't like on the streets. Seems like the past is a giant too, and it has to be knocked down like all the others. So I tell myself, going home, that I have a home to go to, and Annie'll be there, waiting with Nell, stitching clothes for the new babby. And sometimes when I get in and the evening sun glints on them through the window, I fancy I can see something glimmering, just for a moment, into the shape of a boy and girl, standing behind Nell and Annie, and leaning forward as branches of trees lean toward water, or flowers to the sun.

AUTHOR'S NOTE

A long time ago, on a farm very close to where I live, a farmer and his wife took in two children, boy and girl, from the workhouse, to help with the run of the farm. As the years passed, people began to notice that the children never got any older. But the farm was isolated, people kept to themselves, and only when the mother of one of the children came looking for her did the truth finally emerge. The farmer and his wife had been working the children to death, and replacing them with similar-looking children from different workhouses.

No one ever discovered how many children had been disposed of in this way.

As soon as I heard this dark history I knew I wanted to write about it. It became the factual basis for my fictional story—though in the course of researching it I discovered that it was not so unusual as I had initially supposed. In the 1830s there were several enquiries into the deaths of workhouse children who had been placed in apprenticeships. Charles Dickens himself became involved in one while writing *Oliver Twist*.

There are other factual elements in this story. Manchester was granted a Charter for Incorporation in 1838. Until that time it had been run as a feudal village, by the manorial lord. Rapid expansion and industrialization meant that the struggle for political representation came to the fore in the 1830s.

One of the key figures in this struggle was Abel Heywood (1810–93). The son of a weaver, Abel Heywood worked in the town center from the age of nine, and was educated at a Sunday school on Bennett Street. He established the radical paper *The Poor Man's Guardian* in 1828, and on different occasions was imprisoned and fined for distributing it cheaply, i.e. without the Stamp Tax, which would have made it too expensive for the working people he wanted to reach.

Abel Heywood went on to have a long and illustrious career, becoming alderman of the city in 1853, and mayor in 1862. He refused all other titles, remaining devoted to the cause of the urban poor. It is said that on his inauguration as mayor, Queen Victoria refused to stand with him. His association with Joe, Annie and Nell in this story is entirely fictitious.

The Mosley family were the manorial lords of Manchester. As Joe discovers, it was a Nicholas Mosley who bought the township and surrounding lands in 1596 for £3,000. At the time of the story, Sir Oswald Mosley was the manorial lord, and he was well regarded and philanthropic, helping to fund the new hospital in Ancoats and subsidizing Poor Relief. His cousin, Sheridan Mosley, is a fictitious creation, though Mosley Street and the Portico Library still exist.

Dr. James Phillips Kay (1804–77) was one of a small but energetic group of doctors who devoted themselves to the urban poor. He worked in Ancoats, where the life expectancy was only fourteen and, in 1832, at the height of the cholera epidemic, served in all the most dangerous districts, finally publishing that year his classic *Moral and Physical Conditions of the Working Classes*. He eventually left Manchester after a breakdown, but continued to publish investigative medical journalism and is one of our main guides to health conditions in the 1830s.

John Sanderson was a weaver who injured his hand while weaving, and stayed on to work at the hospital, eventually becoming governor. He was known for his humane administration—particularly where the so-called "lunatic wards" were concerned—which were exemplary at a time when the treatment of those suffering from mental illness was hair-raisingly brutal.

Livi Michael

GLOSSARY

anyroad	anyway
bad nick	bad state, condition
bandy legs	bow-legged
beadle	parish official
blaggers	crooks
Blue Locusts	the police
bob	one shilling
boggart	supernatural being, often associated with a particular place, e.g. swamp, pool
bole	trunk
bowking	coughing hard
braces	suspenders
catarrh	phlegm
chuffed	proud
clemmed	starving
drubbed	beaten
frit	frightened
furmety	dish of grain boiled in milk like porridge
gaol	jail
gibbet	gallows
ginnel	narrow passage between houses
governor	head, person in charge
gurned	griped
jerkin	man's close-fitting jacket
Jinny Green-teeth	boggart (see above)

Lammas	harvest festival; first day of August
libbed	torn apart
meat pudding	meat and gravy in a crust
midden	rubbish heap
mizzle	mist, drizzle
mizzy	confused state
nick	steal
nowt	nothing
Owd Nick	the devil
owt	anything
palaver	nonsense
picking oakum	untwisting old ropes to make new
punters	customers
right wally	idiot
scally	urchin, thief
scunnered	frightened, spooked
skelp	glancing blow
slavering	drooling
slutch	muck, sewage
thistlefluff	thistledown
tow-haired	very fair hair
wainwright	wagon builder
wezilled	shrivelled, wizened